# MAN

## IN THE

# MIDDLE

## KEN MORRIS

bancroft
press

Baltimore, MD

Published by Bancroft Press ("Books that enlighten")
P.O. Box 65360, Baltimore, MD 21209
800-637-7377
410-764-1967 (fax)
www.bancroftpress.com

Cover and interior design: Tammy Grimes, Crescent Communications
www.tsgcrescent.com • 814.941.7447

Author photo: Michael Campbell, Michael Campbell Photography

ISBN 1-890862-25-8 (cloth)
ISBN 1-890862-26-6 (paper)
LCCN 2002117219

Printed in the United States of America

First Edition

1 3 5 7 9 10 8 6 4 2

*To my wife, Amelia, and my four sons Brett, Scott, Tim, and Colby.*

I love you with all my being, and thank you for the lessons you teach me each and every day about humility and humanity.

# PROLOGUE

---

Blood-red stripes ribbed the horizon while an ocean breeze, wed to the scent of salt and seaweed, rustled past. Later that day—perhaps unaware of the morning's tragedy—children would splash in the La Jolla Cove, playing Marco-Polo through peeking eyes. It was a setting that made San Diego's North Coast so unique, validating citizens' claims that this *was* "America's finest city."

Nicholas Zerets, however, cared nothing for clear skies, May sunshine, or the citizenry as he moved with effortless strides down this gold-plated stretch of real estate. Past a steak restaurant, a valet booth in front of an eight hundred-dollar a night hotel, and a newly built bank building boasting a hundred billion in assets, his heels click-clacked as if a ticking clock. When a San Diego City police car turned a corner and headed in his direction, he leaned back on his heels and slowed to a stop. He withdrew a tin box from a hip pocket, opened it with one hand, and removed a dark papered Djarum. He set the Turkish cigarette on its slow burn and watched.

Once the black and white accelerated and sped past, Zerets dragged deeply on the lit weed and continued his march. At his side, and chained to his wrist, hung a steel reinforced briefcase crammed with stock trade-confirms, notifications of maintenance calls, and final requests for additional funds—a substantial commemorative for those who would later investigate. Back at his apartment, on a computer monitor, was a screen full of stock symbols—each signifying a past trade—and nearly every one a miserable loser. It wouldn't take a MENSA to understand the why of his actions.

Zerets continued across the street toward Jackson Securities' branch office. He already knew the brokerage firm filled the ground floor of this six-story, two-year-old building. A half-dozen retail brokers were visible through glass doors. Some chattered on phones, others, like puppets putting on a show, sat face-to-face with clients. Sales assistants took notes at cramped desks outside their boss's offices. And all of this took place in a tight area of less than two thousand square feet.

Entering, Zerets snatched a brochure, musing over the assertion, in block letters no less, that Jackson was at the forefront of capital formation:

## DO YOU WANT TO GET IN ON THE GROUND FLOOR OF THE NEXT MICROSOFT?

Jumping to the brochure's end, he read:

> *We are in the business of finding undiscovered investment gems while they are still in their raw, uncut form. That's good for American business. That's good for our clients.*

He dropped the promotional material to the floor and announced with a slight accent, "I am Zerets, here to see Cannodine."

The young female receptionist he spoke to sat behind a desk that swept across ten feet of lobby. "Mr. Cannodine is expecting you."

Zerets looked across the room to the spread-legged security guard. The cop cocked his head at the exit sign. Zerets nodded back. "I am aware of which is his office," he replied.

He continued across the carpeted floor to a solid-wall office with the nameplate, *Erik Cannodine—Branch Manager.* Zerets knocked and opened in a single motion.

Cannodine had slicked-back hair and skin stretched across fat cheeks. He looked up, then snatched a dark jacket from behind his chair and whipped it over his shoulders.

"Mr. Zerets," Cannodine said, "I am sorry about your trading account. Had we known you had access to a million in cash, we'd never have liquidated to satisfy your margin debt." He rubberbanded a smile and offered his hand.

Zerets ignored the proffer and did a quick inventory of the office. Oak desk, white carpet, built-in bookshelves, a degree hanging from the wall, and branch office records stored in a row of locked floor-to-ceiling cabinets lining a back wall. Along one shelf, and adorning every piece of flat-topped furniture, were family photos of a peppy trophy wife and three kids, all looking like carbon copies of their old man. Cannodine was at least fifty, so Zerets figured this was a second marriage.

"I see you're admiring my kids." Cannodine's delivery was salesman smarmy but laced with a nervous tremor. "You have any tykes, Mr. Zerets?"

"No." Zerets continued to survey the surroundings.

"Not to worry. You're young enough. I had my last when I was forty-seven. Poor me, eh?"

"I am not much on chit-chat, Mr. Cannodine, and I feel urgency to complete my mission."

"Of course, let's move on." Cannodine's tone made it clear he understood they were busy men. "And, well," he continued, "I just wanted to let you know I feel bad about the way things unraveled for you. Very unfortunate. But with so many day-traders losing so much money, our back-office is forced to liquidate when super-active clients get below twenty-five percent of their equity value. And you didn't respond to margin calls. It wasn't until later I discovered you were connected."

Zerets ignored the administrator's apology. "You were instructed not to mention this visit. You were discreet?"

"Of course, Mr. Zerets."

"I assume you have no problem accepting large amounts of cash?"

Cannodine sat and opened a folder. "No, sir. Cash shouldn't be a problem. We have to make certain disclosures, of course." He began stacking paperwork. "A few things to sign. Would you like a cup of coffee?"

"No." Zerets unfastened the chain from his wrist. The briefcase lay propped open on the far edge of Cannodine's desk.

"I know you've had some misfortune with a few of your trades," Cannodine said, "but I'm sure your luck will change. We've got a guy who dropped a cool half-million, then made it—"

"Come here," Zerets said, "and I will show you what I have inside my valise."

"Is it really a million?" Cannodine drew closer. "It's amazing that so much money can fit into a briefcase. You'd think it'd take a big box."

"Yes, you would think so."

Stepping to his left as the manager passed by, Zerets waited, then struck with a hatchet-like palm across Cannodine's soft neck. The fat man bounced off the desk and crumpled to the floor.

From inside his briefcase, Zerets clutched the first of six M-67s. He pulled one pin, placed the device under Cannodine's body, yanked a second pin, and rolled the two and a half-inch fragmentation grenade against the file cabinets. He put two additional spheres in each of his jacket pockets. Calmly, he walked through the office door.

Noting with satisfaction the armed guard's departure, Zerets removed two grenades from his right pocket. He positioned himself with his back to the rear door. Pulling both pins, he tossed one of the two explosives over the reception desk. The girl looked up through a puzzled smile. He lobbed the second to a far corner.

Zerets activated and rolled the final two grenades as the first explosion blew open the office door. Splintered wood and Cannodine's remains filled the air. From his protected position, Zerets saw one of the flunkies slap her hands to her face. Immediately after, the second explosion shredded the contents of Cannodine's file cabinets.

Zerets spun and grabbed the rear door handle.

"Shit!" he yelled as a rare drop of perspiration zigzagged down his neck.

He kicked the bolted door. It was solid.

Instinctively, Zerets flew towards the glass-faced front door thirty-five feet away. A single stride later, a series of four explosions obliterated what remained of Jackson's offices.

Including Zerets.

# CHAPTER ONE

**"I AM SORRY."** The voice sounded old. "Hannah was the best…"

Peter Neil had heard this sentiment a hundred times over the last five days, and each time he had, it resurrected the image of his mother's body, mangled in the crash. But nobody had eulogized Hannah Neil more effectively than Jason Ayers, his words coming slowly, as if wrenched from his heart.

Ayers—sixty-two years old, Stanford Law School, respected, revered by some, wealthy, and a man seeming to have everything—had aged a decade in the two years since Peter last saw him. What, Peter now wondered, did this important man want with a zero like him? It was strange. And painful. In the fifteen minutes since pecking at the front door, Ayers had proven himself to be a hundred and sixty-pound pillar of salt, rubbing against Peter's wounds. Their exchange had been restricted to condolences and heartbreaking testimonials as to how wonderful Peter's mother had been, none of which Peter needed to hear. His suffering was kiln-hot without additional stoking.

As Peter stepped from the kitchen, balancing two cups of scalding, espresso-strength coffee, his normally broad shoulders sagged under a mountain of regret. Regret that he had done little in his twenty-eight years to have made his mother proud. Regret that he was stuck in deep shit without a clue as to how to get out. And regret that he had answered the door this morning.

Before sitting and planting his own elbows on the card-table separating them, he placed one cup in front of the older man. As Peter squirmed, unable to get comfortable, the freeway traffic, not many yards outside the west wall, zipped by in a noxious migration to nowhere.

Ayers picked up the mug, blew steam, and took a small sip as his untethered head wandered. Peter found the awkwardness of this tête-a-tête less troubling than the sense that no end was in sight. Ayers gave every sign he was dug in for the long haul. Peter doubted the man even had sufficient energy left in his bones to get up and leave, even if he wanted to, which he clearly did not.

Peter decided to clear the air. "I know about you and Mom," he began.

Instantly, Ayers' hand—the one clutching the mug—went limp, causing scalding liquid to flood across the table. Peter sprang up, grabbed a pile of paper napkins from a wicker basket, and threw them over the spreading puddle. Ayers' hand was wet and red, but none of what must have been excruciating pain registered on his face.

"You know...about...Hannah and me?" Ayers asked. "What happened?"

Peter reached across the table and snatched the half-empty cup. With a fresh napkin, he mopped Ayers' hand. "You should see a doctor—"

"Oh my God." The words were faint. Then, full of urgency, Ayers craned forward like a broken-necked giraffe. "What do you know?" he said. "Tell me."

"I know," Peter began, hoping to calm the distraught man, "you and Mom were intimate. She never told me, but I knew. I also knew she broke it off years ago."

For the first time in many seconds, Ayers exhaled. "Lovers? That's what you know..."

"Yes. I understand it was a brief affair. And believe me, I don't blame anyone. Listen, Mr. Ayers," Peter continued, "Mom didn't fault you. And she was grateful for what you did—getting her the job. She called you her dearest friend..." The words *the day she died* stuck inside Peter's mouth.

"No matter what happened," Ayers said, "I loved her."

Before Peter could respond, his mother's pet calico—now Peter's—waddled past them.

"I always liked Hannah's cat," Ayers said distractedly. "What's his name?"

"Henry."

"Yes. Henry." Ayers cleared his throat. "I, I have a confession to make. As you know, I was close to Matthew at one time, not just your mother."

Peter nodded, recalling that Ayers and his father were college roommates and friends for years after. Their families at one time had frequent dinners together, but to Peter it always seemed an odd social mix. While Ayers was successful, Matthew Neil rarely had paid next month's electric bill before it was due. Even so, Ayers was like a sycophant to Peter's dad, clinging to their friendship as if it were oxygen administered to an asthmatic.

Then, out of the blue, the year before Matthew Neil grew ill, Ayers was no longer a welcome guest in the Neil household. Nobody—not Peter's mother, not his father—ever offered any explanation for what had happened. But whatever the reason for their falling out, Ayers took the initiative, contacting mother and son shortly after the elder Neil passed away. That was ten years ago. The prodigal friend assisted them by insisting Hannah enroll in a program, become a paralegal, and join the law firm bearing his name. Peter had no choice but to be grateful, and that meant he must suffer through whatever this wreck of a man now had to say. He gripped his chair and held tight.

"I need to do something for you, Peter."

"This isn't necessary—"

"Let me finish." Ayers raised his damaged hand, continuing to show no signs of discomfort. "I understand you quit your job this week."

Peter wondered how Ayers knew about that development. "Mom's death made me re-evaluate my priorities," he confirmed. "I was fed up with pushing overpriced mortgage loans on unsuspecting clients."

Peter decided not to mention that he had handled his resignation with blowtorch subtlety, telling his boss, Craig Hinton, he thought the man crooked for making side-deals with mortgage lending institutions that concealed their bloated interest rates in confusing terminology. He'd said a few other things as well, none of them endearing.

"A person needs to have a job he enjoys." Ayers' head turned and locked on a wedding picture of Hannah and Matthew Neil propped atop a side table. Peter followed his gaze. In that photograph, cake covered the newlyweds' smiles like thick makeup. Jason Ayers—slightly out of focus—hovered off to one side, hoisting a champagne glass in an apparent toast.

"Yes," Peter half-heartedly agreed. "I guess they do."

"Peter. This is hard for me to admit..." Ayers paused to clear his throat. "But I did additional checking. Your mother told me she didn't approve of your girlfriend—Ms. Goodman."

"No, she didn't," Peter said. The suspicion in Peter's voice wasn't meant to be disguised. "I broke up with her the same day I quit my job."

Ellen Goodman's image filled his mind in a blaze of glory. On the one-to-ten scale, with ten being knockout, she was a twenty-three, but the woman had the morals of an alley cat and, to make matters worse, had been a co-worker. Her sleeping with their boss, in what she regarded as a career move, was another reason why Peter quit his job and romance simultaneously.

"I already knew about your breakup," Ayers said. "Ms. Goodman has a reputation. Well-founded I am told."

"You could know these things—" Peter said, making no effort to hide his displeasure or the challenge in his voice "—only by hiring an investigator to pry into my life. Did you?" He didn't dare ask how much more about his life Mr. Jason Ayers had dug up.

Immediately, the man grew nervous and apologetic—even seemed surprised that what he had done might be interpreted as inappropriate. He said he did these things with the best of intentions. He had promised Hannah, he said, to help Peter if anything ever happened to her. He was, he reminded Peter, a link to the past. Practically family.

"I swear to God," Ayers continued, "I never meant to upset you. I didn't know any other way to keep my promise to Hannah."

One after another, the rationalizations flowed as if Ayers hoped one or two—like argument spaghetti thrown against Peter's brain—might find their mark and stick. As he listened, Peter's emotions ran the gamut from pissed-off at the invasion of his privacy to pity over the neediness in Ayers' pleas. In the end, Peter went with sympathy. He reminded himself of his and his mother's debt to Ayers. That damn debt.

"Would you like to learn to trade stocks, bonds, currencies?" Ayers asked, sounding hopeful. "You'd work for—"

"I appreciate the gesture, Mr. Ayers, but it's not something I'm interested in."

"Stenman Partners is a hedge fund. They manage billions of dollars," Ayers continued as if Peter had said nothing. "I am their counsel. They would hire you in a minute on my recommendation." He explained that Peter had a lot going for him: he did well at UCLA, was good looking and athletic, and people gravitated to him. "All you've lacked is motivation."

"You mean to make money?" Peter asked.

"I know it sounds crass, but yes. By the time you're thirty, you could be making more money than you ever dreamed—"

"Not now, Mr. Ayers. But thanks anyway."

Ayers tried several more times, unsuccessfully, to sell Peter, then said, "There must be something I can do."

Partly to calm Ayers, partly to address some leftover questions he had about events just prior to his mother's death six days ago, Peter said, "Maybe you can help explain a few things to me."

Ayers' head lifted. "I'll try."

"The morning Mom died, she came to see me at work. She seemed disturbed."

Ayers looked away. "About what?"

"The explosion in La Jolla. She said she knew that man Cannodine at Jackson Securities. When I asked, she seemed frightened and evasive. Was that related to your law firm?"

Ayers made a twitch-like nod. Leeman, Johnston, and Ayers, he confessed, handled legal affairs, on a retainer basis, for Jackson Securities. He and Hannah met with Cannodine a couple of times.

"That explains how she knew he had young children."

"Yes. Mr. Cannodine had pictures of the kids and spoke of them."

"She felt sad, knowing his kids would suffer. She also said the others who died weren't guilty of anything. Do you know what she meant by that?" It was highly unusual for his mother to hide things from him, but when they had met that morning, she seemed evasive. She had also been nervous and near tears, and all he gave her were five minutes on his way into work. He should have done more—at least had a cup of coffee with her. He now hoped Ayers might throw him a bone of understanding, something to hold onto that might explain her unusual behavior. In his desire to hear something new, Peter didn't notice Ayers' face turn even more ashen.

Ayers shook his head. "I don't know what she might have meant, other than the obvious: a number of coworkers died with Mr. Cannodine." With an escalating voice, he continued: "Did she say anything else? Think, Peter! I need to know."

Ayers' passion startled Peter. He paused, shook his head, then said, "Some of your clients upset her. I think she meant this Cannodine guy, but Mom wasn't specific."

"Did she mention anyone by name? Or say what Cannodine had done?" Ayers' hands massaged his brow as if he might erase wrinkles or tear skin in the process.

"No, but she did say lawyers represent…what was it?" Peter closed his eyes and replayed the meeting. His mother had surprised him outside his office only minutes after he'd first heard about the Jackson Securities tragedy on his car radio. She huddled under a stairwell in the shadows, shivering despite heated Santa Ana winds blowing south from Los Angeles.

As Peter reassembled that last conversation, he continued: "Clients, she said, did evil things—she used the word 'egregious'—and, despite that, attorneys acted as their advocates."

Ayers claimed to have no idea what Hannah meant. When it seemed the conversation had run its course, Peter made a show of looking at his watch. "I'm sorry, Mr. Ayers, but I need to get ready to go. I have a meeting with the attorney who handled Mom's finances."

Peter herded Ayers to the front door. Before leaving, Ayers begged one last time. "Please, Peter, consider the job offer. If you don't let me help, I won't survive."

Tired of the topic, Peter said he'd think it over. With that, the melo-drama thankfully ended, and Ayers retreated back inside the shell he'd car-ried through the front door an hour earlier. Though Peter knew Ayers was upset, something beyond sadness hung in his eyes. Adding to the mystery of the last hour, Peter wanted to know: what did helping him find a job have to do with survival?

---

An hour later, the strange meeting with Ayers still kicked around the back of Peter's mind as he drove to meet his mother's financial attorney. The lack of information coming from Ayers had added to his confusion. Too much about the day his mother died remained a mystery. That an off-duty cop witnessed the crash and provided details—"she drove too fast…hit a piling…the car burst into flames…death came instantaneous-ly"—provided little insight. Was his mother simply upset with work? Was that why she drove so recklessly? That didn't seem possible. Was there more to the connection with Cannodine and Jackson Securities? If so, why had

Ayers downplayed matters? Peter worked through the details but got nowhere.

For one of the few times in his life, Peter had an overwhelming desire to open up to someone. But he couldn't push a nonexistent button. The Neils had been independent to the point of stubbornness, especially Peter's father. The elder Neil had kept his feelings private, unwilling to burden friends. It became a family trait.

At the thought of his father, Peter reached into his pocket and felt the face of his moonstone—a gift from Matthew Neil fifteen years ago. The white gem, his father had told him, could relieve all anxiety if one passed a thumb over its smooth face. Peter believed him and rubbed whenever tense. Like now.

Moving along the packed interstate at a breakneck five miles per hour, and ignoring the knocking sounds of his multi-injured VW Jetta, Peter replayed his concerns. He remained puzzled over what he'd seen the day of his mother's death, on his first trip back to his childhood home to rescue her pet cat—a familiar twenty-minute drive south on Interstate 5 and east on Balboa Avenue. The route took him past the baseball fields where his father had coached him for nine years. Cattycorner to Peter's final turn, he viewed the high school track where he had starred as a middle-distance runner. He next passed the home of a best friend from childhood, long ago abandoned in a move to a more prestigious address.

Similar to most homes in the suburb of Clairemont, the Neils owned a single-story stucco on a cramped eighth of an acre. Two blocks away, furious traffic burdened the city's main streets while strip malls and fast food restaurants ran in unbroken lines for blocks, and groves of signposts outnumbered trees ten to one. *Modest* was the best way to describe this northeast corner of San Diego. Matthew and Hannah Neil had bought the home twenty-five years ago. Back then, young families populated the neighborhood. In the Neils' household, there was enough roughhousing to raise the roof, but the roof hadn't been raised since Matthew Neil had died. As he neared his destination, Peter felt anxious. Could he stomach entering the house, he wondered, knowing it was no longer anyone's home?

Peter parked at the curb and approached through the front-yard just as a dark sedan drifted past, speeding up slightly when he absently looked up and over. A half step later, a dry leaf crunched underfoot, directing his attention to the walkway, now cracked where tree roots had worked their way underneath. Alongside the sidewalk, the sparse lawn had turned to rust brown, a victim of ongoing water shortages in Southern California. A local evening paper—dated the previous night, the night his mother died—rested atop the steps leading to the porch. Peter recalled reaching down and picking it up. *Odd*, he had thought. His mother always retrieved her paper when she came home from work at six o'clock. The police officer said the accident occurred around half past nine in the city of Carlsbad, twenty minutes north and west of Clairemont and thirty-five minutes north of downtown San Diego, where she worked. Where was she headed that night? She never went out late, and, as far as Peter knew, she didn't have any friends in that part of North County. Had she worked longer than normal hours? Had she met with someone? If so, was there a person who might share a last conversation? Peter had a deep longing to know these things.

He had entered the house through the front door. Henry immediately bounded over, then snaked his way in and out of Peter's legs, rubbing calico fur against his jeans. The animal purred like a small engine.

"You're scared, aren't you, Henry?" Peter asked.

With the blinds drawn, the entranceway was dusk-dark. He looked over to the living room and the oak floors, chipped and dented with nearly three decades of hard-use. The area rugs had worn spots at their edges, and the house smelled musty. Surveying the rest of the room, he noted a pile of papers, threatening to spill off the cedar work desk. Peter went over and opened the top drawer. It was empty. He wondered if his mother was looking for something and dumped out the contents. Another strange thing: the computer was turned on, the screensaver dancing with floating checkerboards. When he slid the mouse, his mother's file window popped up. After shutting down the computer, he had considered taking a tour of the house—his old room, the den, his mother's bedroom—but decided to wait for another day. He felt too drained to weather the sadness.

He noticed a flashing light on the answering machine, which sat on the window ledge separating the kitchen from the dining area. He shuffled over and hit *play*. The machine-voice announced there were seven messages. The first message came in at 6:03 p.m. That call began and ended with a hang-up. The other six messages ended similarly, except for the third call, where a hoarse male voice pleaded: "Please pick up." The steady flow of calls, the last coming at 11:04 p.m., confirmed his mother had not made a stop home before driving to Carlsbad.

With Henry standing alongside his empty food bowl, Peter realized the animal hadn't been fed the previous night—another unsettling curiosity. His mother went out of her way to take care of her pet, and not coming home—at least long enough to feed Henry—was unprecedented. It also meant the computer had been left on that morning. None of this made sense, then or now. His mother rarely forgot even small tasks.

From a hook near the phone, Peter remembered retrieving a set of keys. One was an extra to his mother's destroyed Subaru. The other key, undersized, looked like a bicycle-lock key with a round, nondescript insignia and some kind of numerical code stamped across its face. Peter removed the smaller key and slid it onto his key chain. One day, he suspected, he would discover whatever the key unlocked—maybe some trinkets or memories locked in a drawer or a box somewhere in the house.

He next fed Henry, gathered up the animal's bed, litter box, dishes, and food, and put them in several grocery bags. Scooping up the cat with his free hand, he left. Peter loved this house, but he had driven away without a look back.

---

On the lengthy drive to Smitham and Jones, Estate Attorneys, Peter had too many questions and too few answers. Arriving at the Solana Beach law office, Peter put these concerns on temporary hold. Jerome Smitham had said certain matters needed to be decided sooner, rather than later. The man's concerned tone of voice had made it clear: there were unpleasant, pressing financial issues. Time to address a whole new set of problems.

Peter entered and the receptionist immediately escorted him to Smitham's office. In his sixties, the attorney, at six foot-six inches, resembled a preying mantis, his skin taut like pulled taffy, and his joints sharp and severely angled. He also jittered like a man who had inhaled five cups of house-blend. Hound-dog eyes, however, gave his face a sympathetic look.

After a few minutes of brutal overview—in which Peter learned more than he cared to about red ink—Smitham informed him, "I advised your mother to declare personal bankruptcy," as if explaining why he shouldn't be sued for malpractice.

"No way she'd do that," Peter said. He didn't bother to explain about the Neil family pride. His father had laid it on the line: pay your debts, and meet all your obligations, no matter what.

"You're right," Smitham said. "The suggestion of bankruptcy offended her. I've been advising Hanna *pro bono* off and on for the last five years at the request of Jason Ayers. He sends substantial referral business my way, so I was happy to do him a little *quid pro quo*. That means—"

"I know what *quid pro quo* means, Mr. Smitham. I also know *pro bono* means you've been working for free." Peter immediately regretted his tone of voice. "Mr. Smitham, I appreciate what you did for my mother."

Smitham nodded.

Peter looked over the ledger pages lying on the table and tried to make sense of the lines and rows of numerical entries. "Excuse me if I sound stupid," he said, "but it looks as if Mom still owed money from Dad's hospitalization."

Smitham gave an almost imperceptible nod. "Unfortunately, yes."

"How could there still be debts after more than ten years?"

The attorney explained about the medical costs associated with Matthew Neil's illness. "They were gigantic," he said. "Peter," he continued, "if Hannah were still alive, I wouldn't say anything."

"About what?" Peter asked the question, despite knowing he didn't really want to hear the answer.

"Your schooling was another drain on her finances. In your junior year, a tuition check bounced. Jason Ayers picked up the shortfall."

Peter's guts sank. "That can't be. She and Dad set up a trust. She said everything was paid for."

"Saying it didn't make it true. Hannah had nothing—as I already implied, her entire income went to pay bills and debt service."

Peter surveyed the attorney's office while he absorbed all this new information. Diplomas and pictures of Smitham's family hung in precise rows: a son, a daughter, several grandchildren, a plump wife. A picture of him in a fishing outfit, a bass flapping in a net, was blown up into a three-foot by four-foot glass-fronted frame, and made the centerpiece of an entire wall.

Despite its cavernous dimensions, the office felt confining. Overstuffed furniture, standing lamps, pine filing cabinets, and over-filled bookshelves shared the room with billowy live plants whose broad leaves selfishly demanded space.

Worse, the room felt jungle hot.

Peter removed his jacket and slung it over the arm of the leather chair. His knees bent into his chest. He felt like a leaf-eater waiting for the next predator to take a bite.

"I need to know what you intend to do about your mother's mortgage," Smitham said.

"Mortgage?" Peter had no notion his mother still owed money on the house. He quickly came to a new understanding: he didn't just have nothing, he had less than nothing. No make that *substantially* less than nothing. "How much?" he asked.

"Unfortunately, your mother secured loans against her property. Little or no equity remains. If you don't repay approximately fifty thousand dollars, creditors will force sale."

"I grew up in that house, Mr. Smitham. Mom would never have wanted me to give it up."

"If you can manage the payments, I should be able to convince the creditors to let you keep the place."

"Fat chance of that. I've got no job, and, because I opened my big fat mouth when I quit, I've got a former boss who hates my guts and won't give me a reference worth shit."

The phone rang. On the third ring, Smitham said, "Excuse me. I must take this call."

The desk separated the older man from Peter by ten feet. Smitham spun in his swivel and began to speak in a low voice. Over the high-backed chair, Peter saw only the top of the attorney's head. As he waited, Peter continued to eye the numbers on the ledger. His parents, it seemed from the lines of debits and credits, never had a dime of savings. He wondered: was being poor an inherited trait? While he pondered his financial morass, Peter thought he heard Smitham say, "Jason" and a moment later, "debts." Less than three minutes after picking up, Smitham spun and again faced Peter. "Excuse me, where were we?"

For the next few minutes, they reviewed Peter's options. Smitham then asked, "Do you have any assets?"

"Squat. Owe money on my car. Rent's due. I have maybe a grand in accrued salary and commission, and that's more than spoken for. Basically, I'm tap-city." Peter reflected inwardly long enough to blame himself for getting into this mess. If stupid were smart, he told himself, he'd be Einstein.

The attorney nodded as if he'd heard those thoughts and agreed with them. "I understand you have a standing offer from Jason Ayers."

"That was Mr. Ayers who just called?" Peter asked.

"Yes. He wanted me to reiterate—in the face of what you've learned about your mother's financial situation—his offer to set up a job interview. Stenman Partners is a prestigious and potentially lucrative place to work."

"I know nothing about the capital markets beyond what I learned in Econ 101, and I couldn't pick Stenman from a police lineup if someone helped me."

"They prefer to train their own traders. Commitment, loyalty, intelligence, and hard work are what Stenman seeks in an employee."

"Thanks, but I think I'll pound pavement. See if lightning can strike. Can you keep the creditors at bay for a couple of weeks?"

"Under the circumstances? Yes. Perhaps you have other relatives who might loan you some money. An aunt or an uncle? A grandparent?"

"Nope, but even if I did, I wouldn't ask."

"Don't forget Mr. Ayers' offer," Smitham said. "He sounds sincere."

"Yeah. I'll keep it in mind."

"He cares, Peter. Like…well, perhaps like a father."

Peter recalled Ayers' own son. Curtis had died just after their families stopped seeing each other. Maybe Ayers *was* reaching out to him as he might a son. Peter was skeptical, but it might explain some of his bizarre interest. The thought also brought to mind Ayers' daughter. Peter wondered what had happened to skinny, freckle-faced Kate.

"I recommend you call Mr. Ayers and talk it over."

"As I said," Peter answered, "I'll keep it in mind while I see what I can manage on my own. Thanks again, Mr. Smitham."

The attorney offered a painful smile as Peter stumbled from his office.

When the elevator arrived and Peter stepped in, his eyes roamed to the acoustic panels in the ceiling. He spoke to the tiny holes: "Hey, God, if you haven't heard, I need a job."

# CHAPTER TWO

STANLEY DRUCKER TOOK A DEEP SWALLOW. The alcohol burned its way down his throat, warmed his stomach, and began the daylong process of numbing his brain. He enjoyed the solitude of Saturday mornings—his ex had left a year ago, and he didn't miss the bitch, not for a nanosecond. And since she had no idea he had offshore money in the low seven figures, he reveled in the knowledge that he paid her next to nothing, despite California's Community Property laws. Fuck her. She went back to Iowa and good riddance.

He stretched and yawned, then took another sip. Drucker liked his house—half an acre, two master bedrooms, and view of the ocean from above the beaches near Malibu. Secluded, too—thick oleander and two dozen pepper trees sheltered the main house from nosy neighbors. He had a satellite dish that got him a couple hundred stations and twelve pro football games on Sundays. Wolfgang Puck's latest hot spot attracted the in-crowd, only a mile or two away, and, in a weekly show, Drucker liked to waltz in and order fifty bucks' worth of gourmet-to-go as if he were at Mickey D's. He drank only expensive booze, Starbucks' double tall cappuccinos from the nearest joint two blocks away, and got laid at least twice a week, even if he had to pay for it. Los Angeles wasn't such a bad place to live so long as you had enough dough to afford the good life, and he did. And he planned to have a lot more as he began to publicize his investment success to some of the rich cats in Beverly Hills. With almost no overhead—a small office, some equipment paid for by the brokers he sent business to, and a secretary who made minimum wage plus a buck—he would be raking in a couple mil per year in the not too distant future. Not bad, he thought, for a guy who went to J.C., and then to Chico State, where he amassed a whopping C-minus GPA. No sir, not bad at all. He deserved to feel like king of the damn hill.

And he lived such an easy life. Except for the inquisition by that anal compulsive government prick last week, there were few problems. Managing a portion of Stenman Partners' money was a godsend. Most of the time, Morgan Stenman's people even told him what to buy and what to sell. Money flowed in, Stanley put it to work, and charged the partnership 1% of assets under management per year. Stenman, in turn, charged back to clients that 1% *and* a hefty percent of profits. Since Stenman had near perfect insight and returned ungodly profits to investors, nobody minded the big fees. Everybody felt happy as pigs in shit, especially Stanley "King-of-the-Damn-Hill" Drucker.

A heavy knock on his front door shook Drucker back to the present. He rose from his chair and stood six feet from the solid wood door. He reflexively looked to the clock on the wall: five minutes after nine. Since the bitch had left him, he never had uninvited guests on Saturdays. This was his time to sit back, drink, watch a day of sports, and go bar hopping at night, looking to get lucky. That was the routine. If this was a door-to-door salesman, maybe he'd just kick the damn salesman's ass.

Drucker took a quick shot of scotch, then grunted, "Who's there?"

Instead of an answer, the door slammed open. The bolt ripped from its screws and wood splinters flew like darts. In a reflex, Drucker flung his hands over his face at the same moment his kidneys weakened.

An enormous man, six-foot-two and at least two hundred and fifty dense pounds, cast an impressive shadow. He wore his hair in a thin pony-tail and had a flattened nose, seemingly without cartilage. After he stepped in, a much smaller man with the face of a damaged ferret followed. An ugly grimace pulled the second man's upper lip into a sneer, revealing polished, even teeth. Drucker guessed he was Mexican. Both wore tailored suits with open jackets and handguns strapped to their chests. Behind them a woman followed. The two men parted, looking like uneven pillars, allowing her to take center stage.

Through full lips, she said, "My name is Sarah Guzman. These two gentlemen are my associates. You are a loose end."

*Loose end?* Her words made no sense. Neither did the name Guzman—no way this woman was Spanish or Mexican. If she had a single feature that wasn't Anglo-Saxon, Drucker couldn't find it, and he stared hard enough to notice. For once, Drucker wished his house had fewer trees and less brush. In fact, he'd have happily allowed every one of LA's four million miserable losers to see into his yard, to witness this criminal act of breaking and entering. While his mind raced to figure things out, he kept asking himself *what if.* What if these men elected to pull their guns and use his head as a bull's eye? Nobody would care. In LA, people minded their own business. What a horse-shit city. *Help*, he wanted to scream, but the word had no voice.

"I am from Ensenada Partners. You know us?" the woman asked, seeming to feast on his confusion.

Unfortunately, Drucker knew quite a bit about Ensenada—none of it good. "Yes, ma'am," he mumbled, humble and contrite. "You're the Mexican connection—the one that funnels funds—"

"You talk too much, Mr. Drucker." She nodded and the small man struck Drucker's jaw with the back of his hardened knuckles. Drucker recoiled, acting the part of a whimpering dog.

"Huh," he said, rubbing his cheek. "Talk too much?" Adding to everything else, the steel edge in her voice cut through to his spine, making it difficult for him to remain erect.

"I have it from a contact of mine that you are someone the SEC intends to investigate," the woman said. "Could you enlighten me as to your conversation with an Agent Dawson last week?"

Drucker attempted to look pliant through a steady head-bob. Despite the dreaded men flanking Guzman and the pain of a swelling cheek, he couldn't help but focus on her. About the size of a child, yet possessing full cleavage and perfect hips, the woman had alluring, deep-set blue eyes that seemed entirely dead to him. In return, she regarded him as she might an annoying gnat, in need of extermination. What was she doing here? he wondered. She clearly didn't mind putting herself at risk, showing up personally at his door like this—she probably enjoyed the danger. She would bust his balls, and when he went down, spit on him. That's what he saw in her face.

"This guy Dawson," Drucker began, "said he had interest in how I managed such big returns. He said I seemed to have a sixth sense when trading in my aggressive fund—the one I manage for Stenman Partners."

"What did you tell him?"

"That I use stock and currency charts—technical analysis. I showed him the paperwork...I know the drill. Everything documented."

"Did you book those other trades?"

"Other trades? You mean the ones losing all that money?"

"Yes. Those." Sarah gave a subtle nod and the larger man began to clean up the shards of wood. The other moved a step closer to Drucker.

"Yeah, I booked them. Why anybody'd want to lose so much money over the course of a couple days beats me, but I do what I'm told."

"Did you find those losses stressful?" Sarah looked down the deep corridors of fear in Drucker's damp eyes.

"Uh, uh. Not my money." Drucker took a half step back, but a hand pinched his shoulder. He froze.

"Have another drink, Mr. Drucker." Sarah nodded in the direction of the open bottle resting on a table next to an armchair. As she did so, the thick man finished cleaning the pieces of door and switched off Drucker's television.

"No thanks."

Drucker swore at himself for panting like a dog and stuttering like a damn fool. In the middle of Drucker's silent tirade, the scar-faced smaller man shoved the bottle to his lips. Drucker choked as expensive whisky flowed half down his throat and half down his shirt. He tried to scream, but the needle that struck his neck put him to sleep in half a breath. As if the bones had been yanked from his body, he folded and sprawled across the white carpet.

*Where am I?*

This was the first thought popping into Stanley Drucker's battered head as he regained consciousness. Every bone ached. As he lay on his back, railroad tie rigid, glass shards dug into his skin. He looked up a sheer brick wall, while the smell of urine—some of it his own—hung in the fetid air. He'd awakened, he determined, shivering in an alley. Twenty inches above his face, the scarred man who had attacked him, who had stuck him with the long needle, looked down at him through gun barrel eyes. With flaring nostrils, the man resembled a baby bull, ready to attack. Drucker bent a weakened arm to his face, hoping to remove a pair of sunglasses blurring his vision. He pulled, and immediately tried and failed to scream.

"Time for a challenge, *Señor* Drucker."

Drucker struggled to lift himself, but a vicious heel kicked his raised shoulders back down, causing his head to bounce off asphalt.

"Not yet, *mi amigo*. You must learn the rules first."

Drucker flopped side to side like a dying fish on a dry dock. He struggled to focus on his tormentor's expression, but the heavy tint of his glasses prevented that.

"Let me explain how we play this game." The voice came across as a whisper, sounding almost intimate. "Your sunglasses have been attached to your head with epoxy, and your tongue, injected with a toxin, is swollen."

*I can take care of any investigation. I'm an asset.* Drucker listened to his gurgled sounds and nearly choked over his thickened tongue and the saliva building inside his mouth.

From his jacket pocket, the male enforcer, Ferret-Face, removed two rectangular metal boxes, each fitting into a palm. He then reached down and yanked Drucker's half-naked body to its feet, forcing a box into each of Drucker's hands. Ferret-Face clamped Drucker's right thumb onto a raised button on the first box.

More awkwardly, and never releasing the first hand, he did the same to Stanley Drucker's left thumb. Tears dribbled down Drucker's cheeks, and teetered on his upper lip until they built up and cascaded over, falling five empty feet to his blistered toes. With his gaze following that salty flow, he became aware of spider-webbing wires connecting several pounds of explosives strapped to his legs and hips. Barely visible across his naked chest were the words: *Death Death.* He recognized the building across the alley and street as the police station.

"Here are the rules," the man said, his words sounding rehearsed. "If you take either thumb off either device, you will explode. If you try and disconnect any wire, you will explode. If anyone else presses either of these buttons, relieving you, you will explode—each button is sensitive to your thumbprint only. In thirty minutes, no matter what you do, you will explode. This should be challenging. Do you understand?"

Drucker understood all right. He clasped the detonators, putting maximum pressure on each of his thumbs.

"And by the way," the man said with a smile, "I will have saved you *mucho dinero.* You are not going to require a casket, I think."

Turning a corner, the well-dressed Mexican used a cell phone to call a local television station, alerting them that a suicide crackpot, lurking near the police station, had explosives strapped to his body. He even identified the man as one Stanley Drucker, violent alcoholic, divorced, unstable, and manager of a local fund that lost millions of dollars just this week.

———

Rancho Santa Fe estates average four acres of grounds and more than 10,000 square feet of house. Nearly every one has a tennis court, a pool, and a stable of horses. Ayers' estate went beyond even these lofty averages.

Jason Ayers loved riding his favorite horse along the community trails. The aroma of Eucalyptus was soothing, and the tree's shedding leaves and bark padded the trails and muffled the sounds of the outside world. In addition to these tall trees, Ayers' property boasted close to a hundred lemon and orange trees—so many that he paid someone to harvest them twice a year and cart off the excess fruit.

In the past, at night, with an absence of street lamps and sidewalks, Ayers felt at the edge of the world, alone and at peace. He cherished his home and had come to reconcile himself with his wife, Anne, these last few years. After his son Curtis had died ten years ago, he grew even more devoted to his daughter. Kate became the center of his life, and he would do anything for her.

Longing for some of this former tranquility, but finding none, a diminished Jason Ayers spent Saturday afternoon slumped in a slip-covered chair, finishing a third scotch. "Oh …my… God," he whispered. "How could I have let this happen? Hannah, why?"

Sounds of footsteps at the door startled him. Anne Ayers stood inside the door frame, her gray hair scattered like detached spider webs. She had aged right in front of her husband, grown heavy and wrinkled. Was that why he had sought Hannah? Ayers had asked himself this question a hundred times. Was it a shallow need for younger, more vibrant company? He knew the answer was no. Hannah represented much more. He needed to help her, love her, and take care of her and her son. If he had been able to do so, he would have made a first installment on his debt to Matthew Neil. Now, everything he had attempted had turned deadly. And surely things were bound to get worse before they got better, if they ever got better.

He looked at the wall clock. The hands blurred on their way to three o'clock.

*Why, God, am I such a weakling?*

"You shouldn't drink so heavily," his wife said.

"Yes. You are right, dear." Ayers continued to sip.

"Come get something to eat, Jason."

He couldn't know how long Anne had stood in the library. Had they been talking? "No. No thank you. I, uh…I think I'll watch some news. Take my mind off of…"

*At three o'clock, you will turn on your television and wait. We have a message for you.*

Carlos Nuñoz had spoken those words to Ayers late last night. It was now five minutes before the appointed time. Suddenly, time slowed, then crawled. The television voices droned on—talking heads saying nothing important. Three o'clock came and went. Nothing. Five more minutes passed and still no news. He flipped channels. Could this be a cruel hoax? He prayed *yes* but believed *no*.

At 3:20, he felt hopeful. Then, in the middle of a boxing match, came a news flash. A reporter's excited voice filled the room, but Ayers absorbed the images, not the sound.

TV crews captured live the frantic movements of a lunatic with explosives strapped to his body. As one camera focused on the word *DEATH* scrawled twice across his chest, the TV anchor identified the man as Stanley Drucker.

Ayers knew Drucker, the same way he knew Cannodine. Hannah Neil had also known Drucker, just as she had known Cannodine. She also knew their crimes.

The newscaster's words found their way into Ayers' brain:

> *From what we have been able to gather, Drucker is an aggressive stock fund manager who's apparently distraught over the loss of millions of dollars in investors' money over the past several days.*

The deep voice then mentioned the tragedy at Jackson Securities just days earlier. The newscaster concluded by saying:

> *Psychologists believe that with the current volatility in the markets, these sorts of mental breakdowns could become all too common—much like people jumping out windows during the Great Crash and Depression of the 1920's and 30's.*

Without warning, Ayers felt himself pressed against his chair-back.

Drowning out all other sounds, the explosion vibrated the television. The video caught what appeared to be shards of brick hurtling from the disintegrating building next to where the man identified as Drucker had stood.

The commentator's voice first turned hoarse, then went silent.

A moment later, Anne re-entered the study. Ayers' white face must have unnerved her because her voice trembled. "Let's go someplace," she said. "You need to get out of the house."

She took her husband's hand and pulled him up and out. Without a will of his own, it was a simple thing to do.

---

The forty-nine dollar a night hotel room came furnished with cold linoleum tiles and ragged towels that scratched skin but couldn't absorb water. The dump also had battered walls, and the overhead lights flickered and hummed. All night long, the sounds of connubial banging in the room next door infiltrated the fabric-thin walls. Sleep had not been an option.

The stooped man with thick glasses tapped his bony fingers on the bedside table while pressing the phone against an ear. SEC Agent Oliver Dawson was small enough to shop in the boys' section of Sears, and his suit draped a couple sizes too big. His haircut was discount, as was the wide tie riding too high on his collar. He wasn't much of a physical specimen, either, with crayon lips, a pointed jawbone, and intense eyes. As he waited, he sipped a can of disgusting cola, his third in an hour. He wished the goddamn beverage machine had Diet Coke instead of this generic discount-crap. It tasted like metal and the bubbles were too fat.

Dawson's attention refocused as a female voice informed him, "The report from the Director's office yielded only dead-ends. I'm sorry, Oliver. The documents had no fingerprints. We may never know the source of this information on Jackson Securities or Mr. Drucker."

"Whatever happened to those FBI lab geeks being able to walk on friggin' water?" Dawson immediately regretted the outburst. "I'm not mad at you, Angela. Just frustrated."

After she disconnected, Dawson slammed the phone down. This was a kettle of month-old fish-stink. His two biggest leads, and now both obliterated. He wanted to believe neither the FBI lab nor the Security and

Exchange Commission's Enforcement Division had leaks, but he knew one or both did. And he had been so close to squeezing Cannodine and Drucker.

"Some squeeze I managed," Dawson mumbled to himself. "I'm worse off now than when I started. Now the bastards know who I am and that I care." They'd be watching, whoever *they* were.

With his leads down the toilet, he doggedly began to pack his bags for the trip back to Washington, D.C.

"Not giving up," he told himself, "just waiting for another break."

# CHAPTER THREE

IT WAS A DISHEARTENING FEW WEEKS OF UNEMPLOYMENT. At least twice, and as many as four times a day, Peter called, interviewed, and generally impressed those he met, only to get dinged when they contacted his former boss for a recommendation.

On several occasions, he tried pretending he'd been unemployed for the last couple of years, but that didn't fly too well either. Being a bum didn't exactly inspire prospective employers. One interview began to sound like the next, and Peter often forgot what dead-end job he was pursuing from one hour to the next. He even dipped into the marginal job market—those paying near minimum wage. Most of those employers wanted to know why a university educated man, who graduated near the top of his class, felt hell-bent on getting a shitty low-paying job working next to high school dropouts. They suggested he might quit the minute he found something more lucrative, as if moving up the job ladder were an option. Quitting his old job before having a new one had proved another of his less than brilliant strategies. At least he had the excuse of stress at his mother's death and a sudden compulsion to move his life in a direction she would have approved. Still, not a smart move.

Compounding this desperation, he needed to decide between rent payments and car payments. He elected to pay on the car—he could sleep in the back seat, but he couldn't drive his apartment to an interview. Since the landlord had no empathy for Peter's plight, he'd let it be known that after eight more days of unpaid rent, he'd evict both tenant and cat. And things got worse. Peter had just one more week to find enough money to service his mother's mortgage commitment or risk foreclosure. Recalling a bit of high school French, he summed up these sentiments with a rueful chuckle: "*Sur moi le déluge.*"

In his bathroom, prepping for yet another day of defeat, Peter stared at the mirror and spoke to his reflection: "Hello. My name is Neil. I want to work for you. I will do anything. What? The job pays a buck-fifty an hour? No problem, so long as there is ample opportunity for advancement."

Pulling his tie knot to his throat, he wondered if it was strong enough to make an adequate noose. Next, Peter imagined his slim wallet saying: *feed me.* "Sarcasm's a good thing," he said. "Shows I'm resilient through thick and thin." Once he finally finished dressing, he approved. He was jobless but looked prosperous. As he exited the bathroom, the phone rang, piercing the dull air. Peter veered towards the extension on the bedside table, but considered not answering. Why bother? The string of bad news was endless. Would this be any different?

He stood along the west-facing wall and window and listened to the swoosh of speeding cars. At night, he pretended this never-ending traffic was rolling surf. He wished, however, the waves didn't honk every few seconds. Flipping a mental coin on the fifth ring, he elected to pick up. When Jason Ayers said, "Hello," Peter immediately wanted to reconsider his decision.

"I spoke with Jerome Smitham," Ayers began. "He told me you were interested in finding your own job. Any success?"

Peter stared at a dark smudge on the wall. "It's an avalanche of opportunity," he said. "There's this assistant manager's job at a Jack in the Box restaurant. I'd make six bucks an hour and report to a nineteen-year-old. I'm considering it. Paper delivery routes are available. Also frozen banana dipper at the amusement park. Lots of things. I'm sorting out the opportunities."

"At least you've kept a sense of humor."

"Gallows humor. I'm looking at an eviction notice. With rents having escalated, my landlord is dying to get me out of here."

"Sounds bleak."

"I'll manage."

"Jerome says you're behind on Hannah's mortgage payments. How about letting me handle those?"

"No thanks, Mr. Ayers. You've done enough. Mr. Smitham told me you paid my tuition when Mom ran short of money."

"Jerome's got a big mouth."

"Anyway, thanks."

"That was the only money Hannah ever took from me, and she only did so because…" The voice faded to nothing.

"I'm glad he told me," Peter said. "I owe you for a lot of things."

Ayers paused to clear his throat. When he began again, he sounded tentative. "It was nothing. Under the circumstances, why don't you reconsider the position with Stenman Partners?"

"I appreciate the offer, but I don't want a make-work job. It's too much like a handout, and that's something I can't take."

"That's where you're wrong, Peter. Morgan Stenman makes everyone earn his keep a hundred times over. If you don't cut it, you're *ipso facto* out. Just come by my office for a chat."

"I don't know, Mr. Ayers."

"Hannah took *this* job and did outstanding work. She became, far and away, the best paralegal we had. That didn't amount to charity."

"She had to take that job—"

"Flipping burgers sounds good to you?" Ayers asked.

"No."

"Just a talk. I've got some free time around noon."

Peter agreed. "I'll see you in three hours. I appreciate the concern."

As Peter prepared to cancel the day's other interviews, Henry hopped onto his lap. "Whatta you think, old man?" he said, stroking behind the cat's ear. "Take the job for a month or two until we get back on our feet?"

Henry's throat vibrated in a contented hum.

———

Peter approached the elevator with four other people—three men in their mid-thirties or early forties, and an elderly woman. He wondered if they could hear his heart racing or see the small ballooning of his pulse against the soft part of his neck, near where the tongue attaches to the back of the throat. He attempted to will himself into a state of calm, but had mixed success.

The three men elbowed ahead, imitating pigs at slop time. One after the other punched a button for a floor, glowering at one another as if the order of floor input might affect arrival time. The numbers three, five, and six lit up. Peter allowed the woman in ahead of him while holding the door, making certain it did not retract while she entered. She glanced sideways, but gave no other sign of acknowledgement.

The woman tapped seven, the top floor, which was also Peter's destination. Peter moved to the back of the box and leaned into a corner. At least sixty years old, the woman had a serious face, smooth for her age, and she smelled like musty geraniums. After moving to the elevator's rear, she leaned on an aluminum cane with rubber-tipped tripod legs. Her indifference hung heavily in the tiny space.

When the first man—a fat guy with heart attack scrolling across his face—got off on three, they all rearranged themselves to maximize their territory. Next, a slender man with an eye tic stepped forward. On the fifth floor, he rushed off, turned left, then spun and reversed his course. On six, the last man, thick-limbed with a swollen and discolored eye, bounced on his toes while waiting for the door to open. He wore torn jeans and shit-kicker snakeskin boots. His clothes held the stink of twenty-five cent cigar, and his forearms bore a biker tattoo—it looked like a red, black, and white Harley-Davidson banner. Expensive silver and turquoise jewelry circled his forearms. Exiting, he bounded to the first door. Peter read the logo: *Harkness and Jameson: Specialists in Criminal Law*. Without knocking, the man barged in. As the elevator doors closed, Peter wondered what crime the tattooed man had committed. His demeanor suggested something monumental.

The elevator churned its way to the final floor. Five minutes before noon, Peter exited, trailing the suddenly unfrail woman. She carried herself with agility and speed down the hallway. Leaning on her cane as she stepped, she made it to the door with the Leeman, Johnston, and Ayers: Attorneys at Law nameplate several yards ahead of him.

As the office door shut in Peter's face, he stared at the grain of the wood and thought about the importance of the next hour of his life. He had rejected this job twice. Now? Now he wanted the position enough for his knees to knock. And wanting it so much made Ayers' possible change of mind a potential back-breaker for Peter. And broken backs, he understood, were hard to fix.

Feeling foolish as he stood like a flagpole in the hallway, Peter took a deep breath and grabbed the polished brass doorknob. He pushed, stepped in, and peered across the open space. The office held the quiet air of a university library—Peter could almost feel the moon-brains working behind these desks, billing clients at the rate of a couple hundred bucks an hour, every mind filled with millions of legal facts and precedents. He felt like a thrice-failed second-grader by comparison.

In a far corner office, where his mother had once worked, sat a book-ish clerk with an eager-beaver face. A pang struck across Peter's chest, caus-ing the air to thicken as if he were in a freshly watered sauna. In an effort to seal his grief, he swallowed, then redirected his attention. An African-American woman in blue business attire and stylish wire-frames sat behind a formal-looking reception desk. Handsome, in her fifties, she had gray hair and wore a phone headset, thus freeing her hands for other chores. Her nameplate read: *Elaine Robinson.*

Observing his approach and making eye contact, the receptionist nodded and held up a forefinger, signaling she would be right with him once she finished her phone call. After taking a message and hanging up, she said, "Mr. Neil, Mr. Ayers will be a few moments. I am sorry about your mother. I was a dear friend, and we all loved Hannah. Especially me, she was my…"

Elaine Robinson couldn't finish. Peter nodded his understanding, thanked her, and stepped to the coffee table and sofa set up for visitors to cool their heels. He skimmed the *Wall Street Journal* headlines and was reading about a coordinated attack on a third-world central bank when a voice hailed and distracted him from across the room.

"Peter Neil?" A mid-twenties woman whisked over to him. "I couldn't believe it when I heard you were coming to the office." She had a husky voice that easily carried the twenty-five feet.

An understated skirt and open jacket moved in rhythm with the bob of her rounded shoulder. And something about freckles dotting a cockeyed smile made her seem familiar. But who *was* she? he asked himself.

Just before she introduced herself, a movie-clipped-memory project-ed itself. Her hair still hung long and thick with a chestnut shine, but she was no longer skinny, nor did she wear braces. When she said, "I'm Kate. Kate Ayers," he had already guessed.

Fourteen years had passed since their families' occasional dinners, but this was the grownup version of that girl. Peter could not suppress his delight, a response originating in his toes, flowing up his spine, and onto his face, culminating in a hearty smile. She had a warm aura, and an odd mix more cute than pretty, but better than both. When she grabbed his hand, Peter said, "Little Katie Ayers. Damn. This is quite a surprise."

Ten minutes of catching up later, Peter asked, "You work here?"

"I'm embarrassed to say so, but yes. I just graduated from UCLA Law, and I'm working as a third-year legal associate for part of the summer. Naturally, I got the job on my merits…" She smiled, then laughed. "Okay, okay, Father had something to do with it. But I'm working for nothing. I didn't want to take one of the spots away from another intern; I'm *pro bono*. I've got to head back to LA in mid-July, so I couldn't commit to a full summer anyway."

"You're going back in July? How come?"

"I'm assisting one of my law professors on a textbook—on personal injury and tort law. Kind of a snooze, but it looks good on the old resumé. While I do that, I study for the bar exam."

"That's impressive. Are you going to concentrate on securities law?"

"Nope. Way too boring. I'm heading for criminal. That's if I pass the exam."

"You'll pass. I can see the intensity in your eyes."

"My eyes?"

"They're smart eyes."

"I'll take that as a compliment, though I can think of something a little more endearing."

"I'm tongue-tied. Perhaps I should have said you've got a certain *je ne sais quoi* about you." Kate curtsied, the tilt of her head hiding what Peter guessed was a smile. He continued, "By the way, I rode up in the elevator with a potential client." The image of the tattooed man with the deep bruises still gave him the creeps. "I hope you find a better class of criminal once you take the plunge."

"Even the guilty need counsel," she quickly replied, half-serious. The remark kept the mood light but hinted at her principles. As she spoke, Peter recalled his mother's comments about representing evil. "I'd like to start out in the Public Defender's Office. I don't know where I'll go after that."

"Mr. Neil," the receptionist gently interrupted Kate. "Mr. Ayers is ready."

Peter nodded. When he said, "I enjoyed seeing you again after all these years, Kate," he meant the words. She eased the tension he'd felt all morning by drawing him back to a happier time in his life.

"It was fun," she replied. "I don't know if you remember, but you used to make fun of my freckles. The first time you did, I cried because I didn't want you to think I was ugly. I had a crush on you."

"I was too busy being a thirteen-year-old to notice. Long belated apologies. Anyway, you've blossomed—*blossomed*'s a dumb word—but you've…well, you get my point."

A light blush accompanied an appreciative nod. "You want to get together?" she asked. "I'm free tonight."

"Tonight?"

"I'll buy dinner."

"You'll have to," Peter said. "I'm broke."

"Good. I like my men beholden." She laughed. "You can tell me if you take the job."

"You know about the Stenman Partners position?"

"Of course I do. Father tells me everything. If I were you, I'd accept. If you've got what it takes, you'll do very, very well there."

"You know Morgan Stenman personally?" Peter asked.

"My godparent. Father's been the partnership's counsel for thirty years."

"That's a good recommendation—"

"Excuse me, Mr. Neil, but they're waiting." The receptionist stepped around her desk, ready to lead him away.

Peter and Kate agreed to meet, seven p.m., at Bully's in Del Mar. As he made his way to Ayers' office, he wondered if he'd heard correctly. Had the receptionist said "*they're* waiting"?

If so, who besides Jason Ayers?

Kate's words, "If I were you, I'd take the position," bolstered him. He prayed he'd have the opportunity to take her advice. If so, he vowed to work ten times as hard as anyone else.

The overworked moonstone radiated friction-heat as Peter dropped it into his hip pocket. With a deep gulp, he knocked on the solid door. For the first time in weeks, he had a good feeling. He prayed it wasn't a head fake.

"Come in," Ayers said through the solid door.

Leaning forward, Peter obeyed.

# CHAPTER FOUR

AGENT OLIVER DAWSON ROSE FROM HIS DESK AND STRAYED TO HIS fourth floor window, grabbing a quick look at the Washington, D.C. scene. A June gloom hung over repugnant air spewing from the exhaust pipes of Fifth Street's bumper-to-bumper traffic. He turned the latch and slid the window open, breaking cobwebs in the process. Immediately, the sounds of revving engines and horns in staccato blares filled the room. He stared at the sky, filtered through gauzy air. Squeezing a dent into the can, he clutched his fourth Diet Coke of the morning—a ritual that kept his head buzzing and his mind racing. Behind him, the inaugural photos of the last eight presidents hung in a row. "The rogues' gallery," Dawson called them. Ronald Reagan's photo had his autograph scribbled across his chest. Dawson wished he had President Kennedy's signature instead, but he was too young to have met JFK.

It had been a depressing few weeks, as unfulfilling as any time in his life. When he returned to Washington after the Cannodine and Drucker fiascoes, Dawson handled a small insider trading case. A CEO's in-laws had traded shares of his company ahead of a takeover bid. Having settled this brief investigation with a paltry fine, he now had additional time to feed his frustrations. For the last fourteen of his thirty-nine years, the agent had dedicated himself to enforcing the nation's securities laws. No matter how hard he tried or cared, it wasn't enough. Tight budgets, sophisticated law-breakers, the explosion of wealth around the world—all made his efforts less than the proverbial drop in a bucket.

It was like everything else in his life: one mountain to climb after another. He was always the smallest person in class, had shitty eyesight, no athletic coordination, was far from brilliant, and a social misfit. Only his dogged determination had kept Dawson from getting lost behind life's eight-ball. He had persevered, gone to law school at night, and worked his way into this job.

Oblivious to the spent-petroleum smell in the air, he threaded his way through the maze of boxes, each of them containing sloppily labeled manila folders stuffed with pages from cases current, pending, or dismissed. It represented detritus that continued to build as the years wore on. The tiny office was made even smaller by protruding snap-on bookshelves that jutted from every wall. Dawson's footsteps tapped against the chipped and dingy linoleum, over to a dog-eared cardboard box with *STAPLES The Office Superstore* printed across its red front. He bent down and removed a stack of clipped papers. Arching upright, he tossed a shock of bangs from his forehead and, with the pad of his palm, pushed his horn-rims up the bridge of his nose. Opening the folder, he held it outright as a parishioner might hold a hymnal. He read his own note: *no indication of source.*

No indication who had mailed him those pages from San Diego a month ago? How could that be?

Somebody with access to confidential records on both Cannodine and Drucker had found a conscience. Someone anonymously sent to his attention several photocopies of receipts with Cannodine's signature, suspicious trade confirms from numbered foreign accounts, and evidence of funds transferred from the Cayman Islands. With what he had, Dawson confronted Jackson's branch manager and suggested he might become the target of an SEC investigation.

"If you haven't done anything illegal, Mr. Cannodine," Dawson had said, "then you have nothing to fear."

When Cannodine's body flinched and his face took on the look of a dehydrated apple, Dawson became convinced the man knew plenty. By the third visit, a threatened subpoena seemingly in his future, Cannodine had asked about immunity. Immunity inquiries, anybody in law enforcement knew, often marked *the* big first step towards gaining cooperation.

But then, a day-trader's rampage cut Dawson's inquiry short. *Bullshit.* If Zerets, or whatever the hell his real name was, hadn't blown himself up, nobody would have bought that idiotic story. Now, the agent remained alone in his lingering doubt. He didn't believe for a minute Zerets committed suicide. Someone set the swine up—Dawson didn't know how, but the murderer was just another disposable pawn.

Same with Stanley Drucker—a dimwit who couldn't lead a barbell to gravity—yet somehow had managed to move hundreds of millions of dollars in and out of his managed accounts at a numbing velocity. And except for recent losses, he had made ungodly returns on his investments. Then, after an initial visit by Dawson, came his monumental suicide. And everything fell so damn conveniently into place: Drucker loses millions of dollars and is depressed. According to his ex-wife, he has a history of alcoholism and violence. A search of his house uncovers materials and instructions on bomb-making. Since not a molecule of Drucker remains, there is nothing more to pursue. The Director of Enforcement's Special Assistant, Freeman Ranson, even suggests that Dawson had pushed too hard and set Drucker off.

And because of Ranson, the pressure on Dawson increased daily. Ranson took every opportunity to criticize—claimed Dawson felt bitter over having failed with the Treasury manipulation case he'd brought, and failed to make stick, against Stenman Partners a few years back. That he always pushed too hard and needed to back off and be less passionate. Some of what Ranson said was true. Dawson *was* bitter—damn bitter— but that had nothing to do with this case. People had committed crimes that dug deeply into the financial system, maybe deeply enough to stagger a few Wall Street institutions. Dawson felt the filth in the joints of his bones and it pained him. He cared about the law. To him, it mattered.

"You don't listen to anyone and you're dangerous, Dawson," Ranson had said in front of the Director. "You've got a weak case and you go nuts, threatening people. Somebody needs to clip your wings."

"Ranson's an asshole," Dawson now said as he clamped shut the file. "A flaming asshole." The agent found himself wishing he stood six-foot, two inches and weighed two hundred and twenty pounds, instead of five-six and one hundred and forty. If he had the size, he'd kick Ranson's ass. Maybe not kick his ass, but threaten to kick his ass and scare the shit out of him.

"Mr. Dawson? Oliver?" Angela Newman, the secretary he shared with two other agents, stood at his door. "Did you need something?" she asked.

With his office door always open and the walls paper thin, Angela had heard his outburst.

"No. Talking to myself." His head bent down to his thick-soled black shoes. He put the more scuffed of the two behind the other. It was a clumsy attempt to hide the fact that in over a year, he had yet to get a shoeshine.

"If you're sure." She turned and stepped away.

"Angela," Dawson said, reacting to an impulse. "Can you ring the FBI lab? Find out who did the tests on those materials I got in May from San Diego?"

"Certainly." Angela, raw-boned, with a narrow chin and crooked teeth, smiled. "Anything else?" she asked.

Dawson felt flush. He liked Angela and wished he wasn't such a coward. Nobody would care if he dated his secretary. Ask her if she's free for a drink after work, he urged himself. "Uh, maybe if you…" He stalled.

"If I what?" She batted her eyes.

"…if you wouldn't mind making that call now, I'd appreciate it."

"Of course, Oliver."

*Dammit*, he scolded himself.

Fidgeting, he watched her turn and leave. Her dress draped long and limp, a floral pattern with bunched shoulders and a pink ribbon cinched around her tiny waist and tied in a bow. Stringy, dirty-blond hair brushed against her collar in the back just before she disappeared around the corner. The others in the office made fun of Angela, calling her the old maid. She was thirty-five—younger than him. Not old, he thought. And even if the others didn't like her looks, Dawson found her expressions kind.

One day, he vowed, I'm going to ask her out.

Dawson picked up his soda and downed the last three ounces. He pulled open his drawer and grabbed another can, listened to the hiss of the airborne carbonation—a whisper of his addiction—then took a deep swig and waited. Waited for a break. Waited for someone to step forward and give him another lead. Waited for Angela Newman. Waiting—that's something he had long ago become accustomed to.

Fifteen minutes later, Angela returned to his open door, "The FBI lab technician?" She had tears in her eyes.

"Yes," Dawson asked, attempting to present as pleasant a look as possible.

"Had an accident."

"Terrific. Let me guess. He's off work for a month and I can't get my damn files back."

"It's—" Her voice shook. "It's worse. He was with another agent. Killed. Shot in a horrible accident."

"Dead?"

She nodded.

"When the friggin' hell did that happen?"

She hunched over. "Two or three weeks…" she said.

"What a coincidence. About the same time Cannodine and Drucker are getting blown to bits." Dawson seeped his rage through Angela's tears—and softened. "I'm sorry. I care. Sometimes I get too emotional."

"Yes, sir."

"What the hell is going on?" Dawson asked. "Angela, are you okay?"

"I think so." She bit her lower lip.

"When you're ready, see if I can get back the originals I sent for analysis—that would include a short letter, copies of ledger pages, notes, and two transcripts of phone calls." He put the soda can against his burning cheek.

"I already asked," she said. "They refuse to release any records until the deceased's cases have been reassigned and the technicians have had a chance to evaluate his work."

"How long will that take?" Dawson stood and trudged around his desk. Finishing his soda, he crushed the thin aluminum can and slammed it into the trash container. The clang echoed off the sides of both the can and his skull.

"Several weeks," Angela said.

"Tell them this is top priority. Tell them I want everything as soon as possible."

"Yes, sir. Shall I tell them anything else?"

"Yeah. Tell them…No. Forget it. I guess I'm just going to have to friggin' wait."

"Is that all, sir?" she asked, struggling with the words.

"Yes, I guess it is."

The second she left, Dawson went to the open window, stuck his head out, and yelled, "Fuck it all!"

Through the noises of downtown D.C., his words died before they hit any ears other than his own. His voice barely qualified as sound.

Figures, he thought.

---

The door hinges chirped as Peter entered Ayers' office. The attorney, propped upright against the front of his desk, greeted him with a wan smile. When Peter took a step forward, Ayers straightened up and offered his hand. The attorney stood an inch taller than Peter, and, with fingers like thick noodles, offered a limp handshake. Dressed like the millionaire he was, Ayers had regained much of the dignity he'd lost the morning he'd come to Peter's apartment and broken down. Peter also looked refreshed in a blue suit—not a designer label like Ayers', but still neat and a good fit. An outsider would not have recognized these two from their rendezvous over two weeks ago.

The office air held the scent of pungent flowers—somehow familiar— but mixed with tobacco smoke. Ayers' face pointed away. Peter turned just as a woman's voice said, "Hello, Mr. Neil."

The woman from the elevator now eyed him as she leaned over her cane, all the while coddling a cigarette wedged inside a slim, plastic holder. She didn't inhale deeply, but managed an endless stream of exhale.

"I didn't see you when I entered," Peter said, stumbling over his words.

His mind had just enough time to wonder who she was before she said, "I am Stenman."

"You're Morgan Stenman? I assumed..." Peter felt exponentially disoriented. Suddenly, knowing this was Stenman, the metal cane became an extension of her metal arm, her metal chest, shoulder, neck, and head. Cast in iron, she was an element of the earth, basic and impenetrable. Beyond flesh and blood.

"You expected a man," Morgan said.

"I confess, I did. And that makes me a moron." Peter's face reddened. If his pants had fallen to his knees, exposing his privates, he couldn't have felt more foolish.

"I gather you don't watch much investment television," Ayers said in Peter's defense. "Morgan is an advisor to presidents and a glass-ceiling breaker of the first order."

"Being flat broke, I watch no business TV. My portfolio consists of a couple boxes of cereal and a pint of milk for my cat."

Stenman nodded. "Clever."

Peter didn't think she sounded sincere. "Put a foot in your mouth often enough," he said, "and you develop strategies for getting the damn thing out. Nice to meet you, Ms. Stenman." He offered his hand.

"I do not shake hands." She leaned back, creating a few inches of additional space between herself and Peter. "From this point forward," she continued, "if you intend to work for me, refer to me as Morgan."

"If I intend to work for you?" Peter's voice wavered between unbelieving and hopeful.

She took a calculated puff.

Ayers chimed in, "Your choice, Peter."

Peter did not risk a moment's hesitation. "If it's up to me, then yes."

"Good," Ayers said. "Morgan informs me that you'll start out doing trade processing and projects. If you are half as intelligent as I've assured her, you will progress quickly to more important assignments."

Stenman held up her hand and Ayers immediately fell silent. "I am not offering you a job just because my long-time friend and attorney says to," she said. "If you accept the challenge, then know this: your value as a human being will be measured by how much money you make for my firm, yourself, and me. You must make the necessary sacrifices. That is understood?"

Peter guessed her manner of speaking and accent were Eastern European. He blinked for the first time in a minute. "That's the American way." His face turned red over the triteness of his response.

"Indeed. The American way," agreed Ayers. "Your beginning salary will be minimal—seventy-five thousand—but once you pass your probationary period, in a month, that will increase to a hundred. If you make it through year end, you will be eligible for a bonus."

Peter doubted he had heard correctly. "Seventy-five thousand *dollars*?"

Stenman gave him a harsh look. "That is inadequate?" She had charcoal eyes—cold now but combustible.

"No, no," Peter said. "Fine. More than fine."

Peter knew he had failed to hide his shock. Seventy-five K was nearly twice what he'd been pulling-in writing mortgage loans. The thought of a hundred K and a down-the-road-bonus knocked his heart against his backbone.

"Now, Peter," Ayers said, "about the loan secured against your mother's house…"

Peter mentally switched gears. "The loan? Once I verify income, I can schedule repayment."

"No," Ayers said. "Stenman Partners will arrange to pay off the second mortgage—and keep the house from going up for sale. You should be able to handle the original loan on your own. With Morgan's permission, I've already cut a check for fifty thousand dollars. The amount will be deducted from your year-end bonus."

"Am I dreaming?" Peter asked, looking to Ayers.

"I erase your debts," Stenman said, "because I do not want my employees' attention diverted from business. Any other questions?"

"When do I start?" Peter asked, thinking they had way overpaid for him. He would have been happy to work for half what they offered and been satisfied with the annual five percent raises the rest of the world lived with. When you've had dose after dose of shit luck, you get used to the smell. He tried not to, but worried there had to be a catch.

"You begin tomorrow. Five-thirty," Ayers answered. "New York markets open at half past six, but foreign markets trade all night."

"I don't know what to say," Peter sputtered.

"Show up on time and do what it takes *not* to fail." Stenman's voice sounded guttural.

"Dress is smart-casual, Peter." Ayers chuckled. "Only Martha Stewart knows what that means."

"You report to Howard Muller—third floor." As Stenman spoke, obliterating Ayers' attempt at lightening the mood, Peter's head jerked back to her. "Now," she said in a dismissive tone, "I have other matters to discuss with my attorney."

Ayers guided Peter away with a hand on his elbow. As Peter stepped out, the older man said, "Good luck."

The office door clicked shut before Peter could respond. He closed his mouth and stumbled across the firm's main floor, shocked a bombshell hadn't exploded at the last second and shattered this amazing karma. Before exiting, he glanced toward the corner of the room where he had first seen Kate Ayers. She held a phone to her ear, but mouthed the words to Peter, "Goodbye, see you at seven."

Peter nodded and drifted down the hallway. At the elevator, he punched the air with his fist in a subdued celebration. What a turnabout, he thought. Seventy-five plus bonus. Going to a hundred if I make it.

"I'll make it all right," he swore. "For that kind of money, I'll learn everything. Do what I'm told. Do whatever it takes."

Once Peter stepped outdoors, the sun penetrated his clothes and warmed his flesh. The air smelled sweet. The traffic rang vibrant. He now understood what it felt like to be at the center of a universe with all matter revolving around you. It felt exhilarating.

# CHAPTER FIVE

BULLY'S RESTAURANT HAS A LOUD BAR AND DECENT STEAKS. At night, it is always crowded, attracting off-track bettors who migrate in as a clique to drink and distort their successes. The place is perpetually nighttime dark, smells of dripping fat, has crisscrossing wood beams, and yet it managed to feel intimate in the half-wall booth where Peter and Kate shared fifteen years of stories.

After several minutes of catch-up, they got around to ordering a bottle of Cabernet. Once the wine arrived, Peter said, "You look great. I can't believe you've grown up into...well, into this..." He spread his arms, palms upturned in the gesture of a man offering up something special.

"Little ol' me?" she asked, flapping her eyelids in mock Southern Belle style. "You mean this beautiful, alluring, sexy diva?" Kate smiled, then laughed. The combination represented a pattern both genuine and frequent.

"My thoughts exactly." Peter put his hand over hers and rubbed. The gesture reminded him of the last time he had seen his mother alive. As they stood in the shadows of the building that morning, he had taken her hand and circled the back with his thumb in an attempt to calm her. In a reflex, Peter abruptly withdrew his hand from Kate's.

"Did I do something?" she asked.

He exhaled deeply and regretted the sudden melancholy, but his emotions had just caromed around a place he found difficult to escape. Peter wondered if his mother had seen Kate at any time over the years. And did Kate suspect her father and his mother had once been intimate?

"Did you..." He wanted to ask, but if she didn't know about the affair, wouldn't it be better to keep it buried?

She reached across and covered his hand. Her flesh felt comforting.

"Did you ever see my mom, these last few years? Since our families stopped being social friends, I mean." He stared, vainly searching for clues.

"A couple of times at the office. I meant to say something—how sorry I was, but I didn't know how you'd react." The wet sheen over Kate's eyes built into droplets that she wiped away. "Father says he worshiped your parents. And even though your father broke off their friendship those last few years, Father never stopped admiring him."

"Jason's been a good friend."

They worked their way through the painful conversation and by the time dinner arrived, they were back to sharing happier thoughts. Later, just after Kate paid the check, Peter said, "I'll repay you for dinner once I get my first paycheck."

"Not so fast," Kate said. "I don't want your money. What I want is for you to reciprocate. You can buy *me* dinner next time."

"Sounds good. I'll call."

She wagged her head. "When a guy says he'll call, it's a blow-off. I'm not letting you off so easily. Your paydays are the fifteenth and the last day of each month. Next Tuesday you are once again solvent."

"You know what day I get paid?"

"I told you: Father and Morgan have a relationship that goes way back. Our firm has a department that handles payroll for many of our clients, including Stenman Partners. We do most of their paperwork, banking, even some client billing. When I heard you got the job, I peeked at some of their records. Don't tell anybody, but I know Father's computer password and user name. If they found out, they'd change the entire system. Supposedly impenetrable."

"Then how did you tap into the thing?"

"I was doing some work at home, over a weekend. Father was having a hard time—I think it was the weekend your mother...well, it hit him hard and he'd been drinking. He left his laptop on and I remembered his password: Hannah-anne-kate. Your mother's, my mother's, and my names, all pasted together. I also have a semi-photographic memory and recalled his ten-digit username." Her mouth pleasantly stretched. "Okay, so I don't have a photographic memory. I'm nosy, and I wrote the letters and numbers down. So today, I gave it a try. Bingo-bango. I had Stenman Partners' payroll records staring at me."

"That's a lot of trouble, but at least I can alert my landlord he'll be getting paid soon. With that settled, how's Friday of next week for dinner?"

"It's a date."

"On another topic," Peter said, "maybe you can tell me something about Morgan Stenman."

Kate nodded. "She's gruff, but she's been like a kind aunt to me."

"Can you tell me anything about her partnership? I know nothing, yet I'm about to dive in and swim amongst the sharks, so to speak."

"Some, though I'm far from an expert on stocks and bonds."

Stenman Partners managed, she said, a hedge fund that made leveraged bets on everything: stocks, bonds, currencies, and commodities. They went long all of these instruments—which meant they owned the asset. They also could short each asset category—which she explained was a transaction that allowed the fund to make money when the asset value went down, rather than up. "Shorting has something to do with borrowing stock, selling it, then buying it back later at a lower price. Don't ask me how it all fits together, because I still don't get it."

"That makes two of us," Peter said.

Kate next detailed some of Stenman's overseas interests. "They're aggressive, moving quickly as they acquire information from their global network. And the partnership is phenomenally successful. They have money flowing into and out of developed countries in addition to Eastern Europe and dozens of underdeveloped markets. Morgan is considered one of the most astute traders in the world."

"I noticed she speaks with a slight accent—maybe Slavic."

"You have a good ear. In the early nineteen-forties, according to my father—and I guess he ought to know—she escaped Poland. Her family was Jewish and she was rescued, but not her parents. The Nazis captured them and they disappeared."

Peter became enthralled by Morgan's tale. She had no money when she arrived in the U.S. With a few poor relatives working in the navy yards in San Diego, she eventually made her way through U.C. Berkeley, then nurtured family contacts from Eastern Europe who had prospered after the war.

"She began investing money for some of them," Kate said. "Over time, her track record attracted international attention. The rest is history. Morgan and her staff get paid one percent of assets under management, plus twenty percent of profits."

"How much money does she manage?" Peter asked.

"I'm not sure. She has dozens of offshore accounts, and the money flows in and out so fast from overseas that the amounts fluctuate, but at any one time, I'd say several billion in client funds are under management."

Peter whistled. "Say it's five billion. The one-percent fee totals fifty million. If Morgan's making as much money for her investors as people say, twenty percent of that would be what? Another four hundred million dollars? Maybe more. Who makes hundreds of millions of dollars a year?"

"It sounds ludicrous, doesn't it?" Kate said. "And you may have under-stated the amounts. It's possible Morgan controls ten to fifteen billion dol-lars. Only she and a few close associates are privy to that information. Not even Father knows for sure."

The numerical insanity clotted Peter's sensibilities enough that he felt mounting intimidation. *Deal with it,* he counseled himself.

When they later left the restaurant and arrived at Kate's Jag, Peter offered his hand. She shook her head and said, "I'm no longer a little girl." Her voice then became breathy. "When you say goodnight to me, buster, you better do it right."

She yanked him from behind his neck, pulled, and kissed. Hard. A moment later, a grinning Kate slid into her sleek auto and drove away.

Peter ran his tongue over his lips. Outstanding, he thought.

Peter drifted down one of many sleepy streets towards his own cheapo-car. He peered into a bookstore, then jaywalked to the far side of Del Mar's main boulevard. He stumbled past a local library in an old church building, a couple of real estate offices, and multiple stop signs. Families of four slept in suburban homes half a block away. A train, flying over a trestle, blew its whistle from the bluffs just west. The sound mingled with an ocean breeze that licked his skin with a light dew. The full moon illuminated his path.

The wine. The company. The prospect of tomorrow's employment adventure, all spun like an out-of-control top through his mind. Before dawn, he'd confront things he'd barely heard of: longs and shorts, puts and calls, bids, offers, index options, straddles, strips, futures, IPO's, share repurchases, fixed incomes, foreign currency trading.

More compelling than any of this was the wealth. Nobody at Stenman Partners had discovered a cure for anything—not cancer, not the common cold, not even a hangnail. But they earned four hundred million in income

a year, maybe more, for betting on winning investments.

"Am I selling out?" he wondered out loud.

"No," he announced to the street lamp. "Dad was a financial failure. Mom lived in a sinkhole of debt. Life is what it is."

He drifted farther down Del Mar's main street. Rich people lived in Del Mar. Maybe one day he'd live in Del Mar or Rancho Santa Fe or La Jolla. Maybe he'd have a view of the ocean instead of the freeway. A block from his car, a woman with a small dog on a tight leash passed in the opposite direction. The cocker spaniel defecated in a patch of ice plant. The woman placed her hand in a plastic bag and scooped up the steaming feces while Peter's head filled itself with foolish gratitude for cat litter boxes. The wine's affecting my brain, he thought. Or maybe it was the kiss.

In bed, twenty minutes later, he rubbed his moonstone hard enough to raise a blister.

———

Carlos Nuñoz arrived at the compound at five a.m. Although the guards recognized him, they nonetheless held rifles at the ready.

"*Hola, Señor Nuñoz. Como está usted?*"

Carlos depressed the button activating the driver side window and said, "*Bien. Y tú, Manuel?*"

"*Muy bien. Gracias.*"

Manuel, like the 20 other mercenaries patrolling the parameter of the Guzman estate, wore an olive-green uniform, topped off by dark glasses and a soldier's cap with a black brim and thin rope adornment across the front. Alongside him, a German shepherd lightly tugged against a steel leash.

Manuel yanked a lever that popped open the trunk while the dog sniffed for material that might make a bomb. The dog also had the ability to detect drugs, though that skill had limited relevance with the recent changes in their mix of business. Manuel, his rifle slung over his right shoulder, next raised the panel housing the spare tire. He allowed the dog to poke its head inside. Both satisfied, they worked their way to the engine. Manuel reached beneath the hood, unhooking then lifting it. He and his friend next inspected the interior of the car, focusing on the space under the front and rear seats.

A moment later, the guard used a mirror, mounted on a curved pole, to examine the chassis beneath the hundred-fifty thousand-dollar, steel-reinforced Mercedes sedan. Every car and guest underwent a similar methodical search, with absolutely no exceptions. The word *trust* had no meaning in this part of the world.

"*Gracias, Señor Nuñoz*," Manuel said as the arm of the barricade swung open.

Carlos coasted through the gate and down the hundred-plus yards of driveway towards the sprawling Mission-style home. He loved Sarah Guzman and did not mind that she was an Anglo. He loved her intelligence. He also admired her estate, where every one of the thirty rooms had a view of the Pacific Ocean and her mile of private beach.

He was loyal because she was unwavering. After the death of her husband, Sarah Guzman had become the family's *madama*—the head of their house. And he believed in her black magic, the spell she held over men and women. Carlos wished, above all else, he could have been of her blood so he might have inherited her intelligence, been born of *her* loins, not his own mother's disgusting *choca*.

As he pulled his car up to the front door, an armed valet bowed and took his keys while Carlos fantasized how *he* would handle Sarah's brother-in-law, Fernando Guzman. One thing he knew with certainty: Sarah Guzman's solution to this uprising would be genius.

Carlos approached the outer gate with its stone pillars and wrought iron spikes. When he snatched the lion's paw door-knock and prepared to announce himself, drops formed on his upper lip. Every time he arrived at this place and took in its unimaginable wealth, he felt humbled.

Knocking, Carlos pointed his face at the camera mounted just inside the courtyard. The guard, already alerted by those at the front entrance, verified Carlos' identity and buzzed him into the patio. A noisy fountain, spewing water from the mouths of posed statuettes—naked cupid-like creatures with tiny penises—greeted him as he stepped toward her house.

He continued along an open-air esplanade lined with red tile and adobe archways. Above him, additional soldiers with high-powered weapons nodded in deference to him—as an important man, they respected him.

Carlos turned, went up a flight of stairs, and down a second open

walkway. A sea breeze, swirling off complex architectural angles, flowed through his slicked-back hair, parted with a razor's edge on his right side—an extension of the long mound of tissue distorting his face.

He signed the Catholic cross against his chest, whispered the words of the Holy Trinity, and knocked.

A half-second later, she said, "Enter."

---

Carlos stood just inside the office door and waited. "We have three hundred million set up with a two-trade," Sarah Guzman said into the phone. "Second broker-bank is First Cayman. They have booked a gain of three ten, looking to clear ten net of the transaction. Understood and acceptable."

Sarah listened to the voice on the other end, then said, "Yes. I am aware the Thai Baht declined eight percent last night. I agree. That is a good spot to book gains and build up the account value. Howard, I leave those details to you."

Sarah glanced over the top of her reading glasses at Carlos. She liked the boy and admired his intensity. He was her husband's twenty-eight year-old nephew, and one of several bright family members she retained after Enriqué Guzman had died three years ago. Short at under five-foot-seven, Carlos had pockmarked and oily skin but a lean, strong body. Because of his looks, he became her husband's least favorite relative—another reason for her deep affection.

Sarah sat behind a hand-carved mesquite desk. In a corner, an arched adobe fireplace showcased a bonfire that roasted every corner of her thousand square foot office. Fur area rugs—glass-eyed brown bear and mountain lion—warmed the Spanish tiles beneath an umbrella of oak beams crisscrossing a peeked ceiling. She noted the raised tissue zippering across Carlos' right temple and down his cheek, chin, and neck—the result of a knife-fight at the age of twelve. The boy received a disfigurement, but his two attackers had landed in paupers' graves. Since that day, Carlos had no annoying second thoughts when doing whatever she found necessary to maintain order.

He removed his aviator sunglasses and slid them into a breast pocket.

Once she hung up, Sarah said, "That was Howard Muller. We have moved another four hundred from our Tijuana friends to our investment partners."

Carlos only nodded. Sarah understood he disliked Muller. So did she, but, to her, likes and dislikes had nothing to do with business. She hoped the tension between these men never boiled over. It would be such an unfortunate mess.

"I understand that the aftermath of the Cannodine and Drucker affair has been satisfactory," she said.

"*Si, señora.* We have laid those matters to rest."

"Good." The only thing Sarah regretted about that unfortunate affair had been the necessity of sacrificing the man calling himself Zerets. On several occasions in the past, he had proven an asset. But, better than anyone, she understood unpleasant choices sometimes had to be made for the long-run good. Still, she grew angry when slip-ups demanded such sacrifice.

"Now," she continued, shaking free of these thoughts, "you indicated another matter required my attention."

"Regretfully, yes. Fernando Guzman."

"My husband's brother? He is causing problems again?"

"*Si.* He tells the family he is tired of your ascendancy. He calls you a *gringa* who married his brother and stole the family business. He says we should never have forsaken the old ways. That you need to be replaced."

"He wishes to go back to the dangers of brokering drugs when we can broker money, safely, more profitably? He is a dangerous fool."

"I agree. What would you have me do?"

Against Sarah's snowy skin and white hair, rage appeared like a red mask, flaming her cheeks. She considered the situation for a moment. "You will get a large, wooden box. It will have enough space to fit Fernando Guzman and three days' water and food. You will put a hole in that box. You will attach an eight-foot pipe—a hollow pole—to that hole. Air will flow through, just enough to keep the traitor from suffocating. You will bury that box, with Fernando in it, six feet deep, in a cool, shaded spot that no person will pass by. Like our Lord Jesus, on the third day—that is, after three *complete* days and nights—you will take several of the family members on a picnic near that shady grave. You will comment on that pole, poking from the ground. You will organize the men and dig until you solve this mystery. When you uncover the box, with my dead husband's stupid brother, you will open it. Before you raise Fernando from the dead, you will tell him: 'It is a lucky thing Sarah Guzman suggested this picnic.' He will understand."

"This is a good plan, *Tía*. I believe we cannot kill the fool, lest we create additional dissension. Some do not believe your husband, Enriqué, committed suicide—that such a devout Catholic would allow his soul to be damned."

"They believe a man, such as my husband, would buy and sell drugs, and have men murdered for stealing a gram of *cocaina*, but would not commit suicide?"

"Indeed. It is *loquera*. Still, you make a wise and merciful solution to the problem of Fernando."

"You will have no trouble completing this task?"

"None. I will use people unknown to the family."

The rumble of thunder gave a gentle shake to the house, while the scent of ozone filtered through the window.

"That is good, Carlos," Sarah said. "Since we have now completed our business, feel free to help yourself to food—the cook has put out fruit, breads, an ample bounty in the sitting room. If you wish to avoid the approaching storm, stay here today and tonight. My home is, as always, your home."

"*Muchas gracias.*" Carlos bowed and backed away.

As did most of their conversations, this one ended with many unspoken understandings.

# CHAPTER SIX

FROM THE AGE OF THIRTEEN, PETER HAD WORKED AT LEAST TEN FIRST-days on the job. His various occupations had included construction, gardening, motel clerk, camp counselor, and a host of other non-memorables whose only attraction was the paycheck that kept him marginally solvent. But this represented more than simply a new job. It was a high-paying job for which he had little grounding. It was also something he sorely needed.

For six hours, Peter spun in his bed, filled with the anticipation of a runner, waiting endlessly for the starter's pistol to fire. His mind, reviewing and re-reviewing future roads he might travel down, allowed little more than a snippet of sleep. He didn't mind, though. He had almost enjoyed the agony of the long night, filled with the anticipation of the upcoming day. If this were any normal day, he would have been exhausted from a night of tossing and turning. Instead, he now felt like he could put his feet together and vibrate his way to Stenman's offices. A gallon of adrenaline guaranteed that fatigue would not be part of today's agenda.

Instructed to arrive at half past five, Peter didn't mind the predawn start. He knew the New York Stock Exchange closed at one in the afternoon on the West Coast, so that meant early in, early out. Maybe leave by three or at the latest four and still be able to put in ten or eleven hours' work. After turning off North Torrey Pines Road onto a two-lane private road, he encountered an automatic gate-arm beside an enclosed guard post. Once he stopped, a floodlight beamed through his window. Cupping his hands over his brow, Peter rolled his window down. Appearing, rather than arriving, a lanky man—looking like a drill sergeant—asked, "You are…?"

"Peter Neil. A new employee."

The man produced a clipboard, ran an index finger down the page, then said, "I need to see a picture I.D."

Peter caught a glimpse of a holstered pistol, looking so natural on the man's erect body that it might have been a piece of bone. Peter fumbled to find his driver's license before handing it over.

"Credit card, please."

"What's this all—"

"Credit card. Please."

"Sure, but why all the security?"

The guard ignored the question.

"You may retrieve these at the end of the day. We will run a check concurrent with your other tests."

The guard shoved a form and pen under Peter's nose. Peter signed and continued on. He drove past pine trees towering over yucca and cactus, all groomed to look natural. Etched into an overhanging copper-coated roof, the letters *S.P.* were the only indication Stenman Partners owned the building. Having grown up a few miles east, Peter thought he knew this area. He was wrong. He never imagined such a fortress existing off the main road leading past Torrey Pines State Park and Golf Course. The building exterior—beautifully crafted in natural stone—looked sturdy enough to qualify as a bomb shelter, or, more accurately, a West Coast version of Fort Knox. The image of his pockets full of gold coins flashed through Peter's hyperkinetic brain. Despite arriving thirty minutes earlier than he'd been told to, the parking lot was already half-full. Peter's VW looked ridiculous beside six-figure works of automotive art.

Although sunrise was half an hour off, spotlights chased away all hint of shadow. As Peter approached on foot from where he parked, the nighttime dew traced his face like an icy sweat, the wind snapped his loose cotton slacks, and he angled a shoulder to ward off the draft. Still a hundred feet away, he spotted two armed guards, looking as hard as bronze. The sight made him wary. One man simply stared, his head immobile. The other glanced side to side as if he had a nervous tic or head palsy. Had he landed in Russia as a suspected spy? Was he marching into Sing Sing? The questions didn't seem so outrageous as Peter kept a steady pace, feeling the closed circuit cameras observing him like a hundred eyes, peering at him from the carport, every third or fourth light post, and the building front.

*Scanning for what? Protecting what?*

Peter took deep breaths of cool air and reached for his moonstone—his habitual anxiety-reducer—but did not withdraw the gem from his pocket. With all these guards, guns, and cameras, he didn't want anyone wondering what he might be clutching. It seemed like a shoot-first, ask-questions-later kind of place.

With his eyes, but without moving his head, Peter scanned the silhouetted horizon. Through the dim light, he made out the rough edges of the one hundred-foot bluffs overlooking the beaches tying together the coastal communities of La Jolla and Del Mar. From the look of the place, Stenman had elected to buffer her headquarters with at least two acres of undeveloped grounds, with every square inch sharing an ocean view. How much had this property cost? In the tens of millions, he guessed.

Once he reached the front door, the guards glanced at Peter's paperwork. He then signed in and was led to *Security,* where a nurse drew a vial of blood. "A drug test," they said. A set of fingerprints followed. Efficient. Practiced. Everything performed in less than four minutes. These people knew their business.

Minutes later, a Dr. Parker wired Peter's fingertips and pasted electrodes across his chest and neck. He spoke in a monotone, explaining that he had a few questions. Wanted to talk about issues. Peter—like a good new employee—dumbly nodded as if he understood.

The doctor's appearance defined the word "bland." He was man without affect, and almost too perfect a caricature of a psychiatrist. He wore wire-frames and had a large forehead and a pasty face, shaded by a well-cropped beard. The lace of gray at his temples looked painted on. When Parker began by asking questions about Peter's family, school, grades, and social activities, Peter obliged with short, to-the-point answers.

After ten or twelve minutes of mundane conversation, the lab-coated psychiatrist asked, "And your mother's death: how did that happen?"

Peter did a double-take at the sudden change in topic. He briefly tried to figure out what possible relevance his mother might have—unless it was some kind of Oedipal Complex test—but went ahead and volunteered the details provided by the police. He also mentioned some of his mother's professional concerns.

For several minutes, the shrink continued to press this line of questioning, so much so Peter thought the guy might be suffering from an obsession of his own. When Peter had had enough, he asked Dr. Parker about the relevance of the interest in his mother. The doctor at first looked taken aback, then nodded and answered: "We are a stressful working environment, and you have experienced a tragic loss. Our concern is for your mental health. If you prefer, though, you may refuse to answer." The man's expression, however, seemed at war with the conciliatory words. "Dealing with guilt," he continued, "is often a difficult thing to do. Sometimes parting conversations with loved ones have great psychological significance. We tend to blame ourselves when a parent dies. At the end, did your mother share anything else?"

Peter stared at his questioner. "Like what?"

"Anything. Maybe something struck you as curious or out of character." Dr. Parker made a notation in the spiral notebook perched on his lap. "You earlier said something about her concerns with the law firm's clients."

Peter shook his head. "As I already told you, my mother didn't like the fact that law firms defend certain kinds of people, but she didn't go into specifics."

"I see," the doctor said. "Now, I want you to close your eyes and visualize that morning. Are you certain she didn't give any other clues as to why she was upset?"

"Visualize?"

"Yes. Mentally replay the morning."

"She said something about feeling tired all the time. I doubt you'll find much psychological significance in that."

"If you give a psychiatrist enough time, he'll find significance in anything." The doctor smiled as if to say, *See, I'm really a good guy, after all.*

A moment later, in what struck Peter as an abrupt move, Parker hit the intercom and announced to his secretary, "Mr. Neil and I are finished."

Instantly appearing and illuminating the room, a knee-knockingly beautiful blonde pranced in. She placed a hand on Peter's shoulder and brimmed.

"I hope you don't mind walking, Mr. Neil," she said. "It's two flights, but then you look in good shape." She sized him up. When she deposited him in front of a locked double door, she said, "My name is Katrina. If you need something…anything…I'm on extension twenty-two. Twenty-two—that's also my age. Maybe that'll help you remember."

"Thanks. I'll remember," Peter said. He watched her tight hips and narrow waist sashay down the stairway. She reminded him of ex-girlfriend Ellen Goodman.

He turned and faced the last barrier, a heavy metal door, believing—hoping—he'd made it to the big-time. At least he was on a payroll and had survived the initial scrutiny. Building up his resolve, Peter stroked his moonstone and knocked. A click indicated the disengagement of a dead bolt. When he entered, the simultaneous cacophony of a half-dozen voices deluged his senses. Other than the blasphemies polluting the air, not a word of what he heard made any sense at all.

---

Two hours after Peter first entered Stenman Partners' building, the warm rays of dawn lanced through the trading room windows. He felt like an unarmed Don Quixote surrounded by fire-breathing dragons, knee deep in trash. It wasn't exactly a bad mix of emotions that washed over him—more a jumbled mass of confused fascination. The room—his new workday home—was a pigsty of coffee cups, paper scraps, greasy brown bags, leftover fast food, and soda cans. The smell was a combination of a packed McDonald's restaurant, burnt coffee, and sweat. Accompanying this stink was bedlam. Shuffled, scrunched, and torn paper coated every surface. Bodies popped up and down. A pen was flung against a computer screen. The place could have been a ward for the attention deficient.

Three steps in, Peter halted in petrified fascination. A pyrotechnical voice echoed from a skull scaled to a body twice the size of the one it sat on. The face was a vast oval with Aryan eyes framed by a brow running in a single unbroken bush over the nose-bridge. In his late thirties, the man with flapping lips was at least six-four. He had out-of-kilter ears—tiny, like apricots—almost no more than holes in the side of his head. His looks— the sum of scary, mean, and downright weird—intimidated Peter more than his foghorned vulgarities. The man stood at the door of the only office on the floor and was clearly in charge of the other hyperactive traders. Peter realized this person had to be Howard Muller, his new boss.

"Hit the damn bid, Numbnuts!" Muller yelled. "This is a no brainer— I could get a signpost to do your fucking job."

The trader, looking to be about Peter's age, seemed unfazed by the bizarre man's assault. Numbnuts had a day-old shadow and, like Peter, his scruffy brown hair was too long. He was physically average, with corneas that darted every which way. Numbnuts nodded as Muller slammed the office door. A moment later, Peter heard the young trader scream into his phone, "Hit the bid! I don't give a rat's ass about squeezing an extra nickel on the trade. Do it!"

Peter stood, his spine rigid, grateful he had been far enough away that Muller's angry spittle hadn't doused his face. Peter's reactions went unnoticed, however—he might as well have been part of the atmosphere since not one of the twenty or so bodies paid him an ounce of attention.

The office area looked to be a four-thousand square-foot rectangle, running some sixty- by seventy-feet. Through the glass wall of a conference room, Peter saw what he assumed was sophisticated teleconferencing equipment and a fifteen-foot table. In a corner, there was a sink, refrigerator, built-in bar, and microwave. Interrupting this survey, from across the room, a tiny man with a beet-red face yelled, "Shut the fuck up you shit-for-brains!" He then slammed his phone against the desktop three times. When he finished, he pulled the shattered mouthpiece out of a plug, dropped it into his trashcan, and reached into a drawer for a replacement. Once he'd plugged the new headset in, he punched a button and began speaking to someone else as if that outburst had not just occurred.

Peter's sight line next roamed down the tight rows of traders. Littering the desktops were computers and flat-paneled slaves packed with stock, commodity, currency, and worldwide market indices. Each piece of data flashed in real time, overwhelming Peter's senses in the way that a planetarium awes those trying to make sense of the universe.

Every individual, including assistants at smaller desks, had phone banks with at least thirty incoming lines, a dozen or more pulsating at any one time. The bodies sat elbow-to-elbow without so much as a divider between desks. But the intensity of the players precluded anyone from attending to anyone else's affairs. No time to waste on office intrigue, he realized. This seemed like professional Mardi Gras, and, feeling his own pulse racing, Peter sensed an overwhelming desire to understand and belong.

"Report to Howard Muller," Stenman had said. After weaving through piles of crap and bodies in motion, Peter studied the nameplate mounted on the glass door: *Howard Muller. Chief Investment Officer.*

Muller leaned into a speakerphone, his back to his door. Beyond where his new boss sat, Peter noticed a wall's worth of Civil War memorabilia, locked in glass cabinets. Tattered Union and Confederate flags hung alongside unsheathed swords. The display also included muskets, pistols, war photos, belt buckles, and even a Confederate uniform with what looked like bullet holes and blood stains.

When Peter opened the door, Muller sensed the intrusion and spun around.

The CIO hit the hold button, cutting off an agitated voice in mid-sentence. He glared at Peter. "Nobody comes into my office unless I tell them to."

Muller sat behind the biggest mug of coffee—more like a German beer stein—Peter had ever seen. The aroma filled the air, an indication that this was a stiff brew. As if this guy needs artificial stimulation, Peter thought.

"Sorry," Peter began in a respectful-to-your-new-boss voice, "but I'm—"

"I know who you are, Asswipe. Go sit with Numbnuts. He's the one I yelled at when you came in. He'll teach you what little he knows—that should take all of twenty seconds. Now, get out."

"Should—"

"What word didn't you understand? Out!"

The words hit him like sucker punches and Peter sagged from the pounding. He dutifully backed up, afraid to turn his back, and not sure he still had a job. Once the office door shut, granting him some measure of safety, he worked his way back through the room.

When Numbnuts turned, Peter said without thinking, "Hello. I'm Asswipe. The anger management dropout told me to come sit with you."

The trader's intensity melted into an involuntary smile. He held out his hand. "For new meat, that's damn funny," he said. "Hope you last longer than the last four or five losers. I'm Stuart Grimes, a.k.a. Numbnuts. I'm jammed up my ass, so just watch. When the markets close, we'll review things…"

Stuart's voice sounded adenoidal, as if he had a sinus condition. Abruptly, the trader must have caught something through his peripheral vision because he spun around, turning Peter off. He punched a flashing button labeled *GSI* with one hand and grabbed his phone with the other.

"There. You happy?" he asked. "The stock's ticking at three-quarters. If you hadn't noticed, that's last sale—a zero-plus tick—and the company can pay, so do it! Hit their damn bid before some other bright boy beats you to the punch." Stuart paused. "Fine," he added. "Eight cents a share, you greedy bastard. Put it up, on the hop."

Peter began to write: *Last sale? Zero plus tick? Put it up? On the hop?*

*Company can pay last sale? Ticking at three-quarters? GSI? Eight cents a share? Hit their bid?* At this rate, he thought, I'll only have a couple thousand questions before lunchtime. He hoped Stuart was patient and tolerant of ignorant people. A sense of humor wouldn't hurt either, he decided.

When Stuart grabbed a red-bordered ticket and slid it into a machine that thumped, Peter felt encouraged. He had figured out—on his own—that this was a timestamp. When Stuart wrote *1,200,000 STQ*, then *66*, Peter again deflated—he added more questions to his list.

A moment later, *12.00000s STQ @ 66.75* scrolled right to left across one of the screens. Another phone light flashed, this one labeled *PB*. Stuart punched, lifted, and spoke: "That's us. Thanks for marking-up Selection Tracking. I'll send something your way, later." He hung up.

"I hope this job doesn't require mind-reading," Peter said below audibility.

He added, *PB, Selection Tracking,* and *send something your way* to his list of terminology-related questions.

Sitting back for the next few hours, Peter listened as much as he could, all the while studying thousands of numbers and symbols looking like energetic fireflies. As people continued to ignore him, the tidal wave of stimulus overload threatened to crush him. No wonder the last four or five employees had failed. He gripped his stone and thought of his father. His mother. His cat. Unemployment.

A voice yelled, "The bid's been raised! Get ready to sell. Nobody's gonna pay a higher price than these flaming assholes—not for this piece-of-shit company."

Peter's head whipped from face to face in an attempt to understand. Failing that, he pressed pen to paper, adding yet another item to his endless list of questions.

---

After taking a gulp, Jason Ayers placed the decanter under the sink and made his way across his office. Two fingers of scotch glowed through a crystal tumbler pressed between his white knuckles. Leaving a message wasn't the smartest move, but since he didn't intend to spend the rest of the day—maybe the week—waiting, he had no other choice. He took a second sip and closed his eyes as the liquid scorched his throat and raced to his brain. His secretary's intercom-voice cut through the air, snapping him to attention. He depressed the open speaker button.

"Yes, Carolyn."

"Ms. Stenman returning your call."

Ayers' hands shook. He put the glass down, flipped open a breath mint box, and grabbed and swallowed half the candies in it. With his breath flowing cold across his tongue, he opened the speaker attached to line two.

"Morgan?"

"What?"

"How did Peter Neil do?"

"I'm busy," she said.

"The polygraph? Did he pass the polygraph?"

"You sound apprehensive."

"No, no. I only wanted to know what Peter said."

"Is there something I should know about Peter Neil?" Stenman asked, her words feeling to Ayers like poison-darts. "Perhaps concerning his mother?"

The attorney regretted calling. What if Peter did know something about what Hannah had done? He sipped, and put the glass down, but didn't let go. "I would have told you—that is, if I thought there was anything else taken from our offices by...." He couldn't finish.

"If the polygraph were a problem, you would have known by now," Stenman said.

Ayers flopped down and sank into his chair. Thank God, not a problem. Change the subject, he thought.

"I really called to discuss the new offshore bank accounts."

"A necessary change because of sloppy security at your law firm," Morgan said coldly. "I want to hear that there will be no more Hannah Neils."

"No. No more such problems. I know you're busy."

It took another minute to wrestle free of the stress-filled exchange, but once he did, Ayers breathed a deep sigh. Knowing Peter had no additional information came as an enormous relief. Now, with the issue settled, things might work out well for Peter. This was a perfect job for him and, if he thought seventy-five thousand a year was serious money, wait until he realized the boy sitting next to him made ten times that much—and that others were paid well over seven figures a year.

"I really do want to help," Ayers said to the walls. "And yes, Peter—" he whispered, feeling better than he had in weeks, "—maybe this is how I begin repaying your parents. Give you something they never had. Make you rich."

With a final tilt of the glass, Ayers finished his drink. Clutching the breathmints a second time, he tossed the rest of the box into his mouth. He then took the glass to the sink, rinsed it with soapy water, and replaced it on the shelf above the wet bar.

All evidence of indiscretions gone, it was time to get back to work.

# CHAPTER SEVEN

Shortly after one p.m. on the West Coast—corresponding to the close of the U.S. markets—a second contingent of traders began to trickle in. During the overlapping shift, which lasted well into the afternoon, thirteen traders and at least that many support people reconciled positions and confirmed the hundreds of trades done during the morning and afternoon.

Peter learned that traders tossed their completed trade-tickets into out-boxes. Every few minutes, runners—looking like ants hustling after spilled sugar—dashed up and down the rows and collected these tickets. The handfuls of trade-records then made their way down chutes to the first floor, where trade-processing took place. These back-office professionals immediately keyed the information into in-house computers. The traders therefore had computer access to positions with only a brief time lag. The first-floor back-office was also responsible for comparing trades with the hundreds of confirms flooding Stenman Partners' offices every day from dozens of worldwide brokers. Reconciliation of a trade break, a fail-to-deliver, or a *Don't-Know-the-Trade* became a life and death priority.

Stuart Grimes, in a brief moment of peace, mentioned that these workers also arranged for share borrowing to facilitate short sales, monitored receipt of rebate income on short sales, negotiated margin interest rates, ADR fees, and a dozen other mumbo jumbo functions, none of which made any sense to Peter.

Close to three o'clock, Stuart spun around his chair and said, "Let's grab the conference room and begin your education. I'm meeting a New York broker for drinks and dinner at five, so that'll give us a couple of hours."

Before rising, Peter asked, "What's a New York broker doing in San Diego?"

Stuart put a paternalistic hand on Peter's shoulder. "We're gods, dude—that's what they're doing here: paying homage to the money. We fork-over a hundred million a year in commissions to brokers. Every trade, every time we buy stock in a secondary or IPO, some institutional sales-person makes some serious scratch—we have several sales-traders who make over a million dollars a year, just off our account. These bozos come to town all the time to brown-nose. Wait until Christmas."

"A hundred million in commission?"

"More than that," Stuart answered. "I have no idea what Howard Muller pays out on his shit. And that doesn't even include Stenman's farmed-out money."

"What's 'farmed-out' mean?"

"Morgan's taken some of the money she's raised offshore—that means money domiciled abroad—and turned it over to outside money managers. You remember that guy Stanley Drucker? The one that blew himself up?"

Peter nodded. "Yeah. Hard to forget."

"He was one of the managers that had a small chunk. Guys like Drucker charge us 1% for their efforts. We still get to keep 20% of the profits. Between you, me, and these walls, even though the money is supposedly invested at the sole discretion of these outside managers, Muller and Stenman tell them what to buy and sell."

"Why not manage it ourselves?" Peter asked, confused by such a convoluted scheme.

Stuart took his hand off Peter's shoulder. Across the room, Howard Muller filled the doorframe of his office. "I don't know," Stuart said, sounding tense.

"Neil! At five. That's when I'll have time for you."

Peter nodded. "Fine...good. Five. Okay, Mr. Muller."

The CIO shook his enormous head as if what Peter had said was idiotic. "Fine, good, okay," he mimicked. Muller turned and shut his door.

"Is he always such a prick?" Peter asked.

"Pretty much a two hundred forty-pound blood blister," Stuart confirmed.

"A misanthrope," Peter said.

"A what?"

"He's a misanthrope. Someone having an aversion to his fellow man."

"What're you? A dictionary?"

"He's a jerk," Peter said, wishing he hadn't stretched his vocabulary. "That sound better?"

"Yeah, he's a hammered-shit jerk. But—and it's the almighty *but*—Muller's got contacts in high places, and he'll pay you some big-bucks if you learn how to make him and this firm money. What'd you think of his hobby?"

"The Civil War stuff?"

"Strange, don't you think?"

"Is there a story to that?" Peter asked.

"Muller is a closet bigot, I think—wishes the South had won. He'd like to have slaves working these phones."

"That's funny," Peter said, smiling at the thought of traders chained to computers, and Muller, in a golf cart, whipping them to make more money.

"Not that funny. The man's schizo in the head. Last time he overindulged in my presence, he talked about his Nimrodic war theories. That was after the SEC dropped the Treasury manipulation investigation. Morgan treated us to Dom Perignon—a case of the stuff. A small reward for all of us circling the wagons."

"Treasury investigation?" Peter asked.

"A long story with a happy ending. I'll tell you about it another day. Anyway, Muller drank too much and let his hair down. I had to endure a profane lecture on why the South lost the Civil War. He thinks the Southern generals weren't, in his words, 'fucking ruthless enough.' When Northern generals like Sherman marched through the South, they burned plantations, raped women, murdered everyone in their path. If Lee and the South's other gentleman-generals had done the same thing, the North would have capitulated. At least that's Muller's theory."

"Sounds a tad revisionist. The South lost because they had limited resources, no manufacturing, and—"

"Who gives a rat's-ass, dude?" Stuart said, hiking his shoulders into his neck.

Peter felt stupid for debating the issue. "You're right. Who cares? I used to collect baseball cards."

Stuart leaned back and said, "Anyway, with Muller it's more than a hobby; it's life. He looks at creating wealth as warfare—and in a way, he has a point. His theory about the effectiveness of ruthless tactics applies. This is a business where the weak perish. Scruples are…anyway, it's all about making scratch, no ifs, ands, or buts."

"Okay. Since you brought it up, how the hell does one make all this money for the funds?"

"Good question. I should write a book, but then I'd end up in jail." Stuart grinned.

"Jail?"

"I'm kidding, dude. Back to making money. First, you gotta learn the various trading vehicles: options, futures, stocks, bonds, currency, commodities, whatever. Then you gotta develop relationships with CEOs, specialists on the floor of the exchanges, analysts, syndicate managers, anybody and everybody. Find out what punches their button, then punch away. That's why I go out with these brokers when they travel to San Diego—that and occasionally getting laid. Then squeeze everyone and everything for all their worth. Gain access to the best sources of information. Use money as leverage to acquire what you need to know—commission dollars are as good as cold, hard cash. If commissions aren't an option, then…well, you'll figure that out in due time."

"To that end," Peter said, "let's get me up to speed." He pointed his head at the empty conference room.

"They told me to take you under my wing, so might as well get started. By the way, when you finish with Muller, you ought to come join me with the salesperson from Gordon, Ashe. She's a hotty and she's bringing along a co-worker."

Peter thought he saw a shameless leer overtake Stuart's grin.

Once inside the conference room, Peter plowed through his list of questions, but each answer produced a new set of questions.

Another two hours later, standing outside Muller's office and waiting to be summoned, Peter felt his head ache with an overdose of information.

———

Peter waited a couple of minutes for Attila the Boss to notice him. He leaned against a pillar off to one side. Once Muller made eye contact, his brows furrowed and his eyes rolled. Peter took that as an invitation to enter.

The moment Peter stepped in, Muller snatched a phone and pasted it to his ear. Turning from Peter, not bothering to excuse himself, he said, "At

4:07 Pacific time, the dollar cross-rate was: 3.32. I buy one billion. Sold at…" Muller lifted and bent his left arm, exposing a heavy gold wristwatch. Peter noticed he wore a wedding ring. Poor woman.

Muller continued: "It is now 5:02 p.m., and the cross rate is 3.11. I'm selling one billion back to you." The CIO entered something into a hand-held calculator. "I am netting sixty-six million, two hundred twenty-five thousand, one hundred. That goes against Grand Cayman, booked to…"

Peter couldn't hear the rest.

Once Muller hung up, he reached inside a drawer and removed what looked like a sophisticated television remote control. He aimed it at a metal box, sitting on the near corner of his desk, and began pressing buttons. He next picked up a black-bordered trade ticket—one that Peter now recognized as a buy ticket—and inserted it into a slot in that box. An electronic hum announced a time stamp. Muller wrote something on the face of the ticket.

Finished writing, Stenman's CIO aimed the remote a second time. This time he grabbed a red-bordered ticket—indicating an asset sale—inserted it, then removed it. He made a few notations, clipped the buy and sell tickets together, and crammed them inside a Plexiglas vacuum tube, into which they disappeared. These transactions, or whatever they were, took less than three minutes from start to finish.

Muller refocused on Peter. "Sit down." He aimed his finger like a gun at the leather-bound chair angled across from his desk. Peter obediently complied. "I will explain this project one time—" Muller's eyes darted between three computer screens as he spoke "—so I want you to shut up and listen. We've done a crap job of monitoring commission payments. Most of these piece-of-shit brokers we do business with receive more money from us than they're worth. Your job is to review year-to-date pay-outs to each deadbeat firm, then go to my traders and get them to rate how useful these idiot-sticks have been. Is that clear?"

Peter unbuttoned his jacket, pretending relaxation. He then cleared his throat and said, "You want me to correlate—"

"I said: shut up."

Peter nodded, grateful Stuart had explained how the brokers made money from Stenman's trading. Without that, even this elementary request might have passed a mile over his head.

"Uh—" Peter cringed, knowing an attack was inevitable "—who do I contact to get this information?" That his voice sounded apologetic seemed unavoidable.

"Listen, Asswipe. That's for you to figure out. And I expect this project not to interfere with your workday—you're going to stay married to Numbnuts until I decide whether to fire you, or give you more responsibility. Now get out."

Another phone must have flashed because as Peter prepared to slink out, Muller picked up a headset and said, "Oil futures trading at…"

It seemed like a lot had happened, but the entire episode had lasted less than seven minutes. Remembering Stuart's suggestion that they meet for drinks and dinner, Peter decided to do just that.

On the way down the elevator, he committed to coming in to work at four the next morning. "If Muller wants a dedicated worker," he said to himself, "then a dedicated worker is what he's gonna get."

Fifteen minutes later, Peter leaned across a table in a crowded hotel bar and shook hands with Aimie St. Claire, sales backup from Gordon, Ashe International. Across from her, with Stuart's arm already draped around her shoulder, sat Louise Hartman, lead salesperson on the Stenman Partners' account.

Two glasses later, the champagne had just enough of an effect that Peter forgot everything. Everything, that is, except how to have one hell of a good time.

# CHAPTER EIGHT

**O**N FRIDAY, PETER ARRIVED AT WORK HALF-AN-HOUR LATER THAN HE had intended, but still early. Faces he did not recognize worked the phones—many traders spoke in foreign languages. Peter sat, listened, and observed. With about half the number of bodies as later in the day, the room felt more subdued, but the intensity was still evident. These workers seemed like nocturnal animals, creeping around in a mysterious world where everything they did arose from instinct or impulse. But Peter already understood the difference between decisions made in milliseconds and a lack of thought. See, react, trade, move on, then do it again and again and again. As impossible as it seemed, he'd seen Stuart Grimes make a hundred such decisions over those few hours yesterday, most of them yielding positive financial results.

In the background, janitorial personnel silently worked between desks, careful not to distract traders' concentration for fear of inciting already frequent, verbal attacks. Plastic sacks—dozens of them, filled with enough paper to denude a small forest—lined a rear door, ready to be hauled away.

Peter sipped French Roast and took everything in, grateful his intelligence had counseled him not to drink to excess last night. While he now felt tired, at least he wasn't hung-over. Sniffing his fingers, he rewound the evening's events. Obviously, Stuart Grimes and Louise Hartman had had carnal knowledge of one another before last night. Their public groping preceded a disappearing act—to her hotel room—around eleven o'clock.

That left Peter and Aimie St. Claire alone in the hotel bar, enjoying expensive cognac, her hand camped on his thigh. The girls acted aggressively—not *girls*, Peter reminded himself. Both were in their late thirties and built for action. They didn't show cleavage—didn't need to. Instead, they chose colorful cashmere sweaters with statically launched strands begging to be stroked. Crow's feet around their eyes presaged a raunchy worldliness.

Better than their physical allure were the stories they told of exciting

Wall Street trades done on behalf of important clients, and of sexual escapades and scandal. They gesticulated, laughed, and whispered when speaking salaciously, and made it all sound wonderful and thrilling and fun. And they seemed to know everybody in the securities industry. Early in their careers, they'd been to Mike Milken's Predators' Ball during Drexel, Burnham's heyday, before the firm went belly-up and before Milken went to prison for a few years. Back then, Drexel professionals dished out morsels of information like they were *hors d'oeuvres* designed to whet the appetites of powerful money managers. Drexel's one-hundred millionaire investment bankers, in turn, sold junk bonds to these grateful fiduciaries as if the high-risk paper were as precious as everlasting life. "Milken even had the nerve to insist his people call those crap bonds, 'high-yield.' You used the term 'junk,'" Aimie had said, "and you were likely to be canned *and* blackballed for life."

Louise told an equally compelling story about handling a trade with Ivan Boesky in a company magically acquired in a take-over the next week. She'd been smart enough to piggyback the trade, she said, and sneak a few thousand shares into one of her secret, personal trading accounts—she'd made forty grand on that little investment, back in the day when forty grand meant something. They dropped names like "Blade," "Skyball," and "Helmet Head" as if Peter knew these people. He learned that when professionals used the term "Wall Street," they meant the financial markets worldwide, not just in New York. Everyone considered Morgan Stenman, in fact, a *Street* icon and, as such, that officially made Stuart, *and* Peter, fellow citizens of Wall Street. And as silly as it seemed, knowing this made Peter happy.

And Peter didn't particularly care that much of what he heard confused him. The evening was magical. And though he had suspected it was in the offing, he hadn't intended to sleep with Aimie St. Claire—at least not until her hand moved from his thigh to his crotch. Now, less than two hours after rolling out of her king-sized hotel bed, her scent lingered. Before he'd allowed himself to be seduced, he wished she had told him she was married. With the clarity following meaningless sex, he now vowed: *never again.*

Behind him, a gruff voice caught Peter's attention, pushing last night's indiscretion to a back corner of his mind. From a second row of desks, a trader with a red-snaked nose spoke into a headset wrapped from his ear to his mouth. The conversation was in French. Peter understood a few words, but in the context of the conversation, none of them seemed to be meaningful. As soon as that call ended, the rotund man began another call. This time he spoke in what sounded like perfect German. Glancing at the computer facing the trilingual man, Peter watched rows of foreign symbols twitching ever-changing prices.

The trading room, Peter figured out, operated twenty-four hours a day, employing three semi-distinct shifts. If yesterday's activity was indicative, these shifts overlapped by two or three hours. That put the minimum workday at ten hours, the maximum at twelve—before special projects and nights out.

When the man finished this second conversation, Peter introduced himself and asked what time Stuart Grimes normally arrived. "At half past five," the trader said. Peter then asked where he might go to begin his project on tracking commissions.

The man's breath smelled flammable, undoubtedly the result of recent eighty-proof shots. With Peter's second question, the grizzled man lost his remaining splinter of patience. "First floor," he said, spinning and punching a button on his phone bank, spewing rapid-fire French, and tuning Peter completely out.

With forty-five minutes to go before Stuart's estimated arrival, Peter took the stairs to the first floor.

———

At six-fifteen, an hour after arriving, Peter left the Head of Administration and Support, feeling pretty good about his progress. Carl Butler was harried, but at least he had referred to Peter by his given name, and, when Peter mentioned that Howard Muller had assigned him this project, the name-drop worked like magic. Butler's eyes wobbled the moment the word "Muller" vibrated against his eardrums and defiled his brain. The suddenly nervous man showed Peter how to log on and download the information he needed. With a few formatting hints, Peter felt he could complete the first part of his task over the next few weeks. The biggest problem would be gaining the cooperation of the traders, since, to assess brokers' usefulness, he needed their opinions.

"One step at a time," he told himself.

Bounding to the third floor, Peter spotted Stuart Grimes the moment he buzzed in. Stuart, barking into a phone, flapped his arms like an ostrich trying to fly. Amazingly, he exhibited no sign he'd consumed massive amounts of alcohol the night before or spent the night and morning doing the nasty. He had clean eyes, and was operating on a million cylinders.

How'd he do it? Peter wondered.

Peter made his way past animated bodies, their voices a garbled lace of frantic commands and profanity. By the time he got to Stuart, the trader had a second phone pressed to the other ear. He spoke back and forth, sliding one handset to his mouth, then pulling it into his neck while speaking into the other. All the while, Stuart's eyes scrutinized his computer screens, absorbing bits of data on currency, bonds, foreign indices, and a multitude of other mysterious indicators.

"You say your guy's preparing to address the sales force?" Stuart asked into the left phone.

Peter leaned in and heard a voice spill an answer. "Yes. He's raising his estimates on Global-Tech by fifty cents for this and next year."

Stuart lowered the left headset while pulling the right mouthpiece up. "Take the Global offering at fifty-five," he said.

Just loud enough for Peter to hear, a second voice said, "You want them all?"

"Fucking hell, Lloyd. I said take the fucking offering. And you're held!"

A moment of silence followed as Stuart clocked a buy ticket and wrote:

*502,000 GLTS @ $55 — Held*

Peter did the math. Stuart had just purchased $27 million worth of stock. He counted the zeroes again, just to make certain he hadn't miscalculated.

Stuart acknowledged Peter's presence with a nod. Pinching the right handset between his ear and shoulder, he tapped a pen against one of his screens, drawing Peter's attention. In an unmodulated voice, he explained, "This is NASDAQ. I'm buying a block of Global in London, before the stock begins trading in the U.S."

"What's *held* mean?" Peter asked.

"It means I'm not giving idiot-stick Lloyd any discretion to screw things up."

Peter didn't understand, but he let it slide for the time being, making a mental note about this and the infinite number of curiosities clogging his brain. Over Stuart's shoulder, on the NASDAQ terminal, Peter focused on the letters GLTS and a long line of brokers displaying prices. The market showed a best bid of 55, a best offering of 55.15.

Stuart turned his attention back to his phones. "Fine. I'm buying five hundred and two thousand GLTS at fifty-five, double net."

Stuart dropped the right headset but still held the other to his left ear. He stamped the GLTS buy-ticket a second time. In a box along the left edge of the ticket, he checked OTC, then scribbled the word *London*. In a column labeled "broker," he wrote CKLSN. "That stands for Clarkson Securities—they're the U.K. broker I used to buy the stock," he explained.

Stuart dropped the buy-ticket into the out-box for processing. In a nonstop motion, he scooped up a red-sell ticket. He wrote: 302,000 GLTS. Under broker he wrote: STTN.

"STTN stands for Stratton Brothers. I'm waiting for them to come back with a bid for the stock." Stuart again pointed to his NASDAQ machine. "Look, Glo-Tech's already moving higher. Market opens in five minutes. Nobody wants to get caught short, not with Stratton's analyst issuing an aggressive buy and raising his estimates—the guy's the number-one rated industry analyst. When he opens his pie-hole, institutions listen. They're gonna waddle in like lemmings to buy this stock. I told you, Petey: you can't have enough information."

Peter watched while prices in Global Technology ticked higher. First Stratton Brothers' trader showed a 56.50 bid, up a point. Other market makers followed as the news of an important analyst's upgrade announcement raced up and down Wall Street. By the time the market opened for trading, the bid had climbed to $57.30 per share. A couple minutes into trading, with Glo-Tech's volumes huge, Stuart responded to a bid from Stratton Brother's trader.

"I'm selling you three hundred two thousand GLTS at 58.20, net," Stuart said.

Watching Stuart check boxes and scribble the details of the transaction, Peter did some quick math. In less than ten minutes, Stuart had cleared three dollars a share on three hundred thousand Glo-Tech shares, or nearly a million bucks profit.

"Not bad for a few minutes work," Stuart announced.

"The other two hundred thousand shares?" Peter asked. "You holding out for a better price?"

Stuart brimmed as he punched the direct wire to Gordon, Ashe. "Nope. Gonna sell them right now."

He gave an order to sell the two hundred thousand shares. Before he hung up, Stuart said to his counterpart on the other end of the phone, "And that order is to the credit of Louise Hartman and Aimie St. Claire. Thanking them for dinner."

Stuart shrugged and explained to Peter: "Gotta pay for what you get in this business. That trade should cover their expenses. Later, I'll shoot them more commission to cover extras." His teeth flashed like a drive-in movie screen. "How much was getting your rocks off worth, dude?"

Peter didn't answer. Even without understanding everything he'd seen over the last few minutes, the fog blanketing his new business began to lift. This game, he thought, just got easier to understand.

---

Oliver Dawson glanced at his watch: 11:04 a.m. For two frustrating hours, he had been reviewing a stack of option trades done in advance of a recent takeover. Despite suspecting people had bought on inside information—the call option volume just ahead of the announcement was triple the normal activity—he also guessed most of these crooks had parked their gains in offshore accounts. Too many countries had banking secrecy laws: Cayman Islands, Switzerland, and more recently, Mauritius Island, off the coast of Africa, to which hedge funds had taken a recent fancy. The more sophisticated funds moved money through dummy accounts from one place to another, making the already difficult trail impossible to follow.

It was the same old story. The only ones ever nailed for insider trading had the brains of a lead-eater—like a mid-level manager using a mother-in-law to buy stock or options, figuring that because she had a different last name than his, he wouldn't get busted.

"What's the point?" he said to himself.

Angela Newman interrupted his frustration. "Sir, I need to speak with you."

He took a sip of Diet Coke. "Certainly, Angela."

"Is this a good time?"

"As good as any," he said, anxious because his secretary's voice wavered.

A moment later, Angela fidgeted in a straight-backed chair as Dawson locked on her expression.

"I have been your secretary for over two years," she said through a stammer.

"And you've been outstanding," Dawson replied with over-the-top enthusiasm. "I hope I've let you know that."

"Yes, sir…yes, Oliver, you have."

He exhaled. He didn't care that others couldn't appreciate her.

"But…but I have…" She turned away.

"But what, Angela? Did I do something wrong?"

She inhaled, then exhaled in a rush. "I have asked for and received a transfer to another department."

"Why? You're tired of my swearing, aren't you? You must hate me."

Angela looked surprised. "How can you say such a thing, Oliver? You *do* swear too much, but *hate* you? You are such a stupid man."

*Is that why she's leaving?* he wondered. *I'm stupid?* "I can change. Please don't leave."

"I have to."

"Why?" he asked.

"How could you not know? I'm leaving because—" Dawson leaned on the edge of his seat, ready for a double-barrel of bad news "—because I care for you, personally, and all you do is ignore me. Being around you makes me sad."

For the first time in his life, he felt a rush from unbelievably good news. With rare confidence, he asked, "Will you have dinner with me? Tonight?"

The tables turned. Now it was Angela Newman's jaw that dropped.

# CHAPTER NINE

---

**A**T WAR WITH THE FIREPLACE'S SIX-FOOT FLAMES, A STIFF BREEZE FILLED the room, bringing with it a hint of seaweed and salt. Gulls barked and swooped, visible through the open window making up half the west wall. The echoes of the violent Baja surf contributed a low rumble, more soothing to Sarah Guzman than music. She manufactured a smile as her guests entered her office.

"Fernando," she began, "we were shocked to hear of the torture you endured. Unimaginable: trapped in a box, expecting to die, choking—barely enough air to breathe. Praise God for the accident of discovering you before you died."

Carlos Nuñoz had wheeled the sixty-year old Fernando Guzman, two days rescued, into Sarah Guzman's office, the old man's hands already strapped to the arms of a wheelchair. His features had decomposed—the eyes reflected nothing, olive skin hung like bloated bags, and bones bent like saplings, barely holding him erect. His head rocked.

"Unfortunately," Carlos explained, "*Tio* Fernando has had a break-down—perhaps a small stroke. Even the joy of salvation has not yet over-come the agony of what happened. He listens and understands, but he seems so distraught that I fear he might do something irrational to himself or to others. It is sad. We are searching for those who did this dreadful deed. Former enemies of your husband's, we suspect."

Sarah nodded, expressionless.

"What shall we do with your husband's brother?" Carlos asked.

"He shall live here, with me. Nurses will attend to him until he is bet-ter. Guards will surround him at all times, for his protection, of course. I will take a personal interest in his welfare. Tell the family I love my Fernando. I will take care of my Fernando. I will take care of any of my family, if necessary. Tell them for me, Carlos."

"I shall."

"Now, if you could wheel poor Fernando to the kitchen, the maid will feed him flan. Perhaps a cup of tortilla soup."

"*Ciertamente.*"

The wheelchair's rubber wheels rolled silently across the tiled floor, their suspension absorbing the tiny indentations between the clay squares, then handling the trip's remainder over thick area rugs. Before Fernando vanished, Sarah Guzman imagined a small spark in his eye.

"Good," she said to herself. "That will save so much time in the future."

———

At the end of his first month, Peter graduated from probationary status. Stenman personally called to inform him that he had an impressive report card. His salary jumped not to one hundred thousand, but one hundred twenty thousand.

"The largess," she said, "is meant to keep you motivated."

And she knew what she was doing. Peter often stayed behind at the end of Stuart's shift, and sometimes well into the night—seventy hours many weeks, displaying stamina that qualified as extraordinary, even by Stenman Partners' warped work standards. He even managed to endear himself to a couple of the late traders—enough to sit as a piece of furniture and observe. He learned that the trades done on behalf of Stenman marched around the world as the night progressed. Tokyo, Australia, Malaysia, Hong Kong, Singapore, Korea, Thailand, in the afternoon and early evening. Later, the activity migrated to Eastern Europe, Norway, Finland, Sweden, Switzerland, overlapping with France, Germany, Italy, Spain, and the UK. In each of these and dozens of other markets, Stenman had local relationships—brokers, bankers, politicians, company CEOs, and military leaders.

In addition to trading and back-office professionals, Stenman employed fourteen analysts whose job it was to maintain a steady flow of information. These researchers occupied half of the second floor and did fundamental balance-sheet and income-statement analysis, as well as top-down economics—estimating country and regional GDP along with assessing sovereign risk. Their most important job, though, was to dig for insights like good investigative reporters. They sought tips, uncovered significant sexual indiscretions, identified greedy executives and politicians,

and did whatever they could to provide Stenman and her traders an informational edge. These resolute people, Peter discovered, also displayed no more social skills than their trading counterparts—at least to those lacking the information they craved.

It took longer than Peter had hoped, but around the end of his fifth week, he managed to put together a thorough analysis of the commissions-paid project assigned him by Howard Muller.

Throughout, Muller never warmed to Peter, but that didn't matter—the CIO treated everybody like hammered shit. That Morgan Stenman had received a positive report on Peter was much more important to his professional prospects.

From his assigned project, Peter confirmed that the commissions paid were even more than Stuart had estimated. In fact, they were mind-boggling. Adding in Muller's trades, the total payout amounted to nearly two hundred million a year. No wonder brokers brown-nosed Stenman on a constant basis.

As Peter wrapped up his work, he had one unexplained item. Nobody seemed willing to discuss why Stenman Partners paid a number of small regional-brokers—many of whom Peter had never heard of—an inordinate share of commission dollars. Of particular interest, because of recent events, was the firm of Jackson Securities. In the last six months, Stenman Partners had paid them eight million dollars, but had ceased doing business with this third-tier firm after the explosion at their La Jolla branch. As he did with all outstanding curiosities, Peter solicited Stuart for an explanation.

"You in a rush, Stu?" he asked, having finished reconciling the last of Stuart's trades—a job he had begun a week earlier as part of his training. "I've got some questions regarding that project Fat-Head gave me."

Stuart surveyed the trading room. Few people remained. Worldwide markets had closed and, since it was Friday, would not reopen until Sunday afternoon on the West Coast. "No problem, Petey," he said. "Conference Room. Put our feet up and shoot the shit."

Stuart led the way. Looking at the back of Stuart's blue tee-shirt, Peter felt gratitude and admiration. After the close of business, Stuart always took time to review his trades. As a result, the confusing language began to make sense, as did the various financial instruments routinely used by Morgan's employees. Stuart even allowed Peter to participate in some of his transactions—like working orders on the NYSE whenever Stuart traded a listed stock.

Reaching the conference room, Stuart began by saying, "You're catching on fast, Asswipe." Both men grinned. For several weeks, nobody, including Muller, had used that name when referring to Peter.

"How come Muller still calls you Numbnuts?" Peter asked.

"Term of endearment. Not many of us get permanent nicknames."

"Lucky you."

"I never told anyone this…" Stuart shook his head. "Forget it."

"What? You can't start a confession, then just drop it."

"Yes, I can. What's your question?"

Picking up a remote lying on the table, Stuart aimed and pressed. The curtains, bunched in the corners of the glass-walls, slid shut, granting them complete privacy. With a second shot, Stuart adjusted the lights, making the room dusk-dark. Reaching into his pant pocket, Stuart removed a vial. He tapped white powder onto the glass sheet protecting the oak table. He then removed a freshly-minted hundred-dollar bill from his wallet. He used the edge of the bill to line up the powder. Rolling the bill, he bent over, inserted the tube into a nostril, and sniffed. The first line disappeared. Without looking up, and shifting to the other nostril, he inhaled the second of four lines.

Sighing with satisfaction, he ran the back of his index finger along his upper lip and blinked at Peter. "A Friday ritual. Your turn, dude."

Peter showed no reaction. He'd seen coke ingested a hundred times at school and parties, and in the back of buses on the way to football games. He shrugged. "Not my poison," he said.

"You'll change your mind once you start carrying some hundred-million-dollar positions…whatever."

Stuart did a repeat and consumed the final two lines. He leaned back with his feet propped on the table, his breathing seeming to keep time to a hip-hop or rap beat, every sense enjoying the rapture. With both hands, he raked his fingertips across his scalp. Under the lids, Peter saw his friend's eyes dart in violent circles.

When the spell broke, Stuart spoke again. "Your project—what is it you want to know?"

"How come our fund did so much business with a firm as small as Jackson Securities? What do they offer that's worth millions of dollars a year in commission?"

"Drop this one, Peter." Stuart's body tensed as he shook his head.

"Drop it? Come on, Stu. Don't treat me like an outsider. What's the story?"

Stuart sniffed, then brushed the back of his hand across his nose. He said, "Don't quote me."

"If you say so."

"Several reasons. First, they're a local firm—we get community good-will." Stuart reproduced the vial from his pocket.

"That's thin," Peter said. "There's lots of local firms we don't do squat with. Why them?"

"I didn't say that was the main reason. Next, more importantly, they do tons of small cap deals—many of them micro-cap, below fifty million. They give us whatever allocation we ask for."

"Their deals tend to go up in price in the aftermarket?"

"Temporarily. You heard of churn and burn?"

Peter wagged his head.

"It's also called pump and dump."

"That doesn't help me," Peter said.

"It's simple. Jackson Securities brings a company public—they did a ton of Internet crap before the sector went baballoo. You know, companies with no earnings, no revenues, no business plan, but with *dot com* at the end of their name. We take a million shares of Bum-fuck Dot Com at ten bucks. Jackson's brokers then hype the company to all these crackerjack mom and pop clients of theirs, get them excited thinking this is the next Amazon.com in its heyday."

"That's the *churn* in churn and burn and the *pump* in pump and dump?" Peter asked.

"Yup. These yahoos jump into the stock and it opens at twenty-five bucks a share when it starts trading. We sell our shares to all these shit-for-brains piling in at inflated prices."

The light went on in Peter's head. "We dump our stock at a big fat profit. Later, when the stock drops like a rock, they get burned," Peter said.

"Ergo: churn and burn, pump and dump. Very descriptive phrases."

"Exactly. We clear fifteen million in low risk profit. We do that with them twenty, thirty times a year."

"For a total profit of some three hundred million dollars over twelve months."

"That's it, genius. We also did business with them for another reason."

Peter leaned forward, cupping his chin.

"They're owned by a Swiss bank. They have overseas clients who like to lose money."

"That makes no sense," Peter said.

"Through their Swiss parent, Jackson brokers for phantom offshore interests."

"What's the significance of that?"

"Banking laws, Petey. Untraceable accounts."

"I still don't get it. Jackson is an intermediary between us and a Swiss bank that's brokering for some other client? Who and why?"

Stuart reached for his cocaine, this time satisfied with doing two lines. When he finished, he said, "Sometimes Muller has me do his grunt work. Same as you do for me, only his stuff is mega—not this nickel and dime stuff we do in the trading room."

"Whoa. I'd hardly call making a few million bucks a day nickel and dime."

"Peanuts. Muller'll hand me a stack of twenty or thirty matched buy and sell tickets booked with Jackson Securities—currency and commodity trades mostly. My job is to go through these tickets and calculate the P&L, then report that number to Muller. A couple times, Muller's accounts made a fortune trading with this untraceable Jackson Security account. I'm talking a hundred million or more, in a morning. That means the other side is losing that much money."

"Must be somebody stupid."

Stuart cackled. "You're a beauty. *Stupid*? I don't think so."

"If they're always losing money—"

"Maybe Howard Muller's the smartest damn trader that ever lived. Did you ever consider that possibility, dude?"

Without warning, Stuart began to laugh. At first controlled, the chortle grew in intensity until he sounded like a small child, tickled by a relentless parent. He hugged his ribs with crossed arms, but failed to settle down.

Through watering eyes, he snatched the vial, used his forearm to mop the table of all powdery remnants, got up, and said, "That thing I almost told you earlier?"

"The thing you never told anyone else?"

"Yeah. You'll keep it a secret?"

"Sure." Peter leaned forward.

Stuart choked the words from deep in his throat. "Muller. Him and me is related…" Stuart folded his forehead into his crossed arms, trying to stifle his laughter, coughing in the process. "Thank God," he struggled to say, "I didn't get that elephant noggin. Oh man…this is so damn funny. Cousins…Can you imagine my poor aunt giving birth to that head? Must have been like…"

It was contagious. Peter laughed, also out of control. "Ouch! That head, in the birth canal…" Peter couldn't finish the thought.

"Dart boy," Stuart managed to say. "Drop the dude, and his head falls fastest…Baby Howie's feet sticking up in the air…like a dart…or a lab experiment gone very wrong."

Peter felt like he might cramp, as if he had done drugs with Stuart. "That head, on that body—he looks like a Stonehenge column and top."

"You're cruel, dude."

"He's in New York," Peter continued through his own guffaws, "at Thanksgiving. The Macy's Parade. They're gonna tie rope around him and pull him alongside Garfield the hot air balloon."

"Oh, my God. Funny…" Stuart choked.

"Billed as the giant, floating head. Weird, scary, floating head." Peter wondered how he got on such a roll. He couldn't stop himself. "Muller trips…on his head…his skull would dent linoleum. Break bricks. Here, Howie, mind banging your gourd against this cement wall?…Need to knock it down…"

Stuart sniffed, then swabbed a tear from his cheek with a sleeve. "Hey, I can't take no more. Maybe the guy's just the best damn trader in the whole friggin' world…that's what got this laugh-riot started. That's rich. Gotta go."

Stuart left the room, his high-pitched cackles silenced once the sound-proof door clicked shut. Peter's mania immediately subsided. Why, he wondered, did Stuart think the comment concerning Howard's trading prowess was so hilarious? Everybody knew Morgan Stenman and her CIO

Howard Muller were two of the best—if not *the* best—traders in the world. The President of the United States, members of Congress, Third World central bankers, heads of states—all called for advice.

"Has to be the drugs," Peter said under his breath.

———

At home an hour later, Peter put Henry's food bowl on the kitchen floor, the episode with Stuart a dismissed curiosity. He changed his clothes and got ready to pick up Kate. It would be their fourth or fifth date in the last few weeks.

He wondered about their relationship. Were they more than friends? Kisses goodnight and handholding, but friends do that.

"Gonna go slow, old man," Peter said to Henry. "Don't want another Ellen Goodman."

Peter grabbed his car keys—to his new BMW—and stepped out, noting that the keys to a Beemer felt different than those of a Jetta—heavier, as if made of gold. He jangled the key ring in a hand as he patted the sides of his jacket. For the first time in memory, he forgot to drop the moonstone into his pocket.

With his thumb, he repeatedly pressed the button on the key chain that activated the car door-lock system, listening to the high pitch go on and off as he neared his forty-four thousand dollar machine. Beep, beep, beep, beep—unlock, lock, unlock, lock. His moonstone never sang to him, he thought. One more beep and the door unlocked a final time.

# CHAPTER TEN

**T**HE LAW OFFICES OF LEEMAN, JOHNSTON, AND AYERS WERE DOWNTOWN, overlooking the San Diego Harbor. A forest of masts and sails, moored to a labyrinth of docks, bobbed along the shoreline below Jason Ayers' windows. Farther south, the arch of the Coronado Bay Bridge cut through his view of the marina and the ocean. At eye level, cumulus clouds looked frozen in place, back-lit by the late-day sun. For Ayers, the view was nothing more than an anchor, to keep his vision from floating around his office.

Usually law associates worked slave hours, billing clients at the rate of fourteen hours a day. Friday was the only day the firm tolerated—even encouraged—moderation. Most associates and partners left the building by six p.m. On this Friday, as Ayers pretended to be busy, Kate and two others remained in the outer offices, finishing projects deemed of sufficient importance to ignore Friday's early-out-the-door rule.

Ayers jumped to his feet and began to pace. He staggered in the direction of the picture window, turned left, and shuffled towards a wall of built-in bookshelves filled with six-inch hardbound legal volumes. Along another wall, photographs stared down at him. One picture in particular stole his attention—a forty-year-old photo, framed and preserved. A boy, twenty-one years old, wore a grass- and blood-stained football uniform. Tucked under one arm, he held a battered helmet. The jock's other arm draped around a grinning, skinny, bright-bore of a boy, dressed in a blue and gold sweater. That day, Matthew Neil had scored three touchdowns and caught eight passes for over two hundred yards. The last statistic remained a school record. Jason Ayers scarcely recognized himself as the geek in the photograph. He still recalled how warm he felt, being the best friend of the best player on one of the best teams in the country. Matthew had been *his* best friend. And what had it gotten his friend? Endless tragedy. And the duplicity had not ended. Not by a longshot.

"Nothing I can do, either," Ayers said, as if explaining life's unfairness to the ghosts of the two side-by-side buddies. Hidden somewhere, he suspected, were additional pages—and the life of anyone unlucky enough to discover those pages would become worthless. Peter Neil was the most likely candidate. Worse than that, if Peter became a target, so did anyone he cared for, including Kate.

"Insanity, Hannah. Why, Goddammit. Why?"

With exaggerated care, Ayers pushed an ice-cube floating in his drink. Licking the scotch off his index finger, he held up the tumbler, allowing the setting sunlight to plait through the light amber. He gulped, then set the glass down. With this last dose of courage coursing through his brain, he rang for Kate, wishing, more than anything else, Peter didn't remind him so damn much of Matthew Neil.

When she entered, his resolve wavered. If only the stakes weren't so high, he thought. "Sit down, Kathryn," he said. "We need to talk."

"This has to be quick, Father. Peter will be here in ten minutes. We're having dinner with his friend Drew Franklin. He and his wife just found out she's pregnant with their first child, and we're celebrating."

"That's what I wanted to discuss. Do you want a drink? I think I'll help myself to one."

Kate shook her head. He took his cocktail tall and neat. Without turning, he said, "I do not want you seeing Peter."

"Is something wrong with tonight?" she asked.

"Not tonight. Not ever. End it."

Kate ran a hand along her temple, moving a shock of hair over an ear. "I don't understand. You can't mean what you're saying."

"He is no good for you. That's all there is to it."

"You're the one who got him his job. You're the one who told me what wonderful people his parents were."

"I forbid you." Ayers regretted the words the moment they flowed from his dry throat.

"You forbid it?" Kate's face strobed red. "You have no right, no authority." Anger and confusion laced her words.

"Listen, Sweetheart. I know what I'm talking—"

"You can barely get the words out of your mouth. You're drunk, Father. You've been drunk most of your waking hours for over a month, and I'm going to chalk this conversation up to intoxicated dementia."

"That's not true." Though he tried, Ayers couldn't hide the fact that his speech *was* thick-tongued.

"Whatever's wrong with you, Mom and I are praying it passes. And while I love you, and I am sympathetic to your problems, I will not have you dictate who I can or cannot see. I am not a little girl, and I do not need you to run my love life."

"Please. Peter isn't his parents."

"No. He isn't. But he has a conscience. He's smart. And I think he cares for me. Maybe not love—maybe it never will be love—but I'm going to find out. I go back to LA next week, and that leaves me a small window to reach some kind of understanding."

Ayers' hands shook. He wished he could think clearly. Goddamn alcohol. What to say?

"Hannah Neil and I were lovers," he blurted out. "I considered leaving your mother for her." Ayers wondered if the lie showed on his face. "Peter could have ended up as your step-brother."

The blood drained from Kate's cheeks with the speed of sound. Her red-rimmed eyes burst with silent tears. "You're making that up." One tiny teardrop managed to escape and run down her cheek.

With the damage already done, Ayers elected to push for an end to Kate and Peter's relationship. "No. It's true. Ask Peter. He knows. He's known all along."

"She's the one, then?"

The question threw Ayers off. What did she mean, *the one*?

Kate's voice shook as she continued: "Mother and I knew there was someone."

"You knew I was unfaithful?"

"How could you do this?"

"I was weak. I cared for—"

"I don't mean the relationship with Hannah Neil. I mean, how could you call me into your office, and tell me these things in an effort to poison my feelings for Peter?"

"This is extremely…" He couldn't bring himself to mention the danger.

"Peter practically gave his mother's house to an indigent family—a man without a job, struggling with a wife and four kids. The man's paying only a hundred a month for a place that's worth a coupla thousand, but Peter said that, with his job, he didn't need the money. Did you know that?"

"I never said he wasn't a good person. But beware, Kathryn. He's making more money than he ever imagined possible. He'll be able to obtain anything in this world money can buy—and that's just about everything. Where will you be then? Little, sweet, Katie Ayers? Beware. He will change—everybody who gets rich does. He'll hurt you."

"No. He won't. If this doesn't develop beyond friendship, that's okay with me. But he will *not* hurt me."

"He's already paid fifty thousand for a new, sporty car. BMW, isn't it?"

"So what? It's only a car."

"Now he's moving next door to his trading partner, Stuart Grimes—into a three thousand a month condominium above the racetrack. Whitewater views—"

"How do you know that?"

"I know many things, Kate." Ayers, near the window now, stood with his back to Kate and continued. "Peter slept with a salesperson from Gordon, Ashe—she's ten years older than him and married."

"I won't listen to this."

"You must listen. He's going to get a substantial bonus after the first of the year—that's after the forgiveness of his loan. Then next year, as he assumes some real responsibility and buys into the program—"

"What do you mean, 'buys into the program'?"

"He'll be just like the rest. It'll sneak up on him…" *Shit*, Ayers thought. *Shut up, you drunken fool. You'll get yourself killed.*

"You're wrong. And all you've done is hurt me, not dissuade me." Kate rubbed the dampness from her eyes as she shook her head. "If that is all, my date is waiting."

The reverberation of the closing door sealed Ayers into a familiar tomb of wood, alcohol, and regret.

When he left the office, ten minutes later, Kate and Peter were gone—long gone.

———

Peter sensed Kate's sadness. He asked, but she said it was nothing. The evening's events, he hoped, might turn around her mood. She seemed excited about meeting Peter's best friend and his wife, Monica, for the first time. Peter had explained to Kate that he and Drew had gone to UCLA together, roomed on campus together the first two years, then shared an apartment off campus until they graduated. At school, they pushed each other academically and attended each other's athletic events. They partied together at the end of each term and, five years later, remained as tight as they ever had been. Hannah had been like a second mother to Drew, even throwing a surprise party when he got into medical school. Since Drew's own mother lived on the East Coast, Drew Franklin had spent vacations with the Neils. At his friend's wedding, Peter had been best man.

Once they got inside Drew and Monica's warm one-bedroom apartment, Kate thawed some, especially with Drew's white teeth smiling vividly against his black skin, his easy laughter deep and warm. When Drew told her about nicknaming Peter *"White Bread"* the first time they met, she laughed for the only time that night. She seemed happy for the couple's good fortune and brought a pair of green knit booties for the baby-to-be. "Pink for girls, blue for boys, green for I-don't-knows," she had said. They applauded her good judgment.

Monica served lasagna—Peter's favorite—salad, and bread with olive oil to dip in. Kate said she loved the food, yet ate next to nothing. She smiled in all the right spots, but the electric joy she brought to other occasions was missing. At one point in the evening, she announced that by the end of next week, she would return to UCLA, a couple of weeks earlier than originally planned. Maybe this change in schedule bothered her, Peter thought. But why? LA was a relatively short drive away—two hours or so. Easy enough to arrange a visit.

Peter worried in silence. He knew he cared for her. He felt part friend and part attraction, mixed with a healthy dose of respect for her heart and her intellect. When they said goodnight to the expectant couple and climbed inside his car, Peter decided to push for an explanation.

"Kate. Don't tell me it's nothing." The powerful European engine hummed under his voice, the transmission sat in neutral, the parking brake keeping them from rolling down the gentle hill. "You're upset. Tell me."

"I don't know if I can." She looked out the side window, away from Peter.

"Look at me," Peter urged.

She didn't move.

He put a gentle hand behind her head and applied a guiding pressure.

She allowed her head to rotate, but fixated on her hands resting on her lap. She still wore her work clothes—a dark blue jacket with matching skirt. In the way she dressed, she looked the part of bright young professional. With a quivering lip, swollen eyes, and shaking jaw, she exhibited a fragile ego that seemed ready for transition into monumental depression.

"Katie. We're friends. More than friends. Tell me."

"Are we, Peter? Are we *more than friends*?" she asked with more than just hope in her voice.

Peter understood she had meant the expression differently than he had. "Yes, we are," he said, praying he would not regret the white lie.

"I had a meeting with Father this evening."

"I saw you leave his office. He told you something?" Peter dreaded what she would say next.

"Yes. A few things…" She stopped. Her chest heaved.

"You know about the affair between my mother and your father."

"Yes." She nodded.

Peter turned off the engine. The vapid air had cooled and now bordered on cold. The light from a street lamp cast Kate's silhouette against a row of trees sashaying in the moonlight. The couple remained parked at the curb, along a cul-de-sac.

"Are you hurt by knowing? Are you upset I didn't tell you?" he asked.

"A little hurt, but not upset about you keeping it from me." For a moment, the car held a pre-storm calm. Kate broke the silence: "Peter?" she asked.

He nodded.

"Do you feel betrayed by your mother?"

"I'm not proud of what she did," he said, carefully considering his words. "Mom was in deep grief when my father died. He had suffered for two years with stomach cancer. In his prime, Dad was over six feet tall, weighed one hundred ninety-five pounds, and was the strongest man I ever knew. I mean, he was a man's man. All-American wide receiver in college, a sprinter, and personally courageous. For me, Paul Bunyan and George Washington all rolled into one. Then, just before he died, he became so weak I had to carry him to the bathroom to use the toilet. He weighed nothing."

"I shouldn't have asked," she said.

"My father dreamed big dreams. He moved from business to business and failure to failure. Despite that, Mom wanted him to live forever, even if he'd been only a shell of the man she married. She reached out to your father, and I don't blame anyone for their weaknesses—I've got enough failings of my own...So no, I don't feel betrayed."

"I don't blame your mother," Kate said. "But I do blame Father—he took advantage of a woman in need. I know what it's like to be taken advantage of. I wear my heart on my sleeve, and my feelings for people never go away."

Peter said nothing and listened to Kate's deep breaths. A few moments later, she began again: "There's something else. My father's confession had nothing to do with feelings of shame."

Peter gave a puzzled look.

"Father told me these things because…"

The bucket seats restricted him some, but Peter turned as much in her direction as he could. His right arm draped across the divide created by the stick shift. His hand rested on her left shoulder. He squeezed.

"I need you to explain something to me," she said.

"I'll try."

"Why did you rent your mother's house to someone you didn't know, for essentially nothing?"

"That's a strange question."

"Please. I need to know."

Peter paused in thought. "I had to—that's the simple answer."

"Why?" she asked.

"A compulsion brought on by the spirit of my mother. She was compassionate and would have wanted her belongings to benefit someone in need."

"Is that how you feel?"

Peter sighed and looked out the front window towards the lights of a nearby high-rise hotel. "I'll try to explain, even if I don't know why you're asking."

"Thank you."

"I guess at first I felt sorry for the man—who wouldn't? He's an African-American father, with four kids, little formal education, and less than no money. He answered my rental ad. He expected a job to come through and planned to use his salary to move into a better neighborhood. He'd have paid his entire income to move his family out of Southeast San

Diego. The drugs, the gangs, the violence. Clairemont isn't exactly La Jolla or Del Mar, but as middle class neighborhoods go these days, it's a hell of a lot better than where he was."

"He didn't get the job?" Kate leaned into Peter.

Peter shook his head. "It devastated him…No, I take that back. I think it humiliated him. And I had other reasons. I thought about Drew and his family. His father took off before Drew turned six. His mom went on welfare and hated it. If not for a football scholarship, he'd have been another victim of 'no-thank-you.' A black man with no hope of escaping the neighborhood. Now he's in medical school. He'll save lives and make a difference." On a nearby street, a siren wailed. Peter waited until the sounds faded before continuing. "Then, when I couldn't get a job, I would have been in deep trouble without your father's help. I told Mr. Jefferson—that's my tenant—he and his family could live there for free, but he's a proud man. Said he'd pay me a hundred a month and work on improving the property. In the first two weeks, he's already made good on his promise. In between looking for jobs, he spends his time fixing and sprucing…" Peter felt he had failed to explain himself. "This is a long-winded way of saying Mr. Jefferson is a good man and deserved a break."

"You are special, Peter."

"Not really, but thanks for the kind words. Mind if I ask *you* something?"

The way she said "No, I don't" came across as *maybe, maybe not.*

"Why did you need to know these things?"

"Something Father said. It doesn't matter any more."

"What?"

"He said you'd change. Turn into…never mind, Peter. Take me home."

Peter could see her head moving in the fractured light. He understood she was still upset. "Of course. We can be at your apartment in ten minutes."

"No. To your apartment."

"I…I don't think we're ready—"

"I don't care if you don't love me," she said. "And I won't tell you I love *you*. Hold me. If you don't feel like making love, don't. Just hold me."

"I—"

"Please."

Fifteen minutes later, they arrived at Peter's apartment. When they entered, they had to weave their way around packed boxes.

"I'm moving tomorrow—I already told you that, didn't I?"

She nodded.

Just then, Henry came sauntering in. When he looked up and saw a stranger, he stopped and cocked his head.

"That's the infamous old man Henry," Peter announced.

"He doesn't look so old. Come here, you handsome devil."

Kate bent down on one knee and put her hand out. Without hesitation, Henry strolled forward. Kate greeted him with a palm down his back. She then took a finger and began to scratch behind Henry's ear. He purred and plopped on his side.

"You've made a friend for life," Peter said.

"Are you talking about you or the cat?" she asked, half-seriously.

"I meant the cat. Us? We're already buddies."

"I'm glad I got to see your apartment before your move. I like it."

Peter took her hand. "You won't once I give you the tour. Excuse us, Henry."

"I may have been born an L.L. Beanite," she said, "but I like modest digs. And this qualifies as modest." In a surprise, she laughed.

Peter felt relief. Messy apartments and lazy cats were good medicine, he decided.

"Here," he said, taking her hand. "Let me show you the most disgusting bathroom in the history of bathroomdom." In a successful attempt to create an abstract nightmare, Peter's landlord had selected orange floor tiles, a blue toilet seat, and bright yellow walls. In addition, all the fixtures were a third too-small, making them look as if they belonged in a nursery school. "This"—he opened the door to his rainbow-outrageous bathroom "—is a bad dream, disguised as a bathroom. It's suitable only for color-blind midgets."

He flipped on the lights, illuminating the room and Kate's face. "Oh my, God," she said, shaking her head. "I'm having a hard time coming up with a word for this."

"Dreadful," Peter deadpanned.

"No. Wonderful. At least in a bizarre kind of way. Can two fit in that tiny bathtub?".

"I don't know."

Kate immediately stepped out of her shoes, dropped her shoulders, and gave a left-right shrug. Her jacket rolled off her back, piling at her heels. Before Peter could react, she unzipped her skirt and stepped out, displaying pantyhose and white cotton panties. She reached into the tub and turned on hot. Stretching her hose at the waist, she pulled them off in a smooth left leg, right leg march. Peter stared. She didn't have former paramour Ellen Goodman's perfectly sculpted legs, but they were smooth, white, and lovely. Kate also had narrower hips, with a less round backside. Maybe she wasn't as beautiful as Ellen, but he found her infinitely more attractive. Without a word, Kate unbuttoned her white blouse. She clutched the garment in her hand and dropped it on top of her skirt. All that remained were her panties and plain white bra.

"We have two options, Mr. Neil," she said, sounding professorial. "Either you get out of here in the next five seconds, before I strip and step into this tub, or you stay, take off your clothes, and we see whether or not this sucker will actually hold two adult bodies."

Peter stayed.

---

From a sedan that had tailed them from the moment they left Leeman, Johnston, and Ayers, a stranger took telephotos of the couple. He had pulled to the curb across the street from Peter's apartment and parked. *Good, but not great stuff,* he thought as his defrost fought to keep his windows clear enough to take unencumbered close-ups.

"Need to do better than this, George," he had said to himself over the click-click of his camera. At under six feet, dressed in jeans, Adidas running shoes, and wood-cutter plaid shirt, he appeared intentionally unremarkable.

Ten minutes after Peter closed and locked the front door of his apartment, George slithered from his car, careful to keep away from the orange glow spraying from a solitary street light. The private detective approached the second-story apartment from an alley in the rear of the building, carrying a high-tech recording device—slung across a shoulder—as if it were an unused walking stick.

Where he stood, looking up at Peter's lit window, he appreciated the indigo nothingness. His current location had no overhead lighting, no moonlight, and a six-foot fence dividing this property from the next. "Very good logistics," he said in a low voice.

George twisted the five-foot pole, taking care not to bump the mounted microphone. He slid a link, extending the stick like a television antennae. He made this move one more time, producing a twelve-foot pole. He put a set of headphones over his ears, then positioned the mike at the window with billowing steam, escaping from a hot tub of water. He began to listen and tape-record just as the female voice said: "take off your clothes…"

For the next hour, George enjoyed the voyeuristic aspects of his job. When the couple moved to the bedroom, he repositioned himself and, though he hadn't thought it possible, the show got even better. He guessed he'd get a bonus for this work. Too bad Peter Neil didn't have a first floor apartment. He'd have loved to have a set of *those* pictures.

When the couple fell asleep around three, the private investigator left. On the way home, he replayed his audio tapes, fast-forwarding to the good parts.

———

For three weeks, Oliver Dawson and Angela Newman worked separately, and left the office separately, then met for dinner. If happiness were an earthquake, Dawson measured a ten on the Richter scale.

Intimacy, once it came, nearly overwhelmed him. In orchestrating that bold next step, he had trembled, afraid that Angela's love wouldn't manifest itself in the same achy physical way his did. When they entered his apartment that night, it was different from the handful of earlier visits. Relaxing classical music hung in the background, while muted light veiled the living room. He had spread a thick blanket across the floor and piled pillows against his sofa.

"I feel like an adolescent," he had said. "I love you, Angela. How could we have been so afraid to tell each other for over a year?"

"People like us lose their courage. If others could see through our eyes, Oliver, they would understand beauty more fully."

Every time she spoke, Dawson felt as if he were a student, learning lessons about life.

He took her hand and led her to the sofa. A smile spread across her face, giving him additional resolve. When guided to the floor, she had put a hand through his thinning hair and combed his scalp with her slim fingers. He closed his eyes, amazed at how wonderful the gesture felt. She leaned over and kissed his ear. He turned and looked at her through moist eyes.

It had begun slowly—like a ballet, he imagined. An hour later, she engulfed him and he felt only contentment. He had never imagined he might bring pleasure to another person. From that moment, they spent every night together.

Now, Saturday morning, a week into their new lovers' routine, Angela's head rested on Dawson's slim chest. "You aren't angry I went ahead with the transfer, are you?" she said.

At first Dawson had tried to talk her out of changing departments. Now he was glad he had failed. While nobody would care if two ugly duckling co-workers dated one another, it was easier this way. On the one hand, she was still in the building, so they could see each other on an intermittent basis during the day. On the other hand, their relationship was not the subject of lewd speculation.

"No," he said. "I agree. It's better this way."

"Monday, I start my new job. I'll miss being outside your office, but I'd trade that for seeing you, touching you, having you in this way, any day of the week."

Her words aroused Dawson. As if she sensed his need, she reached under the sheets and touched him. "Oh my. I do believe you like me, Agent Dawson."

Oliver Dawson spent the next hour proving her correct.

# CHAPTER ELEVEN

PETER AND KATE AWOKE, STILL ENTWINED. THEY TOUCHED, KISSED, THEN gave in to their passions all over again. Afterwards, Kate pushed herself from the bed. Peter watched her float towards the bathroom, naked and wonderful. Henry, grateful for the restored peace, reclaimed his spot at the foot of Peter's bed. For Peter, a tinge of guilt lingered. When Kate gave him the option to hold her all night and not make love, he had intended to do just that.

"This is a problem, and I'm an idiot," he said to himself as Kate disappeared around the corner.

Peter sank into his down pillow, fingers laced behind his head, sheets pulled mid-chest. What the hell had he gotten himself into? If it had just been a casual acquaintance, like that salesperson from Gordon, Ashe, the uneasiness might quickly pass. But this was different, and he felt the guilt leaking from his brain to his heart. He cared for Kate. Did he want this relationship to progress? Peter suspected the question wasn't easily answered. Something intimidated him—the C-word. Commitment. She'd want that. So would he, in time.

Was he ready? No, he didn't think so. The timing was bad. His career had just taken off. For the first time in his life, he was making significant money. He had freedoms he never imagined. He could travel and eat at the best restaurants any time he wanted. Later today, he would move into a new, expensive co-op with an ocean view. He drove a fancy new car. He knew famous people in the investment world. One day he might do multi-million dollar trades, even take part in some esoteric billion-dollar transaction—similar to cornering a Treasury auction like Stenman had done a few years earlier, after which Kate's father deflected the SEC's investigation. A serious relationship now could steal hours from his work, cause him to get soft, make him lose the edge he had. He wanted badly to win at this game of making more money than anyone else. He'd try not to hurt her, but he might need to distance himself from her for awhile.

He heard the toilet gurgle, water splash against the porcelain sink, and then her footsteps leading away from the bedroom, in the direction of the kitchen. When Kate re-entered the bedroom several minutes later, she was dressed and casually sipping from a cup of steaming tea. Peter felt disappointment. He sought to look through her clothes and imagine the body that had so energized him last night and this morning. Her dark brown nipples and small white breasts. The long, delicate ribcage that stretched when they made love. The intimate spot on her neck—just below the left ear lobe—that elicited a groan when he kissed it. All of this held his imagination. With a will of their own, his eyes moved to her hips and those legs that had wrapped around his waist and hugged him deeper, refusing to let go, even when overcome with physical exhaustion.

"I'll be leaving." She put her mug on a copy of a *Sports Illustrated* lying on his dresser.

Peter refocused on the rumpled suit shielding her flesh. The starch in her white blouse was limp. She hadn't bothered to put on pantyhose—but her legs, he thought, looked better for the oversight. Had he known she intended to come back clothed, he would have followed and watched, enjoying the reverse strip-tease and memorizing every detail.

"I'll shower when I get home," she said. "I've already called a taxi. It'll be here shortly."

"We could shower together—or take another bath," he said, not certain whether he wanted her to say yes or say no.

"I'd rather not."

Peter jerked himself upright. "Don't you want breakfast? I'll get dressed. We'll go out."

"You're so old-fashioned, Peter. Somebody must have told you that after sex, the boy has to buy the girl breakfast."

Peter tried to sound jocular: "You mean we don't? Heavens, all that breakfast money wasted?"

Kate sort of smiled. "Good for the service economy."

"I'll call you."

"You forget, Peter. I know that's just a line guys use—especially the morning after. I'm glad we got to talk last night about…about your tenant and our parents. Thanks for caring enough to ask why I was sad."

Peter nodded, but he was thrown aback. She acted like she didn't expect anything more—not even another date. Her flippancy made him a little uncomfortable, like he had no control over what was happening.

"You leave on Wednesday?" he asked.

"Yes. I'll be working on the textbook and studying for the bar. If I pass the first time—and I'd better—I'll become a full-fledged attorney by year-end. If you turn to a life of crime, give me that call you alluded to."

"I'd like to take you to dinner, before you go."

I'm begging, Peter thought. Why? I've been plotting to distance myself from her. Now she's handing me an opportunity on a solid gold platter.

"We'll see," she said, smoothing her jacket with her flattened palms.

He squinted with an unspoken question.

"I needed this closeness," she explained. "I took advantage of you. I know that. And thank you."

"For what?" Peter asked.

"You'll think I'm perverted—maybe I am…I shouldn't say this, but I've never had an orgasm before." Her candor dumbfounded Peter. He couldn't even nod his head. "I don't mean I haven't been with a man," she continued, "only that I'd never felt the earth move before, so to speak. And though it's not for me, I guess I now understand why some people have sex just for the fun of it. And relax, Peter, I don't expect you to feel the same way I do. In fact, I'm not sure how I feel. I'm confused about everything."

Numbed, Peter watched her take several rapid steps toward the bed. She kissed his cheek, then gave a gentle brush across Henry's flank. Inhaling, she said, "I can still smell our lovemaking. Sorry about your sheets…we made quite a mess." She laughed lightly. "See you, lover." She began to pad away from the bed.

Henry stretched, sprang to his feet, hopped down, and followed.

"Kate?" Peter asked. She turned her head. "Let's see how we feel over the next few weeks. While you're away, let's talk, email, see each other a few times. When you come back as a high powered legal-eagle, can we revisit our feelings?"

Million-watt delight lit up her face. "Yes. I'd like that." She took several steps away from him before halting in mid-stride. She turned one last time, and said, "No. I'd love that." She blew him a kiss, then disappeared.

An hour later, Peter sipped coffee and pondered how this had turned out the way it did. Far from clinging, Kate was willing to blow the whole thing off as a needed emotional interlude. If nothing else, she was capable of keeping him off-guard.

"I think you'd have gone with her, old man," Peter said to Henry.

A knock came from the direction of the kitchen, in the back of his apartment. Peter looked at his watch, puzzled over who might be visiting at such an early hour and why they chose the rear door, rather than the front door. "Come on, Henry, let's see who's a-visitin' us this fine morn."

Once inside the kitchen, Peter saw a man's head through the glass door-panes. A combination of shadow and a tilted Cubs cap hid the face. The man held up a clipboard for Peter to see. In a voice loud enough to carry through the glass, he said, "Got a delivery from a…" the man squinted at the writing on a slip of paper. "Can't read the name, but delivery's for a Mr. Peter Neil."

Peter immediately guessed that Kate had sent him something. Flowers? Candy? He felt like a cad. He should have been the one to send something. Still, it was typical of her. Sensitive and kind. Peter nodded. When he unlocked and opened the door, he saw a second man, his features also hidden, standing behind the first, three steps down.

With the swiftness of an athlete, the first man struck Peter across the neck. By the time he hit the linoleum floor, Peter was unconscious.

---

"We reported four hundred twenty-two million, one hundred-fifteen thousand, three hundred-fourteen this week." Sarah Guzman calculated the numbers a third time as she spoke into her speakerphone. "I checked with Howard and we are in agreement."

"How is the marketing campaign progressing?" Morgan Stenman asked.

"We have reached agreement with the second of the four cartels in Colombia, and made contact with the others," Sarah said, removing her reading glasses and setting them on her desk. "They are interested in an arrangement similar to our Mexican clientele."

"That you could organize the enemies of your dead husband and make them eat from your hand is impressive." It was a rare Stenman compliment.

"Not so much so, but thank you. Giving up our share of the north-south traffic, then burying our organization, was an enticement. Your financial sophistication has simplified my efforts."

"Please," Stenman said, "finish your report."

Sarah replaced her glasses and looked back at her numbers. "If we can close on the three organizations we are pursuing, we will double our take. But can you can handle this many transactions?" Sarah heard Morgan exhale filtered cigarette smoke.

"We can," Morgan answered. "I will get our attorneys to set up additional accounts."

"How is the flow from your end?" Sarah asked.

"The Russian money is impressive. It is convenient. The politicians, like those in your world, are participants."

"And there are no developments with the Neil situation?" Sarah asked.

"No, but we shall all continue to monitor the one person likely to find anything, if it exists. Now, I must go. Thank you for the update. Things are good."

"Yes," Sarah agreed. "Good."

Once they disconnected, Sarah Guzman pulled up the computer file on Hannah Neil. She read:

*HANNAH NEIL:*
*Husband, Matthew Neil, deceased, cancer, age fifty-one.*
*Son, Peter Neil, age twenty-eight.*

She stopped reading. Clicking the down arrow, she scrolled through several pages of photographs. She stopped when she reached a close-up of Peter. She studied that picture and two others that followed. He had a square jaw and a rugged, handsome face. Brown hair. Broad lips. She returned to his bio. He was six foot, one inch, one hundred and ninety-six pounds. No close relatives. Best friend, Drew Franklin—Sarah Guzman highlighted the name. She continued: no athletic scholarship, but ran track and cross-country at UCLA; earned a double major in English and math; outstanding grades. Obviously, she concluded, he had also been a financial underachiever. Until now.

Just before closing the computer file, she nodded approvingly. "Intelligent eyes."

Opening an unrelated file, she went back to work.

Peter came to with Henry licking his face. Still on the floor, he rubbed the point of impact below his right ear, guessing a metal rod did the damage. The bruise went deep.

The outside door was open, and despite mingling with freeway stench, a stiff breeze brought welcome relief. Pushing himself to his feet, he swooned, clutched at a nearby counter-top, and noticed his small microwave was missing. A robbery? Everything he owned, including the microwave, was antiquated junk. An untouched dirty skillet sat on a burner next to a jelly-jar glass.

Thank God they didn't use the steak knives to slit my throat, he thought.

Peter managed to stagger to the living room. Sprawled across the floor were the contents of his moving boxes. Spiral notebooks with college class-notes had been strewn throughout the room. Elvis Costello tapes not taken. That qualified as the first piece of good news. A box of photos, dumped. A framed picture of his mother, missing. Why?

"What happened, Henry?" Peter's voice sounded ragged. "You're my only witness."

Peter suddenly noticed his color television was stolen. "What's the point?" he asked himself. "The thing's four years old and cost two hundred bucks, new."

The six-year-old stereo, also gone. His wallet lay open, tossed on the floor. Ten, twelve dollars was all he had. His new credit card, still unauthorized, gone. Through the open bedroom door, he saw evidence of additional ransacking. The mattress was askew. Someone, apparently expecting to find something underneath, stripped the sheets off his bed. Also taken was the clock radio.

"What a bunch of morons," Peter shouted to the walls. "The damn clock radio ran twenty minutes slow."

Peter heard a knock on his front door. For the first time, he realized his diver's watch was missing from his wrist. *Brilliant. That's worth about three bucks.* Still tentative in his steps, Peter made it to the door and peeked through the watch-hole. Thank god, he thought, when he saw Drew Franklin's face outside his door. Drew's arrival meant it was noon—the time he had agreed to come and help Peter move.

Drew, entering the opened door, saw Peter's face and the neck bruise. "You get in a fight?" he asked.

"Not exactly," Peter answered. "Somebody beat on me to steal eighty-nine bucks' worth of crap."

Drew examined Peter and determined the injury wasn't serious. "They either knew just the right spot to knock you on your ass without serious injury, or you were damn lucky," he explained.

After Peter's quick summary of what had happened, Drew found himself equally bewildered. "Doesn't make a bit of sense," he agreed. "Probably drug addicts, desperate for a fix. We see them all the time at the hospital."

Peter shook his head. "This guy, the one who hit me, he didn't move like someone impaired. Too quick to be a druggie. I'm no slouch when it comes to moving fast, but he caught me flat-footed. And while everything they took was crap, they were thorough and fast. Methodical, I'd say."

"Let's call the cops," Drew said.

"We do that and I'm stuck here at least another day. You and I both know they'll never find anything or anybody."

Peter reached into his left trouser pocket: empty. He patted his other pockets. Nothing. He went to the kitchen and checked the floors.

"What are you looking for, White Bread?" Drew asked.

"I can't believe it," Peter mumbled.

"Can't believe someone robbed you? It's not as if you live in the safest neighborhood—"

"Not that. Never mind."

Bad enough they stole crappy appliances and took his sheets and pillowcases to cart the stuff off in. But why, Peter wondered, did they take his moonstone?

It took the rest of the day to move out, but by dinnertime, Peter, Drew, and Stuart Grimes sat comfortably on Peter's ragtag sofa in his new home. They sipped Heineken and enjoyed an ocean view on one side and colorful sightseeing balloons on the other.

Stuart took a deep swig and said, "Well, neighbor—glad I talked you into moving here?"

"Yeah," Peter began, "especially after getting my head dented as a send-off."

"I'll tell you something, dude: as bachelor pads go, you and I live in the best. You'll have bimbos hanging from chandeliers."

"If I fall into that trap, Stu, Drew has instructions to castrate me."

While the three men bullshitted their way into the evening, Peter watched Henry explore his new home. The calico liked the place. Three bedrooms to claim as his new territory, rather than half-of-one. A new, oversized kitchen. Even a new food dish. By the time the others left at ten o'clock, the animal had deposited a layer of fur throughout.

The two roommates—Peter and Henry—went to bed an hour later. They heard real waves through the windows, not the horns, screeching tires, and occasional fatal accident they'd become accustomed to. Before he fell asleep, Peter resolved to call Kate. Ask her to lunch. Maybe invite her over and show her around the new pad.

After all, this bathtub was twice the size.

# CHAPTER TWELVE

On Monday morning, a new voice echoed through his intercom, and Oliver Dawson found it disconcerting. His new secretary, Carol Larson, came from the secretarial pool, assigned to him while he and the other two agents sharing a secretary interviewed and agreed upon a permanent replacement for Angela. Young Carol had a pretty face, but it was her full breasts, straining the buttons of her blouse, that drew everyone's attention. At ten o'clock, this newest attraction at the SEC Enforcement Division rapped on Dawson's door.

"Come in," he called out.

"This just came for you, sir."

Carol batted her eyes as she handed him an oversized envelope. On the outside it read:

CONFIDENTIAL—TO BE OPENED BY ADDRESSEE
ONLY (Under penalty of law)
OFFICIAL BUSINESS
FBI Laboratory—Washington, D.C.

At first baffled, Dawson suddenly remembered his request for the lab results, and for the original documents anonymously sent to him in the San Diego case. He used an index finger to rip apart the seal. Reaching inside, he withdrew the contents.

A short cover letter read:

Attention: Agent Oliver Dawson
Re: Tests
From: Dr. Isaac Hermanson

Apologies for the delay, but we found it necessary to inventory Agent Carlson's projects. I have included a summary of the lab findings already sent to your offices by Carlson, short-

*ly before his death.*

*To reiterate, a clear set of fingerprints (unidentified) was lifted from these pages. We additionally determined that the weight and texture of the paper, on which the letter was printed, was an expensive grade used by an exclusive clientele—mostly law firms.*

*The manufacturer of this paper—as identified by their watermark—is International Paperworks, Inc. out of Portland, Oregon.*

*In each case, as you are undoubtedly aware, we were instructed not to conduct additional follow-up. If that directive changes, please advise.*

*Sincerely,*
*Dr. Isaac Hermanson—Federal Bureau of Investigation*

Dawson slammed the packet on his desk. He retrieved and fished through his files on Jackson Securities. Hadn't he been told the investigation turned up no fingerprints? He was sure he had. Flipping pages, though, he found nothing in writing to confirm his vivid recollection.

"How the hell did I reach that understanding?" He drew a blank.

He phoned Angela, hoping she had an answer. After a brief exchange of soft endearments, she asked, "Do you have a problem, Oliver?"

"Yeah. Brain lock." He then asked about the evidence from the lab. "Who informed us about the results, and when?"

"You were in San Diego. I relayed the information."

"That's right." He shuddered at the memory of the cheap hotel room, the sleepless night, and the mission's failure. "Where did you get your information?" He tried to contain his mounting wrath.

"Let's see…"

Dawson stared at the FBI letter while he waited for Angela's answer. With what the lab had now concluded, he was certain it could identify who had contacted him, if he asked. "What a damn waste of time," he whispered into the back of his hand, the one covering the mouthpiece.

"Did you say something?" Angela asked.

"Uh, no. Any recollections?"

"Yes. I got a call from Director Ackerman's office."

Dawson had known Donald Ackerman for ten years—before Ackerman became an SEC director. Their respect for each other stemmed from their equally strong commitment to their work. So why did Ackerman try to scuttle the investigation?

"Ackerman said the tests were negative?" he asked.

"Not the Director, his office. Maybe his assistant. Yes, I'm certain. Freeman Ranson notified us. I don't think we received anything in writing, though."

Dawson knew for damn sure nothing had been sent in writing. Writing left a trail. This way, Ranson could deny having said any such thing, or he could simply claim misunderstanding. Dawson's dislike for the man quickly ballooned into hatred. Ranson had always been far too interested in matters that did not concern him. Prior to this latest outrage, Dawson had considered the director's assistant merely a prying annoyance. Now, he had other suspicions. What did he know about the man? Thinking deeply, Dawson recalled that Ranson, before joining the SEC, had worked in compliance for an investment-banking firm. Was there a connection or a conflict of interest going on here? Dawson would give odds on it.

As a follow-up, the agent made a quick call to a friend in the SEC's personnel department. Ranson, he discovered, had indeed worked for the investment bank Stratton Brothers prior to joining the Securities and Exchange Commission seven years ago. His educational and professional history suggested he had been a top-notch attorney, ambitious and connected. Now, Dawson wanted to know, what had possessed Ranson to leave a much higher paying job in the private sector for the SEC? It didn't make sense.

That Freeman Ranson had come from Stratton Brothers represented another potentially disturbing piece to this puzzle, Dawson decided. Stratton was one of the two brokers in bed with Stenman Partners at the time of the Treasury manipulation investigation. And it was well-known that Stratton Brothers and Stenman Partners had a long-standing relationship—a relationship that predated Ranson's leaving the investment bank. It was circumstantial, but Dawson's instincts told him Ranson hadn't been playing straight with him.

"Freeman-fucking-Ranson," he said under his breath.

An hour later, Dawson convinced Director Ackerman to meet him in Dawson's car, heading toward Silver Spring, Maryland. The director's six-foot frame scrunched into Dawson's undersized, unkempt Toyota. Director of Enforcement Donald Ackerman had slate eyes and the tan face of an outdoorsman. Now fifty, he had achieved quick success at the SEC—a byproduct of his smarts and political savvy. Dawson believed him to be among the most competent people he knew.

"I like you, Dawson," Ackerman said, "but this had better be good."

"Sir, bear with me. As much as I hate to say it, you may have become an unwitting part in what I believe is massive securities fraud."

Ackerman's skepticism stretched his face. "You are on the thinnest of ice, Agent. Does this have to do with your dead-end investigation in San Diego—those two suicide crackpots who busted a brain-vein and went nuts? Tell me that's not what you're babbling about."

"Not a suicide-murder, sir."

"Good. What is it then?"

"I don't believe Zerets committed suicide—I think someone, and I don't know exactly how—set him up. These same people murdered Cannodine because of my investigation. And Drucker—"

"Oh my God, this *is* about San Diego. You're anal-compulsive, Dawson. Turn this heap around and get me back to my office."

"No, sir."

"This is insane. You can't kidnap the head of SEC Enforcement."

"Nearly fifteen years, sir—that's how long I've knocked my head against a wall. Tried to enforce the laws with piss-ant results. This time, we've got some big fish dangling. Hear me out. Please."

"You've got until we reach the Maryland border, then home. That's fifteen minutes. Make it good."

"I will. And thank you."

"Don't waste your time thanking me."

Dawson lifted his foot off the accelerator, enough to cut ten miles per hour off his speed. Then, after laying out the coincidences, he asked, "Why didn't you see the lab report indicating there *were* prints on the letter? Not told the paper was distinctive? Why did Ranson give me misinformation? Any potential source of information in this case seems likely to end up involved in an accident, suicide, or a murder. Someone leaked information.

It wasn't me, and it sure as hell wasn't you."

"We're a huge agency and sometimes there are slipups. Shit happens."

"This toilet's stopped up and overflowing, and Ranson's the one sitting on the pot."

"In my book," the Director said, "Freeman Ranson's an exemplary employee. You have ten seconds to reconsider and withdraw your accusations."

"No thank you, sir. I may be wrong, but I'm willing to go with my gut, and my gut tells me I'm on to something."

"You willing to put your neck in the noose on this one? 'Cause that's where it's gonna be if you're wrong."

"Yes. Even if I'm proven to be full of shit, I need to know. So do you."

"If this were anyone else in the department, I'd say go to hell. But you're a good agent, and I can't ignore something this big. Let's hear the plan."

"We go around Ranson…" Dawson explained how. "Then I work in the background to determine where those documents came from—I work solo. Without anyone's sanction, not even yours. It will take some time, but I've waited my whole life for this kind of an opportunity, and I'm willing to take it slow and easy."

"Why without sanction?"

Dawson sensed the heated stare and felt naked, subjected to ridicule by this important man. Dawson's skinny chest began panting. No turning back now, he knew. "Because eventually these sons of bitches are gonna figure out I'm involved. If they think this is official, and think the SEC is launching a full-blown investigation, people and their families are gonna get buried—literally. If they think it's just me, they're more likely to opt for damage control."

"If what you say is true—and I suspect ninety-plus percent of your story is self-delusional—that makes you a possible target too."

"Maybe. But if I disappear or end up dead, it'll be hard for them to explain. If anything does happen to me, then at least I'll have proven a point. Correct?"

"If you die in a freaky manner, yes, I'll buy into your thesis. Hell of a way to make your point, Oliver."

Dawson's head swung from the road to Ackerman. In all the years they had known one another, this marked the first time the director referred to him as Oliver. He felt foolish for the happiness this small gesture brought him.

Still warmed by the informality, Dawson continued: "I'll go to San Diego. I'll pay my own way. When I find out who in San Diego sent me those documents, I'll take some time off and investigate on my own time, in violation of agency guidelines. If I'm caught, you read me the riot act. If I create too much of a stink, you fire me on the spot. That should convince Ranson I'm acting without agency approval."

"This is nuts. I don't think such extreme—"

"Excuse me for interrupting, sir, but if I lose one more lead, this case will disappear—and I'll feel responsible for additional suffering. Please. Trust me."

"Once you're fired, then what?"

"If we get to that, I'll try to find someone on the inside to feed me information. If this person who sent the Cannodine papers has anything else, or can produce more, I milk him or her. That's it."

"You're a piece of work, Dawson."

"Thank you, sir."

"I didn't mean it as a compliment. I reiterate: you screw up, or smear Ranson—assuming, as I suspect, he's done nothing wrong—and you are history. And until this heats up, you work your normal case load."

"Of course."

"You keep me up-to-date once you make a contact in San Diego—*if* you make a contact. I want reports at least once a week, even if it's to tell me you are up shit creek. Understood?"

"Yes."

"You have six months to get me something concrete—no, more than concrete. Six months to bust this case open or I bust you. That's the deal."

Dawson exhaled, realizing that working covertly, with limited resources, meant slow progress. Even uncovering who had sent him the papers might take weeks or months. If he used up his allotted time without concluding the case, he'd get on his knees, if necessary, and beg for more time. On second thought, looking at the ripples of black around Ackerman's narrowed eyes, Dawson realized begging would be a waste of time.

"You put up or shut up." Those were the last words from Director Ackerman as he stormed from Dawson's car once they reached the office.

Fumbling under his seat for a can, Dawson found a Diet Coke, opened it, and sipped.

"A dog that's got a bone," he told himself. "That's what I am…an ugly mutt, done got a stinky bone, and nobody's gonna take it away from me."

*Nobody.*

———

As the San Diego summer arrived, and the fog hanging over his pre-sunrise arrivals gave way to dry, warmer days, Peter found his financial confidence growing. San Diego, never cold, had transitioned from cool spring to tepid summer. At the same time, Peter had devoured book after book on the markets. He learned about value investing, momentum investing, charts and graphs, micro-economics, macro-economics, even the capital asset pricing model and the theory's absurd assumption that markets were efficient. If they were efficient, he figured, then Stenman and her operatives couldn't be turning in kick-ass performance records quarter-after-quarter, year-after-year.

Peter also enjoyed analyzing companies and picking them apart—by accessing annual reports, year-end 10K's filed with the SEC, quarterly 10Q's, brokerage research reports, and calls to and visits from company executives. He dug deeply for investment insights, using his newfound analytical skills. The learning curve was slick and fast and exciting as hell. The days seemed to last only seconds, the weekends—even when having a good time with friends—lingered, feeding his impatience to get back into the action—so much so that he often came into the office Sunday evenings, with the opening of foreign markets, and stayed the night. He had developed, he told himself, a healthy addiction.

After months of clerking and working orders on the various exchanges at the behest of others, Peter was finally allowed to cut his teeth. By the end of summer, he began to trade independently. By having Stenman Partners on his business card, brokers and executives fed him information and favors. It was as if it were Christmas, year-round. A whisper-number on earnings came a day ahead of the company's press release, and always dead-on accurate. When a gigantic institution hit the market with a buy order in a given stock—one big enough to push the price up several dollars—a broker might let it slip that Peter should buy a few shares ahead of that event. With a research recommendation pending, he'd be told: "Buy some, Peter. You won't be sorry."

Gifts, bestowed every hour of every day. Was it all perfectly legal? he asked himself. Probably not, but it was business as usual, and it wasn't smart to refuse presents from people he might one day need.

In a jam, like when lugging a non-performing stock position, Peter learned to create a technical breakout—buy more, and take the stock higher, through a previous price-resistance level. A call to one of the Street's top-rated technical analysts—along with the promise of future remuneration—could generate a technical, short-term buy-recommendation, thus driving the share price even higher, just long enough for Peter to dump his position. "Tricks of the trade," Stuart told him. It was a smaller version of the good old pump and dump, only tailored to his specific needs. Information and influential friends—Stuart had been quite right about their importance.

Once fall rolled in, Peter began to make substantial contributions to the hedge fund's profits. In some things—fundamental stock research for one—he actually became more proficient than his mentor Stuart. Peter's energy and passion grew daily. Even an occasional stinker trade couldn't diminish the thrill of making significant money by day's end, and of winning, where the final score was determined simply by numbers of dollars. In the case of a hot deal, Peter might make a hundred percent increase in a single trading session. And because of Stenman's financial muscle, when he asked for it, he always got gigantic representation on these ultra-hot deals. Everybody understood the unwritten rule: generous stock allocations went to those who paid the most in commissions. And nobody paid more than Stenman Partners with their four- or five-hundred percent turnover per year in funds under management.

Now that he understood the process, Peter felt like a pump-cart in a room full of locomotives. He longed to dabble in the big numbers thrown around by more senior traders—those who tucked their ears into their phones, protected their sources of information like a well-guarded treasure, and made tens-of-millions in magical profit on a near-constant basis.

And beyond these wizards were Howard Muller and Morgan Stenman. They had the resources and touch that could turn a "pittance"— a hundred million or so—into a fortune of several hundred million or even a billion dollars. Peter could recite stories he'd heard of how mysterious overseas partners raked in more money than many countries' governments had stored in their central banks. This was heady stuff, and Peter imagined the day he could taste that kind of raw financial power.

By October, nobody doubted Peter's passion. "A machine," Stuart said of Peter's seventy-hour weeks. "A natural," Morgan Stenman had said more than once after reviewing his performance numbers.

The brokers who covered him enjoyed his pleasant manner, and bent over to give him preference on deals, insight, and knowing winks and nods. Company executives, accustomed to a browbeating whenever someone from Stenman Partners called, seeking information, appreciated Peter's politeness. He sometimes received a proprietary nugget or two as a reward for his uncommon civility.

On the first Friday in October, Peter closed out a trade and took a quick look around the room. With his turret close enough to Stuart's that their elbows brushed, Peter noticed Stuart's nose dripping like a leaky faucet. "Fucking-A, Stu, it's noon," he said, muffling his voice. "You need to get a grip." Stuart's eyes rolled so fast they made Peter dizzy.

"Lighten up, dude," Stuart said. "Friday ritual. A treat after a week's hard work."

"Can't you at least wait until the market's closed? How can you function with all that shit floating around the scrambled eggs between your ears?"

"Usually helps. I got a great idea…since you got nothing to do, mind reconciling for me today?" Stuart's leg jack-hammered off the ball of his foot.

"Nothing to do? You know better than that."

"Fact is, Petey, you're right. I am a little messed up. And I got too many…" Stuart paused to wipe his nose. "Muller had me take down some of his trades…I've got to reconcile them. Help me out, just this once. It's not as if I haven't taken you under my wing, helped build your budding career and all that."

"Yeah, yeah." Peter began to play an imaginary violin. "Just this once. Whatta you need me to do?"

Peter recalled Stuart disappearing that morning into Muller's office just as Muller left for a meeting. When Stuart emerged, an hour later, he had a stack of fifteen or twenty tickets that he now withdrew from a side drawer. Stuart dropped them in front of Peter.

"The P&L ought to add up to…uh…shit, how much was that?" he asked himself in a voice loud enough for half the room to hear.

Stuart patted the desktop with both palms like a man trying to put out a small brush fire. Spinning his head, he said, "Oh yeah, oh yeah, oh yeah."

He then darted to Muller's office. With a rapid series of punches, Stuart typed a seven-digit password into a keypad, opened the door, and went in. A moment later, he reemerged and pulled Muller's door closed. Stuart wore a ridiculous drug-fueled grin and looked as if he might be humming to himself. He waved a slip of paper as he bounded towards their desks on the balls of his feet. In the background, one of the clerks dinged a bell that signaled one p.m.—the stock markets had closed for the week.

"Here," Stuart said, flopping into his chair, facing Peter. "This is on the QT. If Fat-Head knew about this, he'd cut my balls off, hang 'em up to dry."

"What number am I trying to reconcile?"

Stuart rolled his shoulders to a silent rhythm as he squinted at his own handwriting. "Two hundred twenty-one and some change."

"Two hundred and twenty-one what?" Peter asked.

"We're dealing in millions of dollars." Stuart grinned.

Peter felt bewildered. "You're saying you or Muller or whoever did these trades made that much money this morning?"

Stuart horse-laughed. When he caught his breath, he said, "Yeah. That was me and the freak."

Several traders turned, annoyed at the levity. "Shhh," Stuart slurred, not able to take his own advice. "You mind crunching these numbers while I take recess in the conference room?"

"I don't mind, Stu, but don't you think"—Peter's voice dropped to a whisper. He leaned into Stuart's ear "—that you should go easy on that stuff. You're already messed up."

"Make the money, dude, and nobody's gonna care. See you in ten."

Stuart double-timed it to the conference room. A moment later, he drew shut the curtains. By now, Peter knew the routine. Four lines drawn on the table with a hundred. Roll that bill, inhale, switch nostrils, inhale. Wait five minutes, do it again.

"Get some help, Stu," Peter said under his breath.

Peter picked up the first two tickets. They involved massive day-trades in the Japanese Yen. *Net profit:* $32 million. The account name was coded.

The next two trades were in the British Pound Sterling, similarly large and coded, but something looked wrong with the information on the tickets. The purchase appeared out of whack. According to the ticket, the buy took place several hours *after* the sale. Unless this was a short sale, and nothing indicated it was, the trade times looked ass-backwards. Peter matched the last seven sets of trades—all hugely profitable—and discovered one other with a similar discrepancy. This second erroneous transaction was done through an Irish broker in a stock that appreciated fifteen percent between the purchase and sale. The transaction times also made no logical sense.

By the time Stuart returned, Peter had separated out two sets of confusing trades.

"How'd you do on reconciliation, Petey?"

Stuart's brain, Peter guessed, now floundered in a stupor, light years from reality.

"Stuart—"

"Why you whispering, dude? Got a problem? You need a lesson in addition, subtraction?" Stuart's lids and brows opened and closed in an annoying dance.

"Were any of these trades short sales?" Peter asked.

"Nope. All straight buys then sells."

"So we didn't sell stock or currency ahead of the purchase?" Peter grabbed Stuart's hand and squeezed hard enough to feel bone bow.

"Hey, what're you trying to do?"

Still whispering, Peter said, "These trades are backwards—the time stamps have sales occurring hours *before* purchases. What's going on?"

Stuart managed to focus. "What?"

"Sales before—"

"I heard you the first time." As if he had been caught stealing candy, Stuart looked side to side in an attempt to read others' faces.

"Follow me," Stuart ordered.

The two men quick-stepped to Howard Muller's office. For the second time in the last hour, Peter watched Stuart punch numbers on the keypad lock.

"Muller changes the office code by four p.m. every Friday," Stuart said. "Thank God you…"

Entering, Stuart skipped to a corner and opened a small index-card file, resting on a bookshelf. "This'll be no problem," he said. He took a

# CHAPTER FOURTEEN

FOR THREE DAYS, AGENT DAWSON STUMBLED OVER TORN CARPET, watched non-cable television, ate vending machine sandwiches, chewed cinnamon buns with sticky icing glued to cellophane, and drank burnt coffee and warm Diet Coke. He had hoped to hear from Peter Neil before having to return to Washington. It was now clear that such luck wasn't in the cards. But he had planted a seed, he assured himself. Would it take root in fertile soil? Neil was a bright boy—he'd begin to put the pieces together. The question remained, though: would Neil care? Few people risked everything for principle. Look what happened to his mother. If Neil didn't come around, could he be blamed?

Such were the thoughts mucking around Dawson's tired brain during three days of doing just one thing—waiting. Better to leave, he decided. Go back to work as if nothing happened, and be ready to drop everything if and when he got his break.

On the evening of the fourth day, back in D.C., Oliver Dawson wriggled across his kitchen table to hold Angela Newman's hand. Now that he had made contact with Peter Neil, he needed to ask for her help. Afraid to break the news, he began by beating around the bush.

When Angela couldn't take any more of his rambling, she said, "Oliver, you have something on your mind. You still like me, don't you?"

"Yes. Of course. This has nothing…It's just a good thing that…"

"Good thing *what?*"

"A good thing you no longer work for me."

"I agree, though I suspect you have a new reason."

"You're smart, Angie. I need you to be my conduit to Ackerman. Now that this case is heating up, he needs to be updated. We'll pretend you're contacting him on behalf of your new boss, Jonathan Tinker. You and I can then meet once a week. You pass on instructions from the Director. I'll give you an update from my end."

Angela's eyebrows looked as if they might slide from her face. "We'll meet once a week? We see each other every day."

Oliver looked down at their hands. He intertwined his fingers with hers. "This is important. People are dead. I'm certain Ranson will be monitoring my activities. He must know by now that I received the report from the FBI. Hopefully he doesn't suspect I put two and two together and fingered him as the asshole who misrepresented the lab findings. I don't think anyone in San Diego knows I contacted Neil."

"This is a long-winded explanation for something. Spit it out, Oliver."

"We can't see each other until this is over. Nobody in the office knows for sure about our relationship. If you are to be my back-door to Ackerman, and you're to stay safe, you must stay away from me most of the time."

"No!" she said. "Drop the case. That's asking too much."

"Please. Here." Dawson reached into his pocket, removing an item he smothered in his balled fist. "I want to ask you something, Angie." He got down on one knee, then took her left hand in his. "Will you marry me?"

Inside his now opened hand, he held out an engagement ring.

Angela gasped. Her hand shook as she reached for the diamond, but said nothing. Dawson listened for what seemed a silent eternity. Finally her tender sobs drew his gaze from his shoelaces to her face. Her head bounced up and down, causing her glasses to slide along the bridge of her nose.

"That means yes? Right?" Dawson asked, biting at a snip of air.

"Yes. But this is one heck of a way to get me to agree to do what you ask."

"Thank you…Darling." The endearment sounded new and strange. "Only one other thing," he continued.

"Yes, Oliver?"

"Uh, I don't know quite how to say this…"

"What?"

"Well, until this matter is settled…"

"Yes?" Angela slipped the ring over her finger.

"Until we are no longer an undercover team, you can't wear the ring or tell anyone we're engaged."

"You have got to be joking."

"Ranson finds out you and I are—"

"I get it, Oliver. All I have to say is, you better get this case cracked and send the bad guys to jail, soon. Real soon."

# CHAPTER FIFTEEN

PETER DIDN'T QUITE UNDERSTAND WHY HE HADN'T MENTIONED HIS Dawson run-in to Ayers or anyone at Stenman Partners. It wasn't as if he believed any of the ridiculous accusations tossed around by the agent. And he hoped nothing more would happen if he ignored the whole episode. As it turned out, his anxiety over Dawson's visit did begin to subside. To placate himself, Peter even phoned Dawson's D.C. number. When the agent picked up, Peter disconnected, relieved that his tormentor no longer haunted Southern California.

Despite the unpleasantness at Sammy's Restaurant, Peter passionately loved his job, especially the daily adrenaline rush. That everyone measured their worth by the money they made put them all on an equal footing. Make it or fail. Period. He also appreciated the fact that everyone minded their own business and kept their activities a well-guarded secret. The most successful people on Wall Street had built their personal dynasties on this simple formula. One day he might be placed on one of the pedestals reserved for Wall Street's legends, if only he stayed the course. And I will, he silently swore to God, stay the course.

Things progressed uneventfully until the end of October. On a Saturday, Peter stumbled onto an opportunity. He decided to buy a personal computer. He went to three separate stores, only to discover PC's to be in short supply. His frustration sparked a trading idea.

Arriving at the Stenman offices on Monday, he began to work the phones. He made calls to a number of PC manufacturers, assessing inventory levels and accounts payable and receivable. He confirmed that sales had very recently exploded. This revelation flew in the face of dire headlines and a severe price decline in computer makers' stocks. By midday, he felt confident. He ran his idea by Stuart.

"Just a few weeks ago, PC manufacturers pre-announced lousy earnings for this quarter. Their inventories grew bloated when retailers began returning units right and left. These companies initiated discounts, and planned to reserve against unsold product—most earnings estimates had these companies losing money over the next four or five quarters."

"I read the papers," Stuart said, "and it's a ten-hankie story. What's your point?"

"These guys went ahead and lowered prices," Peter answered. "At first, ten percent. Sales went up, but not much. Then they lowered prices another ten percent. Guess what happened?"

"They lost enough money that half of them are going out of business by year-end?"

"That's what I thought, until I tried to buy a PC this weekend. They hit a price point where elasticity of demand was huge."

"Elasticity of demand? You read too many fucking books, dude."

"I'm saying sales went through the roof. Inventories are down—way down. *Ergo*: no write-offs as previously announced. Soon, as early as next week, we're going to get an about-face on those profit warnings."

"No way, Peter. In fact, Howard has a huge short position in these stocks and he's tight with someone at Guerren, Clark in San Francisco. Between you and me—and I mean only you and me—his contact's head of Corporate Finance. The guy's information is perfect 'cause Guerren, Clark underwrites half these companies' stock deals. If what you say is true, Howie-Boy would know."

"Maybe not," Peter said. "None of these companies is contemplating selling stock to the public—not with their share price in the shit-can."

"That's true," Stuart conceded.

"That means corporate finance business is at a standstill. Muller's guy might not be up-to-date—when there's no business pending, these guys are lazy assholes—you're the one who told me that."

"If I said so, it's true." Stuart leaned back and chomped on a stick of gum at a hundred miles an hour.

"Also, this is a rapid turnaround," Peter continued. "That last price cut was recent. The stock-out's recent. I called several CFOs. They confirmed inventories are historically low. And as they sell add-ons to all the computers moved in the last few weeks, the current Street estimates for next year will also go up. These shares are going to double—no, when this news hits the marketplace, they'll triple in price."

"You sure, Petey? If you're right, Howard's going to get his ass handed him. He's not used to losing money, and not even heaven's gonna save the guy at Guerren, Clark."

"I'm certain," Peter said, his body coursing with excitement.

"You gotta run this by Muller. He's got a position, and you can't go long the group while he's short stock."

"Do I call him?" Peter asked.

"He's not going to be a happy camper, dude. You better go knock on his door. Say something nice about Robert E. Lee to cut the ice…" Stuart grinned.

"Why are you smiling?"

"No reason. Go." The smirk grew.

A moment later, Muller grudgingly beckoned Peter into his office. When Peter explained what he'd told Stuart, Muller exploded, "Fundamental research is for losers. I have my facts first-hand. Sit down, shut up, and try not to shit in your pants."

Muller phoned Stratton's second floor analyst on the PC industry. The man confirmed: "The industry is in deep financial shit."

Next, Muller phoned an unidentified contact. Thanks to Stuart, Peter understood this was Muller's inside connection at Guerren, Clark. He too scoffed at Peter's analysis. "These companies are hopeless losers," he confirmed. "We've written them off as clients until this cycle turns, and that might take two years."

"Now, Neil," Muller said at the end of this second call, "get out."

In the past, assuming he was wrong, Peter would have hung his head in shame. This time, feeling he was on solid ground, Muller's dismissal merely pissed him off.

"What did Fat-Head say?" Stuart asked.

"Sadistic bastard threw me out."

"You sure of your facts?"

Peter nodded his head while rage created a moist steam over his eyes. "That's one ass I'd love to kick." He pointed his nose at Muller's office.

"Go to Morgan. She has an open-door policy. She's a bright bulb, knows Muller's a jerk. But beware, dude, if you're wrong, you're road kill."

"If I'm right?"

"If you're right, and it makes as much money as you say it will, you get *beaucoup* kudos from Morgan the Great. I myself would never take the chance, nor do I understand enough about balance sheets and income statements to create a credible analysis. As I told you, my greatest skill is trading money for information. That's all any of us do—except you, of course. Go see Morgan, if you dare."

"What does Muller do if I back-door him on this?"

"Whether you're right or wrong, he hates you."

"He already hates me. He hates everyone."

"Wrong. He has a hard-on for everybody. You haven't seen hate yet. He'll make Sherman's March through Georgia look like a cake-walk."

"You telling me to back off?" Peter asked, more a challenge than question.

"No. That's not what I'm saying. Morgan Stenman's respect is worth any amount of Muller-fallout. You do what you gotta do, dude."

"Then I do it."

From the privacy of the conference room, Peter phoned Stenman. He explained that he wished to outline a trading opportunity.

"What might that be?" she asked.

He reviewed the highlights.

"And you spoke to Howard?" she asked.

"I did."

"His reaction?"

"He phoned our in-house analyst, then a secret contact. They both said I was nuts."

"Are you?" she asked.

"I'm expected to carry my weight. Make money. That's what I'm trying to do. Is there another way to be successful at Stenman Partners?"

"No. Meet me in room 202 at five o'clock. I have been meaning to have a little chat with you anyway."

Peter put the silent phone down. "Short and sweet," he mumbled.

Before returning to work, Peter experienced a vague worry. Why, he wondered, had Stenman "been meaning to have a little chat...anyway?"

---

Stenman Partners' second floor was divided into two sections. The first consisted of offices for analysts. From the elevator or stairs, one had to pass by a male receptionist who resembled a well-dressed paratrooper. Once past this humorless protector, a person had to input a six-digit passcode to enter.

Inside the main floor, ficus trees and hyacinths lined and deodorized the hallways. Besides the hum that accompanies silence, Peter noted that the office trappings tended to get more luxurious and expensive as one progressed down the halls—as did the prestige and incomes of office occupants. At the end of this high-rent alleyway, the head of research had his corner suite. This individual's income went beyond Peter's ability to compute: twenty million dollars in a bad year, a hell of a lot more in a good one.

A right turn at the head of Research's office yielded another set of doors. This led to the Promised Land: Morgan Stenman's hallowed turf.

Stenman shared her half of the second floor with the executive dining rooms, of which room 202 was one. A second set of cameras, infrared detectors, and expressionless men greeted him.

Sign in, metal search, pat down.

"Hiding the Crown Jewels," Peter quipped. The two men could have been deaf.

Once beyond the heavy metal door, the digs got really fancy—even more opulent, in fact, than Peter's unschooled imaginings of New York's white-shoe investment banking houses. Impressionist oils hung from the twelve-foot paneled walls. The hallway—illuminated by crystal chandeliers suspended every twenty feet—had deep carpet that Peter likened to a wall-to-wall yellow-brick-road. He carried with him an intertwining of anxiety, excitement, privilege, and fear—but mostly fear. For the first time since making the call two hours earlier, he began to doubt the wisdom of his action. He suddenly didn't want to jeopardize his position.

Too late? Maybe not, he thought. He'd re-run his hair-brained idea by Stenman, then apologize for the insipid stupidity—admit he had made an arrogant miscalculation. Tell her how much he admired Howard Muller, how much he loved working as a trader. He practiced his verbal back-tracking as he looked for room 202. Once he found the door, Peter had his revised strategy ready. He'd bow his head and make a joke about his ignorance—maybe repeat the comment he'd made at their first meeting about putting his foot in his mouth so often that he was good at getting it out.

With his left hand inside the pocket of his sport coat, Peter rubbed his index finger against his thumb, wishing he had his moonstone. He knocked.

The door opened automatically.

Peter glanced to the small video-cam mounted in the corner of the hall. He entered and saw his blurred image on a screen, one of many electronic devices built into a cabinet along a far wall. Beside Stenman was a second woman. At first Peter thought she was a child. She stood small, but had rounded hips and breasts, and showed no affect through blue eyes. Her forehead rode a bit too high, but led the eye to the complex white-weave of a widow's peak—an imperfection that added to, rather than detracted from, the overall impression. Peter had a difficult time diverting his attention, as if looking at her was addictive. Had this been a poker game, Peter would have folded at the ante.

"This is Sarah Guzman, an associate," Stenman said.

Peter stepped forward and took her hand. "It is…" her delicate fingers felt almost hot enough to burn…"it is nice to meet you," Peter said, unable to manufacture anything other than a pat greeting. With his face stained red, he felt foolish as he tried to guess her age: anywhere from thirty to forty. He wished she had returned his light smile with one of her own.

"I am one of Morgan's partners and an associate of hers for many years. She thinks one day you might be one of the great ones, if you are willing to make the necessary sacrifices. Are you willing, Mr. Neil?"

"Yes," he said, wondering why she was attending this meeting. "That's why I'm here."

Stenman filled a chair, leaning her cane against the outside of the armrest. She nodded to Sarah. "We asked our PC analyst to review your findings," Sarah said. "He did some checking and now agrees with your conclusions. I reprimanded him for his lazy habits."

Peter sighed. He had to prove nothing now. So why did Muller have to be such an ass?

"I'm grateful you listened to me," Peter said, his comments directed to Stenman.

Sarah Guzman glided to the wet bar and began mixing drinks. A glass of Chardonnay for herself. A Perrier for Stenman. "Peter," she said. "Double Jack, a splash, two ice-cubes?"

"Yes. Jack. Just that way," he replied, wondering how she knew. He accepted the drink, sipped, and watched Sarah deliver Stenman's water. He sipped again.

"As I said," he began, "I'm pleased you listened to my analysis. Better lucky than smart, I guess."

"You are too modest, Peter, and it is we who are grateful," Sarah said. "Never before has someone so new to our organization contributed so much."

Morgan Stenman only nodded. In all the time Peter had known her, Stenman never said much. He marveled at how she seemed a master at having others speak on her behalf, as if telepathically directing the show. When Stenman blinked twice in rapid succession, Sarah continued: "This will be a multiple hundred million-dollar swing to the partnership. Tomorrow, Howard Muller will commence covering his short position. Once he has done so, you are free to initiate a long position. Morgan has authorized two hundred million additional to your trading book."

Peter gulped more bourbon. "But I've never taken a position over thirty million," he said.

Stenman spoke: "Do you know what the average bonus will be this year, for those in your trading room?"

Peter shook his head.

"It will average over a million." With that statement, Stenman went back to sipping water.

"I had no…" Peter's head shook, and his Adam's apple danced in his throat.

"Bonuses always have a component of seniority," Sarah said, picking up where Stenman left off. "Loyalty pays dividends. But with this PC transaction of yours, and a few other projects Morgan intends to put you on, you will be up there."

While Peter stood in stunned silence, Sarah Guzman reached for an envelope lying on the dining table. She opened it. "Having said that," she began as if given a self-delivered cue, "this is a convenient time to discuss another matter."

Peter tried to force a pleasant face. Looking at her made his pulse race so fast he felt winded.

"You are loyal, correct?" she asked.

"Yes," Peter said without hesitation.

Sarah's short brown skirt hiked as she moved towards him with slow, fine steps. She had white legs. Light glanced off one knee and highlighted a dark freckle that caught Peter's attention for a split second. When she stood beside him, she seemed a foot taller than her four-foot-eleven inches—she had a way of cocking and swaying her head so that she drew a man's attention down. In her hand she held an enlarged photo, but the image was turned away from Peter. Drops of sweat confirmed to him that something about this situation had activated his autonomous nervous system.

Stenman made her way to the dining table. She picked up a miniature toasted cracker—Beluga caviar was painted across its face in a heavy mound. Sarah waited for her to turn around before continuing. "We have had so much unwarranted attention over the years. The President of the United States calls Morgan Stenman the 'epitome of the American Dream.' He phones to ask for advice on economic and foreign affairs, even while the SEC harasses her."

"I understand," Peter lied.

"Then please, explain this to me...to us." Sarah waved the flopping photograph like a fan.

As Peter looked down at the outstretched hand—the faces on the photo damnably visible—his heart froze.

"This man spends his life attempting to ruin us. He works without agency sanction. Perhaps," Sarah said, "you could help us understand what he thinks he is after."

Peter attempted to respond, but first needed another sip of whiskey. While his brain unscrambled the implications, he stared at the man in the photo, standing over his table.

*You filthy SOB*, he silently swore.

---

Carlos Nuñoz, in room 203, watched Peter's expressions on the closed circuit television and listened, not so much to his words, as to the way he said them. When Peter left, a half-hour's explanation later, Carlos entered the room where the two women waited.

"*Nada*. He knows nothing," Carlos said. "At least not yet. Dawson's visit was a fishing expedition—no contact between the two since."

Stenman nodded.

"I also agree," Sarah said. "But if he ever learns anything, this could become a serious matter. Two of your operatives had to be dealt with because of what Hannah Neil provided the SEC."

"Fortunately not a material loss," Stenman said.

Carlos traced the scar lining his face, fingering the thickened skin as if it were a prize instead of a hideous wound. He remained silent, not yet contributing additional analysis.

"But Dawson," Sarah Guzman said, simultaneously looking at both Stenman and Carlos, "is kicking around because he believes more information exists and that Peter Neil might be a source."

Stenman exhaled a stream of smoke.

Sarah took a seat and crossed her legs. "It is possible Hannah Neil had more documents to implicate a wider network of your contacts. That would translate into serious disruptions. She might even have had documents implicating us directly. It is the unknowns I find troubling."

"What have you discovered about Agent Dawson's visit?" Stenman asked.

"He acted on his own," Sarah said. "Took time off, paid his own way. But it is clear he has identified Hannah Neil as the one who sent him those papers. Once we realized Dawson had requested and received his copies from the lab, we anticipated this development."

"Have you given any thought to taking care of this agent?" asked Stenman. It was clearly Carlos' question to answer.

Carlos glanced at Sarah without moving his head or blinking his eyes. She nodded, and Carlos redirected his attention to Stenman.

"*Sí, señora*," Carlos said, measuring his words, "but it would be a mistake. We cannot simply eliminate a man in his position, for the same reasons we did not make an example of *Señora* Neil. *Atención*. We do not crave unwarranted *atención*."

"*Atención*?" Stenman asked.

Carlos looked to Sarah. "Carlos is saying that people like Dawson cannot be dealt with in the same manner as others because of his visibility. He is now contained, and we do not wish to put a spotlight on him by eliminating him. It is best to give him a little more rope and let him hang himself."

"Continue," Stenman instructed.

"The Director of Enforcement will be made aware of the man's numerous departmental violations," Carlos said. "That should put him in a most uncomfortable position. It is *Señor* Neil we need to concentrate on now. If they prove necessary, we have backup plans. I give the credit to my uncle's wife." Carlos bowed to Sarah.

"Let's just say that if need be, we will turn sympathy away from Peter Neil," Sarah said.

"The details are not my concern," Stenman said, sipping her beverage. "Let's see how Peter reacts over the coming days. He will be made to decide if he is in, or if he is out."

"And don't forget Freeman Ranson," Sarah added. "He swears Dawson is at a dead end. When the director learns of his renegade activities, according to Ranson, he will be suspended or dismissed."

"Maybe," Carlos said.

"You are skeptical," Stenman said.

"It is my nature," Carlos replied. "I do believe *Señor* Neil has nothing now, but that may change one day."

"Let's see what happens," Stenman again suggested. "In the meantime, he seems close to Jason Ayers. I will encourage Jason to monitor the boy."

Carlos rose, went to stand behind Sarah, and put a hand on the back of her chair. "Now," he said, "I wish to discuss another important matter: *Señor* Muller. I believe your CIO is a risk."

Sarah nodded in Stenman's direction, an indication that she agreed with Carlos. She then stood, withdrew to the bar, poured a second glass of wine, sipped, and watched.

"You have a concern?" Stenman asked, showing no hint of surprise.

"*Sí, señora.* He is unstable. Did you know he has a wife? A Japanese woman. He keeps her a prisoner in his house. She is *esclava.*"

Stenman looked to Sarah.

"*Esclava*: slave. His wife is a slave—he treats her savagely. I have no sympathy for abuse of physically weaker beings."

"I understand." A slight frown worked its way onto Stenman's face. Sarah's father, Stenman recalled, had been an original investor, and Stenman had known Sarah since she was a young girl. How her father could have done those things to Sarah was beyond comprehension, and for his despicable acts, Stenman hated the very memory of David Brigston. That Sarah had usually directed her brutality towards powerful men, including her eradicated father, and her vanquished husband, came as no surprise, Stenman thought.

As Stenman's attention refocused on their conversation, Carlos continued, "Not only that, but Muller gives too many interviews. He is drawing attention to himself. I understand he has reached a deal to have a ghost-writer author his autobiography."

"He has crossed that fine line," Sarah agreed with Carlos, "between positive publicity—humanitarian aid, testimony to Congress on matters of national significance, even the occasional interview—and dangerous self-promotion. He touts his investment performance, never suggesting that he may have taken a significant loss on a position."

At the head of the long dining room table, Stenman faced the other two and nodded. "We must not appear omniscient. But, Carlos, I know your personal animosity towards Howard. This remains strictly business, I trust."

"What we do—in our business—must have a rationale that puts our business first. His actions do not. That is why he is a risk."

"I agree we need to maintain discipline," Morgan said.

"And to directly answer your question, *Señora* Stenman, business is *always* business. I hold that first and foremost. If he becomes a larger liability, I may come to you one day and…" Carlos shrugged, his arms and hands bent out and up.

"That is our relationship," Stenman said. "We discuss problems and solutions. Hopefully, all these matters will get resolved in an unspectacular manner. If not, then not. Now, are we settled on this?"

"Yes." Sarah spoke for both herself and Carlos.

"We have another matter to take up this evening. After we have had our dinner, Mr. Ayers will join us to explain more fully. I have initiated a new system of fund transfer that will require us to open new banking accounts."

"New accounts?" Sarah asked, taking her seat. "Our system—your system—has proven effective. When regulators have sought to understand our activities, they have become lost. Why the change?"

"This process will allow us to move money instantly, by phone."

Sarah shook her head. "With maximum security?"

Stenman nodded.

A knock on the door interrupted them. Stenman looked at the screen to her right. A waiter stood with a room service tray stacked with aluminum domes, waiting to begin serving dinner. She activated the door. After setting out smoked salmon and fresh sliced vegetables, the waiter disappeared.

Once the door clicked and locked shut, Sarah picked up where they left off. "How is this transfer possible?"

"Mr. Ayers will explain in detail, but it involves biometrics—speech recognition."

"This is reliable?" Carlos asked, holding a fork with a slice of pink fish.

"Yes," Stenman said. "I am satisfied. We provide specific voice instructions to our banks. They include a statement of transfer, and the account numbers. When we phone in, and after we key in account information, we provide precise verbal instructions. An unauthorized voice will freeze the account. The machinery recognizes our voice patterns, intonations…it is as good as fingerprinting."

"If what you say is correct," Sarah continued, "this means that in the event of an investigation, you could empty all accounts in minutes. Move every penny to other locations."

Stenman again nodded. "If you agree, we will set up these accounts over the next days and weeks."

"I like the concept," Sarah said. "Let's eat. After, I look forward to learning more."

"On another matter," Stenman began, her tone light, her accent non-existent. "I believe Mr. Neil was captivated by you." Her mouth widened. "But then, what man isn't?"

"Only my nephew—" Sarah winked at Carlos and couldn't resist a rare smile "—and, of course, my husband's brother, Fernando. He does not much care for me, does he, Carlos?"

Stenman didn't understand why, but Carlos began an unholy laugh. She had never seen the ugly boy express even a molecule of happiness before this. The cackle was joy, laced with evil. For several seconds, Carlos remained lost in whatever hilarity possessed him.

# CHAPTER SIXTEEN

JASON AYERS STUFFED HIS BRIEFCASE WITH MATERIALS EXPLAINING HOW speech recognition worked. This was to be a $20 million investment in equipment so expensive and state-of-the-art as to be out of the reach of practically anyone in the world—Stenman excepted. With billions passing through the hedge fund's doors, and a ten- to twenty-percent performance fee regularly siphoned off, an investment that hurtled funds to the correct offshore accounts at electronic speed was worth ten times the price. Not to mention the additional attractiveness to those wishing to export assets. Ayers finished his scotch and poured himself another. He looked out the library window at the half-moon and stars.

"So many mistakes," he said to himself. "Too late."

How had he arrived at this sorry state? Thirty years with Morgan Stenman, that's how. In the beginning, he set up tax havens for her. In the mid-eighties, things changed. The markets came alive and everybody seemed anxious to sell information, to get their piece of the pie. With Stenman's international connections, the world was hers for the plucking, and she plucked away with unbridled enthusiasm and success. It proved so damn easy. She started in a big way with her Eastern European connections, many of whom had relocated to Australia, where they owned and ran companies—and seemed eager to share their insights with her.

Then came the development of unregulated third-world markets— Latin America, Russia, the other countries of the former Soviet Union, and Asia. Stenman's hundred million dollars in humanitarian contributions made for good public relations, but were much more valuable as down-payments on political influence and information. She owned a piece of important people in every corner of the world.

The seduction of Jason Ayers had been both methodical and incremental. First, he defended Stenman and her funds from prosecution—that was his job. Next, he helped shelter certain activities by setting up offshore havens, thus avoiding future prosecution. Done with civility, these activities amounted to rule-bending rather than law-breaking—at least until the

Russian Syndicate—the *Mafiya*—and the South American cartel monies came in and raised the stakes. With this current crop of client, things had grown beyond dangerous. Amoral operatives dealt in drugs, carbines, sub-machine guns, missiles, uranium, biological weaponry, and everything else deadly and illegal that brought in big money. With their billion-dollar-a-week cash flows, these criminal financiers needed to launder funds, and thought nothing of eliminating life to protect their interests: Hannah Neil, Erik Cannodine, Stanley Drucker, and hundreds of others. Each elimination sent a message to others: *Don't fuck with us.* Ayers knew they owned him, now and forever. They held his family as leverage. Everybody's family was leverage. Even if he wanted to, he would never find a way out.

He clamped shut his briefcase, stood, put his eyeglasses on, buttoned his coat, smoothed his hair. A legal robot, programmed to do whatever the hell they told him to do. He and his partners were automatons, at the beck and call of Morgan Stenman and, more recently, Sarah Guzman. Soulless machines, they all pretended to be above the fray, but actually operated in a world of legal nihilism.

The phone rang, stabbing his eardrums. Ayers hated evening calls. He had phoned Hannah repeatedly the night she'd died, never reaching her. Since then, death and murder hung in the air each and every night, permeating his brain with the stench of ether.

*Ring. Ring. Ring.* He picked up but gave no greeting.

"Father?"

*Thank God.* It was Kate.

"Daddy? Are you there?"

His heart melted. She hadn't called him "Daddy" since childhood.

"Hello, Sweetheart," he said. "I was just on my way out. A meeting. Is everything okay?"

"I passed the Bar. I'm a lawyer."

Ayers collapsed into a leather-bound chair. "That is wonderful news. I am...what am I? More than happy. I am speechless. What are your plans?"

"I've been offered a position with the Los Angeles Public Defender's office. I plan to accept."

"Are you sure? You could go into private practice. With your grades—"

"I have no interest—you already know that. I have other news."

Ayers also knew not to argue with her. "News? I hope it's good."

"I'm engaged. I'll be getting married in January."

"Married?" The suddenness of the announcement and her intonation troubled him. He tried to disguise his suspicions. "This is a surprise, Kathryn. Who's the lucky man?"

"The professor I worked with on the textbook—you haven't met him. Frederick Drammonds."

The name Frederick sounded ancient. "How old is he?"

"Not that it matters, but he's forty-two."

"That's sixteen years older than you…" Ayers regretted his words.

"Please, Father. Let's not get into it."

"Are you happy?" he asked.

"Of course," she said, not sounding happy. "I'm engaged to a steady man. He's kind, he knows what he wants, and he wants me."

"Dear?"

"Yes," Kate said laconically.

"I'm pleased, of course. And…"

"And what, Father?"

"I'm sorry for the way I treated you. That I told you to quit seeing Peter."

"I forgave you a long time ago. You were right. He turned out to be…"

Silence. Seconds passed. Ayers thought Kate might be holding her breath. His heart wrenched against his breastbone.

"I, uh, I need to call Mom. Tell her."

Kate hung up.

Ayers thought he understood some things about Peter Neil that had escaped Kate's notice. Peter had lost everyone he ever cared for. That made commitment for him especially difficult. He nearly imparted this information to Kate, hoping to make her feel better. He was glad he hadn't. Peter was a topic better avoided.

Clutching his briefcase as if it were a life preserver, Ayers plunged into the endless darkness. Half an hour later, he methodically explained speech recognition—and how it worked—to the three people in his life who frightened him more than death itself.

---

Peter arrived home at six-thirty, still unsettled over what had happened in Stenman's office.

*Dawson, Dawson, Dawson.*

The name stuck in his head like gum on a shoe.

*What an asshole.*

His anxiety made sense. If they happened to find out that the agent—the man with a compulsive desire to tear them down—was in town, poking around, they'd naturally get someone to follow him. Tailing Dawson resulted in that picture of their meeting at the sports-bar. Thankfully, whoever trailed Dawson that night never made it to Sammy's Restaurant. If they had pictures of that meeting, Peter could never explain why he'd run down a railroad track to meet the pain in the ass.

As he entered the kitchen, the message machine strobed. He hit play: "Peter, it's Ellen Goodman. Please call. You're a sweetheart."

"What the hell?" He erased the message. Things were getting worse rather than better.

He hadn't been sweet. He hadn't been anything. They hadn't even talked since the day of their breakup. And the nicest thing Ellen had said that day was that he was a born loser and would regret what he was doing.

After ordering in a pizza, he hesitated, then dialed Ellen's number. Might as well get to the bottom of this now, he decided.

"Hello." Her voice sang.

"Peter. Returning your call."

"I love the cat."

"What cat?"

"The calico. He looks like a young Henry."

Peter glanced at Henry, the furry, fifteen-year-old ball of shedding, gray fur now ensconced in a corner of the living room sofa. "You have a cat?" he asked.

"Of course, Peter. And I'm sorry for having said what I said. We got along most of the time, didn't we?"

"No, Ellen, we hardly ever got along."

"Stop being funny. I hear you're doing really well at your new job. Gosh, Peter, I was a fool to let you get away. I'm glad you—"

In the background, Peter heard a faint purring and interrupted Ellen. "What did you mean when you said I was sweet?"

"Giving me the cat. I named him Peter, after you."

"I didn't give you a cat."

"Of course you did. Are you're trying to be mean?"

"No. Someone else gave you that animal. Try Craig Hinton."

He'd hit a raw nerve, knew Ellen was combusting—he'd heard her huffing before—and promptly hung up.

"Sorry, Ellen," he said to himself, "but I'm not going to get re-involved. No way."

The phone rang. Peter lifted the receiver, then put it back down. He lifted a second time and left the handset uncradled on the coffee table. He took a cushion from the sofa and softened the beeping sounds meant to alert him that his phone was off the hook. When the line went dead, he reassembled his sofa, leaving his phone inoperable.

Two hours later, Peter and Henry dragged themselves to bed. The anvil that was Peter's head hit the pillow, hard. In half a minute—as if on anesthesia—he went under.

---

The following morning, the radio woke Peter to an upbeat oldies tune. He punched the off button. "G'morning, Henry," he said. The cat felt heavy on his feet. "Time to rise and shine. I feel marvelous." He sung the words as he slid his feet into his slippers, pushed himself to his feet, and stretched.

"I love going to work, Henry. I love you, Henry." He ruffled the animal's head-hair. Henry slid off the bed.

As the two shuffled towards the bathroom for inspection, Peter said, "Hope there aren't any ill effects from the tête-a-tête with the boss yesterday. They seemed satisfied, even happy, with me."

At that moment, Peter felt a throb against the base of his skull.

"Nothing prophetic," he told himself.

---

Peter decided Stuart was right. About everything.

For a week, Muller needled and bullied Peter—did everything he could to rattle him. Howard Muller hated him, and that hatred became supernatural in its intensity. At the beginning of the following week, after several companies confirmed what Peter had already uncovered through research, PC stocks soared. Including what he saved Stenman Partners on Muller's short position, the firm's profit tallied over three hundred million.

On Friday of that week, Howard Muller summoned Peter into his Civil War museum.

"You have made a big mistake, Neil," Muller began.

"I'm sorry, but I tried to talk to you first—"

Muller stood. "Your job was to make a convincing argument to me, not Stenman. You never usurp my authority. That is insubordination."

Peter wondered if Muller actually believed such tripe.

"You will regret this," Muller continued. "Thinking you're so damn brilliant, above it all. Watching your back won't do a damn bit of good, either, you miserable nothing."

"Listen, Howard, I didn't mean—"

"Go to hell, Neil."

Peter almost smiled. This was a game he had never played before, but one in which he suddenly felt comfortable. He had four-of-a-kind, and no matter how much bluff and bluster Fat-Head chose to display, four-of-a-friggin'-kind was a three-hundred million-dollar winner.

"Get out," Muller continued.

Peter obliged without further comment.

---

On the following Tuesday, Stenman phoned Peter. "At nine tonight," she said, "you will assist me. Do not be late."

The rest of the day, Peter's head swam in roiled waters. He tried to figure out the implications. First, he hoped he had nothing more to fear from the Dawson incident. More importantly, everyone knew Stenman handpicked only a few traders to work directly with her. He hoped tonight was a first step towards bigger things. If so, the timing was perfect. In less than two months, bonuses would be paid. How much would be in his check? A few hundred thousand? A half million? A million?

"Hey, dude," Stuart whispered in the middle of Peter's financial what-if's. "You and I have a small problem that's got to be taken care of, today."

"Huh? Whatta you mean?" Peter asked, the spell broken. He looked at his quote machine and tried to figure out if any of his positions were under water.

"We're both short Uhlander Pharmaceutical."

"So?" Peter's attention shot to his selective ticker. UHLN scrolled across his screen, trading up thirty cents on the day—no big deal. "Stock's a dog, going lower—Chapter 11 bankruptcy was how you phrased it last week when we initiated our short. Remember that discussion, Stuey?"

"Yeah. I was wrong."

"You had a guy on the inside who said they were out of cash, and unable to raise any more in the market. I checked last quarter's 10Q, called the company—your guy was right." Peter looked at his position: short four hundred thousand shares at sixteen bucks; stock currently at fourteen and change; long two thousand put contracts representing another two hundred thousand shares. All a bet that the stock would trade much lower.

Stuart continued in a whisper. "Give me a friggin' break, dude. Things change. At least I stay on top of my positions—and yours, I might add—unlike mammoth skull over there." He pointed a forefinger in Muller's direction. "I'm told a pharmaceutical out of Switzerland is going to make a takeover bid at twenty-six. They don't care if there's no cash—they want the patents. Bid's coming end of next week."

"Shit," was all Peter could manage. If true, he stood to lose over four million on the position, plus another four million on soon-to-be worthless puts.

"We gotta move," Stuart said.

"You sure about your information, Stu?"

"Come on, Petey. I don't bullshit my friends. Yeah, I'm sure. I got you into this one…but all's well that ends well. We'll cover and get long. End up making money."

"I don't know. Where'd you get the information?"

"Where you think? The Swiss buyer's banker is a contact. Came right out of the bowels of Stratton Brothers' Corporate Finance Department."

"Christ, Almighty. We can't sit around and do nothing."

"We'll split purchases and cover the short. Here," Stuart said, handing Peter a buy-ticket. "I'll get started after you fill in your ticket."

Peter wrote the stock symbol, then coded the ticket with his trading account.

"After we've flattened the short, we'll get long some calls through the offshore accounts—end up making some money on this thing. We'll stay long some puts in case someone asks later—though that ain't gonna happen. But *if* it does, we can claim the whole thing's some kind of esoteric hedge."

"How long to cover?"

"Two days, maybe a little longer. Still plenty of time to get set up."

"And the bid's not coming until the end of next week?" Peter asked.

"Scheduled for the weekend after next."

"This sucks. One day we're certain they're going under, the next we're scrambling to keep from getting ripped a new asshole."

Stuart grinned. "You sure learned to talk the talk. Whodda thought that when you carried your Opie-from-Mayberry ass into this hell-hole six months ago?"

"Cut the bull," Peter said, wishing to concentrate on the excitement promised tonight, working with Stenman. "Let's cover and recover. We're not here to lose money."

"Ain't that the truth, brother?" Stuart said. "The ever-loving truth."

# CHAPTER SEVENTEEN

PETER ARRIVED HOME SEVERAL HOURS EARLIER THAN USUAL. Henry greeted him at the door.

"Hey, dude," Peter began. "Sorry, Henry. I'm starting to sound like Stuart. How you doing, old man?"

Peter looked around his new place. Cool temperatures marked the month of November, but once the morning fog burnt off around eleven a.m., the days brightened and the evenings remained clear. Through the sliding glass door facing south and west, he had a dual view of the finish line at the Del Mar Thoroughbred Club and the white waters of Dog Beach. Living more than a dream come true, Peter sometimes felt the need to pinch himself.

"Can you imagine living on the East Coast, Henry?" he asked. "Temperature's near zero. I'm complaining about fifty degrees, and they're at zippity-do-dah."

Peter walked by the gas fireplace and inhaled the odor of wet lacquer. His interior decorator—borrowed from Stuart—had decided to apply a maple finish to his pine mantle. It didn't look any better than before, Peter thought, only darker and smellier. Through the kitchen door, he traipsed to his refrigerator, opened, and grabbed a beer and a pack of processed meat. Henry stared in at the shelves, his green eyes locking on a half-gallon of milk.

"Yeah, you too," Peter said, balancing the milk, an imported beer, and a package of chicken slices.

Setting everything on the new kitchen table, Peter slipped off his sports jacket and laid it over a reclining chair that faced his fifty-inch high definition television. He opened the curtains to a window showcasing the mountains. In the mornings, in the east, he had the explosion of sunrise through one vantage point. In the evenings, he could watch the sun, sinking below the horizon, in a furious blaze to the west. One hundred and eighty-degree views of paradise. Peter had always assured himself, in the unlikely event he ever came into the chips, he would never change his lifestyle.

Now that he had money, he understood the psychological underpinnings of that rationalization: it was something people with nothing said to control their envy. Having a view to end all views and owning new, wonderful toys wasn't necessarily an evil thing. Kate Ayers was a perfect example. She had an expensive Jaguar, grew up in a mansion with everything laid in her lap, and yet she was as good and pure a person as existed on this earth. Suddenly, thinking about purity, the image of Peter's mother filtered through as a dose of reality. Drew had often said that Hannah was the purest person he had ever known. Peter agreed. And he suspected she wouldn't completely approve of the way he currently lived. The excess. The extravagance.

Peter turned the twist cap on his beer. Foam crept over the lip as he tipped and gulped. He then rolled several skinny slices of salty, processed meat and bit just as Henry purred.

"I know—your turn." Peter poured a generous helping of whole milk into Henry's bowl, then sniffed. "Litter box is smelling a tad ripe, old man—even from here."

He set his beer on the oak coffee table and went to the second bathroom. Henry's bathroom. Peter held his breath and lifted the litter box. Exiting the front door, he proceeded down the six steps, around the corner of a storage building, and across the driveway he shared with four other condos—attached in pods of two—to a dumpster.

Finishing his litter disposal task, he retraced his steps. At his door, a black man, wearing a Charger football cap finished off by graying hair, stared through the open crack in Peter's door. The man was stooped, even hunched, as if he carried an invisible sack of rocks on his neck and back. He began calling in a tentative voice, "Mr. Neil? Mr. Neil? You home, Mr. Neil?"

When Peter got to the bottom of his steps, he heard: "Mr. Neil, it's Charles Jefferson. Guy living in your mama's house." Jefferson craned his head and neck though the front door.

Until he heard those words, Peter hadn't been conscious of how tense he'd become. Remnants of his earlier brush with violence, he guessed.

"Mr. Jefferson," he called.

The man spun, a wide-eyed look of fear on his face.

"Thank the Lord it's you, Mr. Neil. I was afraid you gone and left your door open and somebody think I tryin' steal your stuff."

"What're you doing here? Rent's not due. Is everything okay at the house?"

"Yes, sir, Mr. Neil. It look good as you can believe. I got me a part-time job—nothin' much, but at a nursery, movin' stuff, waterin' plants and all. Maybe turn into full-time after a month. But I got me half-price on some plants. I put 'em into the ground—they look good. You don't like 'em, you can take 'em out, y'know."

"No, no. I'm sure they're fine. Let me pay you for them."

"No way. You the kindest man I ever knowed. No. If I get full-time, I gonna pay you more rent money."

"Forget it."

Peter noticed Jefferson's beat-up car in one of the visitor's spots along the outer boundary of the condo common grounds. He owned a VW bug, and not of the recent retro variety either. Primer and rust spots highlighted jagged holes in the body, and random cracks webbed the windshield. On the bumper, a sticker read, *God is Great.*

"Are the bushes the reason you drove all the way out here?" Peter asked.

"Huh? Uh, no. This."

Peter climbed the steps and stood next to his tenant. Charles Jefferson held something in his thick hands—the hands of an honest worker, Peter decided. Callused with split nails. Jefferson, probably not quite forty-five, had gnarled and arthritic fingers. His bristled cheeks had three or four nicking scars, looking like pink worms against his pitch-black skin. He extended an envelope for Peter to take.

"You brought a letter?" Peter asked.

"It was addressed to your mama. Said *urgent, final notice* on the outside. I was afraid it was a bill and you might get your car or TV or something else taken by the repossessors."

"Thanks, Mr. Jefferson. How about you come in and join me in a beer or a cup of coffee?" Peter skimmed the outside of the envelope. The letter had been sent from a mailbox business in Carlsbad.

"No, I couldn't. But thank you, sir. I gotta go to work now. Working just east of here at the mall on Via de la Valle." He pronounced the name of the street phonetically, so that Valle came across as *valley* instead of *va-yeah.*

"I know the place," Peter said. "Good luck, Charles. And please, call me Peter. I hate being called Mister Neil."

"Thank you, sir." Charles said. "Come by sometime. See the house. Stay for dinner. Please."

"I'd like that, Charles. Say hello to the family."

Charles nodded, then plodded down the steps. Peter watched him amble to his car. It took several tries before the engine coughed itself into ignition. They waved goodbye, then Peter, stepping inside, opened the letter. It read:

> This is a final notice. Your mailbox, number 408, has a balance due of $23.77. If you wish to maintain this mailing address, please contact our office no later than November 23. After that date, we will no longer accept letters on your behalf. Any mail already in your box will be held for two weeks, then returned to sender.

A name and phone number accompanied the note. He had two days before they would close his mother's account. Why, Peter wondered, had she leased a mailbox in Carlsbad? That was at least a twenty-minute drive from her house. It made no sense. *Carlsbad*? His mother had died in Carlsbad. Was that a coincidence?

Peter phoned. He learned that his mother had rented an oversized space with a rental rate of just over twenty dollars a month, before tax. She had paid in advance for seven months. The seven months ended a week ago.

"Is there anything in the box?" Peter asked.

"I do not know. I will check." The woman had an East Indian accent. She had indicated that she and her husband owned the franchise and hated to close out an active box and disrupt a person's mail. They understood people often forgot when their leases ran out. That's why they always sent notices and allowed a grace period.

A few seconds later, she returned. "Yes, Mr. Neil. There is mail. Two registered envelopes. It appears we signed for them and your mother saw them, but put them into her box. That is a strange procedure."

"I don't get it," Peter said. "The registered mail arrived at your office?"

"Yes, it was many months ago—in late March. I noticed when I peeked into her box for you just now. We signed and notified Ms. Hannah Neil. The letters still rest there."

"Anything else in the mailbox?"

"Oh, yes. A letter, also. It is addressed to you, in care of Hannah Neil. And some pizza ads and all."

"Thank you. How do I get the combination to the mailbox?"

"Oh, no. Not a combination. A key."

"My mother is dead. How do I get into her box if I don't have the key?"

"Oh, my. I do not know. Perhaps a court order, unless you have the key. If you have the key, you just put it in the lock, turn, and open. It is simple. I cannot give you another key—that is very against the law. A court order, perhaps."

"Would you do me another favor?" Peter asked.

"If I can, though I hope this means you will pay the overdue bill."

"Yes. I'll pay. Can you check the date of the postmark on the letter addressed to me? Also the return address on the envelope."

It took a few minutes for the singsong voice to return. "It has a postmark of May the twenty-five. The return address is Clairemont." She recited his mother's address.

Peter hung up.

Thursday, May the twenty-fifth?

That would be the same May twenty-fifth stamped on Hannah Neil's death certificate.

———

Peter prepared for his nine p.m. trading rendezvous with Morgan with as much of a nap as he could manage. When he woke at eight o'clock, he had just enough time to get ready. He felt better, but still had nagging concerns. His mother had sent him a letter the same morning she met him outside his workplace, to a mailbox he had no knowledge of until today. And registered letters, tucked away for months. Why? None of it made any sense.

It was dark outside and, with the window open, Peter's room felt clammy cold. His boxers and tee-shirt provided him marginal insulation as he lurched out of bed, feet hurting as if he'd wandered an entire day and night in search of something lost. His hands shook and his jaw vibrated in a futile attempt to generate enough energy to ward off the chill. A few moments later, steam filled the shower. Peter slapped his forehead into the palms of his hands, using the heel of each hand to grind his temples.

Thoughts of the letters brought to mind Charles Jefferson, and the image haunted Peter. It disturbed him that this kind man had so much enthusiasm for every small blessing—happy for a shitty part-time job, and excited about working on someone else's house. On top of that, he had a *God is Great* sticker plastered to his decrepit car bumper. What great things had God done for Charles Jefferson and his impoverished family lately? *None*, was the answer. Poor, ignorant man didn't even know enough to be miserable.

"Stop it." Peter lifted his head in time to see Henry arch his back in reaction to those echoing words. "Sorry, Henry. I was scolding myself. Charles Jefferson isn't the stupid one."

Henry left the bathroom humidity. Peter kicked the door closed, pulled his shirt over his head, removed his slippers, and stood, facing the steamed mirror. He smeared the condensation with the ball of his fist. Through the streaks, he barely recognized the reflection staring back.

Forty-five minutes later, Peter grabbed his keys and started to bound out. He felt better. Refreshed.

"Melancholy gone," he said to Henry. "A blue funk brought on by...nothing. See you tomorrow, old man."

For the thousandth time since someone stole it, Peter rubbed his finger and thumb together, imagining he still possessed his father's gift. When he got close enough to his car, he pressed the button on his key chain. It produced the beep that locked and unlocked the door: lock, unlock, lock, unlock. The action triggered something in the underbelly of his subconscious. What was it? He bounced and jangled the six keys up and down. He climbed into his car, shut the door, and felt for the ignition key.

"Not that one," he said, working to the next key. "Not this small one, either..."

Suddenly, the ripples of an obscure memory spread, reaching finally to a specific time and place: his mother's kitchen, next to the answering machine, the afternoon of the day he learned of her death. He had discovered two keys—one to her destroyed car, the other smaller. At the time, Peter had assumed the second key unlocked a drawer or box somewhere in her house. Turning on the car light, he ran his finger along the jagged edge, recalling his conversation with the Carlsbad mailbox woman. She had said, "Not a combination, but a key" opened the mailbox. Inside was some registered mail and a letter addressed to him.

Needing to hurry, Peter put his curiosity on hold as he inserted the car key and listened to the low hum of his precision engine. Fifteen minutes later, he parked under the bright lights and cameras at Stenman's offices. Two minutes after that, he signed in. Another forty-five seconds and he entered the hallway leading to Morgan Stenman's office. As unobtrusively as possible, he walked in. There, a series of pulsating lights from an endless row of machines—each one tied into some important event, somewhere in the world—greeted him. The show both dizzied and captivated his imagination.

Within the hour, he had dismissed the relevance of his mailbox discovery. He was too busy making history.

---

In her office, Stenman had one other trader present. An old guy, looking maybe seventy, and skinny as a skeleton, sat in a corner. The man's name was Hans. He handled currency trades.

Hans had no social graces.

Before tonight, Peter hadn't even realized that Indonesia's currency was the *rupiah*. Since he'd arrived two hours ago, Stenman and her trader had bought and sold *rupiah* in mind-numbing quantities—over a billion dollars' worth. It seemed hectic, but this was nothing compared to what she expected later, Stenman explained.

"We've only trickled the marketplace—we will shortly flood the worthless piece of shit currency—when it serves our purposes. We are toying with, testing, the Indonesian Central Bank's moronic resolve."

It was as long an explanation of anything he had ever gotten from Stenman, and he doubted she was even aware of speaking to him. When phone extension 4666 flashed, Peter punched the button before the second flash. Stenman's earlier instructions filled his head: "Answer the phone, listen, then repeat everything back to me. Exactly as said."

The accented voice whispered rapidly against his ear, "They are near panic. They've used a billion in hard. U.S., Euro, and Yen—two hundred of each left. Gold sales completed two hours ago. Our meeting set to begin in ten."

The line went dead. Peter feared he hadn't been able to listen and note-take as fast as the man had spoken. It was as if he were listening to a non-stop message left on an answering machine, but without the luxury of a replay button.

"Let's have it, Neil," Stenman barked, her features screwed in a tight ball. "Exactly as said. Do not miss a word."

Peter had scribbled the confusing parts on a slip of paper: *billion in hard, U.S. and Yen and Eur under two hundred each.*

He began: "The man said: 'They're panicked. They've spent...' no, he said: 'they've *used* a billion in hard.'" He studied Stenman, hoping this made sense. It seemed to, so he continued, "U.S. and Yen and..." he hesitated, unable to decipher his own handwriting. Guessing, he continued, "and Euro under two hundred. I mean, under two hundred each. Definitely *each*."

He filled his lungs. It was two hundred *each*, he prayed.

"Anything else?" Stenman asked, her impatience a guillotine hanging over his head.

"Yes. Gold sales completed two hours ago...the man then said: 'We have a meeting set to begin in ten.'"

"That is all?" Stenman asked, her voice intolerant.

That *was* all. *Right?* He asked himself.

"Yes. Nothing else," he answered.

"Good. Hans, offer five hundred U.S. equivalents. Let's see how that affects their thought process." Stenman licked her crusty lips, then put the filter tip to her mouth. She inhaled, then exhaled in several tiny bites, filling the room with nicotine vapor.

Peter continued to stare at 4666.

A moment later, Hans said, "They bought. Man unhappy." Dutchman Hans, on the other hand, laughed like a hyena picking on antelope bones.

"Unhappy? Yes, I think the poor man is filled with nuclear angst," Stenman said with a voice soaked in manic hyperbole. "After eating your offering, that leaves less than half a billion hard," she continued. "They have just flatlined."

Hans nodded. "No IMF. No U.S. Treasury. No bailout. Maybe they call you to ask for advice."

"They aren't going to need me. Devaluation, austerity, fiscal responsibility, economic upheaval. Shit happens."

Hans nodded. "We make money from the inevitable," he said.

Fifteen minutes passed. Extension 4666 flashed a second time. Peter pounced.

The same mysterious voice whispered, "One last request to the IMF for ten billion. Treasury already no. If not, a big, big percent." Again, the line went dead and again the man had set a world record for fast-talk.

"Goddammit, Peter! Spit it out!" Stenman yelled.

Peter had yet to put the phone down. In a rapid run-on, he blurted, "A last request to the IMF. Requesting ten billion. The Treasury said no…"

Peter hesitated for a long second. He had misspoken. It wasn't "The Treasury said no," it was "Treasury *already* no."

"If not—" he concluded, praying to God the slight error had not been meaningful "—a big, big percent."

Stenman picked up an outgoing line, and dialed. "Transfer me to Mauritius." Fifteen seconds passed. Then she said, "Scramble this line." Another few seconds. "Patch me through to…" she recited a lengthy international number. Finally, she said, "They received the request?" She listened, then continued, "Just as you promised. Good. Nothing."

Stenman hung up and asked Hans: "How much *rupiah* do we have left on this loan?"

"One point two U.S.," he said.

"Offer it all. We break the bank, now."

A minute later, Hans turned, flashing bright yellow teeth. "They no longer pay the support—the *rupiah* is bullshit. Look," he said, pointing to his currency screen, "chaos. It has happened."

A little later, Peter studied his Reuters. The headlines read:

**INDONESIA DEVALUES RUPIAH**

**INDONESIA TO ANNOUNCE CUTBACKS IN GOVERNMENT-SPONSORED PROGRAMS— INCLUDING LAYOFFS**

**CAPITAL FLEES INDONESIA**

"That's it," Stenman celebrated. She then said something in German.

Hans laughed at her words while Peter smiled and nodded and played along as if he too spoke German and understood. Maybe he *didn't* get the literal meaning of things, but he *did* understand, and he did share in the joy of the moment. He had arrived, finally, at the top of the mountain and, he discovered, the mountain was made of piles and piles of U.S. greenbacks.

As Peter continued to watch and listen to Hans, he put the mathematical side of his brain to work. He had overheard Hans mention they had borrowed a total of eight billion dollars in *rupiah* over the past two weeks. With now-current levels of devaluation, that meant Stenman Partners stood to clear something like $2 billion in profit by buying the Indonesian currency back at discounted prices and repaying the loan. Good work if you can get it, he mused.

---

Half the night later, Stenman said, "Peter, pick up the phone. Hans will feed you the words—you will learn new lessons."

Hans looked at Peter as if he were toilet throw-up. "You," he said to Peter, "call Bank of…"

For the remainder of the night, Peter learned his new lessons. He sat, spoke, yelled, and did everything they told him to do within the rarified confines of Morgan Stenman's office. He learned the meaning of previously nonsensical words like "pips" and "cross-rates" and "interest-rate differentials." He bought, then sold, then bought back currency at lower prices. Nobody in the markets understood what Stenman and her traders— including a new guy, Peter Neil—were up to. Stuart had said that they used smoke and mirrors in every major transaction. It now made complete sense to Peter. He was a magician confounding the masses.

When he finished with the *rupiah* in London's panicked marketplace, several hours later, Peter reached a decision: he was happy. His former life was a million miles away. He had participated in bringing down a country's central bank, and watched his employer make two billion dollars. Two billion was two thousand million dollars. Two million thousand dollars. He no longer had debts. Had money in the bank. He had made good in a tough world. His career would soon whiz past his friend Stuart's, and maybe soon he would be out from under Howard Muller's control. Agent Dawson was a clown. No longer a concern. All was good. Very, very good. It couldn't get any better than this. Soon, *he'd* be making some of these decisions. Have important people afraid of what was on *his* mind.

Peter couldn't help himself. He grinned until his face hurt.

---

"Adrenaline ought to be sold in bottles," Peter said to Stuart as he folded himself into his desk chair at six a.m., having come straight from Morgan's office. "Best damn drug in the world."

The euphoria had yet to subside, and Peter fidgeted with the aftereffects.

"Where you been?" Stuart asked.

"Making history. You hear about Indonesia, overnight?"

"Do I look deaf, dumb, and blind? Of course I heard, dude—it's got the world topsy-turvy. Latin American markets are going to get crushed— the usual ripple effect. The Crash of '87 is going to be a pancake breakfast in comparison. By the by, we're short those markets: lucky, eh?" He meant his grin to be conspiratorial. "Everyone's assuming that the domino effect will force other developing markets to devalue. U.S. Treasuries: up two points in a flight to quality. Fortunately," Stuart winked, "we were also long Treasury futures up our assholes."

The statement reminded Peter of Oliver Dawson's comments. He'd made a similar reference to Treasuries when describing his aborted investigation of Stenman.

"Whatta you know about the *rupiah* situation?" Stuart asked.

"Nothing," Peter lied. "I reckon Stenman Partners might be a player, is all."

"Already on the news wires, Sherlock. Everybody's calling this another of Morgan's brilliant plays. A few politicians are crying rivers, though."

"Why should they care?"

"These flaming liberal a-holes say that with unemployment and flight of capital out of these countries after they devalue, their economies are going to circle the drain and the poor people will get poorer, blah, blah,

blah. It's bullshit. All Morgan does—at least this is the party line—is speed up the inevitable. Push governments to do what they should have done in the first place."

"Isn't that the truth?"

"Sure, Petey. Truth. We're a bastion of truth, justice, and the American way." Stuart swiped his nose.

"You're getting an earlier and earlier start with that shit, Stuart. Market's not even open yet."

"An appetizer. Enough to give me a mental edge. Look…"

He pointed to a news story indicating that market rumors suggested that Brazil would devalue the *real* against the U.S. dollar within forty-eight hours. Their debt, according to the text, had traded down to forty cents on the dollar, and they had applied to the U.S. Treasury and the IMF for loans to support their currency. According to the wire service reporter who wrote the story, receiving aid was unlikely.

"This'll be interesting," Stuart said. "Guy advising the Brazilian government used to work for Morgan as an economist."

"Stenman and Muller—they seem to be connected everywhere. Or am I overstating things?" Peter asked.

"Nope. The answer is: everywhere. And I mean, everywhere. By the way, we should have the Uhlander Pharm thing covered by end of day. You want me to handle your end?"

"Sure. Makes more sense to consolidate our order." Peter stamped and filled out a buy-ticket. He handed it to Stuart. "Thanks. I shouldn't have gotten so hot yesterday when you mentioned the takeover. You saved me some significant money."

"Not that you need it after all the money you made on the PC play. Maybe in an hour or two—you know, as a little payback for my looking after you all the time—you could cover for me while I take a conference room recess."

Peter agreed, but not before advising Stuart again to take it easy. "You're going overboard with that shit."

"No such thing, dude."

By two in the afternoon, Peter's all-nighter had caught up with him. He headed home with jelly-legged exhaustion one hour after the market closed. He zipped past the state park and the stretch of beach heading north from Stenman Partners' La Jolla location. Although mentally burned-out, he purposely passed the turn to his co-op and made the decision to continue up the coast. Fifteen minutes later, he reached the mail depot where his mother had an address. What was her box number? Four hundred and something—405 or 406? For reasons he didn't understand, his fatigue had vanished.

Once inside the mailroom, he looked for the larger rental boxes. He spotted them along a bottom row, near an exit. He stooped and tried 405. The key didn't fit. He worked his way down. When he got to 408, the key slid in and spun. He pulled the door open, listening to the chirping of hidden hinges. The narrowness of the mailbox had bowed the two registered envelopes—sent *to* Hannah Neil *from* Hannah Neil—requiring Peter to tug hard to free them from their home. Flattening them out, he hesitated to read the handwriting on the envelopes.

What were you up to, Mom? he thought.

Peter then grabbed the scrunched-up wad of junk mail that bunched half-in and half-out of the box. He carried the handful to the trashcans, but went through the sheets one at a time, making certain he discarded nothing significant in the tangled mass. He separated out the mail he'd come for and tossed the rest.

Closing the mailbox, Peter paid the bill and prepaid, in cash, for another six months.

He went to a corner of the office and set the mail on a countertop. He began with the letter to him, from his mother. His hands trembled as he unfolded the typed page and read:

> *Dearest Peter,*
> *I do not expect you will ever read this, and I don't know why*
> *I am writing you. Only that I am nervous. When I heard*
> *about...*

At this point in the letter, his mother had written *Jackson Securities* and crossed it out, not quite enough to hide the words. She continued:

*...certain recent events, I knew I was responsible. I sent some things to a man at the SEC, someone I thought I could trust. He must have leaked the information. I want to believe it is all an unfortunate coincidence, but I cannot.*

*In these registered envelopes are documents that would implicate certain people in a massive conspiracy. I have breached legal ethics by making copies of these confidential papers. I do not know what to do with what I know.*

*Do not open the registered envelopes. The date and seal will prove to any interested party that you have not made copies of the contents.*

*If you are threatened, you must return the envelopes to Jason Ayers, in their current sealed condition. He loves us and will protect you, just as he has provided for me over the years.*

*I wish I had not embarked on this insane crusade. It has already brought so much misery, and I now realize there is no way to win. These people are too powerful.*

*Love always,*
*Mom*

Against his cheek, the pages felt warm, and his mother seemed alive.

Momentarily distracting him, a thick man in a brown suit pushed his way past, nearly brushing against Peter's shoulder. The man stopped and stared less than five feet from where Peter stood. Had he been followed? Peter felt a wave of panic flush his face. He thought about his next move—flight or fight?

In the midst of Peter's confusion, the other man's face suddenly turned soft. "You look upset," he said. "You okay, mister?"

With those words, Peter realized that tears had rolled down his cheek. He wiped them with a sleeve and answered, "Yeah. Just a letter from someone I love..."

The man nodded like he understood. "Love can be a bitch," he said, and exited the mailroom.

As he recomposed himself, Peter debated whether to take the personal letter home with him, but decided not to. He placed everything back into the mailbox and re-locked it. His mother's hiding place had proven effective for this long. Why not a while longer? The temptation to open the registered mail quickly passed. His mother emphasized he should not. Filtered through his taut nerves, her advice seemed brilliant. Sometimes, he convinced himself, ignorance *was* bliss—at least relatively speaking.

When he arrived home half an hour later, Peter had two phone messages. The first was from Drew Franklin: "White Bread. Long time no hear. Baby's due soon and she's gonna be a girl. Yippy. Monica and I want to name her Hannah. I hope that's okay with you? Don't forget your friends. I've left a couple messages and not heard back from you. We still love ya, guy."

Henry jumped into Peter's lap as he pressed the play button for the next message. Peter's smile disappeared the moment the man's words filled the room.

"I was fired from the SEC yesterday. My investigation was unsanctioned, as you know by now. I will leave you alone, of course, since I am no longer a government employee. All I can do is wish you luck. You're gonna need it."

For reasons he couldn't fathom, Peter felt a fresh bout of anxiety coming on. *Dawson fired?* He disliked Dawson. Or did he? He didn't believe anything the agent had told him. Or did he?

"How much does it cost to bribe a dirty cop?" the agent had asked. With the information in the letter from his mother, Peter fought against the feeling that fresh meat hung on the carcass of Dawson's arguments. It had all turned into a confusing mess.

"Dawson got what he deserved," Peter said to Henry. "The man is dangerously misguided."

One thing, however, stabbed at Peter's rationalization. If only former Agent Oliver Dawson had never asked: "How much does it cost?"

# CHAPTER EIGHTEEN

"OH, OLIVER. WHAT HAPPENED?"

When the hotel room door closed, Angela ran and wrapped her arms around Dawson. Her neck folded over his shoulder as they embraced. For two days, she had had no contact with him—had no idea why he was fired. Every Thursday morning they met at a seedy hotel ten miles from the office to exchange messages. This Thursday, she apprehensively waited. When Dawson arrived, she had melted.

After a kiss, Dawson tried to explain. "People know that Neil and I met. Someone then notified Ackerman that I was operating without supervision. I discussed this possibility with the director when we set this whole thing up. It was necessary for him to can me and to do it in front of his assistant, Freeman Ranson." Dawson didn't mention that Ranson had looked like the cat that had just consumed the family parakeet.

"You're not fired then?" she asked.

"No. I am. If I'm right and can prove it, I'll be rehired. In the meantime, the only ones who know I'm working on this are you and Ackerman."

"How can you be working on a case if you aren't an employee?"

"Unofficially."

"I don't understand."

"In truth, neither do I. Did the director give you anything to pass on?"

"Not much. He sure as heck didn't explain that you had his support."

"I'm not sure I do. But this thing with his special assistant is so big he feels he needs an answer. I want you to tell him I'm returning to San Diego. I'm going to make contact with Neil again. This time I'll be more careful."

"You're going back? You can't."

"I have to. They think they've shut me up, so that makes this a good time to go."

"They're killers."

"I'll be careful," he said, squeezing her hand.

"I love you so much. Tell me I won't read you've gone berserk and blown yourself to bits like everyone else who looks at these lunatics cross-eyed."

"You won't."

"You think Neil will come around and help?"

"Given enough time, yes. What I'm afraid of is what happens to him if he slips up and is seen as a threat. Unfortunately, with what happened to his mother, Neil has few reasons to trust me. His mother sends me something in the mail and ends up in a car crash."

"But you were just trying to help."

"How does he know that?" Dawson draped an arm around Angela's shoulder and pulled her into him.

"Because you are a dedicated government agent."

"And supposedly so is Freeman Ranson. So are all those other people who are part of the network that sells information to the highest bidder. No. I need to do something to prove he can trust me."

"Like what?" she asked.

"When he gets in trouble, and I'm certain he will, I'll have to go to the mat for him. Hopefully Director Ackerman will pull the necessary strings."

"You think Ackerman will help when the time comes?"

"If he doesn't, then I hope you don't mind being married to an unemployed lawyer."

"I would live in a hole with you."

"Good. A deep hole, just the two of us."

"I didn't say I wanted to. You go do your job. Get rehired. Now, if I don't go, I'll be late. I am, after all, the breadwinner."

"So true. Go win a loaf for us. I'm airport bound."

"So soon?" she asked, surprised.

"No time to waste. I intend to begin building my friendship with young Peter Neil tomorrow."

Two hours later, Oliver Dawson sat in the last row of an American Airlines jet. With no delays, he would begin his work in earnest in less than six hours.

---

When Peter arrived at work a few minutes after five on Friday morning, a crescendo had already been reached and sustained. He noticed that

Morgan Stenman was in Howard Muller's office. Jason Ayers, also in Muller's office, gesticulated between their frantic bodies as if he were the referee at a main event.

"What the hell's going on?" Peter asked Stuart.

"You read the *IED* yet?" Stuart asked.

Peter looked down at the salmon-colored pages of the *International Economic Daily*, folded on top of his desk. He shook his head. "That looks like some pow-wow," he said.

"I love this shit. I wish I could hear through those walls. Hope Balloon-Head doesn't think to close his drapes."

"You're sick, Stu. What's the story?"

"Morgan's apeshit. She's got our law firm ready to file for libel."

"I'm not a mind-reader. Sue who?"

"Everybody knows we went long Brazilian debt yesterday—huge, despite the risk of devaluation after Indonesia spun the drain. Word was that the Brazilian government would put a moratorium on interest and principal repayment."

"Default on their debt?"

"Essentially, yes. Then, late last night, out of the blue, the IMF and U.S. Treasury come through with a thirty billion-dollar loan. I'm talking thirty-fucking-billion U.S. dollars. The President of Brazil then announces he's going to defend the currency to the bitter end."

"The shorts must have gotten squeezed big-time," Peter said, unable to hide the awe in his voice.

"Killed is more like it," Stuart confirmed. "The bonds we bought at a sixty-percent discount to par are now trading at eighty cents on the dollar. Since we borrowed to buy the bonds in the first place, we generated a one-day return of three hundred plus percent. But some noses are bent. You know Josh Robinson's hedge fund?"

"Yeah. His performance is always being compared with Morgan's. You suggesting he went the other way?"

"He's rumored to have lost three billion."

Peter whistled. "Okay, but. I'm still in the dark. What's this got to do with the *IED* and a libel suit?"

"Some bright reporter with *IED* suggested Morgan profited from information she got from her former employee. The guy who used to work for her and now's an advisor to the Brazilian government."

"Shit. Surely she expected someone to catch on."

"What're you talking about?" Stuart asked, pulling his head back in pretended shock. "She denies having information. The reporter's already been fired, and the paper has promised to print a retraction. She's still going after blood, though. What a Bozo. Morgan's got a net worth a thousand times greater than the value of his entire friggin' newspaper. He should've known he couldn't expect to win. After this, nobody's gonna make that mistake again."

"Hard to believe we'd never use that kind of information, isn't it?"

Stuart shrugged. "I didn't say these things don't happen. I'm saying only a mutant-brain dares speculate about it in print. Guy might end up worse than fired one of these days."

The last sentence smashed straight into Peter's brain.

"Stuart. I'm worried about a couple of things."

"You look like someone killed your dog...no, make that your cat. What's got you ready to wet your pants, Boopy?" Stuart sniffed.

"That damn drug habit of yours for one. Some of the trading practices at this place for another."

Stuart stood and beckoned Peter to follow. While he trailed Stuart to the conference room, Peter stared at the chaos continuing in Muller's office. Morgan Stenman waved her filter-tip like a sword at Howard Muller. Ayers, his head shaking like a bobbing-head doll, looked trapped in a conflagration that could melt his flesh at any moment. Every few seconds, one or another leaned into a speakerphone and screamed something. Just before Peter and Stuart entered the conference room, Muller looked at Peter. Their heads locked. Muller narrowed his eyes and drilled malevolent tunnels through Peter's skull. The curious part of Peter wished to observe the meeting. The fear part of him sent out instructions to avert his attention and shut the door and curtains to the conference room. He went with fear.

A minute later, Stuart had his customary lines of white drawn on the table. The room was dark, the door locked, the curtains drawn. First right, then left, the powder traveled up Ben Franklin's printed face, invaded Stuart's nostrils, passed to his lungs, soaked through membrane, swam into the blood stream, and got distributed to wherever it would create its wonderment. Independence Hall curled around the outside of that hundred-dollar tube, nestled between a thumb and all but the little finger.

Wired, Stuart said, "Okay, dude. Whatta y'wanna discuss?"

"We're friends, right, Stu?"

"The best of." Tightly upturned corners of his mouth fed the words.

"You said something that has got me…" Peter struggled for the right word. "I guess worried sums it up."

"I'm wracking my fried brain, but I don't recall saying anything scary."

"The reporter. You said he might end up worse than fired. What's that mean?"

Stuart did a darting dissection of Peter's face. "A joke," he said. "What's wrong with you, dude?"

"This Brazilian thing. Breaking the Indonesian bank. I've been thinking about the social consequences of some of the things we've been doing as a firm."

"Get a grip. This ain't no petting zoo we're running here. Everybody's nailing everybody, right and left. We're just the best at doing it. So stop whining like a pussy."

"I don't know," Peter said, sounding confused.

"You getting into some kind of complicated self-loathing thing all of a sudden? We're doing what we're supposed to do. And you—as much as I hate to admit it—are the fastest damn study I've ever seen. You're good…better than good. That PC thing was straight-up, too. Nobody in this shop, including Muller, including Morgan Stenman, can do…" The words faded.

"What, Stu?"

"Nothing. The coke's talking too much. Anyway, keep your chin up. When you get a few hundred K after-tax in January as a bonus, you'll go back to seeing the world the right way."

"I got a letter that has me thinking."

"Thinking is dangerous. Who sent you this missive?"

"My mother."

Stuart sprang erect, then put his elbows on the table and leaned forward. "She's dead."

The clarity of Stuart's words startled Peter. "I, uh, found it yesterday. Written a long time ago."

"What'd it say?"

"Mom was worried over ethics, I think. Law firms representing evil. That's why, when you said that thing about the newspaper guy, I needed to ask."

"I told you, it meant squat. What else's bugging you?"

"You and I both know that if Morgan and Muller bought Brazilian bonds, they knew damn well the IMF would initiate a bail-out."

Stuart shook his head. "You've lost all perspective. If you're worried, talk to Ayers. He's our attorney and a friend of yours. Anything else that's got this bee buzzing up your butt?"

"You remember Jackson Securities?"

"Jackson?" Stuart asked. "Sure. You and I talked about them before. So?"

Peter realized he had nothing to gain by floating unfounded theories past Stuart, especially those originating from Dawson. Even what his mother said didn't make any sense. "Nothing. I don't know why they popped into my head. Flustered, I guess."

"Your mother. Did she say anything else?" Stuart asked, his voice cracking with what sounded like excitement.

With a head-shake meant to detach mental cobwebs, Peter said, "Never mind. I need you to explain something to me."

"Go ahead, dude. Shoot."

"How does backtrading work?"

"I don't know what you mean."

"Don't insult my intelligence, Stu. When you and I went into Muller's office to reverse those buys and sells, you said it was backtrading. I saw Muller do something similar that resulted in millions of dollars in profit the first day I went to see him. What is backtrading?"

"You don't want to know, Petey."

"Thanks to you, I've participated. I might as well understand how it works."

"I said no." Stuart pushed himself back. "Let's end this—"

"Let's not." Peter grabbed his friend's hand from across the table and pulled. "What am I going to do? Turn someone in? I'm not stupid. I know I've bent the laws—broken a few with this Uhlander Pharmaceutical trade."

Stuart grinned. "That's true. No exceptions for profiting from material non-public info—doesn't matter that you shorted stock and covered. But ain't ever gonna be anyone who can prove anything. So I wouldn't worry if I was you."

"I'm not worried. I know you're a pro. Same as the others in this room. No footprints."

"That's right, dude. Walking on air."

"If I'm in, then I'm in. Backtrading. You haven't answered my question. What is it?"

Stuart hiked his shoulders into his neck. "You didn't hear it from me. *Capiche?*"

"Agreed."

"Last chance. You sure you want to know? Kind of like losing your cherry. Once it's gone, it's gone."

"I'm no virgin."

"Ask and you shall receive," Stuart said, setting up his pharmacy for another dose of enlightenment. "Backtrading is pretty simple. Someone, let's say Boris Yeltsin's bum-fuck girlfriend, is part of a syndicate—you know, Russian Mob, say. She's smart and wants to get a few hundred million out of that piece-of-shit country. How? She does these trades with a bank—a bank that knows how to keep secrets. Say a Swiss bank. She loses everything in the trades. Every ruble."

"How and why?" Peter pressed.

"Booking trades after-the-fact guarantees loss. Yesterday, the price of manure went down fifty percent. Today, Joe-on-the-take books trades as-of yesterday, getting Bum-Fuck long manure. She then simultaneously sells out for a huge loss. The bank she lost all her money to does another series of similar trades with a second bank, maybe off the coast of Africa. That's what we call a two-trade."

"Another layer of security?" Peter asked.

"Very good, dude. That second bank then trades with Howie-Boy, or Morgan, or me, or you. We make back all that money lost by Bum-Fuck a day or a week earlier. Bum-Fuck's got a tiny account with us or with one of our outside managers. Maybe offshore, maybe not. Depends on her pedigree. Suddenly she has a tiny investment that trades into a great big ol' giant one. All legit as far as the eye can see. Everyone takes some vig along the way, but Bum-Fuck ends up with clean money. Eventually she can buy a building if she wants to."

"The trades are bogus," Peter said. "All we do is shuffle paper, create paper losses in the home country, then create a gain somewhere else, later. Once classified as trading profit, everything's untraceable?"

"Congrats. Like the former First Lady making a hundred grand on commodity trades with squat as an initial investment—difference is: we're dealing in tens of millions, and we don't leave paper trails that can be followed. Adds up to billions in no time. That said, I'm outta here."

Stuart stood, saluted, then exited the conference room.

"Sweet," Peter had to admit. "Not my problem, but still sweet. No wonder there's so much damn money floating around this place."

———

The walk from the conference room was thirty feet. Peter crumpled into his seat and turned on his computer. An incoming phone line flashed. He picked up.

"Hello. Neil, here."

"Morning, Peter. It's..."

Peter scanned the scene still underway in Muller's office. Muller's was the only back not turned. His big mouth widened in Peter's direction—leering, it seemed, like a fox cornering an injured rabbit.

"Hello, Peter? You still there?" the phone voice asked.

"Huh. Oh yeah. I'm here. Who's this?"

"You weren't listening? I told you. We're going to raise our rating on..."

Peter again tuned out and watched Muller's distant head nod against a phone, pressed to his ear.

A moment later, Muller said something to the other two. Ayers spun and looked at Peter. Stenman didn't move.

The insistent broker speaking at Peter continued. "Peter? What's going on? You okay?"

"Raising your rating?" Peter mumbled into the mouthpiece.

"Yes. This is big. If you can get some stock overseas, you'll make some quick cash."

"Thanks." Peter hung up.

———

When the meeting in Muller's office broke half an hour later, Peter was engaged in exaggerated activity. He punched out quotations and read lines of data, all the while working into and out of ten equity positions.

Ayers exited first. He came by the desk. "Peter," he asked, "you have time for lunch? After the close. Around two. Won't take long."

"I'm busy—"

"It'll take less than an hour. Please."

Peter reluctantly agreed to meet.

———

Ayers' Lincoln Town Car was waiting when Peter made it downstairs shortly after two o'clock. A uniformed driver opened the rear door and Peter slid in, next to Ayers. The attorney reached across and shook hands. Ayers' fingers still felt like thick, pliant noodles.

"Thanks for coming, Peter. I wanted to get caught up. After all, I'm the one who got you this job. How's it going?"

"I love trading. By far the best job I've ever had."

"Morgan's happy with your development."

"I'm glad to hear that, Mr. Ayers."

"I think it's time you called me Jason. I hope we're friends."

"Yes. Certainly, Jason."

They spent several minutes speaking of nothing relevant, then Ayers asked, "Any questions you have concerning the firm? Morgan and I go way back, to when she had only a few million under management, and I was an overworked intern."

"Not really. But thanks for asking."

"Would you like to discuss how they operate? They're aggressive."

"I've picked up a few of those habits myself."

"Good for you. This is like war."

"That's what everybody keeps telling me."

"The rules of trading are different, depending on where you play," Ayers said.

He's trying to sound too much like a best friend, Peter thought.

"Take Russia, for example," Ayers continued. "Under the table payoffs are a fact of life. Anyone who plays there, from IBM to the U.S. government, knows the game."

"I've got nearly half a brain. I guess I already figured most of these things out on my own."

"You sound cynical and sarcastic, Peter. Am I reading you correctly?"

"Not really," he lied. "Just wondering where this conversation is heading. Look, I appreciate your concern. And I'm sorry if I'm as subtle as a chainsaw, but I'm tired. If you don't mind, can we cut the crap? I know this business isn't whistle-clean, so save your breath. The way to win a war is by going all-out. Now, I guess that means we're in agreement. I intend to go all-out, all the time."

"Whoa," Ayers said, shaking his head. "Slow down, son. I'm trying to counsel you to be careful with the securities laws, not break them."

"Maybe you need to talk to someone else first. I don't make policy."

"Are you referring to Morgan, perhaps?"

"Perhaps. Look, Jason, I like Morgan, but your preaching to me is disingenuous. So let's drop this line of bullshit."

"Let me state something for the record, Peter. It is Stenman Partners' policy to discourage inappropriate use of information. If you have a question—it's in the employee handbook—you are to ask Compliance. Compliance is undertaken by Leeman, Johnston, and Ayers. Our law firm has someone available twenty-four hours a day."

"Whatever you say. We're encouraged to be aggressive but not overstep the line." Peter rolled his eyes.

"Exactly," Ayers said. "A fine distinction exists between doing good, hard, investigative research and gaining inside information. Even the SEC is having a hard time deciding which is which. Let's take the example of...."

Ayers spent ten minutes clarifying what he meant. It sounded convincing enough on the surface, and Peter nodded in rhythm to Ayers' words while staring out the window.

"Now," Ayers said, switching to another topic, "let's take this Brazilian thing."

Peter focused back inside the car and on Ayers' face. "Good idea," he said. "I'm interested in your spin on what Stenman did in that situation?"

"Again, you sound critical, Peter. Do you think some rules were bent?"

"Bent? Good euphemism for...never mind. Go ahead. I'm all ears."

"I will say this unequivocally: Morgan did *not* have advance word on the loan package, if that's what you think."

"Come on. I'm not saying I care, but the consultant had worked for her, for God's sake. She was the solitary human being in the world who made money on this play. Josh Robinson's hedge fund got hammered, and he's as savvy as they come."

"Listen and you'll understand," Ayers said. "This former employee of Morgan's shares her economic beliefs and values—as former co-workers, that stands to reason. Morgan anticipated his recommendations. That's not illegal. She also knows how the IMF and the U.S. Treasury work. She understood that a major country in this hemisphere, one that has taken on massive reforms—political as well as economic—is important to the U.S. Again, she anticipated that a bailout was more likely to be granted here than in Indonesia. And was correct."

"Okay. Let's say I buy that." Peter had to admit it sounded plausible. "What about Indonesia? Who the hell was on the other end of the phone— the person I passed specific messages from? It sounded like someone inside the central bank." If it shits like a duck, and quacks like a duck, Peter thought, it's gotta be a duck.

"I wasn't there," Ayers reminded him, "but I do know Morgan has people in every country who follow capital inflows and outflows. They poll major market players—including bankers willing to be polled—to gain insight. Deducting bank outflows from estimated hard currency reserves is a game everyone tries to play. Nothing illegitimate in that."

"Down to the last billion, at a specific moment in time?"

"This is a sophisticated world, Peter."

"Fine. You've explained Indonesia and Brazil, counselor. Explain back-trading?"

Ayers shook his head and said, "No such thing. I think I know what you're referring to. Whenever a ticket is incorrectly written, or an error discovered, we file an *as-of* ticket to correct or *backdate* legitimate trades."

Ayers wrote something on a piece of paper as he spoke, using his briefcase as a table. He handed the note to Peter, keeping his hand below the back of the front seat, out of view of the driver's mirror.

Peter kept the slip of paper in his lap and read:

> *Drop this line of questioning. Conference room is moni-*
> *tored. So is this car. Discussions overheard. You are in 100%,*
> *or you are out. Decide and state your decision clearly.*

Peter studied Ayers' face. Deep lines creased the attorney's forehead as he said, "Surely you are aware that errors need to be corrected."

"Yeah, corrections. I guess Stuart's explanation confused me."

Ayers mouthed the word *good*, then said, "It's possible I should review how these error tickets are written and processed. You don't have a problem with any of this, do you?"

"No. Of course not," Peter said with an actor's conviction. "This has been helpful, Jason. Sometimes, when a person is new to something, it gets confusing. But I'm a team player. I'm totally on board."

"That's good, son. On another topic, how has settling your mother's affairs gone? Anything I can help you with?"

With the knowledge that others had overheard earlier discussions, Peter guessed this was meant to be a leading question. Ayers nodded as if confirming the insight.

"Uh, as a matter of fact," Peter said, recalling what he had already admitted to Stuart, "I found a letter from Mom, but I threw it away. It made no sense. She wrote something about the law and clients and such."

"Did she mention that she sent some papers to the SEC?"

Peter's chin dropped. This was a frontal assault for information. How should he answer?

Ayers wrote out another note:

*Say, no.*

"No, she didn't say anything about that," Peter replied on cue. "She did mention something about some documents, but not what or where they were." Did that sound convincing? Peter wondered.

"If you come across anything, you can always run it by me."

"Sure. I'll do that."

Ayers reached for the notes and retrieved them from Peter's lap. He opened his briefcase and put them inside. Clamping the case shut, he spun the locks. The car pulled up to a small restaurant, two blocks from the beach at the north end of La Jolla, close enough for the ocean breeze to ruffle their hair.

As they entered the restaurant, Ayers asked, "And the rest of your life? How have you been?"

They took a booth and faced each other. Peter discussed a few recent events, his new apartment, his car. He then asked, "How's Kate? I've been meaning to call, go see her."

"I don't know if you've heard, but Kathryn passed the Bar."

"That's fantastic," Peter said. "I should ask her to dinner to celebrate."

"I don't think that's a good idea." Ayers shook his head.

"Why?" Peter sounded confused. "I was halfway hoping she'd come back to San Diego after the exam."

"She's staying in LA. Accepted a job with the PD's office. And...she's engaged."

Peter's body whiplashed. "To be married?"

"Yes. *That* kind of engaged."

"Who? When?" Peter really wanted to ask: why?

"The professor she worked with on the textbook. Wedding's scheduled for late January."

"That's a month and change away. I can't believe this." Peter slumped. "It's so sudden."

Lunch was brief. When finished, Ayers said, "I'm going to call for a cab. My driver will take you back to the office." He handed Peter a last note.

Without looking at it, Peter palmed the piece of paper while shaking his head. "Makes more sense for me to get the cab," he said. "Thanks for lunch."

"You sure?" Ayers asked.

Peter insisted.

A few minutes later, Peter's cab sat in traffic while he read through the note Ayers had slipped him in the restaurant:

> *You must not allow anyone to think you have documents from your mother. They are afraid—those papers potentially have trails that go back many years. Do your job and do not rock the boat.*
>
> *I recommend you destroy anything you have. Whatever you do, do not contact regulators. It would do little good anyway. I have done all that I can for you. Please, for God's sake, do what I ask.*
>
> *Destroy this message before you get back to work.*

Ayers had written his message before meeting Peter outside of Stenman's at two o'clock. That meant the attorney had planned this covert communication all along, but why?

"Relax," Peter told himself. "Everything's going to be fine."

*Do not rock the boat.* Peter reread the words. He had never intended to rock the damn boat. What was in those envelopes his mother had left behind? This was one question he had no interest in answering. As the cab struggled to advance, Peter looked out the window. All the cars in his line of vision were crawling, yet all the drivers were desperately changing lanes. Pass, brake, get passed, switch lanes. Catch up, tailgate, stand still. Fall behind.

Katie Ayers engaged: why had that news hit him so hard? Although he had done nothing to further their relationship, her engagement felt like a mortal wound to his heart.

"Mind your own business. Do not rock the boat," he said to himself.

Katie Ayers. Secret messages. Kate. Messages.

"Damn it all," he said, loud enough for the cabby to hear. "Every single thing hanging over my head: damn it to hell."

# CHAPTER NINETEEN

**A**T HIS DESK AFTER HIS CAB RIDE, **P**ETER SQUIRMED AS IF SITTING ON A nest of fire ants. He looked around every minute or two, wondering who was watching. Did Stenman think he was a security risk? Maybe he should say something.

But, no. Ayers had said to do his job. That meant head down, continue to work hard, make money. That was the one thing Peter understood could help right things: make some major profit. Thank God he had already proven he could do that.

And what about Ayers? The man filled Peter with suspicion. Could he be trusted? Was Ayers simply doing what he was told by those he worked for? Maybe this whole thing was a test, engineered by Morgan Stenman. If so, had he passed? The day's conversations saturated Peter's mind the entire afternoon. When he left work, it was dark. Because it was Friday, he understood the commute home was likely to be gridlock. A fifteen-minute drive in good times might take half-an-hour or more now. But he didn't care.

"Time to think," he rationalized.

At least things couldn't get any worse, could they?

The better part of an hour later, Peter pulled into the driveway leading past several other condominiums terraced along a steep hillside. He made his turn and accelerated the last few yards, reaching for and depressing the automatic door opener, then watching. He slowed and timed it so that the roof of his car just cleared the rising door. A dim light illuminated the interior of his garage as he turned the engine off, retracted the garage door, and got out of his BMW.

"Don't say anything."

The muffled words startled him. He spun and defensively raised a hand.

Several feet away, appearing from behind the water heater, stood Agent Dawson. A .38 dangled from a hand draped along his side. He made certain Peter had a good view.

Dawson stepped forward. With his free hand, he grabbed Peter's shirt, at the neck, and pulled. His torrid breath blew across Peter's ear, the clamp on Peter's collar strong.

"The inside of your house is bugged," he said. "I saw them enter, disguised as exterminators. They should have brought tanks of poison—more convincing that way."

"I—"

Dawson released his hold on the shirt and slapped a palm over Peter's mouth. The agent shook his head.

Peter knocked the hand away with a forearm but said nothing. He noticed the window off to the side of the garage was open, unlocked from the inside. A single pane had been cut away, with smooth edges made by a glasscutter. Peter allowed himself to be towed to a dark corner.

"Give me your jacket," Dawson whispered.

Peter did as asked. The agent took the garment and held it by the collar. After setting his gun on a bench, he ran a hand along the lining. He next patted the fabric as if pressing out wrinkles. He searched the pockets. He slid his fingers under the collar. With a penknife pulled from a hip pocket, Dawson made an incision in the lapel. He widened the slit and removed a metallic disk, the size of a small button. He then stood on his toes so that his mouth could reach Peter's ear a second time with a whisper: "A transmitter. Not a microphone, but a tail. Did you leave your jacket behind at any time today?"

Peter nodded.

"Your house is wired for sound. So's the inside of your car. You can bet on it. This garage is the one place they didn't plant a mike."

The conference room at work was wired, Peter recalled, so why not an article of clothing? Why not his home? His car? His asshole if that's what they wanted?

"If the garage doesn't have a speaker, why are we whispering?" Peter asked.

"In case they're using directional mikes, though that's unlikely. They've already thoroughly invaded your privacy."

"*They?*" Peter asked, putting a hostile bite on the word.

"I'm not a hundred percent sure, but I'd be willing to bet Stenman's involved."

"What happened to the phone message where you said I was on my own? I prefer it that way."

"That was a ruse. For your protection."

"I don't want protection. I'm being followed and monitored because of you."

"Listen to me, Peter. This has nothing to do with me. Somebody's interested in you, and since they chose today to make you a telecommunications company, I'm guessing you must know something."

"Yeah, I know something: breaking and entering is a crime."

"I'd keep my voice real calm if I were you, so it doesn't carry."

"I don't know a thing of interest to anyone. And if I did, I'd be a fool to give it to you." Peter recalled his mother's letter. She wrote that the agent she had trusted must have leaked the information. "My mother certainly didn't trust you," Peter blurted.

Dawson caught the implication. "How do you know that?"

Peter hesitated, regretting the slip. "Because nobody trusts you."

"Clever. You didn't look surprised when I said your place was bugged. Unless I miss my guess, I showed up in the nick of time."

"Nick of time? My problems all began with that damn photo of you and me at the sports bar."

"Photo?" The surprise in Dawson's voice made it clear he hadn't known anything about a photograph before now.

"That's right," Peter continued. "A picture of us at the sports bar. I had to talk my way out of that mess. I'm lucky to still have a job."

"No," Dawson said, shaking his head, "you're lucky to be alive. You must have something they desperately want."

"*They*, again? How about you? You didn't show up to get a year-end tan. Leave me alone or I'll phone your former boss and tell him you're harassing me."

"Calling the director—his name's Ackerman by the way—is a bad idea." Dawson kept looking side to side, as if he expected an interruption.

"Oh, that's right. You said the SEC had some people who had crossed the line. I should check with *you* before I call. Convenient Catch-22."

"Whoever you call will relay the message to the director's office. Once his special assistant—a scumbag by the name of Freeman Ranson—finds out, you're history. You do not want them to think they *must* eliminate you."

"You're the one posing the danger," Peter wanted to scream. "They followed you the night they caught us together." Peter pointed a rigid finger at Dawson. "If they thought I was meeting with you again, no telling what would happen."

"Because of that picture of us in the bar, you think they were following me?" Dawson asked. "Are you serious? Did they have a photo of us at Sammy's?"

"No, thank goodness."

"Think. How hard could it have been to follow me a few hundred yards down the beach in my car? It was you, sneaking out the back, using your runner's speed down a railroad track, getting back before anyone missed you, that avoided detection. That piece of pretend-dumb-blond who paid you so much attention was the one following *you*."

Peter's heart beat fast. He didn't have a convincing response. "I'm going into my house, feeding my cat, and relaxing," he whispered: "Whatever's got everybody so interested in me is my business. Mine. Not yours."

"Then it's true. You've found something."

"I didn't say that." Peter reached for the door to the stairwell leading into his condo.

"Watch what you say," Dawson warned, " 'cause someone's going to be listening. When you pee, they'll hear the tinkle. On top of everything else I've said about why you're not dead, I think they're afraid to plant you."

"*Plant me*? Are you trying to be funny?"

"Nothing funny about this, Peter. No matter what your mother thought about me, it should be obvious that I'm trying to solve this thing. To help you."

"I don't want your help. I am tired of being pushed, shoved, prodded, blood-tested, lie-detected, bullied. Who in God's name is afraid of me? I am a nothing."

"Who? Everybody's afraid of you. You're alive because of inconvenience. No. I take that back. It's more than inconvenience."

"I understand you think you're doing your job, Dawson, or at least your former job, but this sounds like a case of paranoia. I'm in enough trouble. Time for me to mind my own business."

"With what happened to your mother," continued Dawson, skipping over Peter's comments, "and the questions that would arise with you working for Stenman Partners, they are being careful to—"

"There you go again. If you're after Morgan Stenman, then you'll have to do it without me. She's aggressive. So am I, for that matter. So is everybody else in the hedge fund bus—"

"You've broken securities laws, haven't you?" said Dawson crossing his arms.

Dawson, Peter figured, had made an educated guess—correctly. For a nanosecond, Peter wanted to confess, to trust this small man with the passionate voice. Instead, his brain defied his heart and forced his mouth to say: "You lost the Treasury case. Now you've managed to get yourself fired. I trust you, I'm history."

"You're going to need to make a deal."

"Deal? With an unemployed SEC agent? No thanks. I'm going back to work and pretend I never met you. If you persist, I'll check with our attorneys."

"I can't force you to do anything, Peter, but one day you're going to realize this *is* your business. Once that happens, I pray you survive. And don't forget what I said before: if it isn't you they go after, it'll be your friends.

"By the way," Dawson continued, "that off duty cop? The one who saw your mother 'crash and burn'? He retired a month later. Says he came into an inheritance from a distant, foreign relative. Guy's got a sweet life, living it up on the beach in Coronado. Another coincidence?"

A pain stabbed Peter.

Dawson grabbed his .38 and tucked the snub nose into his shoulder holster. With that prop back in place, he said, "Don't bother showing me the way. I'll let myself out." Dawson headed in the direction of the open window but, after a couple of steps, spun around and returned to Peter. "Here," he said, reaching over and stuffing a slip of paper into Peter's breast pocket. "If you need to get hold of me." The agent turned and stepped towards the damaged window a second time.

Outside, a dog barked and his master shouted, "Shut up!"

A dull pain hammered deep in Peter's gut. "His name?" he asked. "The retired cop."

Dawson turned. Peter detected a faint smile.

"Name? Ellis. If you decide to visit, I'd make up a story about working for a woman by the name of Sarah Guzman."

"Sarah Guzman?" Peter bit his tongue, wishing the damn cat had gotten to him first.

"You've heard the name?" Dawson sadly shook his head. "No. Let me guess: you've met her. How're you at hitting breaking balls?"

"What's that supposed to mean?" Peter asked, exasperated.

"I'd say that having Sarah Guzman in the vicinity means you've got two strikes against you. Better watch for the curveball."

"I don't know anything," Peter said, convincing not even himself.

"She's Ensenada Partners. You ever heard of Enriqué Guzman?"

Peter didn't show it, but he knew *that* name, too. Guzman had been one of the most notorious drug bosses in Mexico. His death, Peter recalled, had been big U.S. news for a couple days three or four years ago.

"She took over the business. Reorganized. Got out of import-export of the white stuff. Rumor has it she's making more cleaning dirty money throughout Latin America. Her nephew, Carlos Nuñoz—now there's a scary guy—is head of security for her. These two do not screw around when they get unstrung, and it's a short trip to unstrung. Remember reading about the hundred bodies found in that mass grave along the California-Mexican border? That was the aftermath of her withdrawing from the old business. Most bodies were friends and family of those who'd worked for her dead husband."

"Why would she do that? It makes no sense."

"She did it to convince former competitors—the other cartels throughout Latin America—she was serious and had a new business plan that included them as clients. She snuffed-out her husband's former network. Oops, I mean she *allegedly* snuffed-out her husband's former network. Nothing was ever proved. She lowered her overhead at the same time she made a statement about where her new interests lay."

Craning forward enough that his neck appeared to lengthen, Dawson continued: "You scared yet?"

Peter was thankful the garage light was dim and his pallor shadowed.

"And, if you still care, cop's full name is Sean Ellis. Former San Diego City Detective, Sean Marcus Ellis."

Peter wouldn't forget the name.

# CHAPTER TWENTY

Cactus grew inside huge, heavy clay pots positioned below view-windows—windows taking in Pacific whitecaps, seagulls, fishing boats, and the occasional hang-glider. The horizon stretched in every direction without blemish—endless blue sky, connected to endless blue ocean.

Morgan Stenman and Sarah Guzman deliberated with their backs to the windows—they had a view of only each other and Carlos Nuñoz. Because it was a Saturday, all of Stenman's computers were shut down and, except for this meeting in her office, there were no other people on her half of the second floor. Across from the two women, Carlos fidgeted in a chair with cabriole legs, an antique from the time of Queen Anne—not comfortable, but priceless. His right foot rested on his left knee as he tugged at his ankle with an open palm, as if stretching his joints in preparation for a workout.

"Morgan, what did Peter Neil say to your attorney?" Sarah asked.

Stenman inhaled, then exhaled, as she nearly always did when framing her words: "According to Jason, he said he doesn't know where any documents are. The tapes we made seem to corroborate that."

"*Perdoneme, señora*," Carlos said, "but you believe this to be true?"

Stenman merely shrugged.

"Neil is dangerous," Carlos thought out loud. "He has seen a letter from his mother. What else has he seen? I believe it is possible more legal documents—stolen by this Hannah Neil—exist. It is also possible that Neil has them, or knows where they are, or will soon come to know these things. It is *importante* that we retrieve this information."

Sarah nodded agreement. "For the time being, we will wait and continue following, recording, tracking him."

"Maybe some of what you say is true," Stenman said, sounding noncommittal. "I like Peter. I hope this turns out well for him."

"This is a difficult case," Sarah said. "What would *you* have us do, Morgan?"

Stenman flicked ashes into a crystal bowl. "Unless we are forced to, I do not think it wise to harm Peter. Not with what happened to his mother, with the possibility that the regulators may still be interested in his affairs. If possible, we should get needed answers first."

"I agree," Sarah said. "My recommendation is that we buy time. Hope to find out what he knows. But the moment we ascertain he has information stolen by his mother, and we retrieve that information, he must be dealt with. Fortunately, Carlos and I have a contingency plan. You are ready to execute this contingency plan when necessary, Carlos?"

"*Sí.*"

At that moment, Stenman's phone rang. She pushed the speaker button. "I wish to speak with *Señor* Nuñoz," said an accented voice.

"I am here," Carlos said, the impatience in his voice an unspoken threat.

After a rapid briefing, the man said, "He is lost."

Carlos slammed a fist into a wall. "What does that mean, *pelotudo*? 'Lost'?"

In Spanish, the caller explained that Neil had taken off running. Nobody could hope to keep up with him, he moved too fast. At some point, the tracking device must have broken, because the signal died. Off to the side, Sarah gave a whispered translation to Stenman.

"*Ocho ochenta*! Find him!" Carlos slammed a fist into the speaker button, disconnecting the line. "This changes everything," he said. "The transmitter did not accidentally break. He knows."

"Calm down," Sarah said. "Watch his house. This is no reason for panic." She rolled her eyes in Stenman's direction. Carlos understood the gesture, exhaled, and nodded.

"You will solve this problem intelligently," Stenman said, making certain it sounded like a directive. "I do not want anything to happen to Neil that might reflect back on me. Understood?"

To her surprise, Carlos spun in anger. "We do what we have to, *Señora* Stenman. It is more than just your interests at stake."

"Carlos," Sarah reprimanded, "do not forget with whom you are speaking. Morgan Stenman is a great person. She is our friend." Turning to Stenman, Sarah continued, "I am sorry. This is not like Carlos. He is upset that we have lost contact with Mr. Neil."

"*Perdoneme, Señora* Stenman," said Carlos. "I spoke unnecessarily."

"Do not screw with me, Carlos, or underestimate me." Stenman's voice was like a deep freeze, and the room grew frigid. "And do not speak to me in such a manner ever again."

"We will uncover the truth," Sarah explained. "But you must trust our instincts."

"And you must trust mine," Stenman replied, still furious. "I prefer to continue grooming Peter Neil, but I am not in love with the notion. This has gotten complex, and I do not like that. Remember what you said about Howard Muller: he is dangerous because he does things without reason. Do not forget that lesson, either of you."

Carlos' crooked lips trembled. "I will not forget," he said. "Anything."

---

After Sarah and Carlos left, Stenman summoned Howard Muller. He arrived a half-hour later. Stenman recounted to him the day's events.

"Why wasn't I part of that meeting?" Muller drew his eyes together.

"Because our friends do not respect you, and because you have lost your objectivity."

"Who does Nuñoz think he is? Scarface acts so polite, then calls us names in Spanish as if we won't figure out we're being insulted. He thinks everybody's afraid of him."

"*Thinks* they are afraid? Don't be asinine, Howard. He *is* dangerous. So is Sarah Guzman."

"I'm capable of doing as much damage as those two. Maybe we should sever our relationship with them. We don't need her money—you've got plenty coming out of Eastern Europe."

She rotated her head and blew smoke towards a window. "No. Sarah Guzman is the most viciously intelligent woman I have ever known. We will continue together unless she breaks the trust first."

"As for Neil," Muller said, "I happen to agree with Nuñoz. Whatever his mother knew or took is floating around like a time-bomb. And don't forget, I've touched nearly every damn peso, drachma, and ruble that's moved into our funds. I'm the one who finds the places to backtrade. The one who talks to our contacts. If Neil's mother hid anything substantive, it's my ass that's fried first. You want my opinion: find another Zerets and have him hunt Neil down. End it, once and for all."

"You wear your hatred for everyone to see," Stenman said. "Perhaps you hear the footsteps of a bright young man, ready to take over."

"Neil is less than nothing. What I don't like is someone having information that's going to get me investigated by the SEC for the next fifty years." Muller stood up and towered over Stenman. "How do we know he hasn't turned anything over to the government already?"

"Simple: where are the subpoenas? And, according to Freeman Ranson, nothing in or out of the SEC or the Justice Department related to Peter Neil."

"We should nail Neil anyway. I'd love to be the one—"

"Drop it," Stenman said.

Howard Muller dropped the line of conversation, but not the fantasy. He had a plan, inspired by Nuñoz and Guzman. He spun his head, grinned, and imagined the look of terror on Neil's face. His plan was genius in its simplicity, he thought.

And he hoped his plan *did* become necessary.

Just before Peter had left the co-op, he patted his jogging outfit. No transmitters sewn into the clothing, he had convinced himself. He then examined his running shoes, first picking up the right one and searching for a slit around its soles. Finding nothing suspicious, he bent the shoe, thinking something might become evident. Again, nothing.

He ran his index finger down the top of the shoe tongue, to the back, and a spot hidden by thick laces. He felt something small, hard. He held the opening to the light and discovered a disc—similar to the one in his jacket collar—attached to the tiny spot between the tongue and the shoe-top. He never would have seen or felt its presence once the shoe was on. He did not remove the transmitter. He then repeated the process with the left shoe. Nothing.

Peter poured a cavernous bowl of dry cat-food for Henry. He leaned over, stroked the cat's back, and whispered, "I know you don't like dry, old man, but I may be gone for a while." He then took a large bowl from above the sink and filled it with a half-gallon of water.

Peter bolted his front door on the way out and began a slow jog that built to a run. He churned up a hill that led north, through the central business district, pushing himself at a five-minute mile clip—fast enough to ditch anyone following on foot. He then cut through several dead-end street barriers, blocking any car that might be trailing.

Ending a confusing two-mile route, he stopped and removed the right shoe. He reached in and ripped the bug from its hiding place. He placed the circle on the pavement and stepped hard, crushing the insect-sized device. Putting his shoe back on, he took off again, this time at an even more rapid pace. He veered towards Rancho Santa Fe, a three-mile run up hills and over trails.

A mile later, outside the men's room at a mini-mall already decorated for Christmas, he stopped at a payphone to call Drew Franklin. Despite being hidden from view, he remained alert to anything or anyone unusual. He watched as wide-eyed kids dragged their tired parents to toy and electronics stores. A small line formed outside a Radio Shack as someone extolled the wonders of some video-game gadget. Capitalism at its finest, he thought. Despite the innocence of the scene, Peter kept all senses on alert. This qualified as prudence, not paranoia, he assured himself.

After Drew answered, Peter tried to explain things, then instructed his friend, "Meet me downtown Rancho Santa Fe. In the back of that nursery off the main road. I'll need to talk to Ayers, so give me an hour and a half."

"Why not meet you outside Ayers' house?" Drew asked.

"I'm not certain I can trust the guy. If he calls whoever is so interested in following me, I don't know what might happen. This way, I'll take off, no matter what."

Before agreeing, Drew asked, "Does this have something to do with your current employment?"

"I hope not, but probably. And if it does have a connection, I may be up shit creek for more reasons than just Mom's papers."

"I hate to ask."

"I've done some trades that aren't exactly legal."

"You broke securities laws? I can't believe that, White Bread." Peter was grateful Drew didn't sound judgmental.

"Everybody in this end of the business is guilty—you get non-public information, you do a trade based on that information. It's impossible to turn the fact-faucet off—brokers, corporate management, even politicians spoon-feed non-public tidbits to us all day long. Most times, we don't even ask for it."

"If these people call and volunteer information, you mean to tell me it's illegal to use?" Drew sounded bewildered. "Doesn't sound criminal to me."

"That's what I told myself, and even believed was true—I didn't realize until later…" Peter heard the dinging of a garbage truck backing up. "That's all bullshit," he said. "I don't have a good rationale for what I did. But I know for damn sure I need to be more careful from here on out. I think I'm capable of making good money based on legitimately obtained information."

"It sounds confusing," Drew said. "I think I'll stick to blocked arteries and aneurysms."

"That's not all, either. I've got an ex-SEC agent after my ass. I'm in the middle of something ugly, and I don't know how to get out."

"I'll do whatever I can to help."

"Thanks, Drew. I love you, man."

"Me, Monica, and soon-to-be baby Hannah love you too. And, Bread?"

"Yeah?"

"You got the number of my voice mail at the hospital?"

"Memorized."

"I'm gonna give you the password. That way we can give each other messages, then retrieve them without someone listening in."

"Thanks. Mind if I give the number to my buddy Stuart at work? If this gets any hairier, I may need to talk to him on the QT."

"Do what you have to do, Bread," Drew said.

Finishing, Peter hung up. He gave a final look around, then began to jog, still considering which route to take.

The wind blew briskly with the air temperature in the low sixties. "Perfect weather for a run," he told himself.

He decided to take side roads until he got to the Rancho Santa Fe trails. At the trails, he legged his way east, keeping out of sight. His collar lay flat, so he pulled it high and angled his Padre baseball cap, allowing it to shield his neck and face. Fifteen minutes later, he arrived at the outskirts of Rancho Santa Fe, sucking oxygen into his burning lungs. Shadows from skyscraping trees cast a chill over his dripping sweatshirt. He shivered. Bounding forward at a steady pace, he squinted at a street sign and continued farther east. A couple of minutes later, he arrived at the lonely stretch of road that wound down a steep hill to Jason Ayers' estate.

# CHAPTER TWENTY-ONE

THE SEVEN-FOOT GRANITE WALL HAD JUST ENOUGH DEPTH BETWEEN boulders to make scaling possible, and the green wrought-iron that ran along the top of the wall looked more intimidating than it actually was. Once he caught his breath, Peter conquered both obstacles in less than a minute. He chose a corner of the property hidden from the road by trees. No neighbor—if you could call someone an eighth of a mile away a neighbor—could see him entering. A lawn mower buzzed from the back of the house, behind a hedge dividing the three acres of front from the five acres of back. The gardener had parked his truck alongside the six-car garage in a space the size of a basketball court.

Peter hunched over and worked his way towards the front door. He passed a picture window with the drapes drawn. Overhead, a helicopter chopped at a low altitude. The word *NewsEight* ran across its underbelly. Foolishly, while the copter's shadow raced across Ayers' furthest front acre, he ducked even lower, as if hiding from a cameraman.

"Get a grip," he whispered, feeling like a thief.

Just then a cloud blew across the sun, darkening the sky and cooling the air. The wind responded with a force that threatened to dislodge his cap. Peter pressed the brim more securely over his eyebrows and ventured another ten steps. A canvas doormat rested on the slate stoop leading to the main entrance.

At least twelve feet high, the double front doors had arched, etched glass mounted in a cedar frame. Peter remained out of view, shielding his approach behind dense brush running across the face of the house. This monolith of a place not only reeked money, but also defied architectural classification. Dark wood beams framed white stucco walls. The red-tiled roof gave the home a Mediterranean appearance that, taken as a whole, looked flawless from where Peter stood, gaping.

When he reached the entranceway, Peter at first knocked, then rang the doorbell—a chime that echoed. "Time to get some answers, Mr. Ayers," he said, crossing his fingers and hoping this was a good move.

Tapping his foot, he counted to ten. "Don't tell me nobody's home. Come on, dammit, come on."

A minute passed, and he rang the bell a second time. A few seconds later, he turned to retreat, disgusted with himself for having failed even this simple task. The wind picked up again. A few minutes earlier, his body had worked hard to produce enough perspiration to cool him down. Now, sweat turned cold, pasting his shirt to his skin. Involuntarily, he shook like a dog after a bath.

Peter, now tired of waiting, ducked back into the shadows. But the moment he did so, the door opened. Suddenly losing his nerve, he pressed his back against the wall, as if he hadn't planned this meeting in the first place. From where he hid, deep in the brush, he couldn't see the front door, nor could he be seen.

While he stood, as silently as a mute's whisper, he came up with a hundred reasons to abandon his plan. Ayers wouldn't help anyway, he speculated, or, worse, the attorney might turn on him. Or, maybe, he had overblown concerns and simply needed to go into therapy.

"Hello," Kate said, wiping out Peter's resolve to flee. "Is somebody there?"

Katie Ayers' unexpected voice surprised him as much as snow in June. He froze. The door slammed shut before he could get any words through his lockjawed mouth. After a moment's further hesitation, he stumbled forward, the branches splashing against his face, noisy and vicious. He tripped over a sprinkler head, just catching his balance after brushing against red bougainvillea twined up a dark column. He dragged forward and punched the doorbell hard enough to bow his pointer finger.

*Please, please, don't slam the door in my face.* With the Ayers' meeting a thousand miles removed from his consciousness, Peter watched the door open.

They stared. Kate, her hair damp from having just showered, looked as if she might flash a smile. The impulse must have soured in a split second because ice replaced fire in her eyes. Her lips turned down.

"I'm engaged," were the first words either of them spoke.

Despite already knowing, the sentence pierced Peter like a poison dart, dispensing venom to his heart. "I know," Peter said. "Your father told me. Congratulations."

"You don't sound like you mean it."

"I don't. I feel sick."

"You have no right showing up like this."

"I didn't know you were…" Peter stood erect. He couldn't steer his gaze from her face.

"Even if sleeping together didn't mean anything to you, I thought we could at least be friends," she said.

"I don't know what to say."

"Leave." She started to close the door.

Peter stuck a foot inside. "I need to talk to you."

"How did you know I was here? Father hates you, so I know he didn't tell you I was home."

"Your father hates me?"

"He was right. Money did change you—or maybe you were always an ass."

Peter recoiled. Hadn't Jason Ayers gone to a great deal of bother to issue him a warning?

"Peter, what are you doing here?"

"I came to see your father."

"Father? Why not just pick up the phone and call? Are you insane, or did something just pop into your head in the middle of a run?"

"I think I'm in trouble."

"You *think*? How can you not know something as basic as that?"

"You tell me. Somebody, I think Morgan or one of her associates, bugged my clothing and wired my car and my condo. At least that's what Agent Dawson says. My running shoe had a transmitter attached to it."

"Okay, now that we've determined it's insanity, keep talking. When you get to the part about aliens inhabiting bodies, I'll call a good shrink I know."

"Please, Kate. You don't have to believe me—I wouldn't blame you if you didn't—but don't make fun of me. This is serious. I may not be a good boyfriend—or even a good run-of-the-mill friend—but this isn't a joke."

Kate pulled the door wide open. "Fine, Peter. I won't make fun of you. And I'll even listen for a while, at least until Father comes back. But when he does, I'll let him take over. I'm sure he'll be able to set the record straight and sort out whatever mess you think you've gotten yourself into."

Peter mumbled a thank-you and stumbled in. Later that day, trying to visualize the home's palatial interior, he would draw a blank. He didn't notice the marble floor, the spiral staircase, the million-foot ceiling hovering over the entrance hallway, or the chandelier dripping crystal daggers and refracting light. A French provincial sofa and an inlaid mahogany sideboard could have been vegetable crates for all the notice he paid them. A mantel clock echoed off Spanish tile, but Peter's thoughts drowned out the sound. He saw and heard nothing, or whatever he saw and heard never passed into long-term memory. Passionate Kate blanketed his senses, even overshadowing some of his fears.

"I *did* intend to call," he said as he trailed her into the main part of the house. "I wanted to see you. I don't have a good reason for not phoning. I don't even have a made-up bad reason." He restrained a desire to reach out and touch her. "I missed you."

"You've missed me?" Kate violently spun around, driving an exclamation point to her incredulity. "We sleep together, though I engineered that. But then you say nice, sweet things, like all that blather about us seeing where our relationship goes. We exchange a couple of emails, then you stop writing. I call, invite you to some parties. You're too busy with work. Okay, I think to myself, that happens. You still *sound* interested. But that's only because you're too much of a coward to tell me to butt-out—"

"No. That's—"

"Then, I call. The phone might just as well have been a gun, put to my head. Bang. Then bang, bang, bang. I keep firing, only I'm not a good enough marksman to hit my teeny-tiny brain. I leave messages. You know how many messages?"

Peter didn't make a move.

"No, of course you don't. Ten. I left ten messages. At first I worried you'd been hurt. Then, foolishly, I asked myself: why would a nice guy, with manners and charm, who seemed to like me, not return a simple phone call? I didn't have an answer then, and I don't have an answer now. Maybe it's because I was wrong, and you aren't a nice guy. There. That's my summation, Peter."

"I'm a fool."

"Guilty as charged," she said, heading towards her father's library. Peter followed.

Speaking to her back, he said, "When I heard you'd gotten engaged, it hit me. I didn't realize how dumb I was."

"Why are you trying to hurt me?"

"I'm not. And maybe you should marry this professor-book person. I'm in no position to offer an opinion. But I've learned one thing from all this."

"And what's that?" she asked.

"That sometimes the heart is the last to learn. I realize I've done something really, really stupid."

Kate turned and her face softened, but for only a fraction of a fraction of a second. "Stop it, Peter. I don't want to hear any of this. I'm going to marry a kind man."

"I understand. I just wanted you to know I'm sorry."

"Let's skip my problems. Do you need an attorney?"

"You volunteering?"

"Maybe. Let's hear."

Peter hoped the reference to her "problems" meant she had second thoughts about marriage, and he filed the thought away. "I realize this sounds idiotic," said Peter, "but your dad knows things that might help me understand how deep I'm in."

For the next hour, Peter replayed events. He mentioned photos from the sports bar, the intimation that his mother's death may not have been an accident, her letter to him, and the registered envelopes.

Kate fit her attorney cap over her emotions and pretended to be detached, interested in the plight of a potential client-in-need. She listened and then explained that "registered mail is the poor man's copyright. The date of delivery and the seal prove that a document is original. If someone, after that date, claims a document as their own—that is, tries to steal someone's intellectual property—the registered envelope proves the creator's prior claim."

"That's what Mom meant then—that leaving the envelopes unopened should prove I hadn't seen or copied the contents."

"What's in those envelopes?"

"Don't know and don't want to know."

"What else can you tell me?"

Peter highlighted recent trading activities—those he participated in and those he knew of secondhand. He recounted the meeting with her father the other day and the surprise confrontation with Agent Oliver Dawson. When he finished, Kate stopped for a long minute. Finally, she said, "My father warned you not to rock the boat? What do you think he meant?"

"At work, to just do my job."

"Was he suggesting you break any securities laws?"

"No. In fact, he said I should be careful not to. But in the same breath, he tried to explain away all those other situations. Breaking the Indonesian bank. Brazil. Even how paying for information in certain cultures or countries is a necessity. I already told you how we use non-public information to make easy money. You think I've broken any laws?"

"Probably. But it sounds rampant."

"Why does Dawson need me then? With so much illegal activity, why not just come in and clean house?"

"Even if what you say is true, it's nearly impossible to prove. What and when someone knew something, as well as their intentions, are difficult or impossible to prove without internal, corroborating testimony. The fact-patterns you've detailed are easily explained away. It sounds as if my father did an effective job explaining away most of these situations the other day."

"You're right," agreed Peter. "His arguments did sound convincing."

"And records. Obtaining records is impossible if the accounts are domiciled in the right sovereignties. Having said all that, though, did you ever consider that what my father said may be true? That this is nothing more than aggressive risk-taking? After all, you're not a lawyer."

"I hoped that *was* the case. But if it's all so innocent, why am I under such close scrutiny all of a sudden? I open my fat mouth about finding a letter and some sealed papers, and I've got the world's biggest shadow following me everywhere I go. And then there's backtrading? I don't believe it has anything to do with correcting errors. I believe Stuart Grimes told me straight. This is about moving money. Big money."

"For who? You think this Dawson guy was serious about cartel money? Come on, Peter. Not Father. Not Morgan. I've known her my entire life. She's my godmother. No, there's got to be something else. They may well be protecting their interests against Dawson, but who can blame them? He's already fired one shot and failed with the Treasury thing. Now this."

Peter halfheartedly agreed he had blown things out of proportion. But then, as an afterthought, he mentioned Sarah Guzman and her husband Enriqué. When he finished, Kate's face darkened, as if she had made a hidden connection. Peter didn't know how to interpret her look, but he knew the names struck some kind of chord.

"You'll keep everything I've told you to yourself?" he asked.

"Attorney-client privilege. That sounds strange for me to say, since I've never had a client before." She stared into Peter's eyes, then laughed. Although strained, it was the perfect antidote. "I told you," she continued, trying to make it sound light, "I like my men beholden. Not that you're my man or anything…it's merely a figure of speech." Trying not to, she laughed a second time.

"I gotta go," Peter said, grabbing her hand, afraid this small gesture of forgiveness might evaporate. "I don't think I'll stick around to talk to Jason. I, uh, need to think things over. You've been a big help. Thanks. And…"

"And what?"

"Do…do think we can go back to being friends? This time, when I say I'll call, I'll call."

She nodded in slow motion. "I once told you: my feelings for people never change. Friends? Yeah. We're back to being friends."

"Thanks, Kate. That means a lot to me."

"You'll come to my wedding—maybe wear a blue dress and be a bridesmaid."

"I'd be flattered," he said, batting his eyes. Peter looked at his watch. Drew would be waiting. "Time for me to go."

"Where now?" she asked.

"Coronado Island with Drew."

"Why?"

"Gotta see a man about an accident."

"The ex-cop Agent Dawson spoke of?" she asked. "Ellis?"

Peter backed up as he nodded. The impulse to grab her swept over him like a desert flood. "I'll let you know what I discover."

"Be careful," she said. "I'll see what I can learn from my end. Any way to leave you a message?"

He gave her Drew's mailbox information. "If I have something to relay, counselor, I'll leave it there."

Was Kate warming to him, yet struggling to keep her own emotions in check? Peter silently asked himself the question as he stole as many final glances at Kate as he dared. He knew that *he* was light years beyond warm, and that *he* had no ability to hold his own emotions in check. Not wanting his imagination to get the better of him, he left before he did something really stupid—like reaching out to hold her.

———

Ten minutes later, he neared the parking lot of the nursery rendezvous with Drew. He tried to believe that no matter what, he and Kate *could* be friends. He felt better, then worse. It would hurt seeing her, knowing she had married someone else. Why had he always talked himself out of calling? He couldn't figure it out, but he now guessed that somewhere in his misdirected heart was an assumption that they would eventually come together, when *he* was ready.

"What an idiot," he whispered.

A moment later, he saw Drew waiting outside his car, the window down so his friend could listen to the radio. They waved as Peter coasted in on the backs of his heels.

"You look like you've run a marathon, White Bread," Drew said.

"I feel worse than that."

"Where to?" Drew asked.

"You mind driving me someplace, backing me up if necessary?"

"Sounds dangerous."

"Could be, I guess," Peter said, not knowing whether this was a wild goose chase or a dangerous undercover mission.

Thirty-five minutes later, they turned right, having driven the two-mile length of the Coronado Bridge crossing over San Diego Bay. Peter looked at the map and directed Drew towards an expensive vacation home owned by an ex-cop who had a story to tell about a woman, a car, and a crash.

———

Chemistry, left over from childhood, had attacked Kate the moment her father first mentioned Peter's name. That was the day he came looking for a job. Then, when she saw him stride into the law office—tentative and nervous like a little lost boy—a tidal wave of emotion had nearly knocked her over. And today, despite her anger, her resolve had melted. She now fought to interpret all they had just shared, while trying to recompose herself, a task that wasn't coming easily. When he spoke of the heart being the last to learn, she had wanted to believe him. Was he sincere? Did he care for her half as much as she cared for him?

"Stop it, Kate." She reminded herself that Peter had said lovely things in the past and never made good. He had stretched her heartstrings tight enough to break them.

She closed her eyes. A familiar image tarnished her mind. She fantasized about having an automobile accident on the way to her wedding. In this dream, she arrived at the church late and Frederick, in a fit of anger, stormed out of the church, tired of waiting, assuming he'd been stood-up. With that, the engagement ended, then and there. Not her fault, but nevertheless over.

Why, she wondered, did she have such inane thoughts? A shrink would tell her it was because she didn't love Frederick Drammonds—that she dreaded being his wife.

"I don't need a psychiatrist to tell me that." Her words echoed off the ceiling and through her brain.

She began to pace around her father's office, thinking and glancing at the books crammed into the built-in shelves. The thick volumes closed in, causing her scattered thoughts to migrate. How many books were there? Thousands—each crammed with legal cases, precedents, statutes that one day might be used to acquit one of her father's clients—guilty or not—that might be used to get a case, like the famous Stenman Treasury auction case, dismissed. Other books addressed courtroom presentation, comportment, and the alchemy needed to create reasonable doubt where none existed.

The practice of law, she thought, was like a chess game, using strategy and attack to gain victory. Get the black pawn to the end of the board, freeing him to become an attacking queen, but only if the black pawn was made of the right material—gold, silver, or better yet, cold, hard cash.

All of this contemplation came to her because of one thing Peter had said: "Sarah Guzman is the widow of Enriqué Guzman."

Her father had spoken of Sarah Guzman on several occasions over the years. He had arranged Sarah's defense, twenty years ago, at the request of Morgan Stenman. *The charge*: premeditated murder. She killed her father. Not just killed, but stabbed him thirty or more times with a six-inch blade. Back then she was Sarah Brigston, debutante daughter of one of the most visible money managers in New York. Her father had been one of Morgan

Stenman's earliest investors. Justifiable homicide was the defense. The father had molested the daughter—sexually and repeatedly—from the age of seven until she moved out of the house with her mother and brother at the age of fourteen. On Sarah's eighteenth birthday—as if she *wanted* to be tried as an adult—she snuck into his Upper East Side cooperative, used the key she had kept all those years, and punctured him until he resembled human Swiss cheese. She didn't try to hide, and didn't deny her handiwork. In court, to everyone's surprise, she insisted on taking the witness stand.

"Her look beguiled the jury," Kate's father had said years later. "Her words wove a kind of horrific magic over that courtroom. She didn't need an attorney after that. It took the jury less than an hour to return: Not Guilty."

Kate was seven or eight at the time, but later, when she learned details of the case, she remembered thinking it was a just verdict. Over the years, Sarah's name occasionally came up in conversation, and Kate always paid attention. She knew Sarah Brigston had married a successful businessman and now lived in Mexico. Even the name Guzman was familiar. But when Peter mentioned Enriqué Guzman, all the awful pieces fell into place. She knew of the Mexican cartels and the Guzman empire, but Kate had never put Sarah Guzman into that family mix. Now, if what Peter said was correct, she managed a money laundering operation tied directly to Morgan Stenman.

Sadly, it all made sense. Her father was secretive about his business trips, yet Kate learned at work this past summer that he often went to Mexico, Switzerland, the Cayman's, and Mauritius—off the coast of Africa.

Kate now sat at her father's desk, surveying the neat, checkerboard stacks of papers. She retrieved the lengthy User I.D. from her wallet—the one she had copied the day her father was too drunk to remember that he'd left his PC on—then recalled the password: hannahannekate. This time around, her interest had nothing to do with Stenman's payroll policy.

She typed in the User I.D. and waited, her hands trembling. A moment later she had broken in. The cursor drew her gaze to the request for a file name. Not knowing where to start, she began a file-search. She started with *Guzman* but turned up nothing. She tried: *Sarah, Sarah Guzman, Ensenada, Ensenada Partners*, also to no avail. What should she look for? Something to do with money. She typed in *Bank Accounts*. Nothing. Then, *Fund Transfer*. She got a single response: *Biometric Fund*

*Transfer.*

She double-clicked and began to read. After ten minutes, she understood that these operations had nothing to do with legitimately managing money. The sophistication and secrecy involved went beyond anything she had ever seen or heard of. She then read through an agreement granting her father power-of-attorney for Morgan Stenman in the transfer of funds between accounts within Stenman's family of funds. And such an arrangement meant he understood the operation's inner-workings. It also meant that if illegal activity was being undertaken—and that was her guess—he was an insider.

"Oh my God!" the voice boomed.

Kate spun. She hadn't heard him enter, nor had she noticed him step up close enough to see the computer screen and read the text. His features distorted and grew ugly. His face became that of a stranger. He looked nothing like the man she had loved unwaveringly her entire life. Her father had never struck her, but he looked close to doing so now.

"What have you done?" Ayers asked. "How did you get access? First Hannah, now this."

"Hannah? What do you mean?" New suspicions jammed her mind.

"Nothing. This file you violated is just standard securities law—"

"Don't insult my intelligence, Father. Peter told me—"

"Not Peter…"

"Yes. He was here," she said. "I've decided to give him legal advice, if I can."

"What a fool." Ayers picked up the phone and punched four numbers—the first four digits of his employer's private phone—before hanging up. The attorney trembled, and indecision forced his shoulders to drop and his face to sag. "This is such a damned mess. And what makes you think Peter needs representation? He hasn't done anything."

"Somebody's spying on him, and he's seeking answers I think might land him in trouble."

"He'll find trouble all right, but that's all he'll find. Nothing exists that…"

"You choking on your words? Nothing except maybe Hannah Neil's registered mail?"

"He told you of Hannah's activities?"

"That she sent information to an Agent Dawson at the SEC? That there's more incriminating information in cold storage? Yes and yes, Father. Either you tell me exactly what is going on, or I investigate on my own."

"You can't. They killed…"

"They killed who?" Kate demanded. "Hannah?"

Ayers gave no answer, but a tear rolled down his cheek.

"Tell me, Father."

"This is Pandora's Box. If you want to do Peter a favor, tell him to destroy what he has. His information won't amount to much anyway. It might cause some dislocations, embarrassment for a few people, but in the end, the significant damage will be to him. If I say anything, they'll do things to you, to your mother, to me. You can't begin to imagine what unspeakable things they're capable of. You getting the picture, Kate?"

She smelled her own fear. "Cooperate with us, Father."

"No. I cannot. You know names. That's it. I'll destroy these records— not that they'd do anybody any good. Offshore accounts are legal. Peter loves his job, and is set to make millions over the next few years. I don't think he'll jeopardize that. If he does…"

Ayers went to the keyboard and pressed a series of buttons. The files disappeared.

"I never thought I'd say this to you—I love you, Father—but you will never set eyes on me again if you refuse to help."

"Goodbye, then. I won't permit you to be harmed."

He turned, exited the library, and slammed the door.

Kate realized she had nothing concrete, but she also knew that Peter faced serious danger and had to be warned. After she left the house, she stopped at a gas station to use the payphone. She dialed Drew Franklin's mailbox and left a message:

> *Agent Dawson told you the truth about everything. Be care-*
> *ful. Do not phone my father. Meet me where we had our first*
> *date. Tonight, at seven. Do not let anyone follow you.*

By the time she hung up the phone, she had forgotten about promising to drive up to Los Angeles to spend the evening with her fiancé. In fact, in her current intense state, she forgot she even had a fiancé.

# CHAPTER TWENTY-TWO

HAVING PASSED THE CORONADO NAVAL BASE AND THE HOTEL DEL Coronado, Peter and Drew cruised along Central Beach, where condominiums and mansions boasted semi-private beaches. Sailboats, docked a dozen yards from the exclusive boardwalk along Beachcomber Estates, forested their view. Attached in a row were units 1242, 1244, and 1246, each with cantilevered balconies suspended over white sand. Across from this row of dwellings, on the opposite, non-beach side of Sunshine Avenue, were the odd numbered units. Former Detective Sean Ellis' address was 1246, which meant he had direct ocean access. Being at the end of the block, Ellis—more blessed than his neighbors—enjoyed 180 degree vistas of the harbor, ocean, and two-man volleyball.

"A three-story condo," said Drew. "This is an unbelievable spot. Over there." He pointed. "Guy with a flat top, aviator glasses, drinking beer. Probably has a gun under the towel on that table. Looks like the stereotypical steroid cop."

"Yeah. Hope this doesn't get into a wrestling match," Peter said. "I'll approach along his blind side."

"Damn," Drew said. "Must have been *some* inheritance."

"Or he sold influence and told a ton of lies over the years. That's what I need to find out." Peter scanned the street. It was deserted, as if the residents knew enough to stay indoors and out of harm's way.

"What if he did lie about Hannah's accident?" Drew slowed the car, then parked at the end of the dead-end street, half a football field's distance from Ellis' unit.

"If this guy's dirty, then I have to conclude that some of what Dawson said is true. How much, I still won't know for sure."

"You think it'll indicate foul play in Hannah's death?" Drew asked.

"Probably. If so, I nail whoever's responsible."

"Maybe I should take to the beach, like I'm sightseeing. Shuffle in the sand and watch. I'll be near enough to react."

"Just don't do anything until necessary," Peter said, nodding. "I prefer to get answers without a confrontation. If possible."

Peter planned his strategy as he veered towards the co-op. Politeness sure as hell wouldn't work. He decided to try tough. He'd draw on all the vile language he'd learned in the trading room. Drew strode through the dry portion of sand as Peter reached the building's edge. On this protected section of beach, the water lapped rather than broke along the shore, and the breeze smelled sweet, without the briny scent of seaweed. The calm felt eerie, as if the mighty Pacific were powerless.

Peter waited for Drew to make his way to the section of beach off Ellis' porch. Once his friend had positioned himself within striking distance, Peter turned the corner and approached his target. Screwing on a sour face, he flipped his baseball cap, wearing it backwards. "You Ellis?" Peter said, feigning arrogance.

The man rotated his twisted steel-like torso. The motion caused his neck to knot and his shirtless chest to flex. His shoulders rolled into two enormous balls. Evenly tanned pecs, biceps, and triceps danced in readiness.

A furrowed brow indicated to Peter he had the right man. "I got some questions for you," Peter continued.

"I got a question for *you*: get outta here." Ellis had unsparingly vicious eyes and an overmuscled face to go along with the rest of his physique.

"Sorry, Asswipe, but that's not a question," Peter said as he attempted a swagger.

"You wanna be shot, or have your pencil neck broken?"

"Now, at least that's a question. An interrogative, don't ya know, ends in a question mark. A statement is adorned with a period. Maybe you're not dumber than a post, after all." Through peripheral vision, Peter saw Drew wag his head as Ellis reached for a towel. Peter prepared to duck bullets.

"You got a smart mouth," Ellis said, mopping his damp hair, continuing to examine Peter as if at an autopsy. "You've also got too much brass to be a run-of-the-mill jerkoff. So who sent you?"

"Smart boy, Detective Ellis. People who sent me want you to know we've got a little problem. Kind of a warranty issue. Need you to say a few things a second time. Maybe in front of a DA."

"Yeah? Who you referring to that's needing my help?" Neck veins writhed, looking ready to burst evil.

"You expect me to spell it out, Numbnuts? Person who recently helped pay for this pad? Got it yet?"

"You mean the crash thing? They told me that was it. Arrive at the scene, say she drove too fast…you know the rest. I did my job, I got paid."

"Maybe Mizz Guzman needs more."

"You tell that blond witch…" His jaw clamped shut and his Adam's apple rode up and down as he swallowed the profane thought.

"Maybe somebody don't quite believe you—someone's thinking it wasn't an accident," Peter said. "If they figure things out, it ain't just our asses, dude. *Capiche*?" Peter hoped to God this didn't sound as lame as it felt.

"A deal's a deal. I didn't come back and ask for more money after."

"Oh, my. I am so sorry for bothering you. I'm sure *Señor* Nuñoz will understand." The change in Ellis' demeanor confirmed to Peter what Agent Dawson had said: Nuñoz *was* a man everyone feared. "You don't mind if I climb this here plexy-wall so's I don't gotta shout?"

Peter straddled the three-foot Plexiglass gate and stepped over. He took a couple strides and stood next to Ellis. The ex-cop stood an inch taller and weighed at least fifty pounds more than Peter. The monster-man's exposed skin glistened and smelled of tanning oil. Peter felt like a gnat ready to get squished.

"This is got Nuñoz involved?" The ex-cop looked upset.

"I'm a nice guy, but Nuñoz, he's likely to take that stinkin' Coppertone and squirt it up your ass until it soaks your pea brain. If I was you, I'd talk to me."

"This sucks…don't tell that cocksucking beaner I said that. Don't tell him I called him—"

"Relax, Detective. I only wanted to know that you would—" *would what?* Peter wondered, suddenly tongue-tied. Ellis squinted in the way a man does when he suspects someone is full of it "—that you'll confirm in a court of law—if necessary—that you witnessed that accident and crash. That you'll confirm your lie."

The wild dangerous animal reemerged. Ellis trembled with rage, and his buffed arms blew up into something resembling ham shanks.

"*Confirm my lie?*" Ellis asked. "What kind of a dipshit way to ask a question is that? You ain't from Nuñoz. I know when I'm being bullshitted by a bright boy. Who sent you?"

"You dare challenge Nuñoz?" Peter silently said goodbye to his thin cover. "I'll have to tell him—"

"Yeah? Go ahead," Ellis said through a sneer. "In fact, dipshit, I'll call Nuñoz. I'll take my chances that he don't give a rat's ass about me insulting you. Or kicking your ass." Ellis' stiff finger jabbed Peter's chest. The action forced Peter backwards.

Ellis grabbed a cell phone from the table. With his free hand he snatched a 9mm from under a towel, just where Drew had guessed. He held the handset to his ear, the gun to Peter's forehead. It took a few seconds, but before anybody answered Ellis' call, Drew hurtled the fence. His right foot landed on the aluminum rail, using it as a launching pad. His shoulder tucked, his body parallel to the patio surface, he hit Ellis just below the neck with a vicious clip. The dense man's skull snapped back. In the process of crashing, the ex-cop fumbled both items—the gun and the phone.

Ellis' forehead rebounded from whiplash in time to crush a low table, shattering the glass top. Drew bounced off his victim and landed off to one side, his right hand supporting his weight, keeping him from wiping out.

Peter glanced at Drew and understood that they had arrived at an identical conclusion—the time had come to exercise rules number one and two: run like hell, then drive faster than hell. To anyone observing them leap over a chaise lounge and the low wall, then hit the beach and sprint away, the pair would look like athletes in thieves' retreat. They retraced the path Peter had taken ten minutes earlier and flung themselves into Drew's Pinto wagon. A few seconds later, they circled the roundabout and sped off.

"You didn't like his answers," Drew said through winded breaths.

"He's a damn liar. I'm certain Mom *was* murdered."

"I'd say it's time to nail someone." The screech of tires failing to hug a corner punctuated Drew's comment.

"You've got an eight-month pregnant wife. This is up to me."

"What's my wife got to do with this?"

"Everything, Drew. They'll go after your family if they have to. You hang back. Relay messages."

"No—"

"Yes. I've got a plan," Peter lied. "It doesn't require your direct help." Peter sensed that Drew somehow understood the danger, not to himself, but to his wife and unborn child.

"You better keep me in the loop, White Bread."

"I will," Peter said, lying for the second time in less than twenty seconds.

Half an hour later, again on his own, Peter phoned for messages. When he got Kate's urgent directive to meet for dinner, he checked his watch. He had four hours to kill. Fifteen minutes later, he accessed and withdrew cash from an automatic teller machine. With four hundred of those dollars, he purchased a twenty-one speed, all-surface bike. Peter decided he didn't dare rent or borrow a car. For the time being, he figured he'd be much tougher to locate on a bike or on foot.

Peter rode the new bike into Del Mar to wait for Kate. He sat in a corner of a bar, ordered a beer, and watched the front door as nonchalantly as he could manage. At half past five, he checked for messages on his home answering machine and in Drew's mailbox.

He never returned to his table.

———

Howard Muller couldn't be happier. All he needed was for Neil to pick up his messages, phone for instructions, and get his ass to the office. It was nearly perfect. Neil confronting ex-Detective Ellis had everybody paranoid. That Neil alluded to Sarah Guzman and mentioned Carlos Nuñoz by name had sealed his fate.

While Guzman and Nuñoz operated in the background on their own complex plans, Muller had made the unilateral decision to take matters into his own hands. He didn't need Nuñoz' help. He didn't even need to consult with the sub-intelligent wetback. He had figured out a way to solve several problems at once. He'd get those damning papers back, not because he cared about Nuñoz or Guzman—on the contrary, he'd just as soon see their bodies in a state of decomposition—but because his name was attached to nearly every illegal Stenman transaction in the last five years. Even those idiot bureaucrats at the SEC would be able to trace his involvement. In some ways, even more satisfying than settling that matter would be scaring the shit out of Neil. Maybe, as payback, even break him. And once the documents were safe, Neil's life expectancy would be days if he was nimble, hours if he wasn't. Muller laughed. This felt better than watching a company he was short declare bankruptcy.

Muller looked around the room and approved. He had chosen his office as the place of confrontation for a simple reason: he owned every person on these premises. If the unforeseen happened and a problem arose—which he didn't think could happen since he controlled all the information—then he had the ability to erase everything. Stenman's crews were all former government agents, and they knew how to clean up a mess and make it disappear. And they would do anything for the right kind of money, and Stenman Partners had more than enough of that particular commodity.

Muller had only a small fear that Neil might not take the bait. Failing to check for messages in time would puncture his plan. He kept his fingers crossed that Neil didn't screw this up for him.

Near six p.m., Muller's phone rang. He hit speaker.

"You son of a bitch!" Peter's voice sounded like an attack-dog's bark.

Good, Muller thought. He's primed. "Get your ass moving," Muller ordered, having a hard time working the words through a ridiculous grin. "The guards'll wave you through."

"Where is she?"

"I'll look forward to explaining." Muller hung up.

He rose from his desk and went to the file cabinet. He opened the drawer and took out a thin, two-inch by three-inch metal box. He depressed a red button located next to a small antenna. The process made him feel warm inside.

Sliding the metal box across his desk as if it were an attacking queen, he said, through an exultant laugh, "Checkmate, Mr. Neil. Check *and* mate."

---

Peter hung up and reached into his pocket for additional change. He silently cursed himself for having left his cell phone at home. The sloppiness did nothing for his already waning confidence.

Before pedaling the last quarter mile and confronting Muller, Peter phoned Drew at home. Drew picked up on the first ring.

"Any word from Monica?" Peter asked.

"No. Where are you, Bread?"

"I'm checking things out. Don't leave the house unless you hear from her. I'll call you as soon as I find out anything."

Peter hung up, jumped on his bike, and began pedaling through the dark.

None of this made sense, he thought as he struggled to focus on the white curb. Muller had called Peter's home and left a message. "I have a trade in mind," he had said. "Someone's welfare for some papers—I'm certain you know what documents I'm referring to. Check with your friend Drew Franklin. He's missing something valuable."

Peter had called Drew. "Monica's gone," Drew had told him. "Left no message. This isn't like her, and I'm worried."

"I'm sure she's fine," Peter said, not at all sure.

Now, approaching the guarded gate, Peter couldn't figure out why Muller was so mindless as to leave an incriminating message on an answering machine. If the fool had kidnapped Monica and planned to use her as leverage to get those registered letters returned, why leave such a blatant trail? It didn't add up, but Peter didn't have the time to deliberate.

As promised, the guards waved him through Stenman's main entrance. He downshifted and coasted down the hill leading to the front doors, not dismounting his bike until he reached the steps. Ignoring the watchman's gaze, he dropped the bike on the lawn at the base of the stairs, used his pass card to enter, and signed in at the front desk. As he stepped inside the elevator, he saw the downstairs guard make a call.

On the third floor, Peter stepped into the half-lit hallway. Past experience suggested that the only people in on a Saturday evening were research analysts on the second floor and weekend cleaning crews. No cleaning crews on the third floor, though. A mop stood upright, its cloth tendrils soaking in an aluminum pail—obviously left behind by someone told to leave in a hurry.

Reaching the keypad outside of trading, Peter heard the lock disengage before he could enter the password. He opened and stepped into the room, completely darkened except where a crack of light leaked from between Muller's drawn curtains. The main door retracted at Peter's back and self-locked. Feeling his way along the desks, he took care not to trip over trashcans or electrical cords. Disinfectant now masked the predominant weekday aroma—fried food. The silence unnerved him. The place no longer felt familiar.

Peter mentally reviewed what he knew about Muller's office. Stuart had mentioned large amounts of cash behind one panel. Muller kept his desk key in a card file in a far corner, and had Civil War crap mounted behind glass cabinets—probably wired to an alarm in the event of theft. The interior office walls were see-through, like glass, but soundproof. With the drapes drawn, that meant that whatever went on inside would remain private, even if somebody stumbled into the trading room.

What else? He racked his brain. Peter recalled a fire alarm and numerous overhead sprinklers. Also, the locks on his office door were sophisticated. Muller changed the code weekly, Stuart had said.

Before Peter knocked, the door swung open. Looking self-satisfied, Howard Muller sat perched behind his desk with a smart-ass grin pasted ear-to-ear. "I realize you are in a bit of a rush, so please step in," he said.

Peter complied. This door also self-shut and locked. "Where's Monica Franklin?" he snapped.

Muller, a bundle of explosive energy, looked like he enjoyed the confrontation with Peter. "You have something I want: *those* documents. You tell *me*, I tell *you*."

Peter stepped forward. As he did, Muller picked up a metal box and held it outstretched—as a magician might hold a deck of cards for his audience to see.

"Stop right there, Neil. I anticipated your non-cooperation." Muller's fingers folded over the box. Peter fixated on the thumb as it depressed a red button.

Peter looked around the room, moving only his eyes.

The immense skull shook. "Here's what's happening: this is a detonator, tied to a room wired with explosives. In that room, several miles away, is a very pregnant black woman."

"You're insane. What's wrong with you?" Peter needn't have asked the question. Muller's eyes were chutes that led straight to hell and thoroughly billboarded his problems. The man was vile, and his evil was joyous, enraptured, and at the core of his being. It's what made him so good at what he did for a living: lying, breaking the law, unnecessarily destroying people, and amassing fortunes at the expense of others. And for Muller, this current drama was about more than simply retrieving those damning papers. It was about hatred. And sport. About obliterating his most despised opponent.

"You are a pissant, Neil," Muller said, using a tone that confirmed all of Peter's suspicions. "I suggest you listen, carefully." Muller again grinned, as if reacting to an inner joke. "Think back to that moron, Stanley Drucker. It'll save us some time…" Muller gave an explanation identical to the one Carlos Nuñoz had given to Stanley Drucker. "If you try and remove my thumb," Muller said, "the Franklin woman will blow up. If you substitute your own hand—assuming you can do that without this button retracting—she will blow up. The sensors will recognize only *my* thumbprint. So as to make certain we reach a resolution expeditiously, this device will send its signal in twenty minutes, no matter what I do. You may thank Sarah Guzman for the idea. And while I don't much like her personally, she has a formidable mind. Don't you think?"

Peter took another step, placing himself only a yard away from Muller, then stopped. What to do? He didn't have an answer.

"You don't want me to lift my thumb," Muller said, the calmer half of his split-personality now speaking.

Peter watched as Muller's thumb twitched, on purpose, as if a central part of the damn show. "How do I know you won't kill Monica anyway?" Peter asked, buying time to think.

"Trust." Muller laughed a mocking belly-laugh. "That's funny. Almost as funny as you saying I could be a Macy's Parade float." With those words, Muller flipped a mental switch and his voice became hard and crazy, worse than before. "What do you say, Neil? A fucking trade? Huh? Come on, wise guy. What do you say? Hit the bid? Take the offer? How's it feel to be an impotent piece of nothing, you nothing? You have a split-second to decide. Assess your risk-reward. You ready to shit in your pants yet? Sure you are. You've been screwing around with the best. Me. Did you really think you had a chance? Get fucking real—" The man sounded like Stuart on drugs. Only Muller mainlined suffering.

Aware of the emptying hourglass, Peter cut the tirade short. "Shut up, Muller! Tell me: do you have a way to disengage that thing?"

As Peter waited for an answer, something nagged his subconscious. He looked at the Civil War trophy case. The safe. Toward the small desk-key hidden in the index card box. Tape. Matches. He considered all of Muller's words, and then glanced at the man's hand and arm and body. He imagined noise and chaos. How did all these pieces fit together? *Did* they fit together?

"Of course I have a way to disengage things," Muller finally said, not sounding as if he cared whether Peter believed him or not. "I'm here to trade a life for some worthless documents."

Muller stood, holding the detonator chest high, and a bit too casually, Peter thought.

A powerful shudder suddenly passed through Peter's body, rattling his spine and clearing his mind. In that moment, he convinced himself of the futility of negotiating with Muller. He had the seeds of a plan that was less than brilliant, but seemed better than taking his chances with Muller. A tight knot released from Peter's belly like a spring, catching Muller in total surprise. Peter reached out and slammed both hands across the extended box, enveloping the CIO's fat thumb atop the button, making certain he couldn't relax the pressure he had on the detonator. Muller went from bent to rigid in a fraction of a second. With a leveraged twist, Peter wrenched the imprisoned wrist. Pain spread across the man's gigantic face faster than the flash of a struck match.

Peter pulled the twisted arm, circled it behind Muller's back, and lifted. As large as Muller was, he did not match Peter in strength or agility. In a helpless reflex, Muller rose up on his toes, and Peter pinned the wrist and arm against his back in a half-nelson. Muller breathed so heavily that his airborne blasphemies were unintelligible.

Don't let go of his hand, Peter reminded himself in a steady mantra.

"Where is she?" Peter hissed in Muller's ear.

"Nowhere." Tears supplanted sparks as Muller melted. "I wouldn't have had you come…" He coughed, then tried again to speak: "Had you come if—"

"Wrong answer." Peter pulled on the pinned arm. Muller screamed. "Where is she?" Peter repeated.

"I told you…"

Peter tuned him out. Even if Muller revealed where he held Monica, they had too little time to find her and deliver her to safety. Taking another tack, he asked, "How do you disengage this thing?"

"You don't disengage," Muller said. It sounded like a plea.

Peter gave up trying to get through to Muller. *A wireless signal. Radio waves, traveling through walls.* He had earlier formulated an extreme plan and, with all other options tapped out, he decided to go for it. It amounted to a longshot, but at least it was some kind of shot.

Peter did a final inventory of the office contents. "I'm going to tell you to do something," he said. "If you don't, I swear to God I'm going to kill you. You understand?"

"Yes…but a mistake—"

"Your safe," Peter said. "The one built into that panel. The one with all that cash for paying-off scum. Open it."

"No…"

Peter tugged at Muller's wrist, driving a hip into the man's back and forcing him against the wall, near his desk. "Do it."

Muller's free hand depressed a button on the lip of the desk. A wall panel slid open, revealing a two-foot safe with a mounted keypad.

"Enter the damn code. Now!" Peter yelled, compliance with his commands no longer an issue.

Muller leaned in and pressed a series of numbers. The safe popped open an inch. Peter looked to his watch. Time seemed to move illogically, in chunks of seconds. Clutching Muller's hand with his right palm, Peter used his left to finish opening the heavy door. Reaching in, he pulled out two bags and dropped them to the floor. Bundled bills were evident through the canvas.

He then steered Muller to the Civil War trophy case. Peter smashed the glass, activating a burglar alarm. Muller no longer attempted to speak or resist. In a sweeping motion, Peter grabbed one of the two unsheathed swords mounted in a metallic X. He yanked. The pitted blade of the field officer's sword held its mount. Peter made a second attempt, leveraging his weight. This time, the relic released with a jerk. The momentum caused Peter to teeter. Muller limply flowed with the action, but his thumb-grip on the detonator held.

Peter unwound Muller's arm, bringing it from around the back. He then flattened that arm across the wooden desk and raised the blade overhead, clutching the sharkskin wrap of the grip. Aiming, he brought the edge down in a chopping axe-motion. At mid-forearm, the lower half of Howard Muller's appendage separated from his body-main. Peter moved before blood spraying from Muller's stump could soak him.

Peter carried the forearm across the room, thumb still attached to the small metal box, still depressing the red button. Muller collapsed to the floor with a thud.

Peter found the index-card box that held the key to the desk drawer, not daring to look at the gray flesh of Muller's arm. He snatched the small key and returned. Unlocking and opening the desk drawer, he found a tape dispenser. He began winding scotch-tape around the lifeless thumb, pinning it in place against the button. He counted the seconds. He reached eight the moment he stood next to the open safe. He estimated the steel-reinforced walls at four inches. He dropped the taped creation, fingers already gone stiff, through the twenty-inch opening. He swung the door shut.

Would the safe's heavy walls blunt the radio signal when the time limit expired? Yes, it would, he told himself. Four inches of hardened steel should do the trick. It had to.

Peter stepped over Muller's hemorrhaging body to the far window. The overhead lights reflected off skin, making Muller's face look as lifeless as ivory. Peter tried to bury his feelings. He had never brought such physical pain to another person, but this was an unprecedented moment in his life, calling for unprecedented actions. He did what he had to and did it without further pause. And he didn't have the luxury of dwelling on these thoughts. If he survived, he'd have plenty of time in the future for regret. As for now, he needed to move quickly and waste no time. He unlocked and opened the thick-glassed window. The exterior lights, beaming from multiple floodlights, made the ground as bright as day. The sounds of a siren filtered through the opening. The police were responding to the burglar alarm.

Muller's internal phone line—on a corner table—flashed, diverting Peter's attention. Peter picked up and listened: "This is Security…" Peter felt the concern in the hired cop's voice.

When the guard said, "I know you told us not to interrupt, no matter what—" Peter had an inspiration. Doing his best imitation of Muller's vile voice, he said, "Then fucking follow instructions," and hung up. He hoped the guard feared Muller more than the chaotic situation going on around him, at least for a few more minutes.

Peter again stepped over to Muller's desk. He retrieved a gold lighter he recalled seeing moments earlier. He swept the loose papers on Muller's desk into a metal trashcan. Lighting the papers, he opened the windows on the west side of the office, making certain that anyone outside could see the smoke. The overhead vents pushed cool air out, into a breezeless night.

Peter crossed over to, and opened, the south window. He put the lighter to the drapes. It took a precious few seconds for the material to ignite, but when it did, it burned steadily, contributing a rich, dark smoke.

He next yanked the fire alarm on the wall between those two windows. To the sounds of stereo alarms, people began to file out the exits while sprinklers spit a river, cooling Peter's blistering skin. The smoke thickened and billowed with the downpour. *Good.*

A minute later, a second set of emergency vehicles—fire crews and two ambulances—entered the compound. Out front, weekend cleaning crews assembled on the steps. Peter counted four analysts and two of their assistants leaving through the front door. Several security guards used flashlights to highlight the building walls. The sirens grew loud enough to drown out most voices, but not loud enough to break Peter's concentration. He still didn't know if Monica Franklin was dead or alive. He also had no idea where Muller held her hostage. He initiated his hundredth prayer that day, this one shorter than the others—he still had a hell of a lot to do and not much time left.

Grabbing the two bags of cash, Peter leaned through a third window, out of view of the masses assembling in the front, and targeted a thick, low hedge, ten feet from the building. He tossed the first bag and watched it vanish into the dense brush. The second bag followed. Satisfied that nobody on the ground could see the money, Peter returned to the first window in time to see the fire trucks pull up to the fire hydrant at the edge of the building.

He made it to the desk a third time, picked up the phone, and dialed Drew's home number. He didn't know what to say, but somebody had to initiate a search—assuming the explosives hadn't already gone off.

When Drew picked up on the second ring, Peter said, "I'm sorry. I don't know—"

"White Bread. Where are you?"

"It's about Monica—"

"She's home…"

Drew explained that a man had called Monica, convincing her that she needed to meet him in the middle of nowhere. She left Drew a note, she said, but Drew suspected someone broke into their house and removed it. "Her car broke down…it was one small disaster after another," Drew said, the relief evident in his voice.

"She's home?" Peter tried to figure everything out in the few seconds he had left before Stenman's security forces barged in.

"What's all that noise, Bread? Sounds like you're in the middle of a war."

"I am, buddy. I need you to get hold of Agent Dawson." Peter fumbled for the slip of paper Dawson had stuffed in his shirt pocket back at the garage. "Here's his number…"

When they finished, Peter looked at Muller's suffering body and shook his head, disbelieving the insanity—Muller's life, draining away, onto a third-story office floor, and all because of an elaborate ruse? Muller never had a detonator, only a prop made to look like one. It made sense, though. Muller was a classic bully, someone who used intimidation and threat to get his way. Thinking himself smarter than everyone else, he figured he could manipulate Peter with his mind and his words. What an asshole! What did he think I was going to do? Peter asked himself. Sit back and wait for him to admit what he was doing? Laugh at the brilliance of his joke?

Peter trailed over to Muller. Blood drained, forming a pool. Soaking into the gray carpet, it looked like wet rust. Peter took his jacket and wound it around Muller's bloody stump. He pulled the bulky knot tight, hoping to stem the flow of blood. He then reached down and felt Muller's neck pulse. It was weak, but detectable. That done, he returned to the window, away from the lapping flames consuming the drapes, leaned out, and yelled, "Help me! Get a ladder and get me out of here." Peter looked at Muller and shouted, "And get a doctor up here. A guy's hurt. Bad. He needs help fast."

Ten minutes later, two bags tucked under his arm, Peter crawled into the back of one of the ambulances. He had soot smeared across his face, masking his features. He perched with his knees tucked to his chest, coughing convincingly. The medics attempted to put an oxygen mask over his face, but Peter indicated no. They sped off, sirens wailing. Just before the ambulance reached the freeway onramp, Peter insisted they stop. When they resisted, he opened a bag and pulled out a thousand-dollar bill, still crisp despite its age.

"You didn't get a look at me. I held you at gunpoint. Say whatever you want. Just forget as much as you can about me and this trip." When the driver hesitated, Peter pulled a second bill from the bag. "Two grand. That oughta do it." The medics involuntarily nodded and Peter understood—money really could buy almost anything. It could even make people forget.

Reaching into the bag one last time, Peter asked, "Anyone want to sell me their clothes?" Again, a willing seller.

A few minutes later, Peter jogged towards a hotel, up a hill overlooking the freeway. He changed clothes behind some brush and bought a room for cash. He left a message for Kate on Drew's voice mail.

With eyes closed, he waited.

---

When Peter's hotel phone woke him several hours later, he quickly picked up. "What took you so long, counselor?" he said. "I think I need an attorney."

"You're damn right you do."

"You know what happened at Stenman's?"

"No," Kate said. "That's not what I'm referring to."

"What, then?"

"You haven't heard?" Kate's voice cracked.

"If you're not referring to Stenman, Muller, and the fire, then no."

"Ellen Goodman."

"Ellen?" His former girlfriend's was the last name Peter expected to hear. "What about her?"

"Where were you tonight, Peter?"

"At Stenman's. Starting a fire."

"That isn't funny. Where?"

"I told you. At Stenman Partners. Third floor. Howard Muller's office."

"Can you prove it?"

"I think so. The guards saw me. Muller, he…" Peter didn't know quite how to explain. "What happened with Ellen?"

"Ellen's been raped and murdered. Somebody tied her to a bed, spread-eagled, and tortured her. The police are looking for you."

"Ellen's dead?"

"Peter, they think you're involved."

"Me? No way. I haven't seen Ellen since the day I left my job. Dead? Are you sure?"

"I'm positive, and several things have the police convinced you're involved. Your moonstone was in her bedroom."

"I haven't seen that since it was stolen."

"Did you call Ellen the other day?" Kate asked.

"Yes. She left me a message. I returned the call."

"Do you still have the tape?"

"No."

"We'll have to check phone records. Did you give her a present?" Kate sounded like a prosecutor.

"No. Ellen thought I gave her a cat, but I didn't."

"The DA's a family friend. He gave me some information. Said her cat's a calico. Just like Henry. Is that a coincidence?"

"Kate, I'm sorry about Ellen—devastated, in fact—but I'm not involved."

"The cat's tag indicated that Ellen named him Peter. It seems natural to assume that she named him after you. What's going on?"

"I don't know."

"I hope you're not lying...I can't help myself. I still care...You're not bullshitting me, are you?"

"Of course not."

"Good, because there's a lot more. Dark head-hair. Same color as yours on her sheets and pillowcase. A coffee cup in the kitchen. Your prints. A microwave—again, your prints on the door. Semen on the sheets. It looks real bad."

"I've never been in Ellen's apartment. She insisted on staying at my place so her other boyfriends, including our boss—Craig Hinton—wouldn't find out."

"Then we need the DNA results on the semen found on the sheets. They'll show it wasn't you. The rest of the stuff could've been planted— you've pissed off enough people to make that plausible. But in the meantime, you've got to turn yourself in. The labs are running a preliminary DNA test known as PCR. They expect results in two or three days."

"PCR? What's that?"

"It stands for Polymerase Chain Reaction. Forensics extracts the semen and vaginal samples from the sheets, grows DNA in the lab, then compares those to a sample of your DNA. Not as statistically significant as RFLP, but it should be good enough to get you off. The DA tells me he already got a sample of your DNA from a sealed envelope in your apartment."

"An envelope?" Peter asked.

"They got a search warrant. He didn't tell me what else they found, only that he was able to obtain a saliva sample from some outgoing mail you left behind."

"How'd you get all this information?" Peter asked, in awe of Kate's thoroughness.

"I told the DA I thought I could get you to turn yourself in if I knew what we were facing. He believes me. My credibility's on the line."

"Kate, it may be your credibility, but it's my life. I need time."

He then reviewed in detail the day's events with her. "I've got what looks to be a coupla million in cash lying on my bed. Stacks of thousands, hundreds, and twenties. All worn. I'm sure untraceable."

"Your alibi is that you robbed Stenman—" Kate said, her voice near shock "—either killed or maimed Stenman's Chief Investment Officer, set the building on fire, then escaped in an ambulance? This isn't helpful, Peter."

"Can't you do something? At least stall until I can meet with Agent Dawson."

"I'll negotiate with the DA, tell him we're coming in. I'll try and give you until four tomorrow afternoon. After that, I'm screwed. Can you live with that?"

"Yes. One last thing, Kate."

"I'm afraid to ask."

"I still need to meet with your father. Can you arrange that?"

"I don't think so."

"Why? He loves you more than life itself."

"I confronted him. His responses convinced me he's done some bad things. Then he sort of threw me out. And Peter?"

"Yes?"

"He said someone was killed. I think he meant your mother's death wasn't an accident."

"I've arrived at the same conclusion after talking with Detective Ellis."

"If he helps you, Father intimated that he's liable to end up in serious legal trouble, or worse."

"I'm sorry, Kate, but I need to talk to him. Will you ask? If nothing else, I want to understand the past—the history of our families."

"Our lives *have* crisscrossed in a painful pattern. Lovers, friends, and enemies, all intertwined. I'll try my best to set it up."

"Thanks."

"You aren't leading me down a primrose path, are you, Peter?"

"You mean with Ellen?"

"Yeah. Ellen and everything else."

"You have to believe me. I'm being straight with you. Stenman Partners isn't the greatest alibi in the world, but no way my semen is on those sheets."

"I believe you. I'll work on Father and leave a message on Drew's voice mail. You have a way to get hold of Dawson?"

"Drew's got his number and is gonna phone him."

"I'll camp out in the District Attorney's office," Kate said. "By the time you've turned yourself in, they'll have checked out your bizarre alibi. I should be able to get a reasonable bail."

"Unless they want to nail me for what happened at Stenman's," Peter said.

"You said you were justified. Somebody's going to have to do some heavy-duty explaining."

"That's true," Peter said.

"You have any theories on how your moonstone made it to Ellen's bedside table? Your prints on a cup and on her microwave?"

"Beats me," Peter said, "unless Ellen, or maybe even Craig Hinton if he was jealous, had me robbed the day I moved out of my old place."

"You think either of them engineered the theft?"

"Unlikely," he said. "I'm grasping at straws."

"I'll follow up on Hinton, just in case. His relationship with Ellen and the fact that he disliked you makes him a natural suspect. You'll meet me outside the courthouse, tomorrow at four?"

"Yeah. Four. How long before you get my release on bail?"

"Once we confirm things, a day, tops. You should plan to return Stenman's money when you turn yourself in."

"I took the money, hoping to trade it for answers. Under the circumstances, I'm happy to give it back."

Once he re-cradled the phone, Peter flopped across his bed and clamped his eyes. He wished he were back at the old apartment, with its tiny bathtub, bathing with and making love to Kate Ayers. Instead, questions, one stacked on top of the other, weighed like a mountain.

Tomorrow…Peter looked at the bedside clock. The red digits flashed 1:04. "No, not tomorrow. It's today already," he told himself. "Will I find answers *today*?"

Especially to the questions about Ellen Goodman—they had been intimate, and that meant something. But who would rape her? Torture her? "Same person who murdered my mother," he said, almost inaudibly.

The victims were innocent. The game was perverted. And Peter Neil was just beginning to learn how to play.

# CHAPTER TWENTY-THREE

**"I** WON'T SEE HIM."

It was Sunday morning and Kate had just informed her father of Peter's request to meet.

"Peter needs your help," she said. "So do I."

"No. It's too late for Peter. I told you this would end tragically if he persisted. Now he's wanted for murder, and that cockamamie alibi of his isn't going to hold."

"He didn't kill that woman. If you'd only—"

"For God's sake, Kate, wake up to what's happening. Stenman's guards deny seeing Peter last night. According to arson investigators, a cigar, left burning, started the fire. Morgan denies the theft of any money. Howard Muller is vacationing in the south of Mexico as we speak. The ambulance drivers claim they drove somebody, but whoever it was forced them to stop. And they don't recognize Peter as that person. Even if he was there—and I'm not saying he was—he still could have murdered the woman. The time of death may have been mid-afternoon. Even this Drew fellow told police he left Peter before two."

"The initial DNA tests will be ready tomorrow or early the next day," Kate said. "They'll prove he's innocent."

"You're not doing him any favors by pretending to be his attorney. You're smart, but you have no experience. He needs a real lawyer."

"He needs a…a friend. You can't be this cold-blooded. Somebody murdered Hannah Neil. You as much as said so yesterday. Peter confirmed that with Ellis."

"He went to see Detective Ellis? No wonder…"

"No wonder someone set him up?"

"I didn't say that." Ayers went to the cabinet near the sink. He reached for and retrieved a bottle of Jameson. He filled a six-ounce tumbler.

"It's not even eight in the morning," Kate said, her voice a knife's edge. "You're killing yourself, and rather than do something noble to ease your mind, you wallow, morning, noon, and night. Come on, Father. Did you love Hannah? What happened between you and Matthew Neil that caused best friends to quit being friends? Why do you turn your back on their only son? He needs your help."

Kate heard a noise at the kitchen door. She turned. Standing in the doorframe, looking old and defeated, was the forgotten woman.

"M...other," Kate stuttered. "I...I don't know what to say."

"That's all right, Kathryn." Anne Ayers, her chin trembling, looked at her husband of over thirty years. "Answer your daughter, Jason. Do you still love Hannah and her memory? I do—and I forgave both of you long ago...Answer Kate: what happened between you and Matthew Neil?"

"Anne. I'll be with you in a minute—"

"Do not put me off," she said. "I'm tired. Tired of deceiving myself. Tired of your weak and worn explanations. I've known for too long that your firm works for dangerous people. Is it drug money, Jason? I've told myself it isn't, but that's a lie. Isn't it?"

An awkward silence filled the kitchen.

Anne raised her index finger and aimed. "Goddammit, Jason! Answer me. Instead of getting drunk, say something."

"You don't understand, Anne. This is beyond—"

"Beyond your ability to do anything? Is that your cellophane explanation for everything? I'm sick of being your wife. I know I'm too old and worn-out to ever find another husband. I don't care. I'll live alone before I live another day with the man you've become. Thank God our daughter knows right from wrong."

"Please, Anne."

"Curtis overdosed on drugs," Anne said. "He was fourteen. Have you forgotten that? You are partially responsible for his death."

"No! I loved our son."

"You knowingly set up the legal defenses and bank accounts for killers. You are no better than they are." Anne Ayers turned. Three steps later, she stopped. Without looking back, she said, "In fifteen minutes I leave, unless you begin doing what's right. When I'm gone, it'll be forever."

"Don't."

"Then tell Kate and Peter what's happening. If it's still possible, help them."

Ayers took his half-full drink to the sink and poured it down the drain. Kate thought her father looked relieved. Maybe he wouldn't need to spend the rest of his life trying to hide the truth. They had all buried too many secrets, and this one, at least, might no longer eat away at him.

"Kate," he said. "I'll meet Peter in the guesthouse. Tell him to use Furlong Street—it's secluded. I'll leave the rear gate unlocked. But I warn you: no matter what Peter thinks, there's nothing left to do. This has gone too far."

"I want to be there, Father," Kate said.

"No. I have things I need to share with Peter. Alone."

Kate began to protest, but her mother shook her head. "This is between your father and Peter."

"But, Mother—"

"Come, dear. Make your call. Set up the meeting." With a hand on Kate's shoulder, Anne Ayers led her daughter away.

---

An hour later, Peter ducked through Ayers' back gate. He wondered why the man had changed his mind about cooperating, but what mattered most was Kate's conviction that her father could be trusted.

Peter scanned the yard, dotted by fruit and shade trees. The sky was clear and birds were chirping, perhaps warning one another that a stranger lurked nearby. He knew the feeling. Tall hedges ran around the perimeter of the multi-acre backyard, ensuring privacy. Peter bent down and picked up a stray lemon. He sniffed the fruit, aimed at a tree, and tossed the yellow oval. It hit the target, a Eucalyptus trunk, and bounced sharply right before rolling down a gentle slope towards a row of roses.

Crickets, birds, a distant dog, and a fountain—all combined to produce a natural symphony. Ayers' home felt peaceful. Peter knew it wasn't.

A cottage sat back from the main house. That was where Kate had told Peter to meet her father. The structure looked small next to the mansion, but was at least two thousand square feet—or about the size of a middle-class suburban house. The wood shingle exterior was weathered, and the roof was peaked. A red brick chimney, entwined with thick ivy, ran up the near side. Without knocking, Peter entered as a rush of wind blew past him, disturbing a line of dust motes that vanished once he shut the front door behind him.

Inside the guesthouse, Peter glanced at the back of Ayers' gray, motionless head, rising above a leather recliner. Across the surface of a mahogany table, Ayers had fanned out photographs, passing from one time, or year, or season, to another. Faces young and fresh grew heavy and lined. A stack of scrapbooks had fallen to the floor off to one side. They lay in a disheveled mound, pages open, slips of yellowed paper—press clippings it looked like—hanging out, bent and tired.

The room smelled musty. Dusty sheets covered most pieces of furniture. Drawn shutters, the slats closed, blocked out any hope of sunlight. The sole source of illumination came from a standup reading lamp, reflecting off the faces in the aged photographs.

Jason Ayers turned and weakly greeted Peter. As if weighing an extra hundred pounds, the attorney struggled to push himself up with the flats of his hands. He had red-rimmed eyes, strained, Peter suspected, from staring at the thousands of memories scattered across the room.

"I have so…many…" Ayers looked away. He tugged at a fleshy earlobe and took a half-step, stumbled, then tried again. His arms hung long and limp as if they had been de-boned. Wasting no time, Ayers began unloading four decades of pain. "I didn't do anything to help your mother…but not just her. Your father. I killed him."

Ayers turned in on himself as he laid out the story of Matthew and Hannah Neil and his role in bending their lives.

"The university investigated your father, because of me. It was done quietly…" Ayers spoke haltingly, and at length, and Peter listened without interrupting.

Later, when Ayers paused to drink a cup of water, Peter whispered, "So that's what we've avoided all these years."

Ayers heard Peter's words and shook his head. "There's more."

It took Ayers another half-hour to explain how he and Peter's father came to be estranged. Then, as if that weren't enough, Hannah's story followed. "She was murdered because she couldn't sit back and ignore wrongdoing."

Peter had already deduced most of that story. As the tale came to an end, Peter felt no rancor. Rather, he felt pity for everyone, including Ayers. Including himself. Once Ayers' revelations settled in, Peter's brain whirred with thoughts of how to proceed.

Ayers' voice lifted Peter from his concentration. "I want to help," he said, "but you cannot win. Guzman, Stenman, Carlos Nuñoz—none of them places any value on human life. I don't think they intend for you to make it to trial. Kate thinks you'll get bail. She's wrong. They found the murder weapon in your condominium. With all the evidence against you, there will be no bail. Furthermore, your alibi doesn't hold. You were officially never at Stenman's."

"People saw me."

"Who? The guards? Muller? Ambulance personnel you paid to forget? This isn't an American Airlines flight where a couple hundred passengers see you board, take a seat, and order cocktails. This is a secure location with dedicated, highly paid people who long ago sold their consciences to this particular bidder. In addition, Goodman's murder may have been earlier than your Muller visit. I told you—they're thorough. The message machine at your apartment? No message from Howard Muller exists. It was erased or stolen."

"But I'm innocent."

"Remember Cannodine and that Russian who murdered him along with all those innocent people? The man blew himself up. Or did he? Drucker? Did he really go berserk? I don't know how they managed any of it, but nothing is as it seems. Neither will your death, when it happens. Planning and power—they've got more of each than you can imagine."

"What would you do if you were me?" Peter asked.

"Run, maybe. You might buy some time."

"No." Peter's gaze fixed on the photographs. "My father was a good man."

"Yes," Ayers agreed. "The best person I ever knew."

"Courageous and principled?"

Ayers nodded, resignedly.

"Kate said you had power-of-attorney over Stenman's funds. Is that true?"

"If you're thinking I can strip assets, you're wrong. I can only transfer money from one fund to another. I can't take a dime out of the financial empire."

"How's the money moved?"

"Why do you—"

"How?" Peter demanded.

"Half the accounts use biometrics. Voice recognition. We're working on setting them all up that way."

Peter considered what he'd learned about the relationships between the players. Their priorities. How they dealt with treachery. "I have the seed of a plan," he said. "Can you help me set up an offshore bank account?"

Ayers gave a wary nod. "Yes. But why?"

Peter flagged a hand, signaling he wasn't ready to answer questions. "Are you involved in setting up accounts for Ensenada Partners?"

"With the new technology, yes."

"Good. Here's what I want you to do..."

When Peter finished, he said, "I'll explain in more detail later. Most of what happens next depends on Agent Dawson, Morgan Stenman, and Sarah Guzman."

"Stenman and Guzman?"

"I plan to sell them information. Five million sounds good to me."

"Are you insane, Peter? Once they've got Hannah's papers, you're dead."

"Maybe, maybe not. In a few days, I'll need you to set up a meeting with Morgan."

"I hope you know what you're doing," Ayers said. "You realize you can't turn yourself in to the DA if you intend to meet with Stenman."

"You'll have to explain to Kate. She's going to be in deep shit when I don't show up."

"She'll understand," Ayers said. "In the meantime, you'll need a car. A block away, south of the rear entrance, you'll find a green Taurus." Ayers handed Peter a set of keys. "Don't use credit cards or cash machines. If you need money, use the twenties you took from Stenman, not the hundreds or thousands—somebody might get suspicious. Don't forget, when you don't show up at the DA's, there'll be an all-points bulletin issued for your arrest."

"Understood. And thanks."

"Peter. If you need to, you can stay here at night. Use the back entrance and the side streets. Nobody will suspect I'm hiding you."

Ayers clutched Peter's hand. For the first time, Ayers' fingers felt possessed of warmth as a sliver of hope crossed Ayers' ragged face.

"My parents loved you," Peter said, reading Ayers' need. "We've all made mistakes." He understood the need for redemption. They all did.

———

After Ayers left the cottage, Peter mulled over his plan. He had used a trader's discipline in formulating his strategy, balancing the risk and reward of every option.

Committed to a course of action, Peter realized that time, more than anything else, was of the essence. He quickly showered, then took off.

It would be a busy Sunday.

———

Ayers leaned into his desk and reviewed what Peter had asked him to do. He didn't understand, but made the calls anyway. The first was overseas. He set up an account in the name of Peter Neil at Mauritius Trust Bank. Once he got the ten-digit account number, he began the process of opening seven accounts for Sarah Guzman at the same bank. On the last of these accounts, he requested and received a special number.

Why, he wondered, had Peter wanted Sarah Guzman to have an account number identical to his, but with two digits inverted? Before hanging up with the branch manager, Ayers asked, "You can connect Ms. Guzman's new accounts to the voice recognition system?"

"Yes," the deep voice informed him. "The equipment you delivered last month is in place. You will, of course, have her phone us to authorize instructions before we activate."

"Of course. Hopefully today. You can be reached if necessary?"

"For you and your employer, we are on duty twenty-four/seven."

Finished with that task, Ayers next phoned Stenman. When he got through, he said, "We should consider speeding up our account transfers. With all this confusion, I'm nervous…"

Stenman agreed.

"I've already undertaken some of the paperwork for Ensenada Partners," Ayers continued. "We need to set up final authorization."

Stenman informed him that Sarah Guzman was in town on "other security matters." Ayers played dumb, pretending he had no idea what those other matters might be. They agreed to meet in Stenman's office later

that afternoon. Ayers cradled the receiver and considered pouring himself a drink. Instead, he went upstairs. He needed to spend time with Anne, let her know he was sorry. That he loved her. That he had always loved her.

If necessary, he would say goodbye.

---

The loaner car was a godsend. Biking hadn't been a problem before because the distances were relatively short, but from here on out, Peter planned on traveling long, convoluted routes. And he had a long, long list of places to go.

First up, he needed to go shopping. He chose establishments miles away from his co-op—no use inviting trouble. From a discount clothing store, he purchased pullover shirts, another pair of running shoes, and sweats, all off-brand and, except for the shoes, a size too big.

*Next stop*: a drug store. He entered through the automatic doors, hiding his features from the shoplifting camera by hunching down. Scanning the "Personal Care" aisle, he squinted at the kaleidoscope of colored boxes until he spotted something called *Natural Instincts for Men*. He chose: *Lightest Brown*. On the way to checkout, he passed a sunglass stand and snatched a pair of clunky dark shades. Thinking through his intentions, he also purchased a hair dryer, hairbrush, and pair of binoculars. Per Ayers' advice, he paid for everything with nothing larger than twenties.

Once inside his car, Peter removed the dark lenses from the sunglasses and put the thick, lenseless frames over his face. From there, he drove three blocks before locating a barbershop open on Sundays. After getting a cut, he found a public restroom in an indoor mall. He used wads of paper to block and fill the sink. He read the instructions:

> *Put on plastic gloves and protect your clothing with a smock*
> *or towel. Pull tab and lift off the tip on Developer bottle...*

Peter improvised his way to a wet head of hair, squeezed the mixture onto his scalp, then streaked a trace of the chemicals across his eyebrows. Once the dye worked in, he camped in a stall for the required ten minutes. Two rinses later, he had a new look. His short hair looked to be at least three shades lighter than before. Peter used the new hair dryer and brush to finish the makeover.

Wearing a heavy coat with the collar upturned against the cool air, Peter passed a picture window on the way to the parked Taurus. He approved. "I hardly recognize you," he whispered. With a two-day growth of beard, glasses, and the change in hair-coloring, he had altered his appearance enough that anyone viewing his image in a newspaper or on television might not recognize him. At least not immediately.

---

From the Carlsbad Pier parking lot, Peter watched Agent Oliver Dawson enter the Surfside Bar. Shortly afterward, the agent exited, stood at the curb, and waited. When a taxi arrived, Dawson said something to the driver and climbed in. Peter took off towards a specific bus stop five miles south in Leucadia.

Dawson's cab arrived a minute after Peter did. The agent tossed some bills at the driver and slammed the door. He looked around, the scowl visible through Peter's binoculars. With a handful of change, Dawson fidgeted on the bus-bench and waited. He bent over and rubbed his bare arms with the palms of his hands.

As Peter watched, Dawson suddenly bolted upright and locked his sight onto a twenty year-old male shuffling in his direction. The boy, sucking the life from a cigarette, looked innocent enough, with a pierced ear, nose rings, and an orange swatch of hair hanging to one side. But Dawson appeared ready to react, as if this kid might pose some kind of threat. Peter took that as a good sign—the agent was on his guard, distrustful, and ultra-careful. That made two of them. Only after the youth's baggy pants turned a corner did Dawson resume shivering.

A block away, coming from the north, a train rumbled past. Peter had seen enough. If anyone had followed Dawson, he couldn't tell. He released the parking brake and lurched forward. A moment later, he pulled up to the bus stop. With his window already down, he said, "You look cold. Need a lift?"

Dawson stared. "Neil? You look like a punk."

"It was this or dreadlocks."

"Cute. How's life treating you, Neil?" The light tone of Dawson's voice didn't fool Peter. The man's eyes radioed his intensity, loud and clear.

"I'd just as soon hit the road," Peter said. "You coming?"

Dawson jogged to the front of the car and took shot-gun. "You do it?" he asked as Peter pulled away and drove east towards the freeway.

"Do what?"

"Kill that girl? You a love-crazed murderer?"

"That's not funny." Peter slowed down, changed lanes, then accelerated onto the on-ramp to I-5. He merged with the 75 mile-per-hour traffic, content that nobody had turned onto the freeway behind him.

"What's the story with all this running around?" Dawson asked. "I'm sitting at Sammy's Restaurant. Corner table, admiring the view, having a Diet Coke, waiting for you to show up, per our plan."

"Plans change."

"What a runaround. This bartender at Sammy's, an a-hole with an attitude, asks if I'm Dawson. I figure, oh shit, they've made me. I'm worried about you, thinking I'm going to get you busted."

"Thanks for the concern," Peter said, continuing to monitor the traffic from his car mirrors. He slowed to 50 and looked for anyone who slowed down with him. A few drivers gave him the "fuck-you-asshole" stare, and a couple others, upset over the little-old-lady routine, sharply cut in front of him in minor bouts of road rage. Satisfied that he had no tail, Peter re-accelerated to 70 and focused on what Dawson had to say.

"The crumb-ball then says I must be Dawson 'cause I'm the only runt with a rat-face. You call me a runt?"

"I didn't use that word."

"Thanks. Anyway, he says you told him I'd give him a twenty for relaying a message. I give him the money and he tells me to go out the back and run down the railroad tracks to the sports bar. Nice touch, Neil. A little payback?"

"I hadn't thought about it that way."

"He says a cab'll be waiting for me. So I waltz down the tracks and find this cabby who takes me to that shit-hole bar. I go inside and another bartender says he has a message for me. It costs me another twenty. He says to go to this bus stop. Place smells like prehistoric urine. I'm freezing my ass off, waiting for a bus that doesn't come. How come all the cloak and dagger?"

"Trust," Peter answered. "I had to make sure you weren't setting me up."

Dawson reached around and removed several folded pages from his rear pocket. "I had someone make some discreet inquiries into this murder thing. The evidence? I shouldn't tell you, but it's extensive."

"So I've been led to believe." Peter eyed the pages in Dawson's lap, but the fold prevented him from seeing what was on them.

"The DA's people are plenty nervous," Dawson continued. "Some big-time political pressure's coming down on them. My guess: Stenman and her cronies are tightening the screws. They want you brought in or shot trying to avoid arrest."

"Tell me something, Dawson. Are you really unemployed or is that bullshit? Can you really help me?"

"No more games?" Dawson asked.

"No more games."

"Good."

"Yeah. Good," Peter said.

"In that case, I'm reporting to the Director of Enforcement. He's coordinating with the Justice Department and the DEA, and he's the only one—aside from the person relaying messages—who knows anything. This..." he began to unfold the papers, "is a grant of immunity for any illegal trading you engaged in while employed by Stenman."

"That's not my biggest concern right now. You have any influence on this criminal investigation?"

"You turn over your mother's papers, and you get immunity for the white-collar stuff, but I'm not gonna lie to you. Nothing we can do about the murder rap. I warned you, these people are good."

"An attorney I know thinks I'll be murdered no matter what I do. You think that's possible?"

"Yeah—more than possible."

"You *are* an honest guy, Dawson. Just when a well-timed lie might help you get what you want, you're straight with me. I've underestimated you."

"You and the whole world. Get me those documents, and I go after these scum-suckers. Maybe that'll distract them some."

"I've got something else in mind. You keep that letter of immunity warm. I'm going to need it later—if this works out."

"If *what* works out?" Dawson gave Peter a suspicious look.

"I don't want a new identity, and I'm not going to hand over my mother's papers."

"Then we have nothing to negotiate—"

"I didn't say you're not going to end up with what you want. I said I won't be the delivery boy. We keep driving south and we'll be at the Mexican border in twenty minutes. Let's make it a round-trip. In the time it takes to get there and back, you listen to what I want from you. If you agree to follow my lead, I'll see that you get your evidence against Stenman—if that's what Mom had."

"You haven't looked at any of the documents, have you?"

"No, I haven't. Mom sent everything by registered mail, thank goodness. You think you know what's in those envelopes?"

"Names attached to some overflowing accounts. Bank trails. Notes made during meetings between Leeman, Johnston, and Ayers lawyers and Stenman, Muller, Guzman, others. Copies of documents that no longer exist. In other words, dynamite."

"You willing to play ball for a chance to handle some of this dynamite?" Peter asked, already knowing the answer. Dawson was on a professional jihad, and only his SEC investigations made his professional life meaningful. Peter had to fight this fight, or perish. Dawson battled out of principle. And Peter admired him for it.

Dawson peered out the window and ran a fingertip across his lip. Without turning, he said, "It doesn't cost me anything to listen." The feigned indifference didn't work. Peter understood the man was hooked and ready to be reeled in.

Halfway into the return trip home, Peter said, "That's the deal. You in, Dawson?"

"Do I have a choice?"

"Not if you want the evidence."

"Then I'm in."

"You can guarantee your boss—Ackerman—is gonna buy in?"

"Yeah, but he ain't gonna like it."

"Tough. I've still got a lot to figure out. Some things'll change on the fly as conditions warrant. That okay with you?" Peter took the Balboa exit, south of La Jolla.

"Where you taking me?" the agent asked.

"I asked if changes were okay, if necessary."

"Yeah. Where am I?"

"Pacific Beach. I'm dropping you off on Mission Bay."

"I'm parked at Sammy's. Why—"

"Just in case someone spotted your car. I'm paranoid, okay? Here. You can reach me at this number. I'm trusting you, Dawson. Nobody else knows where I'm staying."

Dawson took the slip of paper. "Where's this?"

"Ayers' guest house. He's putting in an answering machine for messages."

"Ayers? Stenman's attorney?"

"The same."

"You certain he can be trusted?"

Peter shrugged. "He's scared. And he thinks I'm going to end up dead, no matter what I do, but yes, I think I can trust him."

"It's your funeral."

"Thanks, Sunshine." Peter slowed the car and coasted into a parking lot on the east side of Mission Bay. "Here you go. This is where you get out. Make your call, grease the wheels."

The agent got out and leaned through his partially open door. "When do I hear the rest of this brilliant plan of yours?" he asked.

"Maybe never. I'll be in touch."

As Peter sped off, Dawson stepped back, slamming the door shut. In his rear view mirror, Peter saw Dawson step off the curb and stare, the agent's head shaking in disbelief.

A left turn later, Peter pressed his right foot down on the accelerator and felt his car surge.

# CHAPTER TWENTY-FOUR

"**I** WANT TO SPEAK TO THE DIRECTOR. Now." Dawson enjoyed giving orders to Freeman Ranson. He hoped one day to order the slime-ball to eat shit and die.

"You're not even employed here any more, Dawson. You should be arrested for impersonating an agent."

This conversational direction and tone did not surprise Dawson. "You mean," he said, "to tell me you refuse to pass on to Director Ackerman that I'm close to a deal? Or that I've got someone high up, on the inside, interested in negotiating?"

"You have no authority to negotiate on behalf of the SEC...or anyone else for that matter," Ranson said. Dawson didn't think it sounded convincing. "Not that I believe you, but who is it you think wants to make a deal?" Ranson tried to make this last question seem like an afterthought, but Dawson didn't bite. He knew the scumbag was apoplectic. And the realization gave him a warm tingle.

"I promised not to say until the deal is signed," Dawson said. "It involves immunity and turning a blind eye to certain future activities. But it'll be well worth the sacrifice if it happens."

"You talking about Peter Neil? We've been down that dead end before."

"Not Neil. First off, I can't find the guy. Secondly, he's turned me down more than once. Finally, he's got much bigger problems with this murder rap." Dawson silently congratulated himself. The lies sounded convincing.

"Not Neil? I repeat: *who*?"

This time Dawson read a Grand Canyon of concern in Ranson's voice. Perfect, he thought. He's buying in. "I can't say."

"Then I have to assume you're full of it—"

Show outrage, Dawson told himself. The agent took a deep breath, and spit into the mouthpiece of the outdoor payphone. "You, Ranson, are a piece of incompetent filth." Then he hung up.

"Okay, Mr. Peter Neil," Dawson said in a low whisper. "That's done. I sure wish I knew why you wanted to get Ranson's bowels in such an uproar, but you surely have."

The agent made one more call. This one was to Angela Newman. "Tell Director Ackerman what happened. Tell him this is part of a plan I've devised."

"I thought you said this was Neil's plan," she said.

"It is, but don't tell the director that. If he thinks I'm being jerked around by a guy suspected of rape, torture, and murder, he might not go along."

"I wouldn't blame him."

"Me either, Sweetheart. Gotta go. Love ya."

Dawson, like everyone else in Peter's plan, could only wait.

---

Sunday night made for a lousy night's sleep. When Peter woke on Monday, the thoroughness of Saturday's cover-up still frightened him. That Stenman controlled so many people boggled the mind. And what of Howard Muller? The man disgusted him, but Peter hadn't wanted to physically hurt him. "On vacation in Mexico"? Maybe on vacation from life, Peter guessed.

From a downtown Rancho Santa Fe gas station, Peter decided to call Stuart at work and get an update. He used Stuart's private line.

"Peter? What the hell's going on?"

"Got a few problems to iron out."

"Where in God's name are you?"

"I'd rather not say. I've been moving around."

"You a…what's that word you used to describe Muller that one time? Misan…"

"Misanthrope. No, not when it comes to you. I just don't trust phones."

"Whatever, dude, but this is a secure line."

"I'm paranoid."

"Can't blame you for that. And for what it's worth, dude, I know you didn't kill that chick."

"That makes two of us." A car honked at a pedestrian next to the payphone. "You hear anything about Muller?"

"Heard he's gone…hold on. I got another call I gotta take. Don't hang up, got some other info for you."

The phone went silent. Peter waited with his face tucked into his jacket.

"Hey. I'm back," Stuart said a minute later. "First off, I found out that damn conference room is bugged."

"Me too. Did you get in trouble?"

"You mean for telling you about backtrading? Making fun of Muller?"

"And your recreational chemicals."

"Nobody cared about the coke thing, but I did get a lecture on my always yapping pie-hole. But since Muller ordered me to teach you the ropes, I guess I caught a break. Fortunately, Muller's war room wasn't tapped."

"You're still employed, so they must've forgiven you."

"They wouldn't if they knew I was talking to you. You won't tell anyone, will you? That's a joke, by the way."

"I already guessed that."

"You wanted to know about Muller," Stuart said.

"Yeah. Did you hear anything?"

"There was a fire in his office, but he was away on a sudden vacation…hold on, got to take another call. I heard something I want to tell you about…give me a sec."

Again, Peter waited. He guessed two minutes passed.

"Stuart! Hello!"

*Shit.*

Peter slammed the phone into the aluminum cradle. He had parked his car fifteen feet away. In seconds, he jumped into the Taurus and listened to the ignition grind, then kick in. With an arm across the passenger's front seat and his head turned back, he floored the accelerator and backed up to the sounds of screeching rubber. Shifting to the brake pedal, he slammed hard and fishtailed. He spun his torso back around, then slid the automatic into drive. The wheels slipped on a patch of light oil before catching enough traction to move forward.

At the exit, a Cadillac cruised past, two blue-hairs talking, unaware that Peter had aimed his cocked auto in their direction. The Easter-green luxury car stopped and waited for a pickup truck to pull away from the curb. Peter went into reverse and spun the wheel hard right, stopped, then pointed his car in another direction.

Self-service pumps were full of obstacles. One car, done getting gas, rolled into his new path.

"Move, dammit," he shouted. Nobody heard.

Peter's car felt like an oven, broiling his brain. He honked, but everybody froze at the sounds of a siren, closing in. Then a second siren, dead ahead. A third came from the rear. A block away, the flashing lights of a black-and-white turned a corner. The cop car sped through a stop sign, the driver knowing exactly where to head. Peter fumbled with, but managed to open, his car door. He flung himself out and hit a full sprint in a single stride. Down the opposite street, another officer spotted Peter, trained his car at him, and accelerated.

*Stuart? My friend?*

Peter tore down a sidewalk and cut into an alley behind a grocery store. He dodged cardboard boxes and a dumpster. He hurdled a vegetable crate and willed himself not to look back or slow down. More sirens. He mad-dashed to the corner just as two unmarked cars spun onto the walkway blocking his path. Peter did a 180. In mid-stride, he froze. Thirty feet away, using his vehicle as a shield, an officer pointed a shotgun directly at Peter's heart. A voice shouted: "One more step and I fire." The detective's hand pumped the gun, reinforcing an already convincing argument. Peter fixated on the black hole. Would he be able to see a bullet leave the barrel? His spine locked.

"Hands behind your head."

Peter laced them where asked.

"Down on your knees."

Peter knelt.

A hand clamped his right wrist with a bone-scraping cuff, then jammed that arm behind his back. The same vicious twisting motion wrenched the left hand, locking it to the right.

"You have the right to remain silent..."

———

Kate arrived at the County Jail on Front Street an hour after the arrest.

She visited Peter, then requested a meeting with the DA. Told "no," she met with a flunky instead.

Assistant DA Francine D'Agostina was a heavy, sour-faced woman of fifty with deep creases webbing along the corners of her eyes and spreading across her face. She had the leathery skin and smell of a heavy smoker. Her office was stark, appointed with metal file cabinets, cheap library bookends, and cold, dirty windows. Even her desk had a metal frame. Frigid, Kate thought. A Woodstock photo, with a skinny Francine as a flower-child, soaking in mud, sat atop a side-table. It seemed ridiculous to Kate that the Assistant DA had ever been thin, or that she had attended a love-in at Yasgur's farm in 1969. And the woman sounded nothing like laid-back when she said, "What the hell do you want?"

"I want my client protected," Kate answered. "I believe he's in danger."

"You do, do you?" D'Agostina tilted back and folded her arms across fat breasts, stuffed inside a blue blazer that fit like a snakeskin in need of shedding. "Ask me if I care. Who do you think you are, promising to have your client turn himself in? The DA isn't going to give you any special treatment after that."

"My client's innocent. If something happens—"

"Yeah, yeah. You're a regular Clarence Darrow. If I were you, I'd go spend some time with my client. He's fish chum." An ugly simper crept across D'Agostina's face. "Check his hands for stigmata. With what we've got, he's already been nailed."

"What do you mean? I have a right to know."

"You have a right to know when I decide you have a right to know. But since I can't wait to see your reaction, I'll go ahead and share a tidbit. The DNA tests? On the semen?"

"You have the PCR?"

"A match."

"Bullshit. Peter wasn't there."

"His little swimmers were."

"PCR isn't definitive."

"It is to one in ten thousand. And we'll get more. We've started RFLP. You know as well as I do that RFLP's gonna create the same match. And the chance for error is only one in five-billion. OJ Simpson aside, I'd say reasonable doubt's not going to be an issue."

Ten minutes later, Kate stared at Peter through a glass partition. They spoke and listened on the jailhouse phone. When Kate said, "The DNA matches," Peter wagged his head.

"What?…It's gotta be a mistake."

"I'm turning this case over to someone else," Kate said, choking up. "I'm too involved, personally—and I don't have near enough experience to help you."

"No. Something's screwed up. Wait."

"How did your semen get on those sheets? Tell me."

"It couldn't have…unless…" Peter clamped his eyelids. The moonstone had been stolen. What else?

"Why did someone give Ellen a calico cat, of all things?" he asked.

"I still don't know that wasn't you, trying to get back with your ex."

"Please listen. I think I might be on to something. Again, why a calico?"

"To tie the gift to you. Make it look like you were pursuing her. That's what the DA's office thinks, so it worked."

"Maybe, maybe not. That morning after you and I slept together, you made a cup of tea. Remember?"

She nodded. "So?"

"How'd you make the tea so fast?"

"Heated some water in your microwave. Found a Lipton tea bag."

"Have you seen any pictures of the murder scene?"

"Yes. Several."

"What color were the sheets?"

"A pattern. Maybe Navajo Indian design. In browns."

"Kate, I know what happened. Here's what you need to do…"

Peter explained everything. As she ran off, she said, "Those sons of bitches. Those fucking sons of bitches."

# CHAPTER TWENTY-FIVE

**"HOW COULD YOU ALLOW YOUR DAUGHTER TO BE HIS ATTORNEY?"**
Jason Ayers held the phone a few inches from his ear. "I not only let her, I encouraged her," he answered with as much aplomb as he could muster in the face of an outraged Morgan Stenman. With no immediate follow-up response from Stenman, Ayers continued, "What better way to stay abreast of what's happening? Kate tells me, I tell you. Isn't that worth something?" The exhale from Stenman's lungs almost tickled his ear.

"Again, you have taken good care of me, Jason. I owe you an apology."

"That's what a good attorney's paid to do. I'm happy you approve. Now, I have some more good news."

"That would be a change," she said.

"Not anything overwhelming, I'm afraid, but the new biometric accounts are ready to go. We have the ability to move money at a moment's notice."

"Hopefully, in the next hour or two, once Neil's out...never mind."

Ayers rushed through the balance of their conversation. If he understood Stenman's slip of the tongue, something was coming down. He tried to reach Kate at the courthouse. She was, the impersonal voice informed him, meeting with the DA.

"Somebody needs to get her a message."

"I'll see what I can do. I'll have her ring you back if—"

"I'll hold," Ayers said. "And please hurry."

Ten minutes later, he was still on hold.

---

Kate stood at the DA's office door, Francine D'Agostina at her side.

"Kate, this had better be good. You made me look foolish." District Attorney Todd Hanson sounded as upset as he looked.

"Sir," the Assistant DA said, "I think you should hear this. Something's wrong with our evidence."

"Wrong?"

"Please, Todd," Kate begged. "I think Peter's life is in danger. He needs to get out of that jail."

"I can't wait to hear."

"You found cat hairs all over the bed sheets, right?" Kate asked.

The DA nodded.

"You assumed they came from Ms. Goodman's calico?"

Another nod.

"I've already had Ms. D'Agostina check. A significant number of those hairs came from an older animal—much older. From Peter's cat, Henry. I'm certain of it."

Hanson looked at his assistant. She nodded.

"Somebody gave Goodman a cat, similar to Peter's, hoping you'd assume all the hairs came from that animal. They got extra credit when you suspected the gift was from Peter and was an attempt to reconcile with her."

"Baloney…" Hanson stopped himself when he saw D'Agostina again wag her head. "Assuming that's true," he continued, sounding as if he were unwilling to concede anything, "they must have known we'd eventually catch on. And that, in and of itself, isn't exculpatory."

"This may have been orchestrated to bring him in, for reasons other than prosecution."

"Please, Kate. Not a conspiracy theory. Based on what? *Cat hair*?"

"Something else strange—on those sheets," Kate said. "A second vaginal sample—other than Ellen Goodman's."

"How'd you know that?"

"Not only that, but…" Kate blushed and her voice shook, "I already gave a blood sample to your lab boys. The DNA on that second stain will match *my* DNA."

"What're you talking about? This is outrageous." The DA sprung to his feet for added emphasis.

Again, Hanson's assistant interjected. "Please, sir. I reacted the same way, but…"

He flopped back down.

"Did you find any semen in Ms. Goodman's vaginal tract?" Kate asked.

Hanson looked down. "She had trauma."

"But no semen. Doesn't that seem a tiny bit odd?"

"Not if you're trying to keep from leaving evidence."

"Oh," Kate said, her voice saturated with sarcasm. "Use a condom in a crime of passion? Assuming that illogical assertion, then how did all that semen get on the bed sheet? You'd have to assume that Peter either spilled or emptied his sperm from the condom all over the sheets. Does he strike you as that dumb?"

"Rapists and torturers aren't known for using logic."

"That flies in the face of your condom argument. Furthermore, I'll wager the sample area was large—beyond what a single sexual event could produce. I know because we made love multiple times and practiced a messy form of birth control."

"This is absurd, Kate. How can you admit to such things?"

"Because my embarrassment is a small price to pay for helping free an innocent man. I agree that whoever murdered Goodman either used a condom or inflicted vaginal damage with an object in an attempt to make it look like rape. But it wasn't Peter Neil."

"We have other evidence," Hanson said.

"Let's address some of that other evidence. On the microwave found at Goodman's, you discovered several prints on the handle besides Peter's. Were any of them Ellen Goodman's?"

"I'm not going to give out that—"

"The answer is no. I see it in your face. However, and hold on to your seat, several of those prints match mine."

"It's true, sir," D'Agostina said.

"The prints, the vaginal sample, the cat hair, the moonstone—all of them came from Peter's old apartment. Months ago, someone robbed him—the morning after I spent the night with him. Check with his friend, Drew Franklin. He'll confirm which items were stolen. Peter couldn't figure out why anyone took the linens from his bed—a brown Navajo pattern—unless to use it to cart things away in, including his microwave—the one found in Ellen Goodman's apartment. My prints on the microwave came from heating a cup of water to make tea that morning. I've already told you how my other deposits came to soil the sheets."

"Sir, I've checked with some of the people familiar with Ms. Goodman's apartment. She had a new, expensive microwave. Missing. The one we found is a piece of antiquated crap. Everything Ms. Ayers says is true...and Kate?"

The familiarity surprised Kate. "Yes?"

"I owe you an apology."

"Forget it. I was an overbearing ass. Todd, I need to get my client released as soon as possible."

"I don't know," Hanson said. "This is too incredible."

"It may be elaborate, but it's still a setup. Thank God Peter put the pieces together."

"I'll have to ask for substantial bail until your DNA is matched to that on the sheet."

"How much?"

"A million."

"Agreed. We'll post bond within the hour."

"And I'll have to personally evaluate the evidence. That might take a coupla hours."

"Fine, but the sooner the better."

"Francine, I want the other boyfriend brought in for questioning. Hinton. Arrest him if you have to..."

Kate didn't mention that Hinton was an unlikely suspect. Let the DA go after other fish. It might make releasing Peter a less bitter pill to swallow.

On her way out, the receptionist said to Kate, "Your father's been holding on line one, for ten or fifteen minutes..."

Kate picked up. "Father?"

"I think something's about to happen to Peter. I phoned the jailhouse, but they wouldn't listen."

"He's being released on bond in the next few hours."

"I don't think he's going to last that long." He quickly explained his fears.

"I'll get the DA to phone..."

Kate ran.

---

"Your bitch attorney requested we put you in a separate cell. Away from the riff-raff."

The uniformed guard had a barrel chest and thick legs that carried him low to the ground. He led Peter down a hallway, along cold linoleum floors attached to walls of unending white. The two men's footsteps clapped in unison. Peter's hands, cuffed behind his back, hurt, and he wore chained leggings that forced him to cut his usual strides in half. The escort's fat palm continuously pushed against Peter's back, making sure he couldn't slow down. They passed through a double door where bookend guards, wearing frowns and sporting holstered guns, stood motionless. When the fireplug shoving Peter along nodded, the other two ambled off.

"I don't want to be moved," Peter said. "I'd rather stay in a place where I can be seen by other prisoners and guards."

"You afraid of something?" The guard smirked.

Through a second, unguarded door, they came to a solid wall-cell, half again as large as Peter's previous cell. The stark room had only a sink, toilet, bed, wooden chair, chipped table, and overhead light bulb encased in a metal wire-frame. The light cast Peter's shadow across the cement floor.

"This should do you," the guard said. He grabbed the back of the chair and placed it under the light fixture.

Peter wore a baggy orange jumper with *SD County Jail* stenciled in black across the back. A lengthy drawstring, the thickness of rope, cinched his waist. The guard removed and folded his sunglasses, then slipped them into his breast pocket. From a pant pocket, he withdrew a second drawstring. He looped the cord, then tied a slipknot. Peter at first ignored him, but as the man put the finishing touches on his creation, Peter began to shuffle back. What was happening?

The guard took the loop and tested it. The length of the drawstring slid through the knot, making it an efficient noose. Peter half-stumbled.

"Where you going, Mr. Neil?" The guard swaggered towards him.

"Someone will find out," Peter said.

"I might get suspended or fired for leaving you with the means to hang yourself, but I'm gonna retire anyway."

The length of the guard's thumb and thick forefinger encircled the soft part of Peter's neck and drove his temple into the wall. Half his senses spilled loose as Peter tried to move, but a bulldog shoulder and hip pressed against his body, pasting him along the rough cinderblock. His throat felt as if it was about to tear apart, even as the guard removed his hand.

Another tug and Peter couldn't breathe. He collapsed to his knees while his jaw jerked up and back. The loop tightened against his vocal chords, as the guard dragged Peter across the floor.

Swirling fireworks burst behind his eyeballs in a spectacular show. Too weak to do anything but gasp for air, and only marginally conscious, Peter felt his wrists uncuffed. Under the armpits, strong hands pulled him to the chair, then up, into a dangling position. In his ear, stale breath flowed from a grunting mouth. Stupidly, he tried to guess what the guard had eaten for lunch. Something with garlic. Lasagna? Carbonara? Veal? Peter became dimly aware of his clanging shackles as he visualized the headlines in tomorrow's paper: **MURDERER HANGS SELF IN JAIL CELL.**

Darkness followed that fleeting image.

# CHAPTER TWENTY-SIX

"**THANK GOD YOU'RE AWAKE.**" Kate nestled her head against Peter's chest and hugged his sides. "The guards were arrested, but they don't know who hired them—or maybe they're too frightened to say."

"What hap…" It hurt for Peter to speak.

"You came close to becoming a jailhouse suicide."

"Is there…" Peter swallowed "…anyone they can't…buy? Where am…"

"You're at County Med. Strained vocals, rope burn, but you're in better shape than the guy who tried to string you up. He claimed he was trying to save you."

"Funny…" Peter pushed himself against the headboard.

"Shh," Kate urged.

"How?"

"Father somehow figured out you were in trouble. Nobody else knows he tipped me off—he said not to use his name."

"Good." Peter's voice sounded gravelly.

"The DA called over to the jail and they sent someone to find you. Just in time. Doctors say you'll be fine in a day or two."

"Need to get out…"

"No." Kate shook her head.

"Got to." Peter dragged his legs and dropped them over the edge of the bed. "Now or never."

"Peter, you were thirty seconds from being dead."

"Let's go, please." He coughed.

Kate put a hand behind his neck and massaged. He pushed himself to his feet. A nurse burst into the room. She barked several commands. Peter ignored her.

"I feel groggy."

"Pain killers," Kate said. "They're designed to make you drowsy."

"I'll stick to…aspirin. Extra strength." Peter's voice still scratched, but he spoke more clearly. "Water?"

Kate went to a sink.

"Here," Kate said, handing Peter a glass. Peter took a delicate sip. He squeezed his eyelids with the first swallow. "Under the circumstances, the DA has dropped the charges," she continued. "All my brilliant persuasion proved unnecessary in the end. Getting hanged convinced the DA of a few things."

"Go. Let's go."

"I'll be right back." Kate left the room.

A half-minute later, she returned, pushing a wheelchair. "We'd better hit the road before they strap you down to the bed."

Kate reached for his elbow and guided him.

"Thanks, Kate."

"No problem. Don't forget, I like my men beholden," she whispered.

A moment later, she wheeled Peter from the hospital.

---

By Tuesday afternoon, despite a lingering neck rash and a voice an octave deeper than normal, Peter had recovered enough to move forward with his plan.

He took a room at a small hotel along Highway 101 in the beach town of Encinitas. The meeting with Stenman was set to go, and he had two hours to accomplish several things before that.

First, he phoned Oliver Dawson.

"You've arranged for a boat?" Peter asked.

"A boat? More like a yacht. This monster's costing me a fortune."

"Good," Peter said.

"You should see this thing. Forty-something-feet long with a cabin that sleeps six, I'm told. Thing also kicks ass in the speed department. By the way, you care that every time I step on a boat I get seasick? Hell, Neil, every time I step on a dock I feel like puking."

"I'm deeply distressed. You'll be ready off La Jolla Shores, tomorrow, before one o'clock?"

"Yes, Massah. You interested in telling me how you intend to orchestrate this miracle?"

"No. The immunity papers for Sarah Guzman drawn up like I asked?"

"The director didn't like it…me either."

"You got them, though, exactly like I asked?"

"Yeah, yeah. Exactly, including the bit about allowing her to transfer assets without interference. If this doesn't work, I'm screwed."

"If this doesn't work, I'm dead, and my death trumps your screwed. You think the director's assistant—Ranson—bought into your story of a potential high-level informant?"

"Doesn't matter," Dawson said. "Ranson has to assume it's serious and report back to Stenman. I'm certain she's aware of our conversation. When this is over, I look forward to busting that prick."

"You ready to take care of Ayers and his wife? Kate too if necessary?"

"Roger to that, but why is Stenman's attorney going to need to disappear?"

"Trust me, he's not going to be a popular guy when this is over. I think we're set, so good luck, Agent."

"Before you go, Neil, tell me what's going to happen to you after I get those papers? No way you'll get out of that hotel room alive."

"That's my problem. You just wait for your cue, get your guy to shore, get her on board, and get your asses down to Mexico as fast as your boat or yacht or whatever it is can take you. After that, you do what you need to do."

Once that was settled, Peter checked Dawson off his list.

---

At noon, right on schedule, Peter's phone rang.

"We're all set," Jason Ayers said. "Morgan's ready to meet. I get the impression she's happy to negotiate the return of those documents. She even shows signs of liking you."

"I'm flattered. She's not considering setting me up, is she?"

"No. Certainly not at my office. Besides, I think the seed you planted with Ranson has her neurotic. She wants those papers."

"My Mauritius Island bank account ready to go? The account numbers as I asked?"

"Just as you requested. And I've set you up with a car rental. A blue Celica, parked just where you asked."

"Thanks. Did Morgan agree to open a joint account to escrow my pay-ment?"

"She did. But why do you want to do that?"

"The account is technically in her...what did you call it? Her *empire* of funds or accounts?"

"Yes. Her various offshore funds are part of her so-called empire of funds."

"And you have the power-of-attorney to move funds from other Stenman Partners offshore accounts, into this new escrow account? As part of your intra-empire fund transfer authority. Right?"

Ayers said nothing. Peter listened for breathing, but heard none.

"Jason. You still there?"

"You're going to ask me to transfer funds from Morgan's big accounts to this joint account of yours and hers. Aren't you?"

"That's why I needed to arrange with Dawson for you and your wife to disappear, at least until we get through the fallout."

"Peter," Ayers began, sounding concerned, "you'll never be able to spend a dime of that money."

"I don't expect to end up with anything. My plan is more complex than you realize. It's time I explained how all this works..."

When Peter finished, Ayers asked, "You think you can do all this with-out Guzman or Stenman catching on?"

"Not sure. A lot has to do with your acting skills. You're the one who's got to sell Sarah Guzman. You still game? I know it's a lot to ask."

"If this works, it'll be worth it."

"It has to work," Peter said. "And, Jason, things are going to get hairy tomorrow, and I wanted to tell you one last thing. On a personal level..."

"Personal? It must have to do with Kate."

"I know she's engaged to be married, and I hope she's happy. But I wanted you to know I love her. I'll do what I can to keep an eye out for her."

"She made me promise not to, but I think I should tell you anyway."

"Tell me *what*?" Peter asked.

"She broke off her engagement."

Before Ayers finished, Peter went from standing to sitting.

"Peter. Did you hear me?" Ayers asked.

"Did...did she say anything about her feelings for me?"

"She didn't have to. She cares, a lot. But she's afraid you might feel

gratitude, not love, in return. You'll have to win back her trust."

"I will. And thanks."

---

A short while later, Peter sat in the back of a taxi, trying to ignore the cabby's constant chatter. Outside his window, he watched a boy kick a soccer ball up and down like popping corn.

"Whatcha got going on downtown?" the driver asked. "You're not dressed like a business guy, but that's all that ever goes to this Leeman, Johnston law place. Suits and briefcase guys. Y'know the type, stuck up, snooty big deals. Never took a regular guy there before. Y'know, dressed like he's going to a workout instead of—"

Peter reached into his wallet and drew out a ten. "I need to think. Mind if I just ride in silence?"

"Sure. Didn't mean to yap yer head off. Just trying to pass the time."

Peter tossed the ten over the front seat. "Shhhh," he reminded the driver. "Unless you see someone tailing us, I'd prefer your north and south lips stayed glued."

The ten bucks worked. The driver nervously scanned for a tail as the creaking yellow proceeded south on Interstate 5.

Peter spent the time mentally reviewing every detail of his plan. He realized that if Stenman wanted him dead, he'd have a bullet in the back of his head before he entered the law-office front door. The thought made his skin tingle, as if he had a bull's-eye hung on his back. The enticement of recovering his mother's papers, Peter hoped, was important enough to keep him alive for at least one more day.

Once they reached Front Street and turned towards Leeman, Johnston, and Ayers' offices, Peter decided to have the driver circle the block before departing. He then asked to be dropped off a block away. Heading down the crowded sidewalk, he tried not to look concerned. At the building entrance, he resisted the temptation to duck and run. Instead, he paced to the elevator, waited for the double-ding of opening doors, and stepped into the lift. No gunshots meant he had survived hurdle one.

Peter carried a canvas bag filled with the bills he'd taken from Muller's safe, appreciating for the first time how light a couple of million dollars felt. When he entered the law offices, the receptionist presented a pleasant face. "Good morning, Mr. Neil. I see you've changed your haircut and color. It looks good."

"Thanks," Peter said. "I'm here to see—"

"Mr. Ayers and Ms. Stenman are waiting. You are to go back immediately."

"Thank you."

"Your voice," she said before he departed. "It sounds deeper. Sexy, if you don't mind my saying so."

Peter nodded. Crushed vocal chords, he decided, were an absolute aphrodisiac.

A moment later, he knocked on Ayers' heavy door and dove in.

---

Jason Ayers greeted Peter. Behind him, leaning on her aluminum cane—an extension of her brittle arms—Morgan Stenman had an almost pleasant expression that unnerved Peter. When Ayers winked, indicating that preliminary discussions had gone smoothly, Peter relaxed.

Peter endured a few informalities before saying, "Here's your money, less a few thousand for expenses." He dropped the bag on the floor next to Ayers' desk.

"I will tell poor Howard you returned the funds," Stenman said. "He will be pleased. But then this money had limited utility for you, didn't it? Cash leaves incriminating footprints when not handled properly. It is satisfying to me that you have learned at least that much while in my employ."

Peter ignored her words. "I want five million. Wired to this account." He held a piece of paper with his Mauritius account information. "I get my money, you get the registered envelopes, unopened, dated before my mother's death."

Stenman showed no emotion. After asking Ayers to bring in some good strong coffee from a shop in the building, not the "crap you make in pots up here," Stenman, like a savvy interviewer, deliberately paused. Peter read the tactic and wasn't fooled—she had already decided what to say, but she wanted to let him hang, maybe get him to reveal something strategic. He didn't bite. He would not initiate nervous chit-chat, as he'd seen others do in her presence. Nor would he offer new, diluted terms while wallowing in anxiety. In a minor inspiration, Peter asked Ayers if he might have a non-fat latté since they were waiting for a caffeine fix anyway. "And a biscotti, if that's not too much trouble." When the attorney cocked his head, Peter understood that his cool had impressed him.

Ayers sent a secretary down to the ground floor to fill everyone's order. While they waited for coffee service, the older man made small talk about how this was the best solution for everyone and five million dollars was not a large amount of money. Then, somehow managing to keep a straight face, he went on to say that when this was over, they could all just get on with their lives, as if Peter's life was worth a drop of toilet water at game's end. Ignoring her attorney, Stenman lit a cigarette that, Peter thought, couldn't have been half as hot as her stare.

When the tray with three coffees and one cookie finally arrived, Peter sipped his latté and chomped on the thick, Amaretto-laced cookie. He didn't like the taste of either but enjoyed Stenman's self-inflicted impatience. He drank delicately and chewed slowly.

A minute into the beverage charade, Stenman finally stated her position. "The price is agreeable, but do not take me for a fool, Peter." Granite-faced, she shoved her full cup of coffee to the side. "I will not send you five million dollars of *my* money in the hopes you will then honor your commitment." She crushed the tip of her cigarette into a crystal ashtray and flung the remains, filter and all, onto the carpet. The grand show had no effect on Peter. He crossed his legs and waited, looking like a bored businessman listening to a salesman's tired pitch.

"Jason," continued Stenman, "has suggested and already set up a joint account, triggered by voice recognition. He deposited your five million dollars this morning. Tomorrow, after the delivery of papers to me, I will call the bank, then you *and* I will read back the account information, activating a voice transfer of those funds to your account."

Peter popped the last morsel of cookie into his mouth. He counted to five, then took a sip of latté to wash it down. Once he'd swallowed, he said, "If I give you the papers, how do I know you'll honor *your* commitment?"

"What do you suggest, Peter?" Ayers asked, on cue.

"We do this in stages," Peter said. He took his index finger and mopped up a few crumbs of cookie from his napkin. He delicately licked his fingertip and squinted with pretended thought. Sagely stroking his palm across his chin and mouth, he said, "And we use Sarah Guzman in such a manner as to make certain I can keep an eye on her. I know she was the one who set me up and had Ellen Goodman murdered."

"If that were the case," Stenman said, not bothering to hide her impatience, "it was because you disappeared and confronted a certain police detective, asking imprudent questions. Then this unfortunate incident with my ex-CIO Howard Muller. So foolish and unnecessary."

"All tough breaks," Peter said without inflection. "I have an idea about how I can watch her while we complete the trade."

Peter outlined his scheme. Stenman, Peter, and Ayers would meet tomorrow, in a place of Peter's choosing. "Some place that'll make sure I don't get ambushed," he said. "Guzman will then receive the first of the two envelopes."

Peter explained that Guzman would open and verify the contents. "With the first delivery, we transfer my five million," Peter said. "After that, I arrange for the second packet to be delivered. If I don't live up to my end of the bargain, you're welcome to have someone put a bullet through my head." Peter then agreed to remain hostage—at their meeting place—until Stenman verified she had the documents she wanted.

Ayers nodded. "The plan has enough safeguards, I think. Do you agree, Morgan?"

Stenman nodded while drawing so hard on her filter tip that teeth outlined against her cheeks.

"Once you arrive at my designated meeting place," Peter continued, "you'll want to check for bugs, mikes, whatever. Check me out too, if that makes you happy."

"When will you notify us of the meeting time and place?" Ayers asked.

"Tomorrow afternoon." Peter turned to Stenman. "At twelve forty-five, you'll be in your limo, heading north from your office."

"In my limo? This is madness." Stenman studied Peter's face.

"I want you moving in the right direction, but I don't want you knowing the final destination. That's for my protection and to make certain there are as few delays as possible. Jason, I'll phone you. You'll then phone Morgan's driver with the information. As far as Sarah Guzman goes..." Peter handed Ayers a slip of paper. "Until you call with her instructions, I want her at this location at noon tomorrow."

Ayers took the slip and studied the address. "This is a diner in

Oceanside. That's twenty miles north of downtown. What's going on, Peter?"

"I want everyone in a different location, moving towards this meeting. Bodies in coordinated motion."

Puppets, Peter hoped, coordinated by a puppeteer.

Ayers shook his head. It was a prearranged protest. "Sarah Guzman will never agree to be a sitting duck."

"She doesn't agree," Peter said, "then we have no deal."

"No deal?" Stenman nearly shouted. "No deal means I initiate some ugly retribution. Somebody better find a goddamn answer."

"Okay," Peter said, rubbing his chin as if he had thought up the solution for the first time. "You," he faced Ayers, "tell her everything will take place in a public place. She's welcome to have Nuñoz accompany her. I'm here to get paid, then disappear. Period. That should do the trick, don't you think?"

This time Peter faced Morgan. He understood she had to agree. She needed to settle this matter, and Peter's asking price was so small as to be stupid. She would have paid several multiples of what he demanded.

"You are a careful man, Peter," Stenman said, just before agreeing to his terms. "But do not get cute with me." She might as well have added: *or you will suffer like no man has ever suffered before.*

After Stenman left the law offices, Ayers guided Peter to a sophisticated recorder. Peter read a series of numbers and a page of nonsense into a microphone with a wire-mesh pop-filter designed to reduce the effects of breath blasts and air currents. The voice recordings, Ayers said, were of a professional quality.

"How does this thing work?" Peter asked.

"In simple terms, we create a voiceprint," Ayers said. "Most systems require a password of choice, plus three or four words for authorization. Our system requires thousands of samples. That's why you had to read all this text. The recording you just made consists of a comprehensive combination of sounds that the computer will recognize and match to your voice. Every word and number in the instructions you give over the phone will be scrutinized."

"And we'll be able to set this up in time?"

"A bank official is ready to input all of the data as soon as we're finished here today. After that, you and Morgan will have an account in which neither of you can withdraw the money without the other's verbal authorization. I will arrange for each of you to read precise instructions when the time comes."

Once they finished, Peter left, opting for the stairs. He exited through a rear door and began to run. He took a route through alleys and around buildings until he arrived at a bus stop, more than a mile from the office. He rode one bus north, then a second east. A short cab ride followed another mile of circuitous running. A sudden cab-stop in mid-block preceded more running and then a second cab. Ten minutes later, Peter picked up his rental car from an outdoor parking lot.

Peter drove the Celica several miles in the wrong direction, intending to lose the tail he was certain had tried to keep pace with him from Ayers' office. An hour later, he reached Carlsbad and removed the registered mail. He took the first envelope to Speedy Delivery Service in Fallbrook, twenty-five miles north and east of where he planned to meet Stenman and Ayers tomorrow. He gave the man delivery instructions: "Tomorrow. Exactly one forty-five p.m. You approach from the beaches north…"

He took the second package to Always Reliable Delivery Service in El Cajon, twenty miles south and east of tomorrow's rendezvous. He told them: "Tomorrow. Exactly two p.m. Through the men's locker room…"

From there, Peter went back to his hotel room, turned on the television, and tried to relax, but couldn't. Beginning at dawn, he would either take the first step on the road to salvation, or the last step to perdition. At this stage of the game, he wouldn't have wanted to make book on which.

At nine, he fell into a deep, dreamless sleep.

# CHAPTER TWENTY-SEVEN

Carlos, alone, entered the Tiger Lily restaurant and looked around. Sarah Guzman flagged him with a raised hand. He crossed the well-lit room and slid into the bench next to her. He leaned on his elbows, looking ready to explode into a violent rage. Sarah understood his feelings. She disliked having to be a messenger to this transaction.

"What is next?" Carlos asked.

"I expect my phone to ring within the hour." Sarah glanced at her cell phone resting on the Formica-topped table. Around them, diners began to exit the buffet line, trays piled to overflowing with Chinese. The smell of grease and soy inundated the still air and clung to hair and clothes. "We will be given instructions at that time," Sarah continued.

"I do not like that we are not in control of this situation." Carlos' eyes jittered, as if impatient.

"We have no choice in the matter," Sarah said. "Morgan wants those documents. So do I."

"*Tia,*" he asked, "why do we agree to this?"

"Because we failed to take care of Peter Neil."

"*Suerte. Señor* Neil has *suerte.*"

"Luck? I am not so sure. He has instincts. We are unable to follow him. Muller presents him with what seems to be an insurmountable dilemma, and Neil slices an arm off and throws the appendage into a safe. He is not one to sit back and wait for help. He has changed over these last months: no longer a boy, I think."

"He is overdue for a mistake."

"Perhaps," Sarah said unenthusiastically. "But Peter Neil is unpredictable."

"We will handle Neil," said Carlos. "I pledge it on my life."

"I hope so, Carlos." Sarah Guzman studied him and nodded.

The minutes they waited seemed long. Her chest heaved, not so much from anger as frustration. She didn't hate Neil. He was a victim—someone in the wrong place at the wrong time. But that didn't change the facts: Peter

Neil would be dealt with the moment they had those documents tucked safely away. Nobody survived screwing them over.

"We have people watching Neil's friends," Carlos said, interrupting her thoughts. "If anything goes wrong, I shall personally order a bullet put through the pregnant bitch."

"Nothing will go wrong, Carlos. You will be at my side."

"*Sí, señora.* I shall make certain we are successful."

When Sarah Guzman took a sip of tea, it burned her tongue.

---

"You ready?" Drew asked, leaning into Monica's ear. "Twelve-thirty—show-time."

"I think so," she whispered. "Are you certain this is necessary?"

"Bread says so. After what happened the other day, with you being lured away, our apartment broken into, I agree."

"What's Peter up to?"

Drew shook his head. "Don't know for sure. But Bread says there's gonna be some heavy fireworks."

A moment later, Monica Franklin began to moan. Her groans grew until they reached screams.

In a voice loud enough to be heard by any eavesdropping equipment, Drew said, "Don't worry, Honey. The ambulance is on its way."

"I'm not due for another month…" She hyperventilated, just as they had taught her at Lamaze class. "These aren't labor pains, are they?"

"No, Sweetheart, but everything's going to be fine."

Drew reached for the telephone and dialed. "Kate," he said a moment later, "Monica's in some kind of severe pain. We're on our way to the hospital. Could you meet us? She'll feel better knowing you're nearby for support."

Kate agreed and Drew went back to his suffering wife.

As the couple stood just inside the open front door, Monica doubled over while Drew attended to her like a concerned husband. The sounds of a distant siren grew stronger. Less than five minutes later, a noisy ambulance, with a handsome expectant couple in the back, sped through traffic to Scripps Hospital and a well-guarded room.

Across the street from Drew and Monica's apartment, a sniper watched through the scope of a rifle and seethed at his bad luck.

---

Jason Ayers phoned Stenman in her limo and gave her the location of the meeting. "You are to get the room number at the front desk after you arrive…"

With that call out of the way, Ayers paid a visit to the Tiger Lily Restaurant. When he entered, he could tell that Sarah Guzman and Carlos Nuñoz were surprised to see him. When he slid along the well-worn Naugahyde booth-seat across from them, Sarah said, "I thought you were going to phone me."

"Morgan wanted us to meet. She's nervous about cell phone calls."

Ayers gave Sarah her instructions. "Go to this section of beach." He described the exact spot. "A beach chair, an umbrella, and a blue windbreak are in place, reserved for you."

He then told her about the first packet. She was to remove her sunglasses if the delivery came off as promised. "You will receive a second delivery, several minutes later. After that second delivery, phone Mauritius Trust Bank at this number, ask for this man—" he put a slip of paper on the table "—and read him these instructions."

He pointed to a brief statement and two bank account numbers. "Morgan has put Peter Neil's five million into one of *your* new accounts. If the materials are complete and sealed as promised, you are to transfer the balance from your account to Peter's." Ayers' finger tapped the bank account number he identified as Peter's. "We're using the new voice recognition technology to make the transfer."

Sarah frowned. "Why bother paying Neil anything?"

"It's only five million, and Morgan wants to make certain this goes smoothly. After the delivery, she has arranged a nearby boat to transport you and the papers to your villa in Ensenada. You should be in Mexican waters within an hour of receiving the final delivery. Now," Ayers continued, "I must go meet with Peter and Morgan. I hope all goes well."

"You did me a favor many years ago, Jason." Sarah's voice carried an unmistakable threat. "I have never forgotten that. But this had better be the last inconvenience."

"I'm certain it will be," the attorney said, his voice strong and clear. "In a few hours, everything will be just perfect."

# CHAPTER TWENTY-EIGHT

MILLIONAIRE DEVELOPERS NAMED AND ESTABLISHED THE LA JOLLA Beach and Yacht Club in 1927. After going through an early bankruptcy, the property sold several times before the name changed in 1935 to the La Jolla Beach and Tennis Club. Since that time, the resort has become a popular spot for sports, entertainment, corporate, and political luminaries. The club's mission architecture consists of adobe-style walls, red-tiled roofs, and sweeping archways leading from one courtyard to another. Gardens, fountains, and a man-made lagoon, all set across twenty acres, give the famous facility an old-world ambiance.

In addition to local members, the facility caters to vacationers. A two-story row of hotel rooms lines the esplanade and looks down at a quarter mile of shining beach. With immense picture windows and full beach and ocean access, it is one of the most sought-after locations in California, or the world, for that matter.

A mile north of the club is the Scripps Institute of Oceanography. The stretch of beach between the club and the Institute is open, public, and crowded. Peter had considered this factor in selecting the site.

Their meeting would take place in a second floor, three-bedroom suite at the northernmost end of the hotel. From that suite's living room, he, Ayers, and Stenman—along with Stenman's armed escorts—could look down on the beach where Sarah Guzman would be seated on a towel, fighting sunburn, waiting to receive her deliveries.

Peter arrived at the brick-faced entrance of the club by taxi. He tossed two twenties into the front seat, indicating he didn't need change. He pulled open the door alongside the curb and took the deep breath of a man preparing to dive under pounding surf. Taking the time to collect his thoughts, Peter watched the cabby nod thanks and speed off.

Fifteen minutes before one o'clock, he entered through the double doors that led to the hotel registration desk. He filled out his forms, paid cash, and clutched the room key.

"Do you need directions, Mr. Neil?" the check-in clerk asked.

Peter said "no" and proceeded through the courtyard leading to the beach-access. Once he reached the red clay esplanade, he turned right and faced north. The room was a fifty-yard straight shot from where he stood. He continued down the walkway, past the men's locker room, then the women's. First-floor hotel suites, some with doors open to enjoy the breeze, flanked his right. Peter felt the jagged edges of the room key dent his flesh.

He reached the room a minute later, made himself at home, and waited.

---

Twenty minutes later, Stenman arrived with three thickly torsoed assistants. All wore identical gray suits and identical aviator sunglasses. A search of the room, using sophisticated debugging technology, followed, as did a strip search of Peter's body cavities. Satisfied, Peter and Stenman sat while her guards stood, flanking them in a triangle.

"Where will Sarah receive her deliveries?" Stenman asked.

"Here," Peter said.

"To this room?"

"Not exactly. If you can manage to wait a little longer, you'll understand."

Not long after, Ayers arrived. "I see everyone's comfortable," he said, sounding upbeat. "I expect Ms. Guzman shortly."

Stenman looked between the two men, and said nothing. Peter admired her lack of curiosity.

Peter saw Sarah first. Carlos, now looking like a joke, trailed behind her, struggling through the sand in his charcoal suit coat and dress shoes, his head in constant side-to-side surveillance. He appeared angry enough to pull the gun he undoubtedly had strapped somewhere to his body and shoot random sunbathers.

"There," Peter said, pointing. "We're ready."

Sarah Guzman, wearing a floppy straw hat, took up her designated spot on the beach, thirty yards south of their hotel room. A slanting windbreak blunted the brisk wind skating off the Pacific, less than twenty feet from her position. As if she felt Peter's gaze, she spun her shoulders. Even though she did not know they were watching, her remarkable face froze in his direction. Dark glasses hid her eyes, but not her intentions. Peter knew that somewhere in Sarah Guzman's poisoned mind, she had already planned his death. Carlos sat along the beach wall, close enough to react, if needed.

The raked sand gleamed, and the warm weather had attracted a healthy crowd of sunbathers. Exactly as Peter had hoped. Plenty of space, lots of witnesses, very public.

A short time later, Peter spied a man in thick black shoes and white overalls struggling down the beach, looking for the blue windbreak and petite blond. Peter nodded to Ayers.

"Excuse me," Ayers said. "I need to relieve myself. I'll be back in a couple of minutes."

---

Ayers went to the back of the suite and entered a bathroom. Nobody noticed or cared. As he locked the door, he pulled his cell phone from his hip pocket. The bathroom was the size of a normal bedroom, with an oversized tub, shower, and brass fixtures. He balanced on the edge of the tub and made his call.

"This is Jason Ayers. I wish to make a transfer of one-hundred-ten-million dollars from Stenman Partners' Swiss National account number four, two, four, seven, one, one..." He gave the numbers precisely, then continued: "...to Stenman Partners' Swiss National account number three, one, nine...." The second account was Peter's and Stenman's joint escrow account. Ayers intended to feed into it as much money in as short a time as he could.

Ayers waited for confirmation. He planned to make four additional large transfers and figured he had at most three minutes before Stenman would miss him.

A bank representative's voice came on and said, "I'm sorry, sir, but your voice wasn't verified. The transfer didn't go through."

Ayers' chin dropped. "Not verified? The equipment must not be working."

"The equipment isn't the problem," the bank executive said. "Perhaps the phone line is unclear."

Something else, Ayers knew. What? He considered the possibilities.

"The acoustics," he blurted. His voice echoed off the porcelain fixtures and tiled walls in the bathroom. The reverberations had altered his voice.

"Hold on," Ayers instructed the bank employee. "I'm going to change rooms." Standing, the gun in his jacket pocket jabbed his ribcage. Ayers reached into the pocket, rearranged the weapon, and prepared to exit the bathroom.

He had already wasted at least a minute and, suddenly, his bad case of nerves got worse. Opening the door, he looked into the master bedroom. During the search for eavesdropping equipment, the room had been ransacked. Stenman's men had pulled the bed sheets and rearranged the furniture. Ayers looked across the mess to a side-wall and the sliding glass door leading to a balcony facing north. He crossed over and went onto the porch. Satisfied that he could not be seen, he crouched and spoke into the phone. He repeated the fund-transfer instructions. Instantly, the confirmation came through. Ayers read off a series of additional instructions, transferring funds to Peter and Stenman's joint account, number 3199216948.

That accomplished, Ayers' confidence grew. Peter just might get this done. It didn't mean the boy would live to see the fruits of his labors, but he just might stick it to these murderous financiers. With a few more carefully orchestrated moves, a lot of the bad people's money would soon vanish.

And, he knew, that was when the real war would begin.

———

Ayers said it would take less than four minutes to complete the money transfers. Peter noted the time, and time was up. He mentally crossed all his fingers and toes and hoped nobody missed Ayers.

Peter joined Stenman and her entourage as they followed the progress of the courier, who repeatedly glanced at the small  slip of paper Peter had given him. Once the courier found and approached Sarah Guzman, the envelope tucked under an arm, Stenman leaned over her cane and into the plate glass window. Peter watched her watch Sarah as Sarah examined the

registered envelope, broke the seal, and spilled out the contents. It looked to be some fifty pages. Sarah Guzman then spent several minutes in examination.

When Sarah took off her sunglasses, signaling that everything was as expected, Stenman straightened herself and said, "Where's Ayers? Anthony," she addressed the man nearest the far door, "find out what is keeping him."

Anthony nodded. Just as he spun to investigate, Ayers appeared through the door. "Shall we make Peter's transfer?" he asked.

# CHAPTER TWENTY-NINE

OLIVER DAWSON, EVEN WITH POWERFUL BINOCULARS, COULDN'T SEE THE concerned faces, or sense the razor-edged tensions, in the hotel room above – too many reflections off the room's main window. Too bad, he thought. He wondered, half-seriously, when he'd hear the gunshot blowing Peter Neil's head off his neck.

The boat rolled an inch and Dawson braced himself. Even a heavy dose of Dramamine hadn't done him much good. He swallowed, hoping to keep his stomach from erupting. He didn't even dare drink Diet Coke for fear of an instant revisit.

Despite the suffering, Dawson was ready. Dry static filled the air, and seemed close to sparking. For Dawson, it felt good. These events would mark his career denouement. No matter how it ended, he'd go home in a few days, hero or goat, and begin loving Angela Newman in public. They'd get married in a month or two. Start a family.

Suddenly, the boat ceased rocking.

With a moment's relief, he re-imagined the activities inside the hotel room. Peter would be going over final details with Stenman. Reaching into his pocket, Dawson clutched his phone and began to input the numbers that would transfer his voice across the country. It took one ring. "Is that you, Dawson?"

"Of course." Dawson answered.

Dawson had phoned Ranson earlier in the day, and had imagined the man experiencing an early-stage heart attack. Then, when Dawson had said he was close to consummating a deal, the director's assistant choked, sounding as if he had a mouth full of his own shit.

Now, Dawson enjoyed jerking Ranson's chain. "We've got our connection," he said. "She's on board." As the boat rocked, he thought: *no pun intended.*

"*She*? Your contact's a woman?" Ranson's words came too rapidly.

"Yes," Dawson answered. "I think I should speak to the director."

"Director Ackerman isn't available. Is this contact another law office person?"

"I better not say anything before speaking to Ackerman."

"Give me the name. I'll let him know right away."

"If all goes according to plan, I'll send you a copy of the immunity agreement—I need to make certain all parties keep their promises."

"That agreement will be worthless unless Ackerman agrees. I'll pass the details on to him. Where are you, Dawson?"

"Come on, Ranson. You know better than to ask. I'll be sending you the agreement by wireless fax as soon as we have Hannah Neil's documents."

Dawson hung up. "That should create some additional confusion," he said to himself.

Squinting at the blinding reflection off the hotel picture window, Dawson gave a hand signal to one of his associates. Three divers, with two hours' worth of oxygen in their tanks, jumped overboard and disappeared as the boat inched closer to shore.

---

Peter read the instructions that Ayers handed him: "This is Peter Neil, requesting the transfer of all funds in Stenman Partners' Swiss National Bank account number 3199216948 to Mauritius Trust Bank account number 7392968127."

The voice verification system analyzed each syllable and cleared him in less than five seconds. Stenman followed with the exact same instructions. The money then moved at the speed of light from the joint account at Swiss National to Mauritius Trust Bank—from one secure location to another. Stenman assumed it was five million. Peter guessed it was at least a hundred times that much.

As if on cue, a second deliveryman, this one in a white shirt and black pants, came marching through the men's locker room. He stood on the esplanade side of the low beach wall and searched for a blue windbreak protecting a petite blond. When he stepped over the wall and into the dry sand, he stumbled. Stenman involuntarily exhaled—as if the messenger carried a bomb. On the beach, off to one side, Peter saw Nuñoz also bolt upright. Everybody was on edge. Peter hoped that was a good thing.

A moment later, the disheveled messenger handed Sarah the envelope, had her sign a delivery form, then departed. She checked the outside. Apparently satisfied, she opened and reviewed the contents. When finished, she produced a cell phone and began to input numbers, referring to a slip of paper—given to her by Jason Ayers at the Tiger Lily Restaurant— that she balanced on her knee. Carlos Nuñoz got up from where he sat and approached her position. While she held the phone to her ear, they spoke. In the middle of saying something to Carlos, she held up her hand, indicating she had made a phone connection.

"What's she doing?" Stenman said, turning to Ayers.

"Perhaps trying to reach us," Ayers suggested. "She doesn't know where we are, only that someone is watching for her signals."

"That is bullshit. She is not phoning us. And who is *that*?" This time Stenman faced Peter while pointing to a silhouetted man shuffling towards Sarah from the south.

"You asking me?" Peter made it sound innocent.

"I said, who is that?"

"Should I go check, Ms. Stenman?" one of the armed guards asked.

"Don't be stupid," she said, her lip quivering. "You are hardly inconspicuous. I hope, Peter, this is not some kind of double-cross."

"If it is, I'm the one getting screwed."

"I better get a damn answer," she said, spinning without need of her cane. She picked up the hotel phone and dialed. "I want Bill Leeman. Now," she said.

Peter did a double-take. With all that had happened, Stenman was lining up her backup attorney, Ayers' partner at Leeman, Johnston, and Ayers. "Amazing" was the only word to describe her instincts.

While Stenman finalized her legal arrangements, they all watched Sarah finish her call and put her phone away.

# CHAPTER THIRTY

THE BAREFOOT MAN WORE A BAGGY SWIMSUIT—BUT LOOKED TOO serious to be a typical nonchalant. He stood as erect as a two-by-four, had Fila shades riding atop his head, and sunshine bouncing off his forehead. He approached Sarah and Carlos as if they expected him and said, in a tone that made it sound as if he were reading from a script, "I am here to escort you to that yacht. Ms. Stenman has arranged your passage to Mexico. She wishes for you to put your delivery in a safe place."

"Ayers already informed me," Sarah replied, making no attempt to hide her irritation.

"I think we will pass on the boat ride," Carlos said to the man. He put a hand on his hip, making it clear he was ready, if necessary, to access weaponry in a split-second.

"This is what Ms. Stenman wants," the man said. He remained calm, as if he had expected resistance.

"Then let Señora Stenman take the boat," Carlos said.

"Miss Guzman, it is imperative that we move quickly. There's too much risk traveling by land. And Ms. Stenman doesn't want those documents destroyed until she's had a chance to analyze them. I'm certain you understand why."

"No, *Tia*," Carlos said. "We do not know this man."

The stranger matched Carlos' deadly stare with one of his own. Clearly, he, too, was no stranger to violence and would not back down. "If this were a setup," he said, "there'd be a hundred agents on this beach, kicking your ass and grabbing those documents." The undercover agent waited for the logic to sink in, then said, "We need to get you into Mexican waters. If you'd rather drive your own car, wait an hour in line at the border, risk the highway patrol, and take chances you won't be searched, then go ahead. But," he continued, addressing only Sarah, "I'd leave ugly-puss behind." He then shifted his gaze and looked straight at Carlos. "If I were an immigration agent, zipper-face would be the first *gilipollas* I'd stop."

"*Chupamela, cabron.*" Nuñoz' breathing came in rapid pants.

"No thanks, *marico*. I prefer women. Are you ready to leave, Ms. Guzman?"

Carlos took a step forward, his hand on the gun strapped to his hip. Sarah shook her head. Carlos' skull might just as well have been made of glass. His deadly thoughts were transparent.

"How long before we are out of U.S. waters?" Sarah asked, resignedly. The documents she held in her hands had the power to destroy her and everything she had spent years building. Not just that, but she had skimmed enough of the papers to realize that Hannah Neil's handiwork also implicated and named many clients. She and Morgan needed to go through these papers thoroughly. Because of all these things, Sarah Guzman would take this opportunity to escape. She had already decided, quite simply, that she had no other choice.

And although these current arrangements did not sit well with her, she had confidence in Morgan Stenman and in the safeguards put in place. Peter Neil, her biggest concern, was vulnerable—Morgan would make him pay if this did not go according to plan. People like Neil didn't have the balls to screw them over. Only fools dared try, and Neil was no fool. Yes, she told herself, this will not become a problem. Having convinced herself, she turned her attention back to the man who would take her to safety.

"I asked you how long before we are in Mexican waters? Answer me."

"Forty minutes, maybe less," the man said. He did not take his eyes off of Carlos. "We'll take that outboard to the cabin cruiser." The man pointed to the boat-launch a few yards beyond the north end of the La Jolla Beach and Tennis Club.

A moment later, Sarah Guzman allowed herself to be escorted down the beach while Carlos, his shoes filled with sand, unhappily followed.

---

Stenman stared as Sarah Guzman and Carlos Nuñoz climbed into a small motorboat waiting at the boat-launch, just below their window.

"Whatever's happening, nobody is forcing them," Stenman said, more a spoken thought than anything she wished to share.

Stenman turned and searched the room with roaming eyes. Peter followed her gaze to the front door. It was open and Ayers had disappeared.

"Where is Jason Ayers?" Stenman barked to her guards.

"He left just this minute," one answered.

"Why didn't you stop him?"

"I didn't know he wasn't supposed to go."

"You." Stenman pointed to one of the men. "Get him and bring him back." Her voice was husky, and darkness engulfed her face. "If this is what I think, Peter, you are dead."

"I don't—"

"Shut up!"

Stenman gave a subtle nod and one of the remaining two guards gave Peter a full-assed cold-cock. Peter fell, not quite unconscious, but close. Under the circumstances, the floor felt better than a feather bed, and he elected to remain down. His cheek grew hot, and the deepness of the bruise pulsated against his skin, but he didn't mind. In fact, he had expected to get pummeled. So long as Stenman didn't give another of her silent cues and have one of these thugs pull out a gun or a knife and finish the job, he was happy to have been right-crossed. That this part of his plan was working— his still being alive—came as a pleasant surprise. So far so good, and he reckoned he had less than half an hour for the rest of his plan to play out. Not too long to withstand the suspense, he thought to himself.

This bit of internal banter was fleeting, however, and replaced by a hailstorm of thought. He didn't want to die, not before he had another chance to see Kate. Had he ever told her he loved her? No. He never had. It was a thing he needed to do, and that desire filled him with resolve. He *would* survive. He had to.

While Peter remained floor-bound, Stenman, intent on following each of Sarah's footsteps, leaned forward, practically imprinting her nose onto the window pane. "She is being taken to that cabin cruiser. What is happening?" she asked, a tinge of panic lacing her hard-bitten voice. Peter assumed it was a rhetorical question. He stretched his mouth and moved his jaw side-to-side. It hurt, but his bones had apparently weathered the knockdown.

The hotel phone rang while Peter struggled into a sitting position. His head still spun but he had the sharpened attention of a person listening for footsteps in the dark. Stenman picked up the handset on the second ring, listened for a few seconds, then said, "You're telling me you just received a fax from Dawson granting immunity to Sarah Guzman? Allows what?"

A moment later, Stenman slammed the phone into its cradle. "Get up, Peter."

A giant hand pulled him to his feet.

"Sit him over there." Stenman pointed. The bodyguard threw Peter onto a sofa as if he were no more than a bag of air. Stenman stood over him. "Sarah Guzman has been granted immunity. She has been given the ability to move assets into the U.S. unencumbered. Jason Ayers has disappeared. I want answers."

"I don't have any idea what's going on. I did my part. I wanted to get paid for those papers—that's it."

"Bullshit. You, Ayers, Guzman, set me up."

"That makes no sense," Peter said, looking frightened, which was easy for him under the circumstances. "Sarah Guzman tried to have me killed. She was responsible for murdering my mother. You think I've hatched a plot with her, of all people?"

Stenman's expression indicated she did not. The phone rang again. Again, Stenman answered. This time she placed the caller on speaker. It was the Swiss National branch manager.

"I've been trying to reach you for the last fifteen minutes…" said the manager. He explained his concern over the transfer of $800 million out of five accounts and the rapid movement of those funds to Mauritius Trust Bank. "I know what you do is none of my affair, but I decided to call and—"

"Are you suggesting that I am missing close to a billion dollars?" said Stenman. "This had better be a bad joke…Who authorized the transfer?"

"I'm not supposed—"

"Who authorized the goddamn transfer?" she repeated, her voice full of death.

"Your attorney. Mr. Ayers. Just a while ago. At first there was a problem—something about the acoustics in a bathroom—but then things cleared up. This isn't our fault, ma'am. Mr. Ayers has authorization to move funds from one account to another. You and a Mr. Peter Neil then authorized the final transfer from your joint account."

Stenman vibrated. Peter tried hard to look shocked. "I…I'll move the money back," he stammered. "I didn't have anything to do with this."

"Here." Stenman handed Peter the phone. "Make the damn call and get me my money back. Now."

Peter pulled the phone number from his wallet and placed the call to his 24-hour/7-day-a-week African banker. When he got through, he expressed a desire to transfer all of his funds to one of Stenman's Swiss accounts.

"I am happy to do so, sir," the banker said, his accented voice resonating from the speaker, "but are you certain you wish to do that? We have a minimum transfer fee of $100 on this type of account."

"I don't care about the fee," Peter said, raising his voice in a manner meant to express impatience. "Do it."

"But, sir, it does not make sense to pay one-hundred dollars to transfer one dollar."

"This is Morgan Stenman," Stenman shouted, "and I demand to know what you are talking about?"

"Mr. Neil? Are you there?"

"Yes," Peter answered. "But what's this about one dollar? I was told that someone transferred $800 million to my Mauritius Trust account from Swiss National. Check again."

After a moment of awkward silence, the unhappy voice returned, "I am sorry, Mr. Neil, but no transfer was made to your account. You have only the one dollar used to set up the account."

Peter took the slip of paper Ayers had supplied him and Stenman for fund transfer. "My account number is 7392968127."

"Well, there," the banker said, his voice registering relief. "That is the problem. The number you just read is not your account number."

"What? Not my number?…"

Peter held up Ayers' instructions and his account slip, pretending to look for what he already knew. Stenman leaned in, then grabbed the two papers and shook. She held the numbers side by side:

*7392698127*
*7392968127*

"The six and the nine are reversed," she said, her eyes wild. "We never sent the money to your account. They set me up."

Peter knew the "they" meant Ayers and Guzman.

"We transferred those funds to someone else's account. Whose account is this?" she screamed into the speaker.

"I've already—"

"Do you know who I am?" Stenman said, practically spitting at the African banker.

"Yes," he said through a croaking voice.

"Then you either tell me, or I ruin you. Who?"

"It was recently opened," he began, "under Mr. Ayers' authorization as a biometric account for Ms. Sarah Guzman. The account has already been emptied, however. Ms. Guzman called, not fifteen minutes ago, and moved everything to a Cayman bank."

"They took my money and got themselves immunity in the bargain," Stenman said, now having heard more than enough.

Peter didn't need to explain. Stenman had figured it out. He and Morgan had sent the money to an account in Sarah Guzman's name, with Morgan assuming it was Peter's account. Sarah then made her call, from the beach, authorizing a transfer from that account to another of her accounts in the Caymans. What Peter would never explain was that poor Sarah only did what Ayers told her to do. Sarah was under the impression that she had moved a mere five million dollars to *Peter's* Cayman account. How was she supposed to remember all of her account numbers? After all, she had so many.

Just then, a shot reverberated from outside. Peter's look of shock was genuine.

A few seconds later, the guard who had taken off after Ayers returned. "I had to, Ms. Stenman."

"You had to *what?*"

"Mr. Ayers. He had a gun. I shot him. He's dead."

Peter didn't hear the sirens. This time, when the police cuffed him and read him his rights, he was oblivious to his own situation. Jason Ayers was dead. This wasn't supposed to happen.

As they escorted Peter, Stenman, and her three friends to the county jail, Peter wept.

A smiling, good-looking man reached for Sarah Guzman's hand and guided her on board the yacht. In the outboard motorboat, bobbing ten feet below the larger boat's deck, Carlos watched and prepared himself to follow. Taking no chances, he had a 9mm in hand and at the ready. Carlos focused on his aunt and the man assisting her up the last rung of the ladder. The moment she stepped onto the deck, Carlos put his free hand on the side of the skiff to raise and steady himself.

At that precise moment, a hand thrust itself from the water and snatched Carlos' wrist, nailing it in place against the edge of the motorboat. A thick man in a black wetsuit broke the ocean's choppy surface and tugged down, using his weight as leverage. Carlos lost his balance as the small craft tipped. The man who had met them at the beach—seated to Carlos' back—started forward, his move perfectly timed. He gripped Carlos' gun-hand and twisted. The boat then rocked in the opposite direction—buckling Carlos' knees a second time—as two additional wetsuits effortlessly slung themselves on board from the far side. In less than five seconds, Carlos had eight-hundred pounds of Drug Enforcement personnel roughing him up. His weapon, now useless, lay at his feet. With a wet, rubber arm around his neck, he could barely breathe.

The moment Sarah took her final step up, the engine of the larger craft revved and the boat lurched. "Follow me, Ms. Guzman," the helpful man said. "We have a surprise for you." He had to yell over the sounds of the powerful engine.

Sarah looked for Carlos, but the boat took a sharp turn and the cabin blocked her view. "Where is Carlos?" she asked, her voice lost in the wind.

The man shook his head and pointed to his ear, indicating he couldn't hear her. When Sarah's straw-brimmed hat flew off and tumbleweeded astern, the now not-so-helpful man made no move to retrieve it. She watched an ocean wave gobble the accessory.

"Did you hear me?" she shouted.

The man shrugged, then tromped towards the cabin. When he turned and motioned, Sarah stumbled forward. Her hair stiffened in the wind like straw. Once they stepped down and entered the cabin, the interior calm was eerie. A small, skinny man with fishbowl glasses sat behind a built-in table. He looked happy and familiar.

It took a second, but Sarah recognized Agent Oliver Dawson from his photograph. It was an epiphany, coming like a searchlight through a previously pitch-black cave. She had never been so unprepared. A trap had been sprung and there was nowhere to go. Impotent rage washed over her. In that moment, her mind searched for novel ways to bring an end to people's lives: Neil? Dawson? Ayers? Friends? Family? Others? "You've kidnapped me," she said, clutching the documents she had just received. "And you're not even with the SEC any more."

"Here," Dawson said, "read this." He handed her a piece of legal-size paper. "A short time ago, I sent a copy to Freeman Ranson and the SEC Director of Enforcement. Congratulations. You are forever immune from prosecution of all crimes connected to these papers you are about to turn over to me. In addition, the money you stole from Stenman Partners' accounts—which I understand included significant funds from several drug cartels—is yours to do with as you please. You may even transfer any of those monies to U.S. investments without interference. Sweetest deal we've ever offered, but still a bargain."

"If you are talking about the five million I transferred to Neil's account," said Sarah, "all I have to say is: who gives a shit?"

"No, no. Not that. The eight-hundred million you moved from *your* account in Africa to *your* account in the Cayman Islands. It was a brilliant stroke, making the account numbers so similar nobody would notice."

Dawson went on to highlight what had happened next. When Sarah had made the transfer phone-call on the beach, in full view of Morgan Stenman and her associates, she had moved a gigantic sum of money into a third account, also in her name.

Sarah acted unconcerned. "I don't need to understand what you are talking about," she said. "When Carlos looks into your eyes, and then slices your skin from your bones, an inch at a time, you will regret this charade. I've eaten and spit out little nothings like you. I will make you suffer."

"Ever choked on a little nothing?" Dawson asked. "And Carlos? I don't think I'll be running into him any time soon. He has his hands full with DEA. With what we're about to learn, thanks to your cooperation with those documents, he'll be under a cloud of suspicion for dealing in drugs and drug money. He'll be held, without bail, while these allegations are investigated. Convenient that Mexico's president is a drug-fighter. We've received his assurances we can do with Carlos as we deem necessary."

"You think so?" Sarah asked. "When he gets out—"

"When?" Dawson interrupted. "*If*... My friends at DEA inform me that the investigation will take at least a decade—and he may end up rooming with Manuel Noriega. You remember him? President of Panama? Maybe you did business with the prick before the U.S. military grabbed him and put him away. He's been asking for a Spanish-speaking, scumbag *amigo* to rot in hell with. Nuñoz might be a good fit."

Sarah ceased listening. Reaching for her cellular phone, she fully expected Dawson to stop her, but all he did was grin, listen, and look full of himself, as she confirmed that she had indeed moved funds to one of her accounts instead of Peter Neil's.

"Fine, Goddammit," she shouted to the banker at Cayman Island Trust. "I want to transfer the funds back. Put them in one of Stenman Partners' accounts."

The SEC agent imagined what the frightened voice on the other end of the phone was saying. He counted to four, then heard pretty much what he expected from Sarah Guzman: "I don't have a damn password, you moron. I want to move the money back. How difficult can that be?"

This time Dawson counted to six before she again exploded: "I can't get the password from Mr. Ayers for the simple reason that he set me up. This is…"

Nice touch, Dawson thought. Peter and Ayers had sucked Sarah in. Not a dime would ever be moved from that account without an all-important password. Peter didn't know what it was. Only Ayers had that bit of vital intelligence.

Sarah's phone conversation ended a minute later as she threatened to murder the banker, along with everyone else on Grand Cayman Island.

"Cartel money in my account is my death warrant," she said to Dawson, her face aflame, "and that simpleton banker says he does not have access to transfer information. What do you want from me?"

"You talking to me?" Dawson asked. "Yes. I guess you are. I've already got everything I need in life. If safety's a concern, I can place you in the Witness Protection Program. You interested?" Dawson's motion sickness disappeared.

"I have my own protection, you fool. You can't get away with this."

"Get away with *what*, Mrs. Guzman? Giving you immunity? That's a done deal. Can't transport you to Mexico? We're halfway there. Can't take those documents?" Dawson nodded and the man who had escorted her into the cabin wrested Hannah Neil's pages from her hands.

"We'll drop you off within the hour," Dawson continued, "and we've arranged for land transportation to your villa. Director Ackerman wants me to express his gratitude for your cooperation."

"I won't cooperate with you. I will renounce this immunity agreement."

"I don't blame you," Dawson said, his smirk widening. "Nevertheless, we will honor the terms. We are men of our word. You are immune, and will remain so."

# CHAPTER THIRTY-ONE

FERNANDO GUZMAN CHOSE THIS DAY TO SETTLE OLD SCORES. To gather courage, he focused on his brother's death. Of one thing Fernando was certain: Sarah Brigston Guzman had done to her husband what she had done to her own father. She murdered them both.

As he approached the front gate without stopping, Fernando drove under the gate-arm, waved to the guard, and passed through without a search. In the old days, the soldiers had been steadfast and professional. Now? Now they were open to auction. For ten thousand U.S. dollars, Fernando could have parked an atomic bomb in the courtyard.

Fernando stumbled through that courtyard and down the esplanade, where he and his brother had once played as children, where he had not been welcome for the three years since Enriqué's death. He continued up the stairs, no longer guarded by men with automatic weapons. A worker with a bucket and mop splashed water and cleaned the rust-colored esplanade. As Fernando passed, the worker nodded recognition before arching his back to continue his labors.

Fernando arrived at the heavy door with the brass knocker. He debated whether or not to knock. Out of habit, he knocked.

"Come in," Sarah said.

Fernando opened the door and stepped in. He still shook at the sight of his sister-in-law. She not only had been a deadly force in his family's life, but had schemed to torture him beyond human imagination. Despite the fact that her beauty had faded these last weeks, she still had the eyes of a devil. And as hard as he fought the thought, being in her presence sent him back into that hole for those three days. At night, he now slept with the lights on, and never again could he tolerate the dark. The risks of losing his mind were too great.

"Get out, Fernando," she said, regarding him as nothing more than a silverfish, nibbling on a scrap of toilet paper. "I do not have time for you."

She was on the phone, whispering to someone. Begging, Fernando guessed, for money, help, understanding, her life. He stood, unmoved and uncaring.

She cupped her hand over the mouthpiece and repeated: "Out, you worthless old man."

She looked away as Fernando pulled a handgun from his overcoat pocket. Nerves forced him to use both hands to steady his aim. But from ten feet, he did not miss.

———

For nearly a month after that climactic day at the beach, Peter and Kate didn't have a single opportunity to talk at length in private. Peter was too busy with the legal system. He had arranged for Dawson to indict him on insider trading, knowing full well that the government would eventually drop the charges. But for the time being, Dawson made Peter look like a target, rather than a confederate. The ruse worked.

With her own mounting and potentially all-consuming problems— with the SEC, her clients, and Sarah Guzman—Stenman thought nothing of Peter. He wasn't even a blip on her radar screen, and would stay that way for the foreseeable future. He was the forgotten man, and that was what he hoped to remain.

On the personal side of the ledger, Peter originally had intended to keep the story of Jason Ayers and his father to himself. It was one of those things, he had thought, better left buried in the past. But with all that had occurred, he understood he had to tell Kate.

"Our fathers were best friends and roommates in college," Peter began, during the first chance he dared be alone with Kate. He told her everything he had learned. That her father had a gambling problem in college, bet on games, got in over his head, couldn't repay his bookies. "His career was going to be ruined before it began. If exposed, he could never have gotten into law school, much less become a lawyer."

"This is about a gambling debt, forty years ago? That's what brought on all this misery?" Kate asked.

"Your father was in a jam, and kept doubling up on his bets. Then he said something that changed everybody's lives. He told his bookie that his best friend was Matthew Neil, star wide-receiver. If it became necessary, he said, he could ask my father to help with a bet."

"What's that mean?"

"Point shaving. Jason intimated he could get my dad to drop a few passes, keep his team from covering the point-spread on a game. He hoped the boast would buy him time. But New York money, interested in betting on a sure thing, told him to put up or shut up. He approached Dad."

"And your father agreed?"

"Dad said no. Jason then told him that the bets were already down, that his own reputation and life were on the line. Dad never admitted anything, not even to your father, but he dropped two passes in the end zone that Saturday. Had he made either catch, the point-spread would have been covered. The school quietly investigated, but with no money changing hands, they cleared Dad."

"He saved Father, then."

"Jason told me he was certain that those dropped passes were the reason Dad never turned pro—shame and concern that one day he'd be asked to help fix another game."

"That's awful, Peter. I'm sorry."

"So was Jason, all those years. That's why he was always trying to make it up."

"All he did was make things worse, though," Kate said. "Why did our fathers have a falling out later?"

"While my father was failing financially, Jason was becoming a super-successful attorney, with loads of money. One night, when all of you came to our house for dinner, Jason, who knew of Dad's financial problems, tried to give him a check for fifty thousand dollars. Dad threw him out of the house and never spoke to him again."

"Why? That doesn't make sense."

"It does if you knew Dad. He had given up his professional football dream for the sake of a close and important friendship, but never even spoke of it. When Jason later offered him money, he trivialized my father's sacrifice, or so my Dad thought. He would never have done what he did for money."

"I think I understand," Kate said.

"Then try and understand *your* father as well. Jason lost a son. Always felt my dad's cancer was the result of anxiety and guilt that he had caused. Then, when Guzman and Nuñoz murdered Mom, he fell apart. He began drinking and became afraid he'd lose you and your mother. I'm not saying he was faultless. He wasn't, but he had reasons for what he did, and his demons were very real. That's why he planned his own death. Aiming a starter's pistol at a known killer amounted to suicide."

"He did that to protect Mother and me, didn't he?"

The way she asked the question made it seem rhetorical, which it was. She knew. Peter nodded anyway. "I'm certain of it. He understood that if he were dead, there'd be no advantage in anyone going after you or your mother. He couldn't have predicted Sarah Guzman's murder or that Carlos Nuñoz would disappear and end up in the middle of nowhere with nobody caring about his civil rights."

A moment passed as they held hands and digested what they'd shared. For the next ten minutes, they sat and spoke of related matters while Peter gathered courage. "Kate," he finally said, softly.

"Yes?"

"Your father told me you broke off your engagement. He also said I needed to work at regaining your trust. I want to. I'd like us to start over, and this time, I'll get it right. I'm not saying I won't make mistakes. I will. What I'm saying is I won't make the same ones all over again."

Kate took Peter's hand and squeezed. "More than friends?" she asked.

"Definitely," Peter answered. This time they shared a meaning.

They kissed, then spoke for another minute. In mid-sentence, Kate interrupted herself: "How stupid of me. I almost forgot." She reached into her purse. "A present for you."

"A present? From you?"

"No. From the DA."

"You mean Hanson? I'm afraid of what it's going to be. After all, he was ready to personally punch my ticket."

"He's not such a bad guy, Peter." Kate tried to keep a straight-face, but her mouth twitched and stretched into a grin. She then completely gave in and laughed. It was a short laugh, but healthy and real. "He's got a good heart and he had a lot of reasons to doubt you. Hard to blame him. Here." Her face glowed with anticipation.

She held out her hand and opened her palm, one finger at a time. When she had completed the dramatic unveiling, Peter couldn't contain his surprise. Or delight. "My moonstone. I can't believe he gave it back. Wasn't it booked into evidence?"

"He owed you, and they didn't need it to make their case. I told you,

Hanson isn't such a bad guy."

"Tell him I said thanks." Peter took the small oval and enveloped it in his fist. But, for the first time he could remember, he did not feel the need to rub it. He slipped the gem into his pant pocket, where the slight weight and heft again felt natural.

"You ready to go?" he asked.

Kate nodded.

# ACKNOWLEDGEMENTS

It is natural that the headlines we read focus on people who abuse investors — that's what sells newspapers and jacks up TV ratings. It is also natural that a novel like *Man in the Middle* contains its share of fictionalized bad apples — that helps sell books and moves the story along.

It is also a truism that evil people abound in the financial markets. I've seen them, been in the same rooms with them, fought trading battles with them (won some but lost a lot, too), and watched, sometimes in awe, at their criminal aplomb. Sad but true, they got away with it in 99 percent of the cases.

I can now say it: My Street experience brought me plenty of good with the bad. It was filled with friends and acquaintances who did their jobs the right way, plugging away, day after day, year in and year out, fighting the fight with the rulebook tucked tightly under their arms. Many of these individuals deserve recognition for the example they set, and the friendship and inspiration they provided me — then and now.

This is also a chance to encourage their email contact. Ten years is a long time to neglect friends and those whom I held in high esteem for so long. My dropping out was one thing, but a decade of no-contact is far too long. (I encourage contact through my new webpage at www.financialthriller.com.)

First, my belated thanks to those who worked with me and whose memory I continue to carry in my heart:

Betty Wood, Palmer Smith, Carole Machold, Jack Gaffney, Scott Schaefer, Ray Fernandez, Ulrike Zeilberger, Priscilla Coker, Jay Rodin, Regina McSloy, Nancy Bennett, George Christophersen, Pat Fallon, Jim O'Donnell, Kevin Ertell, Mike Doherty, Brad Bilgore, Bill Scovin, Allison Campenelli, Helene Pientek, and George Vesos.

Second, I had the privilege of conducting business with a large cross-section of institutional clients I greatly respected and who I continue to hold in high esteem. By and large, they were tough (a necessary trait in their profession), but they were also fair and honest, and thus need to be thanked for their professionalism: Barbara Palma, Lou Simpson, Fiona Biggs, Don Strand, Grace McLaughlin, John Shapiro, Glen Greenberg, Rusty Robinson, David Schaefer, Tony Campbell, Alex Lamont, Andy

Kneeter, Rod Reed, Roger Yates, Billy Joyner, David O'Connell, Allison Hockler, Kathy Burns, Arch Spencer, and Gloria Westlake.

Other Wall Street citizens who I continue to think highly of are: Rod Berens, Mike Gallo, Michael Kaye, Ed Braniff, Bob Boiarski, John Mack, Dick Fisher, Mitchel Fromstein, and Amy Bonoff.

As I was preparing this section of the book, I encountered the name of another man whom I held in enormously high regard—Jim Gantsoudes. Upon checking, I discovered he had passed away several years ago. That news saddened me greatly. I nearly went to work for Jim at Morgan, Stanley's Chicago office before being assigned to block trading in New York. He was talented, kind, and a gentleman. I wish his family well.

To all those mentioned, I continue to look back fondly at our association. To the hundreds of others I may have inadvertently omitted, I beg your forgiveness.

I'd be greatly remiss, too, if I failed to single out my mentor from the day I first parked my wet-behind-the-ears self on the Morgan, Stanley trading desk. One of the most talented block traders in the history of the financial markets, if not the most talented, Dick "Skyball" King had the character of a near-saint and the patience of a kind father, all rolled into one. I could never repay him for the lessons he taught me.

With respect to the creation and dissemination of *Man in the Middle*, I need to lavish special praise on my publisher, Bruce Bortz, and his firm, Bancroft Press, not just for his input in the novel itself, but for his penchant for dreaming big dreams. His work ethic, determination, and doggedness would have made him a Wall Street titan, had he chosen that route instead of the more difficult pathway of publishing.

To my dear friend Leiv Lea, an accountant/CFO extraordinaire, and his wife Deborah, thanks for reviewing the earliest version of this work and the helpful feedback.

I would also like to single out Joel Fishman for pulling my manuscript out of the slush pile and encouraging my early writing efforts. Without his input, *Man in the Middle* would never have been completed.

Finally, to Paul Korngiebel and Hilary Hinzman, your comprehensive review and literate commentary improved the final product greatly. Thank you.

**KEN MORRIS**
Del Mar, CA

# ABOUT THE AUTHOR

A Southern California native, Ken Morris obtained his undergraduate degree from UC-Santa Barbara, and his MBA from UCLA. In the 1980s, he became a stock trader for Morgan, Stanley in New York, and by the age of 31, had become a celebrated, much-sought-after trader operating at the highest levels of the world's capital markets.

In 1992, at the tender age of 39, he stunned and perplexed the financial world by turning his back entirely on Wall Street. Returning to California, he set up a part-time consulting practice, and began devoting himself to his family and to writing. *Man in the Middle*, the first of his financial novels to be published, has already received attention from *The London Times'* City Diary and Jim Cramer's RealMoney.com. His next novel, *The Chosen Man*, is due out in March 2004.

He lives in Del Mar, California, with his wife, a fund manager, and their four sons.